DRINKING GOURD

A Selection of Recent Titles from Barbara Hambly from Severn House

The James Asher Vampire Novels

BLOOD MAIDENS
THE MAGISTRATES OF HELL
THE KINDRED OF DARKNESS
DARKNESS ON HIS BONES

The Benjamin January Series

DEAD AND BURIED
THE SHIRT ON HIS BACK
RAN AWAY
GOOD MAN FRIDAY
CRIMSON ANGEL
DRINKING GOURD

DRINKING GOURD

A Benjamin January Novel

Barbara Hambly

This first world edition published 2016
in Great Britain and the USA by
SEVERN HOUSE PUBLISHERS LTD of
19 Cedar Road, Sutton, Surrey, England, SM2 5DA.
Trade paperback edition first published
in Great Britain and the USA 2016 by
SEVERN HOUSE PUBLISHERS LTD

British Library Cataloguing in Publication Data
A CIP catalogue record for this title is available from the British Library.

ISBN-13: 978-0-7278-8606-4 (cased)
ISBN-13: 978-1-84751-708-1 (trade paper)
ISBN-13: 978-1-78010-769-1 (e-book)

All Severn House titles are printed on acid-free paper.

Severn House Publishers support the Forest Stewardship Council™ [FSC™],
the leading international forest certification organisation.
All our titles that are printed on FSC certified paper carry the FSC logo.

Typeset by Palimpsest Book Production Ltd.,
Falkirk, Stirlingshire, Scotland.
Printed and bound in Great Britain by
TJ International, Padstow, Cornwall.

For Glen
With deepest thanks

ONE

'Well now, Mr Tambo,' drawled the Interlocutor, as the row of black-painted white men ceased their spirited rendition of 'The Bee-Gum Tree' on banjos and bones, and the little backing orchestra – a dark tableau against the painted backdrop, in the mild light that filtered through the canvas walls of the show tent – softened to a gentle plunking, like the beat of a sleeping heart. 'How are you at mathematics?'

Mr Tambo – really Mel Silverberg, skinny in his garishly checkered trousers, the blackness of burnt cork concealing his hundred-percent Caucasian features – rattled his tambourine thoughtfully and replied in an exaggerated 'darky' slur: 'I doan know no *Matthew* Matticks, suh. I knows his brother Johnny, though.'

The audience chuckled, anticipating the joke. Benjamin January, among the musicians at the back of the little stage, vamped on the six-octave upright piano and shook his head. He knew slaves and free blacks almost universally found the antics of white men imitating black ones hilarious. He'd personally never understood it.

On the other hand, ten dollars a week was ten dollars a week . . . and that was all the 'Matthew Matticks' he needed to know, going into the sweltering summer season of 1839.

'No, no!' The Interlocutor waved his white-gloved hands. 'How are you at *figures*?'

'Oh, I beg yo' puddin', suh, I di'n' unnerstan' you! I guess I's pretty good at figures.' Mr Tambo scratched his nappy black wig and looked pleased with himself.

'Then I want to ask you a question.'

'Ask away, suh!'

'Well,' said the Interlocutor – his real name was Owen Tavish, a craggy-faced, wiry Scotsman with eyebrows like a Chinese dragon, 'supposing there were sixteen chickens in a coop, and a man should come along and take out five.' Rumor in the

All-American Zoological Society's Traveling Circus and Exhibition of Philosophical Curiosities held that Tavish had played Shakespeare and Sheridan before the crowned heads of England, before being obliged to flee that Sceptred Isle for either manslaughter or gambling debts or both. He certainly had an 'American' accent that January had never heard from anyone, white or black, anywhere in the United States.

'How many would there be left?'

Mr Tambo writhed his face into a pucker of concentration at this, as if trying to fit all his features into the circumference of a wineglass, and ostentatiously scratched his bottom, a piece of business that drew another gust of chuckles from the good folk of Natchez, slave and free alike. At last he asked, 'What time of day this supposed to be, suh?'

The Interlocutor reared back in exaggerated puzzlement at this *non sequitur*. 'What time of day? Now, what has that got to do with how many chickens is left in the coop?'

A hand thrust itself through the join in the curtains immediately to January's right: a young child's, black, holding a folded piece of white paper. January glanced swiftly toward the audience, lest the interruption be taken as part of the joke. But the line of 'minstrels', and the slight height of the stage on its trestles, kept it from being seen. He plucked it from the child's fingers without missing a beat. Besides the 'Philosophical Curiosities' of the traveling show themselves – a strongman, two midgets, a not-very-convincing bearded lady and the astoundingly tattooed Maryam, Princess of the Desert – there were any number of workers and water-carriers backstage who could pass a message to one of the musicians . . .

A glance at it, however, showed his own name written on the outside of the folded sheet. He set the note on the music rack of his piano, and returned his attention to the living rhythm of the conversation—

'A great deal, suh!'

'Why's that, Mr Tambo?'

'Well, suh . . .' Mr Tambo jabbed a finger at the Interlocutor's silk vest. ''Cause if it was twelve o'clock at *night*, and wasn't nobody aroun', an' *you* should happen to be in the immediate vicinity of that chicken coop, there wouldn't be *none* left!'

In the same instant – Tavish was meticulous about rehearsing his stage crew – the 'minstrels' in the front line struck up their banjos, the back-up orchestra of piano, fiddle, flute, clarinet and drum bounced back into 'The Bee-Gum Tree', and the painted curtain swished shut, permitting January to break the wafer on the folded sheet and read it—

'Dear God!' he cried.

Tavish – who had leaped from his chair and was already halfway to the wings as the Boneless Monzonnis swept onto the stage with their bench and props – stopped behind him, and Hannibal Sefton, hearing the tone in his voice, halted his embellishments with the fiddle and turned his head.

'It's my sister, sir.' January looked up into Tavish's face. 'Isabel,' he added, for Hannibal's benefit: Hannibal knew and loved both of January's sisters and was perfectly well aware that neither of them was named Isabel. 'Sir, I would not, for any other cause, ask this—'

'Where is she?' asked the Scotsman.

'Vicksburg. It may be nothing, but she's six months gone with child—'

'I've heard it that the *Cleopatra*'s one of the fastest boats on the river.' Tavish groped in his pockets, which, being Mr Interlocutor's gray evening-trousers, were empty. 'She's on the wharf, leaving this afternoon. We'll be in Vicksburg Friday. Will you be needing money?' Like most Scots, the exhibition's owner knew how to keep household, but when any of his employees stood in need, January had found the man the living refutation of the tale that Scots were tight-fisted.

Feeling like he was robbing a poor box, he said – which was true – 'I already sent off my week's money to my wife, sir. Five dollars should suffice—'

Tavish – shrugging out of his long-tailed evening coat – led January offstage, and gestured for Hannibal to follow them. The rear quarter of the show tent, behind the curtains where the audience couldn't see, was as usual a very quiet chaos as the next acts warmed up and the minstrels crowded around the single mirror, refreshing the burnt cork on their faces where sweat had streaked it. It was the second of June and the noon sun seemed to slice through the canvas like a knife. Hannibal, too, was blacked up – Americans regarded a white man in a minstrel show, other than the Interlocutor, as 'inappropriate'.

'Don't you go alone.' The Scotsman laid a hand on January's shoulder. 'In New Orleans – aye, and all the way up the river! – I been hearin' tales of slave-nappers that'd curl a man's hair. 'Tis bad enough in New York—'

'I'll go with him, sir,' volunteered Hannibal promptly. 'It's not the first time I've played the master, going up to see *Isabel*.' He threw a glance at January, who nodded, very slightly, at the corroboration of the non-existent sister in Vicksburg. '*Quum Romae fueris, Romano vivite more* – the damn fool custom of a damn fool country . . .' He coughed, pressing his hand to his ribs, and added with deep concern in his voice, 'What is it, *amicus meus*?'

'It may be nothing.' January bit his lip with what he hoped was convincing anxiety. 'I just don't like to take chances since she lost her last one.'

'Nor should you.' Tavish clapped Hannibal on the arm. 'Good man. But ye'd best get that cork off your face or I'll never see the pair of you again.'

In the smaller tent that served as dressing room and, in a pinch, dormitory to the male performers of the circus and Philosophical Exhibition, January unearthed his satchel from beside the bedroll where he'd slept last night, while Hannibal scrubbed cork soot from his face. When he'd packed to join the Philosophical Exhibition, he'd included a tin slave-badge and papers that proved him to be the property of Hannibal Sefton (or whatever name Hannibal chose to forge into the papers – Hannibal had, after all, forged the papers themselves as well).

A prime cotton-hand fetched fifteen hundred dollars on the auction block these days. With the country still struggling to free itself from the effects of the bank crash of two years previously, nobody bothered asking if a slave's protests that he really was a free man might be the truth.

Free papers, January had long ago learned, were the easiest things in the world to tear up.

'Who's the note from?' Hannibal came over and knelt on the rumple of blankets on the pallets at his side. His long hair, wet around the edges, was braided back in an old-fashioned queue that hung halfway down his back: he'd been ill much of the winter and looked like a good-natured cadaver. 'And are we really going to Vicksburg?'

January handed him the paper.

On it was written, *Drummond's Ferry, Vicksburg*. It was unsigned, but January knew the hand, and knew that the man who sent it would not have done so had there been any alternative.

The mark at the top – a star in a circle, like an idle scribble – meant *life and death*.

The steamboat *Cleopatra* still lay at wharf when January and Hannibal made their way down the long, steep slope of Silver Street from the Plaza above. The river was low and the cotton harvest hadn't yet begun, and since the 'cleanup' of Natchez-Under-the-Hill two years previously, the riverfront had a seedy air, more sordid than deadly. January didn't see any saloons actually closed, but the muddy alleyways among the rough-built warehouses, the rickety brothels balanced on stilts and the wooden walkways that meandered among them, were half-deserted under the brazen hammer of the afternoon sun.

He wasn't fooled. The river pirates and the more violent rings of gamblers and thieves might have been driven out, but he guessed they hadn't gone far. Had he been alone, he wouldn't have made it down the mucky slope to the wharves before some plausible-looking white man would saunter up to him with, 'Say, friend, you know this town? Maybe you could help me out . . . Can I buy you a drink?' And the next act of *that* particular drama would be waking up in chains with an opium-headache in a slave pen. As it was, the only ones who accosted them were whores, whose numbers didn't appear to have decreased in the slightest since the last time January had been in the town in the summer of 1836.

In a month, these wharves would be impassable with wagon-loads of cotton, mountains of white fluff going into the presses, or coming out as tight-packed bales that could stop a bullet.

American Louisiana. The 'cotton kingdom'. A different world from New Orleans, and the sugar kingdom of the south.

January never felt comfortable outside New Orleans. Even in his home city these days he tended to remain in the French Town, where he was known to both the free colored community and to the French whites that still held some power. When he'd left Louisiana in 1817, to train in surgery in France, he'd had no intention of ever coming back, and upon his return in the wake of the cholera epidemic of 1832, he had found a city and a country taken over more and more by Americans.

Natchez frightened him, not only because it was the headquarters of every slave-stealer and slave-dealer in the valley of the Mississippi. It was the heart of the cotton kingdom, the American world where every white man looked at him appraisingly; where the concept that a black man might be free or have business of his own never crossed anyone's mind.

And he would not be here – he told himself many times a day, watching white men dressed up as black men portray the sly, clownish laziness of the African race – were there any other way of making ten dollars a week. Any other way of providing for his beautiful wife, his beautiful Rose, in the seventh month of her second pregnancy, with half the banks and a third of the businesses in the country still closed (*Thank you very much, President Jackson . . .*).

He'd have put himself up as the target in a coconut shy for that money, to hold onto the big ramshackle house on Rue Esplanade, until better times came.

But there were some things, he reflected, as he felt the note crinkle in his trouser pocket as they crossed the open mud toward the wharf, that took precedence even over that . . .

TWO

The sun was touching the dark fringe of sweet gum and cottonwood that curtained the flatlands on the Louisiana shore when the *Cleopatra*'s crew maneuvered her into the wharf at Vicksburg. 'Hotel first, I think.' Hannibal, who had spent most of the sixty-mile voyage discreetly tripling their thirteen-dollar war chest in the steamboat's main saloon, added a remark that might have been a classical quotation on the subject of the shortcomings of river travel but was actually Latin for *We'd better not look too eager to get across the river.*

'Right you are, Michie Cyril.' While January carried a slave-badge and assorted ownership documents in his luggage, Hannibal generally travelled with other potential necessities, such as a marked poker deck and the business cards of a number of gentlemen whose name wasn't Hannibal Sefton. He hadn't had call to use the marked playing cards on this trip – on a riverboat you never knew who else would be at the poker table – but given the originator of the note, and the probable nature of the emergency, January had suggested they abandon their own names for the time being.

Whatever they'd find at Drummond's Ferry, he knew already it was going to be a good deal more dangerous than playing with marked cards.

All the thieves, gamblers, confidence tricksters and river pirates who had been ejected from Natchez had made their way, naturally, to Vicksburg, whose towering bluffs dominated the Mississippi for miles. As January made his way among the roustabouts, wood loaders, porters, draymen, pickpockets, slaves and whores of Vicksburg-Under to the steamboat offices in quest of a cab, he kept a cautious eye over one shoulder and never got too near the mouths of those muddy alleys between the warehouses.

When he returned to the wharf it was to find Hannibal backed up against a stack of crates, being harangued by a weasel-faced man in a shaggy beaver hat: 'Boy that size, you can't tell me he was trained as a valet! Why, it'd be a waste of time to put that kind of trainin' into him, sir, you know that as well as me.' He glanced at January as he trotted up alongside the hack, and went on, as if the matter didn't concern him, 'I tell you, you can get a better boy for the purpose in Memphis for four hundred dollars, and I'll hand you, right here on this wharf, five hundred – *five fifty*! – for him. That puts you a hundred fifty dollars to the good—'

Hannibal glanced past Weasel Face as if bored, met January's eye and raised his brows inquiringly. Ears burning with anger, January bowed and said, in his second-best English, 'Here is your cab, sir.'

Hannibal inclined his head slightly to Weasel Face and shook his hand as if he were glad he was wearing gloves, while January handed their two carpetbags to the cabman and said, 'Planter's House Hotel.'

'A pleasure to make your acquaintance, I'm sure, Mr Fenks.' Hannibal's tone implied that it was not one he wished to prolong. January helped his 'master' into the cab, then climbed onto the box at the driver's side. Even at low water, the Vicksburg wharves, like those of Natchez, were crowded with boats: corn, hogs, pumpkins; cheap cloth and cheaper shoes from the mills of Massachusetts; barrels of lamp oil and papers of pins. Slaves and slave-dealers, thieves and whores jostled among the cheap taverns and brick warehouses. Hot light lanced off the water and the smell of privies and horses clogged the brazen air.

Built thirteen years previously on a high bluff commanding the river, Vicksburg offered to the wealthy of the town cool air, prosperous shops and spacious houses, separated from the sordid confusion of the waterfront below.

The Planter's House Hotel was small but handsome, situated on China Street a few blocks from the noise and wagon traffic at the center of town. Hannibal signed himself 'Cyril Pinkerton and valet', of Mobile, Alabama, and inquired for a livery stable. By full dark, January was piloting a buggy back down Clay Street and downriver along the levee, toward where the hotel clerk had told them they would find Drummond's Ferry. Cressets lighted the wharves – three boats were loading to depart, the moon being bright and only a day past full – and a ruddy, sullen glow burned in the doorways of half a dozen saloons. Farther along the riverfront, a rickety whorehouse had all its windows open, the girls sitting in them to catch the river breeze: 'Hey, honey, where you off to so fast?' 'Come on up, handsome, for the best blowjob in town . . .'

'What the hell you mean, fourteen cents a pound?' shouted a man to a warehouse clerk. 'It was *thirty-five* cents a pound two years ago . . .!'

It had been another quiet Mardi Gras this winter. Though January had begun to acquire piano students again, at last – a sure indication that the worst effects of the bank crash had begun to loosen – there were fewer people, either French or American, giving large parties in New Orleans, and fewer 'blue ribbon' balls for the *plaçées* and their protectors. For the third year in a row the opera had closed early, leaving January, Hannibal and every other musician in the town to fend for themselves. He'd been lucky to get the circus, and despite what he guessed was at stake here, he felt a qualm of nervousness at leaving it, even temporarily.

And one never knew . . .

For ten years Americans had flooded into Warren County, and into Louisiana's Madison Parish across the river, men bent upon making their fortunes in these lands newly taken from the Chickasaws. Without slave labor to harvest their cotton, they were nothing: debtors, worthless. The mere thought of their slaves escaping, he knew, threw them into killing rage.

In New Orleans, were anyone to discover that he, Benjamin January, had for two years now been giving refuge to fugitive slaves on their way through New Orleans, in the two tiny chambers he'd walled off in the storerooms beneath his house on Rue Esplanade, he would be fined five hundred dollars – enough to lose him the house – and jailed. This would be catastrophe – Rose and twenty-one-month-old Baby John (not to speak of soon-to-be Baby Rosie-or-Ben) would be left on the charity of his family (with his mother saying *I told you so*, loudly and often) – but being punished by a judge to the limit of the law was still within the limit of the law.

The judges in New Orleans knew January as a prominent member of the free colored community. That community retained enough influence in the town to prevent the jailer from selling him to a slave-dealer and pocketing the money. In New Orleans – at least so far – slave-dealers didn't yet come through the jails 'looking for runaways', as they did in cities like Baltimore and Washington, supposedly to 'return the runaways to their owners' but in fact to take them and sell them elsewhere.

Up here in the cotton kingdom, January was acutely conscious of the fact that the slave-owners regarded the laws of the United States – even of the State of Louisiana – as something that did not understand the local conditions. Where their human property was concerned, nine slaveholders out of ten considered themselves more competent than the legislators in Baton Rouge ('A bunch of Frenchmen,' January had often heard them derisively described) to rule on what should be done to recover absconding bondsmen. More often, they took it on themselves to punish – and warn – those who would rob them of the bodies they had purchased. The country on both sides of the river was still largely unsettled, with miles of cypress swamp, bayou and cottonwood forest between plantations. The vast 'delta' of the Red River lay to the north, a tangled primordial forest. Backed by the poor whites who eked a living from small farms, swamp trapping or cutting wood for the steamboats, the planters were the real law.

White or black, those who helped the slaves escape frequently did not survive to stand trial.

In the dark of the buggy beside him, Hannibal pressed his hand hard against his side to stifle another cough, and January asked quietly, 'You all right?'

'Better than I'd be back at the hotel in a barroom full of planters, trying to look like I gave a desiccated hairball about the price of cotton. *Odi profanum vulgus et arceo*.'

January laughed.

They were past the lighted area of the wharves and saloons. Ahead of them, a pair of lanterns, mounted on a rough archway of pine poles, burned like eyes in the darkness. Beyond them the dark bulk of a vessel lay low in the water. Another lantern burned on its deck. By its gleam, January made out the silhouette of a roundhouse, such as mules walked to turn the grinding wheels that pressed sugar cane. He heard the muted whuffle of a horse's breath, and the clink of harness. A lantern bobbed toward them. 'We're unharnessed for the night, friend. Come back when it's light.'

'I'm looking for Mr Abel, sir. Would this be Drummond's Ferry?'

Boots scrunched the mud. January saw that in the wavering yellow light the bearded man was younger than he'd at first thought, barely twenty. But though his fair beard was as unsubstantial as duck down, premature bleakness had put a line between his brows and creased the corners of his wide mouth. 'You the man from Paris?'

'I am, sir.' January nodded back toward Hannibal, silent in the buggy. 'And that's my friend Mr Freepaper.'

The thin-lipped mouth tweaked into a grin that its owner was clearly ashamed of, because he put it away fast. 'Pleasure to meet you, sir.' He held out a callused hand. 'Saul Drummond. Solomon—!'

A beardless and slightly chubbier copy of himself appeared from the darkness. Even the expression – somewhere between glumness and permanent anger – was identical.

'Get the horses ready. You really a doctor?' Saul Drummond asked, as he and January led the buggy down the wet gravel to the ferry's wharf.

'I am. Is someone hurt?'

'Rex Ballou. Pa's . . .' He fished for a word.

January said softly, 'I've heard of Rex Ballou.'

The horse's hooves clunked on the gangway. Fortunately the animal itself made no fuss about the footing. With the nearest buggy for hire being in St Joseph, nearly fifty miles downriver on the Louisiana side, the beast was doubtless as familiar with the ferry as with its own stable.

'What happened? How bad is he hurt?'

'We don't know how bad,' said the young man. 'Rex was bringing a group of runaways up from Davis' Bend. Mostly the patrols don't ride more'n an hour after full dark. But I heard today, Hugh Riley's man Quinto ran away last night, and patrols was out all over lookin' for him, on account of the reward.' Saul Drummond's voice was rough and hesitant, as if unused to stringing words together, and something in his vowels made January think of a New York banker he knew in New Orleans.

'Rex and them run into the militia patrol just upstream of Lewis' Landing. Rex took a ball in the chest. They lost 'em in the cane-brakes, went to ground—'

'Where?'

'Pa'll take you.'

Young Solomon Drummond kindled three more lanterns in the roundhouse, and the six horses harnessed there snuffled sleepily and shook their manes. 'Git up, Samson. Let's go, Jeptha. *In all labor there is profit, but . . . the way of the slothful is as a hedge of thorns . . .*'

'Did the others get away?'

For a moment, it seemed that Saul averted his face, but it was hard to tell whether the long hesitation that followed his question was from thought, or just the young man's halting speech.

'Yes,' Saul said at length. 'They's all hid. But the patrol found blood, see. They know they got somebody. We put it around that Rex been over in Richmond this mornin', an' we had Boze, our stableman, there in the back of Rex's shop this afternoon, so people'll see through the windows and think Rex is there. But that won't hold more'n a day. He's a barber, an' customers make a fuss if he ain't there on their regular day. So we got to get him on his feet: show it wasn't him that was shot.'

January shivered, despite the night's heat.

'Is he conscious?' asked January. 'Talking?'

'That I don't know, sir. They's hid.' Saul walked back to the thirty-foot steering sweep. The round platform turned beneath the horses' hooves, starting the ferry's two paddle wheels in motion, and the flat, unwieldy craft moved away from the wharf. 'Hid deep.'

In the moonlight January could just pick out the outline of the black arms of half-submerged trees, reaching from beneath the opaque water to grab at the paddle wheels and scrape the shallow hull. Low water had brought bars of gravel and sand to within inches of the surface, invisible but for the riffles flickering over them. Tiny islets, deeply submerged when the river was high, were now formidable obstacles. Saul Drummond leaned on the sweep, deftly threading his way between these dangers seen and unseen, eyes narrowed as they peered beyond the lanterns' hooded light.

'Pa'll take you to 'em,' he repeated after a time. 'Pa an' Rex, they got hideouts all around this country, both sides of the river. Pa don't never take cargo—' the young man used the railroad term that had been adopted for fugitives – 'to the house. Even before Mama died, an' he married Mrs Pryce, he'd never bring 'em to the house. I was sixteen when we come here from New York state, six years ago, an' it wasn't 'til Mama died that he told her, or us – me an' Solomon, an' our brother Davy that died – what he was doin' nor why he'd come down here to preach the gospel.'

'So you haven't seen them.'

The young man shook his head. 'Can't nobody get to 'em in daylight. 'Specially not now, since Drew Hardy's got his dogs out over the countryside on account of the reward Marcus Maury's got out for Quinto.'

Hannibal spoke from the dark of the buggy. 'I thought Quinto was Hugh Riley's slave.'

'He was, sir. Valet. Last winter Riley died, and soon as probate cleared – Thursday, it was – Hugh's brother Gale sold Quinto to Marcus Maury, of Indian Mound Plantation. Quinto ran away Friday night. It was those huntin' him that came on Rex and the others. Maury's offered five hundred dollars reward—'

'Five hundred? What can the man do, raise the dead?'

Saul's mouth and eyes narrowed with disapproval at what January guessed he considered blasphemy, and January put in, 'For five hundred dollars a man could almost purchase another slave.' Most rewards, he knew, didn't exceed fifty.

'Maury paid three thousand for him.' He leaned on the steering oar as the ferry came into the river's main channel, even at low water powerful enough to push the craft southward. 'He's tried for years to buy him off Riley, and turn him into a fighter.'

January bit back a disgusted oath. For the health of his soul, he hated as few things as he could manage in his life, but high on the list of exceptions to his rule were the 'nigger fights' arranged by white men between their black property.

If Quinto were any good, Maury could win back his three thousand dollars in a couple of bouts.

The two tiny glimmers of lantern light that marked the ferry landing on the Louisiana side appeared, and slid inexorably to their right. Between them and the ferry, the river's silvered obsidian surface was dotted with other lights: steamboats, flatboats, rafts of Wisconsin timber like floating islands, four hundred feet long with lanterns gleaming in front of the tiny shelters the raftsmen built on the logs. Though at this point the river was over a mile wide, the water magnified the raftsmen's voices, tall tales and yarns, brags and obscenities traded over cards: 'Who you callin' a cheat, you pussified egg-suck son of a whore? You stand up on your hind legs an' say I'd NEED to cheat a sheep-stealin', arse-suckin' chicken-livered pup that ain't fit to eat with a dog nor drink with a nigger . . .'

'For five hundred dollars,' mused Hannibal, 'I expect every white man in the parish and half those from across the river are patrolling—'

'Oh, we'll get the cargo across, safe enough.' Saul put the oar over, to avoid the first of what looked like a wilderness of snags that bordered the Louisiana bank. 'Not a man in the parish is gonna miss the show that's comin' Saturday. Horse races in the morning, circus at noon – and for them too holy to see the wonders of God's creation manifested, a lying false prophet name of Bickern is setting up his own tabernacle to beg for pennies from the deluded . . . *Beware of false prophets, which come to you in sheep's clothing*, the apostles tell us. *They will turn their ears away from the truth, and . . . with feigned words, will make merchandise of you.* T'cha!' He shook his head, stirred to unwonted speech, January guessed, by the Spirit of the Lord.

'But God turns even the covetousness of the unrighteous into a trap that will seize their heels and break their teeth in their mouths. In that hour we'll get our cargo across the river. Once they're in the 'delta', it'll take more'n dogs to find them. It's all swamp and bayou from Vicksburg almost to Memphis. They'll be safe.'

If the dogs don't find them before they cross the river. January could hear them, distantly, on the Louisiana shore.

He looked back at Vicksburg, jutting like Gibraltar against a patchy black sky, the Walnut Hills behind it swinging back inland. He had crossed the flat, forested jungle that everyone called the Delta: cottonwood forests, thick-clotted laurel 'hells', stagnant ponds and cut-off loops and ox-bows that had once been part of the main river's bed. Few settlements existed there, and those there were lay half-hidden in the maze of nameless waterways where the Mississippi, the Yazoo and the Sunflower had spread and wandered and changed their beds.

'Ho up, Samson.' The boy Solomon tweaked the long rein of the lead horse, and the clump of hooves ceased. The current was weak in these tangled shallows, and the ferry glided gently toward the shore. A pair of lanterns marked the 'downstream' wharf, a mile and a half below the main ferry landing. Snags and underbrush had been cleared, and the dried jumble of uprooted trees and driftwood detritus hauled aside. Gibbous moonlight showed where a trace had been beaten from the plank wharf up to the higher ground of the bank. The rank air, hot even down on the water, droned with insect life.

'Turn upstream at the river road,' instructed Saul as he, his brother and his two passengers maneuvered the ferry into place with poles. 'You'll pass the main ferry wharf to your right. A hundred feet farther, there's a drive down to your left. Pa's waiting for you, to take you on to where the cargo's hid.'

'I'll do for him what I can.' January clasped the young man's hand. 'Thank you.'

'You got to get Rex on his feet.' Saul's eyes were somber in the moonlight. 'Everybody – Sheriff Brister, Mr Maury, Sheriff Preston from Warren County – they know Pa and Rex is friends. They catch Rex, they'll guess Pa's in it with him.'

He dropped the coil of rope he held to the deck.

'Last year,' he went on, 'Sheriff Brister in Madison Parish caught four runaways on their way north. A black man and a white girl was guiding them, a Quaker girl whose family lived in Monroe. A gang of men – Brister claimed later he had no idea where they came from or who they was, and didn't even pretend to try to find out – broke into the jail in Monroe and hanged the girl, after . . . Well, I hear they roughed her up pretty bad. Men attacked her family's home a few days later and burned it. Her family fled the state an' was lucky to make it out. Doesn't matter what the law is, hereabouts.' His eyes were grave and a little scared. 'It is war here. War against the Underground Railroad and all who'd so much as whisper that all men should be free, let alone help them on their way. The men who own slaves are angry, with anger that knows no law. The black "conductor" they caught, the mob beat with chains, before they cut off his manhood, and burned him alive.'

THREE

'It wasn't always like this.' Waning moonlight sprinkled the river to their right, exposing dark shapes moving on the water. A ribbon of woodsmoke momentarily threaded the gluey air. Closer, dogs bayed; a sound that always twisted January's heart with dread.

He guided the rented horse carefully along the rutted track.

'When I was a child, I don't think I ever heard talk of running to the north. For one thing, north was a lot farther off in those days. Ohio, Illinois, Indiana: that was all Indian country still. Around the quarters you'd sometimes hear of a man going west to try to get to Mexico, but nobody could read and nobody had a map or any idea of what the land was like ten miles from Bellefleur.'

'Surely a man could get to New Orleans, and get on a ship?'

'And go where? The only vessels going back to Africa were the slavers themselves – and that's if you could find a crew whose language you could understand. 'Til my mother's protector brought us – Mama, me and my sister Olympe – to New Orleans, we barely even spoke French. And if they caught you and brought you back . . .'

He fell silent, remembering the men in Bellefleur who'd been caught and brought back.

'So where did they run?' Hannibal's light, hoarse voice was barely a whisper in the dark. 'From what I recall of your old master, he's not somebody whose shadow I'd want to live in.'

'They'd build villages,' said January. 'Out in the *ciprière*. Little African villages, deep in the bayous, where the white men didn't come. Maroons, they called them. They'd hunt, or fish, or trade with the Indians . . . And they weren't gone forever. They'd sneak back into the quarters – which was nothing more than another little African village – to visit their families. Up until about five years ago, there was at least one maroon village in the *ciprière* behind New Orleans. It's gone now,' he added. 'You couldn't do it now.'

* * *

The house at Drummond's Crossing stood a few hundred yards back from the river road, surrounded by a belt of young cottonwoods. January tried to recall what he'd been told about Ezekias Drummond, and remembered only that he had been a farmer in Upstate New York, and these days preached hellfire and salvation to a small congregation in Young's Point, a tiny settlement some five miles from the ferry landing on the Louisiana side. The house itself was an L-shaped dwelling built – like many houses along the river – on a six-foot foundation because of the river's floods. The kitchen was a rough shed erected behind it, and extensive stables formed a third side to the quadrangle. In the moonlight January noted cow barns, pigsties, chicken coops, a kitchen garden and the tall chimney of a smoke house. A miniature kingdom among the laurel thickets and cane-brakes that covered most of DeSoto Point.

No light shone in any window of the house, but as they drove into the lantern-lit yard, a shadow detached itself from the darkness of the porch, and descended the long stair. 'You come at a late hour, friend,' rumbled a voice like organ pipes.

Its owner stepped into the pool of light from the buggy's lamps, the original of Saul and Solomon at the ferry, but taller than either – almost January's six foot three – and just as massive in stature. Gray-shot dark hair streamed down onto his shoulders, and a grizzled beard onto his breast. He had his son's square jaw and thin-lipped mouth, and the same grim expression in eyes that were strikingly pale in the dim light.

'Saul at the ferry told us we might be needed, sir,' explained January. 'I've come all the way here from Paris.'

At the mention of the code by which January was known among the other 'conductors' and 'stationmasters' of the invisible route, Ezekias Drummond said, 'Have you now, friend? God sped your feet. We scarce looked for you this soon.'

'Through a thousand years of history, folk have said Cleopatra was fast,' remarked Hannibal. 'Naturally her namesake boat would be.'

''Tis a sorry world,' retorted Drummond, with every bit of his son's grimness, 'when a she-demon of such repute has a boat named in her . . . I cannot say her *honor*. In her memory. Or indeed,' he added, 'when boats are named for women at all. If the

Apostle Paul instructed that they be decently subject to their husbands, how unseemly is it for a good woman's name to be bandied along the riverfronts of America? And how much more unseemly for a bad one's. This is Gibbs Crawford's rig you've rented, isn't it?' He gently scrubbed his knuckles along the face of the white-footed bay between the buggy's shafts. 'Old Saracen here's good for a long pull yet. You'll forgive me—' He came around to the vehicle's step – 'I'll take the reins here, Mr—?'

'St-Denis,' said January. 'This is my partner, Mr Freepaper.'

The big preacher grunted. 'And a shame it is, before the eyes of a weeping God, that a Negro must pass himself off as a slave, in order to move about freely in this freest of republics.' He dug in his pocket. 'Mr Freepaper, my wife and daughter sleep; would it be too much to ask, that you wait here on the porch until my sons and Boze return from the landing? They'll make up beds for you. 'Twill be an hour yet, I reckon, but the night is warm, and the fewer who know the details of our enterprise, the better.'

'As long as your good wife won't come downstairs and be startled to find a stranger on her porch . . .'

'She won't.' Drummond's voice had the decisiveness of an ax splitting kindling. 'Mr St-Denis, you will forgive me if I take the liberty of binding your eyes?'

'*Ibant obscuri sola ab nocte per umbram*,' remarked Hannibal, climbing down from the buggy as the ferryman produced a large blue bandanna. 'I bow to your need for discretion, sir, but I assure you my days of getting drunk and blithering secrets to strangers in taverns are long over – not that I ever knew any secrets worth blithering . . .'

Drummond stepped up into the vehicle, and wrapped the bandanna around January's eyes. 'A man may keep his counsel drunk,' he said, 'and yet – as you say – stone-cold sober he may *blither* away the lives of good men, if he's tied in a chair with his feet stuck in a fire.'

'Er – quite.'

January thought he had seen a curtain move, in one of the dark, open windows of the house, but held his peace. 'Neither my wife, nor my stepdaughter Rachel, know anything of our enterprise here,' murmured the ferryman, as he cinched the knot tight. 'In the morning you shall tell them you were benighted here, having come to visit Henry Foster at Canebrake Plantation – only to find the plantation sold to a man named Jones, and your friend Foster left the county. Forgive me, sir,' he added to January, 'if I put you up in the loft room with the stableman when you return. Before I knew the true light of God's intention, I would not have shared house room with a man of your race, and so I have let the children of this world – yea, even the wife of my bosom – continue to believe.'

'She has no suspicion of it?' January couldn't imagine keeping his activities with runaways a secret from Rose, even if he were concealing them in some other location than his own house. Still less could he picture anyone who began to suspect that *something* might be afoot, not telling at least one friend. ('He's behaving so strangely . . . What should I do?')

'None.'

Oh, HASN'T she? January shut his lips hard on the words. He had, after all, just met this man, and there was something in the slightly smug note to that bass voice that made him think the comment wouldn't be well received. Then the buggy creaked as Drummond stepped down, and he heard his footsteps retreat around the corner of the house, and return again, accompanied by a faint sloshing noise that was, he deduced, a firkin of water – the buggy rocked slightly as the firkin was placed in the boot. Drummond went and fetched something else – food, January guessed, when a smaller weight was added to the boot – and then settled himself on the seat again at January's side and took the reins.

In all that time there came not a sound from the house.

The drive took about forty minutes. *Doubling on his own trail*, thought January, listening to the muted scrunch of the iron buggy wheels on weeds, the slap of branches and shrubs against the vehicle's sides. Occasionally he smelled cattle, and often, the river: DeSoto Point was barely a mile wide, low-lying though thickly overgrown. Often he smelled the wet, green scent of cane or branches closely surrounding them, and once more – distantly – he heard dogs.

Even in his early childhood, under the Spanish King's governors, militia patrols had ridden the Louisiana roads to take up slaves found walking about without permission, or to arrest those who might have slipped away from the maroon villages to encourage their unfree brothers to either escape or revolt. When he himself would slip away to visit the nearest of these settlements – where there was always dancing on Sunday afternoons – he would be meticulously careful to stay out of the way of the patrols, knowing that he would be severely beaten if caught. Adults caught by the so-called 'pattyrollers' were sometimes tortured. He remembered more than one man – and one woman – who had been whipped to death.

At the time – he had been five or six – this had seemed to him normal, the way everybody lived.

The buggy halted. Drummond's big hand closed on his elbow. 'Out you come. Don't touch the blindfold.'

Wet branches brushed his legs. The buggy creaked and his medical satchel was pressed into his hands. 'Stay where you stand.'

Thick brush rustled as the rein was looped around it. Gnats and mosquitoes landed in swarms on January's face. Then a padlock clacked sharply somewhere near. Drummond took his hand, guided him two steps, and near his feet rusted hinges creaked. Warm air rose over his face, rank with the smell of crowded bodies, of a too-close cesspit, of blood. 'Turn around,' said Drummond. 'There's a ladder here.'

'Mr Drummond, sir!' cried a woman's voice from below. 'Thank God you come!'

'I have the doctor.' Drummond's hoarse whisper sounded near to the ground as he knelt. 'How fares he?'

'He's alive, sir.' A man's voice, light-timbred and surprisingly educated. 'I pray God you're not too late.'

'Go down,' Drummond instructed January. 'I shall return in two hours, that we may get Ballou across on the ferry before first light, if he can be moved. Arthur, Isaiah, here is water and food.'

January climbed down twenty-five rungs on a ladder that creaked and trembled under his weight. Hands on his arms and shoulders immediately led him away from the ladder's foot to let Arthur and Isaiah, whoever they were, climb up and get the firkin of water, and the sack or box or whatever it was of food. By the smell of it, too, in climbing up for supplies they carried up a latrine barrel, presumably to be emptied in the river at a place where the patrols weren't likely to pass.

Even before he removed his blindfold January guessed the cellar they were in was small. It was clammy and reeked of too many bodies. Mosquitoes whined in his ears. A toddler's tiny voice muttered sleepily, 'Mama? Mama?' and a woman whispered, 'Hush, Charlie, your mama will be back by and by.'

A man's voice, slurred with weakness, muttered, 'Brother Abel?'

'We have a doctor for you,' murmured the light-timbred voice that had spoken first. 'You'll be all right.'

A single candle's light seemed a glare, after the blindfold. It was set near the injured man, who was lying on a blanket in a corner of what appeared to have once been a root cellar or an icehouse, stone walls glistening with wet. Gnats swarmed like blizzard snow around the flame, and the woman kneeling beside the candle fanned at them with the discouragement of one nearly sick with weariness.

Two men came down the ladder, the larger of them with a small barrel of water on one shoulder, the lighter and more wiry carrying a sack of what later turned out to be bread, cheese and sausage. This man lowered his burden to the others in the cellar and climbed up again, to bring down a small, empty cask with a lid.

'Over here, sir,' said a youth at January's elbow, and led him to Rex Ballou's side.

'We kep' the wound clean as we could, sir.' The woman – the only one in the cellar – came to his side as he hunkered down. 'Brother Abel—' She nodded up toward the shaft into which the ladder disappeared, to indicate Drummond – 'brung us some brandy, and haven't none of us drunk it, but we kep' it for cleanin' the wound here. I heated up some water in the cup, too, often as I could over the candle. But it don't seem to done any good.'

'It's done a world of good, m'am.' January unpinned the wrappings that held the dressing in place. It had the appearance of having been changed recently. 'If you hadn't, I doubt I'd have a chance of helping him.' Looking at the wound, he could understand Drummond's haste in bringing them here at once. 'Mr Ballou?'

Ballou's long fingers groped for January's wrist, gripped it with encouraging strength. 'You got here quick. Thank God.'

'I was only down in Natchez. But clear down in New Orleans, I heard of you, and it's my honor to make your acquaintance.'

The man's lips twisted wryly, and he whispered, 'I could have done without the honor in the circumstances,' and January chuckled.

'We take honor where we can get it, sir. Could you boil me some more water in that cup, m'am?' he added. 'I purely hope that's not your only cup.'

'It is,' said the woman, 'but that don't matter. Gives us all somethin' to do.'

He glanced at a makeshift tin chimney in one corner of the room, with a little hearth of broken tile under it. There was a scrum of cold ash on the hearth, and dribbles of candle tallow. It was clear that no fire had been made there for a long time.

'I ain't heard the dogs for awhile,' spoke up the youth, who'd squatted next to the chimney, and the wiry little man who'd carried down the victuals sack nodded, and passed a couple of tallow candles from the sack to the woman at the hearth.

Faces were nearly impossible to distinguish in the gloom, but January counted four adult men as well as the woman in the cellar, plus two children, a boy of nine or so and the tiny Charlie, who looked about two. Someone dipped a tin cup of water from the barrel, and the woman lit the second candle from the first, and set the water to boil over it on a makeshift little gallows of sticks.

'My name's Benjamin St-Denis.' January held out his hand to the men.

'Isaiah Biggar,' said the wiry man, shaking it firmly.

'Arthur . . . Dane.' Almost as African-black as January himself – Yoruba mother, January guessed, like his own – this man spoke, in spite of the clear care in his diction, fumblingly, as if he'd recently been beaten for speaking at all.

The third man, really a youth of about sixteen or seventeen and so old enough to be put to work in the men's gangs, introduced himself as Ason in a treacle-thick accent common to the Alabama cotton lands. The fourth man, barely older than Ason, big and lumbering and no darker than an Italian, mumbled that his name was Deya, without meeting January's eyes.

'This's Randol.' Isaiah laid an arm briefly around the nine-year-old's shoulders. 'An' that there fine young man with Deya is Charlie.'

Charlie murmured again, 'Mama?' and pushed his tiny ball of a fist into his mouth.

'Hey,' whispered Deya to the child, 'hey, champ, gonna be all right, see? Here we go – you hungry?' From the sack he took a piece of bread, tore the soft center of it out and wadded it into a lump. 'You gotta be hungry, big man. Me, I'm so hungry if Mr Abel hadn't locked that door up there again, I'd'a gone right up that ladder an' eat his horse, shoes an' tail an' everythin' . . .'

The child laughed sleepily, and ate. January suspected they were dosing the toddler with veronal or laudanum. He glanced down at the woman, and met her eyes; he raised his brows, and nodded toward the child, and she responded with the slightest movement of her head and a wince of distress: *Yes*. Fugitives who came through New Orleans – who hid in the ground-floor chambers of his house – had told him of doing the same thing.

Slaveholders knew that once a woman was pregnant, she probably wouldn't run. Once birthed, a baby would make noise – by the time a toddler was old enough to flee, the woman would likely be pregnant again. Mostly it was young men who fled slavery. Women could only endure it.

January took his scalpel and probe from his bag and set them in the water cup to boil, then wet a corner of one of the clean rags that he'd also brought, and gently wiped the wound. Rex Ballou shut his teeth hard, and stared up at the narrowing beehive-shaped roof overhead, where the tiniest shreds of candlelight touched the brickwork. His narrow features were almost European, as was the hank of straight, silky hair that fell over one eye.

'We tried to get the ball outta him this afternoon, sir,' said Isaiah. 'Back home, Auntie Sara said to run the knife back an' forth through a candle flame, so's it'd cut cleaner.'

'Good for your Auntie Sara.' January wondered where a healer-woman in a slave village might have picked up this piece of wisdom which he'd heard from Dr Pelletier, a surgeon at the Hôtel Dieu in Paris, whose 'hobbyhorse' for cleanliness had been sneered at by most of the other surgeons on the staff. January had observed that there were far fewer problems with infection when the instruments had been boiled.

'We couldn't get it,' Isaiah continued. 'An' with just a candle to see by, I tells you, I's afraid to go diggin' around.'

'Good for Auntie Sara and good for you,' amended January, and wrapped his hand in the rag to pick the probe from the boiling water. By Ballou's breathing, he guessed that the lung hadn't been touched. By the fact that he was still alive, neither had the heart. 'Can you turn him? Doesn't look like it bounced off anything inside, thank God. But it's probably got shirting in there with it. Can we risk another candle, without light showing outside?'

When the knife went in, Ballou closed his eyes and gripped hard on the hands of the men who held his shoulders still. '*I will lift up my eyes unto the hills, from whence cometh my help*,' he whispered desperately. '*My help cometh from the Lord . . . He will not suffer thy foot to be moved: he that keepeth thee will not slumber . . .*'

January leaned so close to the wound that he thought he'd light his eyebrows on fire from the candle, and repeated softly, '*My help cometh from the Lord*.'

FOUR

'Can he be moved?'

'Not back to Vicksburg, he can't.' Looking up from the ladder through the trapdoor, January could barely make out the silhouette of Drummond's head against the stars. 'You've said that neither your wife nor your stepdaughter know of this matter. Where would you take him, save to your house? Have you a blanket? The ground is very damp down there.'

'I've a rug in the buggy, a buffalo hide.' Drummond closed the trapdoor over January's head – *Does he think I'm going to pull a sextant from my pocket, to locate his hideout by the stars?* By the sound of it, the ferryman slipped the padlock through the hasp; and then January remembered the Quaker girl in Monroe, killed and 'roughed up pretty bad' for helping slaves to escape. No wonder the man was cautious.

The trap opened again, and Drummond handed down to him the dusty mountain of the buffalo robe, and after it a dirty wool blanket of the sort that cab drivers laid over their horses on freezing nights. 'How long 'til he can be moved? If you and your friend would consent to cross over again tomorrow night . . .'

'If you will, sir,' whispered January, 'I should feel better if I could stay here through the day with Ballou. Can some reason be fixed up for him to be absent from his shop in town? Truly, he cannot be moved now,' he added. 'And I want to be on hand, if his condition worsens.'

Drummond was silent. 'The Lord will make a way straight for us,' he said at last. 'Saul will bear your friend back across the river at daybreak, and put it about that you were bitten by a snake and cannot cross until Monday. I'll come for you this time tomorrow night.'

As he carried the dusty blankets down the ladder, January fought to push aside the wave of panic that stirred in him at the sound of the lock once more snapping shut. *Twenty-four hours.* That time would be critical to the wounded man below. He could have described to Isaiah, Arthur and the woman Giselle the symptoms of bodily collapse, which sometimes followed wounds and field surgeries – the racing, thready heartbeat, the clammy coldness of the extremities – but guessed they had not the experience to either recognize them or deal with them. Yet their lives, the lives of Ezekias Drummond and his sons, and the freedom of the hundreds who would, with luck, pass this way in the coming years, depended on Rex Ballou's ability to heal, and heal quickly – to pretend that he had not been wounded at all.

He made up a bed for his patient, using the wool horse blanket as a mattress and the buffalo robe folded over Ballou as a makeshift quilt. He told himself that if worst came to worst – if this were the ill-fated day on which the patrols discovered the fugitives' hiding place – the others in the cellar would back him in a claim that he was a runaway like themselves. Ballou, they would recognize and kill. Himself, they would lock up in the slave jail in Richmond and send word to Hannibal.

Unless the sheriff of Madison Parish thought he could get away with selling the runaways to a dealer bound for Texas or Missouri.

Are you REALLY going to risk never seeing Rose again – risk letting your son grow up on charity, never knowing his father – for a total stranger?

Rex Ballou risks death every day, to help total strangers to freedom.

And don't you risk death daily in the fever summers when you work the plague hospitals?

He recalled the words of Bacon: *He that hath wife and children hath given hostages to fortune, for they are impediments to great enterprises.*

And against that he heard the whisper of the vow he had made to Rose: *Forsaking all others . . .*

If Drummond had sent his stableman Boze to Ballou's shop to give the neighbors the impression the man was still present, Ballou probably wasn't married. In his mind he heard again the ferryman say, 'My wife knows nothing of my enterprise here,' and again wondered how that could be so.

Shut up, he told himself. *You're here, and the trapdoor's locked. Nothing you can do about it now. Just focus what you came to do.*

'I need something – a pallet, or even some bricks – to raise up his legs a little.' January glanced around him as he and the other men moved Ballou as gently as they could onto the drier bed. 'And I'm sorry, but we'll need to give him more water than the rest of you are getting.'

'Of course,' said Isaiah at once, and the others nodded. With a bitter grin, he added, 'It ain't like we all ain't gone thirsty before.'

'Thank you.' January folded the flap of the buffalo robe over the unconscious man, felt his pulse – still strong and steady – and lightly touched the skin of his forehead and cheeks. Dry but not parched. So far, so good.

Arthur Dane added, 'Will *you* have a little water, sir?'

'Maybe later.' He glanced over at baby Charlie, sleeping in the young man Deya's massive arms. 'Anybody know how well sound carries up that smoke pipe?'

'We hear the dogs sometimes, sir,' replied young Ason. 'Sometimes men's voices. This mornin' I heard birdsong.'

'When first we come down here,' whispered Giselle, 'Mr Abel brung us a little bottle laudanum, to give that poor baby an' make him sleep. We still got some.' She fished it from her pocket and held it up. 'I got to say I don't hold with it, sir – Miz Blanche back home took it all the time, an' give it to her babies – but yesterday it was the savin' of us. It won't – it won't hurt him, will it, sir?'

January shook his head, though he wasn't at all sure of the long-term effects on a child so young. 'He'll be fretful and will cry more for a week or two after he finishes taking it.' He took the bricks that Arthur brought him, from the fallen-in side of the cellar, and made a sort of platform of them, under the wounded man's calves. 'He may be sickly afterwards for a long time. His mama?'

He looked inquiringly at Giselle, then Isaiah, who seemed to be the *ad hoc* leader of the group. '*Your mama will be back by an' by*' could mean anything – from the truth (in which case where was she?) to *Your mama's dead and we don't want you making a fuss about it now . . .*

Life would be terrible indeed, he thought, for a child whose mother had fled with him in her arms, then died on the way, leaving him utterly alone.

It was just slightly too long before anyone answered, but he saw the look that passed between them, Giselle and Isaiah and Arthur Dane.

The look that almost shouted: *Do we tell him?*

No . . .

'We think Cindy got to be hiding someplace near, sir,' Isaiah said at last. 'She – In all the confusion, after Mr Ballou was shot, we lost sight of her . . .'

Another look, eyes meeting eyes – *Was that all right?*

It'll do . . .

What the HELL . . .?

He remembered Saul Drummond's momentary silence and averted face. *Yes, they's all hid . . .*

'She'll be all right,' added Isaiah quickly. 'That is – if anything had happened to her, Mr Abel would have heard of it, an' told us.'

Heads were nodded. Quickly. Giselle added, 'I'll tell her what you said, sir, about the laudanum.'

Ason put in, 'We got us a long way yet to go.'

In that maroon village in the *ciprière*, January tried to remember whether he'd ever heard babies crying. There had certainly been women there – Auntie Jeanne, the *mambo* on Bellefleur, had had a sister there, a *mambo* also: his younger sister Olympe was always running away to see her. And there were older children there as well . . .

All the candles in the cellar save one had been blown out. The boy Randol had fallen asleep, his head on Deya's thigh. Ason took up what was evidently his station, listening at the smoke-pipe; January whispered, 'You think the candlelight can be seen up above?'

'I doubt it,' murmured Isaiah. 'It's twenty-five feet, easy.'

'You know,' said Arthur Dane softly, 'under other circumstances I'd think this was ironic. As a boy I'd read adventure tales, about spying against the British, or the French, or the Turks in the Crusades . . . I used to think them so clever, making shifts to hide one's tracks, to conceal the smoke of one's fire—'

'Read adventure tales?' January stared at him in surprise.

'My parents were freedmen in Boston.' The young man's voice stammered on the words. 'I clerked at Palgrave's – a private bank – and when Palgrave's closed its doors at the end of 'thirty-six I needed a job. Like a fool I answered an advertisement in a Philadelphia newspaper about work.'

January winced at the man's naiveté, and at the ease with which he had been kidnapped in the Pennsylvania city, drugged with opium and smuggled across the border into Maryland, and thence by ship to New Orleans. In New York and other cities, the free black communities had established vigilance committees to prevent such kidnappings, though often there was little they could do. The child of freedmen, raised in freedom, Dane had not, like January in New Orleans, been brought up to always keep one eye over his shoulder. To be perpetually conscious of the possibility of the slave-stealers whose operations – since the beginning of the cotton boom of the twenties – had grown more extensive every year.

He could only put his hand on the man's wrist and give him a little shake: comfort, understanding. He couldn't say, *We'll get you out*, because it was a long, long way to Illinois.

After a moment Dane said, 'Thank you. For two years now there hasn't been a day – not an hour – when I haven't been sick with terror and despair. And it's worse since I fled.'

January understood that, too.

Just after dawn Ballou woke, clear-minded but devastatingly weak. January gave him water, and checked his pulse again. Still strong and steady.

'What day is it?' Ballou whispered.

'Sunday.'

'So in town they'll put it around that I gone over to Young's Point, to hear Ezekias preach.' Ballou sighed. 'I was afraid we'd have to set my shop on fire, so they could say I gone out of town to replace the mirrors.'

January winced sympathetically at the thought of nearly forty dollars' worth of mirrors, destroyed to create an excuse.

'Mr Abel—' He used the code name by which Drummond seemed to be known among the fugitives – 'said that the way would be made straight.' Though he was fairly sure none of the others were listening – Isaiah and Arthur both dozed on the damp earth – 'Is your friend Ezekias a good man in the pulpit?'

'The best of them,' whispered Ballou. 'God speaks to him, and through him.' Lowering his voice still further, he added, 'God sent him to me: that I truly believe. He had his own congregation, his own church, in Genesee County. But God changed his heart, and sent him here to wear the hide of a sinner – you should hear him preach about the curse the Lord set on the children of Africa! – that others might be helped. They are fools who say that God doesn't give his servants the strength to do his will.'

Having spent his first seven years sharing a one-room cabin with parents, sister and another family, January didn't find crowded quarters and the smell of unwashed bodies and clothing unendurable; and in the dissecting theater of the Hôtel Dieu in Paris on hot days he'd smelled far worse than a recently cleaned latrine bucket. When a thread of gray light leaked through the smoke-pipe from above, Isaiah, who had been a field gang driver, handed out rations of bread, cheese, sausage and water, and after eating, most of the runaways lay on the floor and slept.

January too slept, and dreamed of the slave village out in the *ciprière*, the one he'd described to Hannibal. Tiny huts of *bousillage* and thatch, with chickens penned among them. The headman, a slow-moving, wide-shouldered man named Suma, like Ezekias Drummond planned every move, every possibility, every contingency that must be avoided if the village were to remain safe. The few children there were watched constantly, less to keep them from danger than to keep them from wandering far and giving away the village's location. In his dream January was a child again, and one of the village children was complaining to him how *they* never got to wander off into the *ciprière* looking for bird nests and lizards, *they* never got to just go off fishing in the bayous. 'We *always* got to work,' the child complained in the thick patois – far more African than French – that the slaves spoke in the quarters. The maroons fell back on it because no two of them descended from the same tribe. 'Diggin' an' cleanin' yams, an' watchin' the chickens, an' settin' snares for rabbits. Suma says we even got to go shit in different places in the woods every time, so's nobody can find we's here. I wish *I* was in your quarters at Bellefleur.'

'That's 'cause you're stupid,' his sister Olympe had retorted, five years old and ferocious as a wolverine, with her black hair sticking out in all directions, braided with string.

And though January and Olympe were children, he saw Rose pass from one hut to another, Rose as he'd left her two weeks ago in New Orleans, gawky and beautiful in the flowing frock of her pregnancy, her hair wrapped neatly out of sight in a *tignon* and her oval spectacle lenses flashing, smiling her quicksilver smile.

January dreamed of the baying of the dogs, coming closer and closer in the swamp, the shouting of the men on patrol.

He woke in the rank darkness, to the sound of two-year-old Charlie crying, and Giselle whispering a song to him:

'Follow the drinking gourd,
Follow the drinking gourd.
There's an old man 'cross the river
Gonna carry you to freedom,
Follow the drinking gourd . . .

River's bank a very good road,
Follow the drinking gourd.
Dead trees show the way along,
Follow the drinking gourd . . .'

In his mind January saw the map they described, up the Mississippi to Cairo on the Illinois shore, with the seven stars of the Dipper – the Drinking Gourd – always pointing the way in the night sky to the north.

'River ends a-tween two hills,
Follow the drinking gourd;
Nuther river on the other side,
Follow the drinking gourd . . .

There's an old man 'cross the river
Gonna carry you to freedom,
Follow the drinking gourd . . .'

Distantly, down the long pipe of the chimney, he still heard the dogs.

FIVE

'I got to be on my feet,' whispered Ballou, when January emptied the pottery jug they used as a bed bottle into the latrine bucket, and came back to kneel at his side. 'I got to be *seen* on my feet.'

'If you try to go over and piss like the rest of us,' returned January patiently, 'you'll fall in and drown – if you make it that far.'

The day was endless, the cellar like a slow oven.

'They watching you in town?'

'Maury watches everybody. He thinks the world's out to rob him of what's his.'

'This the Maury who wants to turn the late Hugh Riley's poor valet into a fighter?'

'That's the one.' Ballou sighed. 'You heard about that?'

'I heard that's the reason the pattyrollers were all over the countryside Friday night. That sure ain't for you, or for any of these nice folks down here.'

And when Ballou frowned and the others gathered close he realized that this was probably the first any of them had heard about the complication in their plans.

Careful to avoid names, he outlined what Saul Drummond had told him, and when he was done Ballou murmured, 'Damn it. I knew Maury pestered Riley for years to sell him Quinto. Riley didn't hold with nigger fights. Quinto's a good fighter – he's big as you, and fast on his feet as a waterbug. But for him it's just scufflin'. Rasslin' around with his friends on a Sunday afternoon. Not what they do when white men are betting on it. Not for blood.'

January had seen men killed in the fights. Had – when called on – repaired, or tried to repair, damage done in bouts that had no code of rules, no penalties for gouging, biting, strangling or what white men called 'foul blows'. He knew there were slaves who fought willingly – or as willingly as any person did anything when enslaved – content with the privileges that victory brought: better food, comfortable quarters, first choice of the women (whether the woman he chose wanted to have anything to do with him or not). He knew others who fought only under compulsion, with the knowledge that if they failed, their wives, their children would be sold to cover the bets their owners didn't win. He whispered, 'No.'

'You think he suspects?' Arthur Dane's face pinched with anxiety. 'Have you ever helped one of his hands run?'

'No.' Ballou sighed, with an almost comical exasperation. 'That's the damn silly thing. Maury suspects me 'cause I'm friends with – with the Reverend Ezekias Drummond . . .'

His use of Drummond's true name – instead of calling him 'Mr Abel' – startled January for a moment, and he asked, cautiously, 'I thought the Reverend Drummond believes that black men *should* be slaves . . .'

'Oh, he does!' Ballou gave January a very slight nod that said, *That's right, it's as if they're two different people*. 'Rides with the patrols, and his sons with him; came up with this whole system of how God made black folks to serve decent white Christians. I'm the only black face in his congregation and he says, the only decent nigger on the whole of the river. But the Reverend Lemuel Bickern, of the Sanctuary Methodist congregation over in Richmond, has it in his head that Drummond's version of the gospel is heresy and Drummond himself is the Antichrist, and Drummond isn't a man to turn the other cheek no matter what Christ had to say about the matter. He's called Bickern "the minion of Satan" in his sermons, and says he's a false prophet, a Pharisee and a goat.'

'A goat?' Little Randol, who had for hours been struggling to remain manfully indifferent to hunger, thirst and the constant swarming of insects, brushed the gnats out of his eyes and looked genuinely interested.

'In the Bible it says that God's going to divide the good from the evil on Judgment Day,' explained Arthur, 'same as old-time shepherds used to divide the good sheep from the evil, ornery goats at the end of the day.'

'And is this Bickern,' asked January curiously, 'the one who's going to set up a tent-show Saturday to preach the gospel to all those who're too holy to visit the circus?'

'That's the one. The good ladies of Vicksburg have been holding bake sales and fairs and have been badgering their menfolk for years to raise money to build a Methodist church in Vicksburg. They're bringing in the Reverend Jeremiah Thorne from Jackson, and he and Bickern are going to preach wall-to-wall brimstone, turn and turnabout, all day, to bring the money up to their goal, and I will say,' he added with a grin, 'that I surely look forward to seeing which of those two reverend gentlemen gets to actually *be* the new preacher in Vicksburg. The Jackson ladies are set on it being *their* Reverend Thorne, and they're ready to pull the Vicksburg ladies' hair out over it. The Reverend Drummond,' he added, 'is running one of his horses in the race that morning – which makes him six kinds of sinner in Bickern's eyes, and me a scoundrel thief and up to no good for being his friend.'

He sighed, and closed his eyes. 'Better than having me seem like a man who gives a flea's turd about his fellow man.'

January swiped at the gnats thronging around his ears, an exercise in uselessness that he'd pursued for eighteen hours now. At least, he thought, in the substantial *libré* community of New Orleans he didn't have to pretend to be something he wasn't for his own safety and the safety of his family.

For the fifth time that day the baying of Drew Hardy's hounds sounded down the tin chimney pipe, louder this time, and close. In the silence that fell on the cellar, little Charlie began to sob for his mother, and Giselle whispered, 'Shush – shush,' and stroked the child's wet forehead. 'Your mama be here by an' by.'

She threw a quick look at Ballou, who winced, and nodded. 'Give him a little more.'

'I just give him two drops a couple hours ago.'

'They're close.' Isaiah took the child from her arms.

Giselle turned stricken eyes toward January, who looked away. *If they find us, they'll find Ballou. If they find Ballou, they'll go after Drummond . . .*

'I hate it.' Ballou's whisper was so soft that it excluded even Arthur Dane, who sat only feet away. January had to bend over him to hear. 'I know it's got to be, but I hate it like the mouth of Hell. Drummond gives it to his wife, you know – his wife and his stepdaughter. He started with valerian, three years ago when he married Miss Constance. Now it's laudanum. He can't risk them knowing.' He shook his head. 'I don't know what to say to him. You married, St-Denis?'

'I am.'

'Your wife know?'

'My wife,' said January, 'and my niece and nephew who live with us. How old's the stepdaughter?'

'Sixteen. Old enough to know – but old enough to have a mind of her own.'

And how *would* you keep a sixteen-year-old girl from whispering to her friends, if she thought there was something odd about her stepfather's home? Lock her in her room? He recalled those dark windows of the house by the river.

Acquaintance with his niece at that age – and with the Gothic novels his youngest sister, Dominique, consumed like petit fours – assured him that unless the girl was a complete imbecile, imprisonment would only make the situation much, much worse . . . particularly if she hadn't been enamored of her mother's second marriage to begin with.

'How old are your nephew and niece?'

'Fifteen and seventeen,' said January. 'But I never worried about them, 'cause their mama's a voodoo and if either of 'em breathed a word about it, she'll turn 'em into toads.'

The baying of the dogs came near, and silence fell, that lasted long into darkness.

'Made it!' panted Ballou, as he took two steps back to his blankets from the latrine barrel, and sagged down into January's arms. 'Well, damn.'

'Good try,' said January.

'Looks like we're gonna have to burn down my shop.'

'The Lord will provide,' said Drummond, when January emerged gasping from the cellar shaft sometime shortly before midnight, by the stars, and informed him of Ballou's condition. He blindfolded January at once, and left him standing beside his buggy ('Let me stand a bit, I've been cramped up since last night . . .') while he swiftly carried water and food to those waiting below, and brought up the latrine barrel, which he lashed to the buggy's boot. He added, as he finally helped January into the vehicle and they drove off, 'I fear Rex is right, and the shop must be burnt.'

'A pity you can't put it around that Ballou was injured in the fire,' said January thoughtfully. 'But that would look too obvious.'

'Boze is near enough Ballou's height that in his clothing, in darkness and smoke, there will be those who'll attest Ballou was there.' The buggy's wheels splashed oozily into a slough, and water slopped over January's feet.

'At least it'll get Ballou out of the problem of customers coming in later today wanting a shave.'

Drummond grunted. ''Twill have to be done tonight,' he said. 'Boze and I will row across in the skiff – I fear I'll have to ask you, brother, to wake before dawn – ere my wife rises – and cross quietly to the ferry landing. I'll take you over at first light.'

'I could go in the skiff with you, tonight—'

'Too risky. It's been put about in town that you were delayed through snakebite, and this must be seen to be true. Besides, if you went into the town tonight, where would you stay? They'd all see you come into the hotel. And you'll need to wash,' he added matter-of-factly, to which January assented with a sigh. 'You've earned your rest.'

The ferryman drew rein, and pulled January's blindfold free. Beyond the steely gleam of the river, Vicksburg loomed dark against the sky, its waterfront marked with a sullen scatter of gold.

'And I'll need your help tomorrow,' added Drummond. 'Another little game of make-believe, like your friends play in the circus. On such play-acting our enterprise depends. Jubal Cain is in town.'

'Oh?' January's attention prickled at the slave-dealer's name.

'To keep my good credentials, it will be necessary for me to bring you into town with me.'

'All right.' As Rex Ballou had said, some things had to be seen . . . and this was one of them.

If Rex Ballou can get himself on his feet within days of being shot – if Drummond can forgo even the comfort of trusting his own wife – I can do this.

But he remembered the slave-dealer Fenks on the Vicksburg

docks, and the wave of anger that went through him turned him nearly sick.

Limping on his 'snakebit' foot with the aid of a stick, January followed Ezekias Drummond along the brisk confusion of the Vicksburg riverfront the following morning. The blue shadow of the Walnut Hills still lay over the edge of the river, but the day was already muggy and hot. The muscles of shirtless stevedores glistened as they passed loads of cordwood along from the great piles of it on the wharves and into the shallow bellies of the *Gladiator*, the *Otsego Queen*, the *Vidalia* and the *Victory*.

On this occasion Drummond had come to town on one of his saddle horses, a tall stallion of the breed January had heard called 'warmbloods', heavier of bone than the more stylish thoroughbreds but beautifully suited to a man of the ferry owner's bulk.

'They're my beauties,' Drummond had said to him, on the ferry just after dawn, when January had asked him if he bred his horses himself. 'God made man in his own image, and gave him lordship over all the beasts of the field, to have dominion over them – but some beasts are surely wrought with special care by the hand of the Almighty. My wife calls this one Big Brownie.'

He'd shaken his head, as he gently rubbed the animal's thin white blaze, stroked the heavy black-oak muscle of its neck. The horse had responded by nibbling his master's ear gently, without the nervous aggressiveness that so often characterized the uncut males of the breed. 'Gentle as a kitten.'

'Gentler than my mother's cats,' sighed January, 'that's for sure. You don't name them yourself?'

Drummond had hesitated at that, then shaken his head. 'Nowhere in the Holy Writ does it mention the name of a single beast,' he said. In his pale eyes was the closest expression January had seen in them to wistfulness and regret.

Given the control the ferryman seemed to exercise over his sons and his wife – not to mention the stepdaughter deep asleep in a separate wing of the house – January could only assume that it was the slave-groom Boze who had named the sleek, hairy-footed ferry horses after the judges of Israel.

After scrubbing himself all over at the pump behind the barn the previous night, January had not ascended at once to the loft room that Boze had shown him. When Drummond, Boze and Saul had pushed themselves off in Drummond's little rowing skiff, January – with the instinctive caution that dictated his every move outside the French Town – had walked around the outside of Drummond's house and stables within the square of cottonwoods.

By the dim starlight he had seen none of the usual marks left for fugitives: the signs scratched into fence lumber or barn doors, the quilt hung out a window – showed that this house was a 'depot' on the 'railway'. The secrecy here was absolute. Looking up at the lightless windows, January could not keep himself from remembering the two women who slept there, drugged like poor baby Charlie lest they see what they might speak of later.

'*It wasn't 'til Mama died that he told her – or us – what he was doin' or why he'd come down here to preach the gospel*,' Saul had said.

Had that been because Mama hadn't approved of helping other men's property steal themselves and run away to freedom?

What was a man to do, if he had, as Ballou had said, a change of heart? If he felt himself called suddenly, like the Apostle Paul, to save the lives of – give new lives to – hundreds of men and women who would otherwise be trapped in Hell? What was he to say to the wife he'd married before this conversion of thought? *Forsaking all others . . .*

And what of the woman he'd married, the stepdaughter he'd brought to this isolated farm on the Point? Thirteen was an age, January knew, when girls take out their defiance in wild talk, the way his niece Zizi-Marie did with her friends. But when Zizi-Marie described the nuns who taught her as jealous haters of young girls smarter and more beautiful than themselves (like herself), or (upon occasion) as witches worse than the worst voodoo in town, none of her many friends took her very seriously.

The girl's friends – if she had any – would be kin to men who would kill Ezekias Drummond if they heard any blurted secrets, any wild speculations about overheard conversations or shadowy figures spied coming and going in the night.

And then, who would her friends be? There was every chance that the new Mrs Drummond wouldn't hear of her daughter associating with the daughters – certainly not the sons! – of the few crackers and swamp-trappers on this side of the river, and it was unlikely that the daughters of whatever planters there were in Madison Parish, once they reached the age of fourteen, would *be* on this side of the river. They'd be away at boarding school. In Vicksburg itself, in Natchez, or in New Orleans.

No wonder the man turns to his horses for his comfort, thought January, *when he must watch his own every move, his own every thought, even in his own home*.

Coming around the corner of the house on his way up to the loft at last, he had seen across the river in Vicksburg the sudden orange flare of a fire springing up, and had prayed a prayer that the arsonists of Rex Ballou's barbershop would get clean away.

Climbing the steep slope of Clay Street – awkwardly, because he'd wrapped a sharp pebble into the bandage of his 'snakebit' foot to remind himself to limp – January saw the remains of Rex Ballou's barbershop. The white clapboard camelback – with a single-story shop in the front and two stories in the rear – had been nearly gutted, and boards were already nailed roughly over the broken windows. A neat sign had been tacked to the charred door: 'Open for Business Thursday or Know the Reason Why.'

Men grouped idly in front speculated on the cause of the fire ('I told him a dozen times you can't trust them newfangled iron stoves.') or complained that they had to shave themselves this morning ('What the hell's the matter with the man?'), but nobody seemed to be making any connection between Ballou's absence and the man who'd been shot by the pattyrollers on the other side of the river.

Yet.

Know the Reason Why indeed . . .

Everyone seemed far more interested in the poster for the All-American Zoological Society's Traveling Circus and Exhibition of Philosophical Curiosities which someone had pasted to the shop's charred wall, complete with pictures of Martha the Elephant (shown two or three times her actual size – the men in the engraving reached barely to her knee) and Mozambia the Bearded Lady. 'I'm puttin' my money on that bay of Rich Haffle's in the race Saturday.' 'That thing? Runs like it's got two broken legs! Bet on Griffin's Wildfire.'

Jubal Cain was sitting at one of the wicker chairs in the porch of the Planter's Hotel, sipping coffee and reading the *American Turf Register*. He was a big man, broad-shouldered in his well-cut white linen coat, and hard-looking, with that particular withdrawn callousness of expression that January had seen all his life in the faces of overseers, of dealers, of men who have taught themselves to see other human beings as literally no more than animals. Men who could pry a woman's hands loose when she clung to the arm of her child as the child screamed with terror, knowing she would never see her child again: '*Now, honey, don't do no good to make a fuss . . .*'

Men whose method of dealing with a slave's diarrhea was to stuff his – or her – anus with tar so they wouldn't appear to be sick on the auction block.

Men who had evolved a science of systematically breaking the spirits of those they sold, with starvation, rape, imprisonment and carefully calculated beatings.

Cain raised his yellow eyes from the newspaper when Drummond and January came onto the porch, as if calculating January's weight to the pound and estimating at the same time what Drummond's clothing told him about the man's financial position: what he'd take, what January would fetch in the open market.

'You wait here, boy,' instructed Drummond as they reached the hotel's porch steps.

'Yes, sir.'

Cain set coffee and register aside, rose from his chair as Drummond passed: 'Beg pardon, sir, if you have a moment . . .?' His voice was like shoveled gravel. 'Jubal Cain is my name.' He offered a card. 'And I could not but notice what a likely looking boy you have there.' He nodded toward January. 'You haven't ever thought of selling him, have you?'

'If he were my own I wouldn't.' Drummond inclined his head in greeting, but didn't touch his hat. Everywhere in the slave states, dealers were regarded with contempt, even by the men who bought their wares. January was aware of two or three planters, likewise enjoying coffee and a smoke in the chilled light of the pale morning in the porch, observing the transaction, as Drummond had known they would be there to do: a means of confirming his *bona fides*. 'He belongs to a man named Pinkerton, staying here at this hotel – got himself snakebit Sunday when they went out to Foster's on Roundaway Bayou. You, boy—' He signaled to the young man who'd brought Cain his coffee. 'Would you find Mr Pinkerton for me, if he's inside? Far as I can tell—' He turned back to Cain – 'he is a first-class valet. Hardly think it to look at him, would you?'

As January had been virtually certain it would – in a social gathering place like the porch of the Planter's Hotel, at this hour of the morning – this remark triggered a general clustering of the planters, Cain, and the weasel-faced dealer Fenks from the waterfront, and an exchange of opinions about his size, strength, appearance and possible capabilities ('He looks big enough to be a fightin' nigger.' 'Nah, he don't got the eyes for it.' 'Waste of time, puttin' a boy like that polishin' a man's shoe buckles.'). When Hannibal appeared on the porch, feckless and genial as ever with the slight unsteadiness of step that marked a man already a few drinks drunk, January had to stand quietly and hear the whole conversation over again, plus nearly half an hour of attempts by Cain and Fenks to talk his 'master' into selling him to one or the other of them.

Drummond joined in the talk for ten or fifteen minutes, encouraging Hannibal to sell (unsuccessfully) and accepting a drink from Cain 'to thank you for your trouble, sir'. He only took his leave when a handsome, broad-shouldered gentleman, clothed in black and like Drummond patriarchally bearded, appeared on the porch and looked him up and down with an expression of unconcealed disdain: '*Woe unto them that are mighty to drink wine . . .!*'

'Behold,' returned Drummond scornfully, gesturing to the newcomer, 'a prophet greater even than Jesus, who did not disdain to drink with publicans nor to associate with sinners! I thank you, Reverend Bickern, for showing me the holiness of *your* way!'

'Who you callin' a sinner?' demanded Fenks indignantly, but Jubal Cain's yellow eyes only glinted with amusement, and the Reverend Bickern's cheeks and ears flushed bright red.

'*How long shall this be in the heart of the prophets that prophesy lies?*' he retorted haughtily. '*Yea, they are prophets of the deceit of their own hearts—*'

'*They have seen vanity and lying divination—*' Drummond stabbed a thick finger at his rival, his own face reddening dangerously – '*saying, "The Lord saith," and the Lord hath not sent them—*'

'*But the prophet that shall presume to speak a word in my name,*' shouted Bickern, completely losing his temper, '*which I have not commanded him to speak . . . that prophet shall die! Satan himself is transformed into an angel of light: therefore it is no great thing if his ministers also be transformed as the ministers of righteousness—*'

'*God is not a God of confusion,*' said Cain, '*but of peace*. And so, gentlemen, I shall leave you.' He finished his drink and went into the hotel.

All the witnesses later attested that this was the extent of what took place on the porch that morning.

SIX

'How's that foot, Benjamin?' asked Hannibal solicitously, as he led the way – still weaving slightly – into the hotel, January obediently upon his heels. 'I've told the manager to arrange a room for you in the attic, but on your way up, I've laid out my shoes for you to polish in my room – Number Twelve – there's a good chap.'

'Sure thing, Marse Pinkerton, sir.'

'And sort out my shirts for the laundry.'

'Yes, sir. Thank you, sir.' It was just like being in the minstrel show.

Room Twelve was one of the hotel's modest chambers, on the third floor at the back, designed for the respectable indigent: those with little money but with clean collars, top hats, valets and table manners. In it January found, on the chipped marble-topped table, a pair of lace mitts, such as a woman might wear indoors, and deduced that his friend had not been idle in the twenty-four hours he had spent on his own in Vicksburg. He could only hope the lady in question wasn't married.

Or at least wasn't married to anyone likely to come after an errant wife's lover.

'Mrs Passmore,' said Hannibal, when he came in – with perfectly steady steps – a few minutes later. 'A widow of impeccable breeding and refinement, with letters of introduction to prove it. She operates a high-class bordello in Memphis and is in Vicksburg for her health – coincidentally at the same moment that the Reverend Bickern is going to hold his Call to Salvation for those who do not approve of horse races or Traveling Exhibitions of Philosophical Curiosities, and, with any luck, raise ten thousand dollars toward the purchase of land for a new church.'

January said, 'Hmmn.'

'The sight of her turning her ankle on the hotel's front steps just as the Reverend Bickern emerged from its doors yesterday would have made Sarah Siddons blush with shame – *Avertens rosea cervice refulsit, ambrosiaeque comae divinum vertice odorem spiravera*, and all the rest of Virgil's description of Dido . . . It did my heart good to see it.'

'I daresay.'

'Benjamin!' The fiddler looked shocked at his tone. '*Honni soit qui mal y pense!* She struggled valiantly to dispense with the Reverend Bickern's assistance, vowing herself fit to reach the lobby herself and positively demanding to be helped to her room by two porters, only permitting the holy man to follow along – in company with Mr Sorrell from the front desk – to make sure how she did.'

'And how *did* she do?'

Hannibal smiled. 'Very well indeed. I myself had earned the Reverend's approbation a few hours previously by ordering lemonade, of all the disgusting concoctions, at lunch – perfectly genuinely, I might add, they don't seem to have heard of soda water in this benighted hotel. I then won Mrs Passmore's heart by claiming to have met her in Clarke County, Indiana, at a temperance meeting . . . I'd actually seen her dealing faro at Russian Sally's place on Girod Street last year. I shall be very much surprised if she isn't able to make off with whatever funds the ladies of Vicksburg raise for their church, without anyone being the wiser. She and I played a little piquet last night – it was most— Enter!' he called out, at the sound of a quick, soft knock at the door.

January rose – like a good servant – and opened it.

In the hallway stood Jubal Cain.

'Is he well?' The purported slave-dealer stepped in very quickly.

'As well as can be expected.' January took Cain's hat and gloves, and Hannibal brought up the room's bent-willow chair from its place by the tiny writing table.

Cain – or Bredon, and one of the founding members of the Philadelphia Anti-Slavery Society, as he was elsewhere known – looked around him as he took the chair, gauging the cost of these modest accommodations. 'How much will you need for this?'

'Not a great deal, sir,' January replied. 'Friday, the circus comes to town, so we can go back to sharing quarters with the Mighty Hercules and Primula Kelly's University of Educated Canines. Ballou swears he'll be on his feet tomorrow or the next day, but I'd like to go out again tonight and see him. It's no good having him collapse in front of everyone in town.'

'No.' Cain fished in his pocket and brought out a small wash-leather bag, which clinked as he dropped it onto the marble. 'And you—' He jabbed a finger at Hannibal – 'mind you don't leave the lovely Mrs Passmore in the same room with this—'

'What does a poor woman have to do in this town to prove herself trustworthy?'

'Not play cards – or engage in other activities – for money,' retorted January with a grin. 'I'm sure the good subscribers to the Philadelphia Anti-Slavery Society would have something to say if she managed to walk off with their contributions—'

Hannibal snapped his fingers with a good imitation of aristocratic contempt. '*Fere libenter homines id quod volunt credunt.* She has much, much larger fish to fry in the shape of the church funds. In any case, at a dollar fifty a night, plus board, plus your room in the attic – which I'm sorry to say is barely large enough to swing a small kitten in, but it was that or share with Mr Norfolk Drear's valet, who I understand snores like the onset of Judgment Day – I only need to win four dollars and fifty cents per night, which should be easy enough to do and completely inconspicuous. Scarcely worth Mrs Passmore's time or effort.'

'If she hopes to get her hands on ten thousand dollars' worth of church money,' January shook his head. 'I suppose not. Though if it's anything like that amount, as our good employer Mr Tavish would remark, he – and we – are in the wrong business.'

'Well, we all knew that,' grunted Cain. 'But the right business to be in would require you to spend all your time agreeing with the likes of Brother Bickern – and Brother Maury.'

'Any word on that poor valet he's chasing?'

'None that I've heard.' Cain made a face. 'There's going to be nigger fights Saturday – as well as the horse races and hellfire preaching and your Exhibition of Philosophical Curiosities – and I'll have to show up at them . . .'

His heavy brows, a few shades browner than his flaxen hair, pulled down sharply over the ugly little hook of his nose. 'By the way, I apologize for that little comedy on the porch, Ben,' he added.

'It's no worse than watching four New York Jews pretend to be my kinsfolk four performances a week.' January shrugged. 'It's worse for Drummond, if he rides regularly with the patty-rollers. And for you,' he added.

Cain grunted. 'If that chinless muck-snipe Fenks tells me one more time about his "fancy goods", I won't be answerable for my conduct. And now Brister – the sheriff over in Madison Parish – says he wants to ask me about tracking fugitives, so he can find that poor valet – meaning he wants to tell me *his* opinions on the subject . . . and drink. I was a drinking man before I undertook running this section of the railway,' he finished with a sigh. 'But I swear to you, Sefton, socializing with the men in the slave business has made me envy you teetotalers.'

'*When I am dead and opened*,' January solemnly paraphrased the dying words of Bloody Mary of England, '*you shall find Sheriff Brister lying on my heart*. How strong a man is Ballou, sir? Is he up to this?'

'He's strong. He has to be. And he'll do what he has to do, to save this link on the railroad. It's his show,' Cain went on. 'Always has been. He was a valet down in Warrenton: bought himself free in 1825. He had a shop for a while in New York, on Wall Street – he was one of the first members of the New York Vigilance Committee. Whether it was Turner's revolt in Virginia that started him thinking, or just the fact that men were setting up cotton plantations in the territories as fast as the government could throw the Indians off the land, in 'thirty-one he came back to Vicksburg. Ballou knows every foot of the land between Natchez and Memphis. For a couple of years he worked with Harriet Welles – that Quaker girl – in Monroe . . .'

'We heard,' said Hannibal softly, 'about the Quaker girl in Monroe.'

Cain's ugly face darkened. 'That was bad business,' he said. 'Her parents didn't approve of slavery but they had no idea she'd teamed up with a free black farmer to help runaways. They were lucky they weren't lynched themselves.'

'I take it Ballou wasn't working closely with her when it happened?' said January.

'She'd pass cargo along to him from the western parishes. Ballou would connect them with a woman named Eliza Walker in Paducah. Mrs Walker's a runaway herself; she's been leading people through that jungle for years. But after Turner's rebellion it was pretty clear no slave revolt was going to succeed against the US Army, so there were more runaways – and more patrols. And more men keeping an eye on the free blacks, blaming them for the runaways. Ballou went to New York in 'thirty-two with the idea of finding a white partner who'd have more freedom of movement than either him or Walker. He met Drummond at a meeting of the New York Anti-Slavery Society, and Drummond came down here early the following year.

'So, yes, if Ballou needs to be seen on his feet Wednesday, he'll be on his feet. You ride across on the ferry with me this afternoon, Ben, and row back in Drummond's skiff late tonight. Sefton, can you meet him when he lands? The waterfront's crawling with slave-stealers, so don't row back to town. Make for Big Bayou, south of town. If you signal with a lantern before you start, Ben, Sefton should be able to see you from the bluff above.'

'My heart breaks with grief at the prospect of missing this evening's – er – card game with the beauteous Mrs Passmore,' admitted Hannibal. 'Yet I shall contrive somehow to stifle my tears.'

January descended to meet Cain in the long gravel driveway at three. He'd slept for a few hours, washed at the pump behind the kitchen – the customary spot for the ablutions of the slaves, both those owned by the hotel and by the hotel's guests – and changed his clothes. Talk of the fire was the nine days' wonder among the waiters and houseboys behind the kitchen, along with speculation concerning the absconding valet Quinto: 'Men watchin' the waterfront – five hundred dollar, that's a lot of money! An' Quinto, he's big, big as you, Ben. He be hard to miss . . .'

'So where he hidin'?'

Nobody seemed to know.

Inquiries for 'Marse Pinkerton' got January directed to the Ladies' Parlor, into which sanctum Hannibal had been invited by the genteel Mrs Passmore (*Why am I not surprised?*). Tapping at the open door, January discovered his friend holding court with educated compliments and a refined whiff of almost-flirtation: not adultery, as Byron would have said, but certainly adulteration. The tightly-corseted matron in the close-brimmed bonnet to his right was fairly eating teacakes out of his hand.

January guessed immediately which of the ladies present was Mrs Passmore. Far from pretty, with a strong chin and a stronger nose, she was nevertheless warmly attractive, with violet-blue eyes that listened in fascinated absorption to whatever was being said and a voice like dark honey. She spoke seldom, but followed the conversation with the calculation of a fencer in a duel. She only remarked, with hesitant concern, that if the Vicksburg ladies could perhaps not equal the contributions to the new Sanctuary Tabernacle that were being made by the Jackson ladies, those ladies might think themselves privileged to place the Reverend Mr Thorne in charge of the new church instead of dear Reverend Bickern, 'Though I don't really know anything about this sort of thing myself . . .'

'They wouldn't *dare*!' 'It's our Mr Haffle who's assisting in the purchase of the land!' 'Who are *they* to push their way in?'

January estimated that pledges for the church funds rose by about two hundred dollars as a result.

'My aunt Alice did say,' ventured a lovely young woman in a faded dress, 'that the Reverend Thorne, having no church of his own, deserves a place.'

'Your aunt Alice,' retorted the tight-corseted dame, 'is the bossiest woman in the state, Julia Maury, and can't abide the thought of someone not of her choosing being put in charge of what is going to be the handsomest House of God between here and New Orleans! You can't tell *me* that your husband is going to permit those puling Jackson backsliders to buy their way into *our* affairs! The Reverend Thorne indeed! Weak-kneed, cozening, with his milk-and-water talk of tolerating evil!'

'Oh, Caroline,' objected a white-haired lady, 'the Reverend Thorne never spoke of tolerating evil!'

'If you don't know evil when you see it, Laetitia Purley,' retorted Caroline. 'Allowing men to insult the commandments of the Lord by breaking the Sabbath, and heaping scorn on the wisdom of the Bible by refusing to take a stand on drunkenness and gambling – then shame on you! We should never even have permitted him to share the honors of preaching the Word with the Reverend Bickern come Saturday.'

'But, Mrs Haffle, surely you can't expect poor Reverend Bickern to manage the whole day and night alone!' Julia Maury looked distressed. 'What do you think, Mr Pinkerton?' She laid a hand on Hannibal's arm. 'If we're to call out sinners from the moment they begin to gather in the morning, until that – that *shameful* exhibition packs up its tents at sunset—'

'The Lord will strengthen the arm of the righteous,' proclaimed Caroline Haffle stoutly.

'And who else would you have preaching with him?' added a sharp-faced matron in puce. 'That *heretic* Drummond from Young's Point? If he could be hauled away from the horse races himself?'

January had worked three Mardi Gras subscription balls during his time on the board of the Faubourg Tremé Free Colored Militia and Burial Society and knew that blood was about to be shed. He inquired respectfully, 'Anythin' you'll be needin', sir, 'fore I goes to help Mr Cain, sir?'

Hannibal picked up the satchel from the floor beside his chair – January's own medical satchel, in fact. 'Just give him this, would you, Ben?'

'I'll do that, sir. Thank you, sir.' Through the doorway, January glimpsed Jubal Cain, as the purported slave-dealer passed through the hotel's lobby and out toward the driveway. In Latin he added quietly, '*Melius tibi quam mihi*, sir,' and took his leave.

A scrum of men gathered around a couple of wagons on the ferry's deck when Cain and January reached the wharves in a rented buggy. All the details of the barbershop fire were hashed over again among them. Boze – shorter than Ballou but like him fair-skinned – gathered up the long reins of the ferry horses, said, 'Marse 'Zekias say Rex Ballou gone to Richmond early this mornin', after new winder glass. Rex just 'bout spittin' blood, he so mad, 'cause it was his own fault – he didn't rake out the stove in the shop Saturday night 'fore he went to bed.'

'He have fat wood down at the bottom of the ashes?' inquired a tall man in a planter's wide-brimmed hat. 'That happened in my daddy's stables, when I was a boy.'

'So it was, Marse Tremmell. Me—' Boze grinned suddenly, bright in a goblin face that looked like it seldom smiled – 'I ain' never heard such cussin' in my life, 'cept the time my ol' Marse Cox over to Charlottesville caught his glove buttons on his flies an' near to dammit gelded himself.'

January led the buggy toward the center of the ferry, while Cain sat in its shade and gazed out across the brown waters to the Louisiana shore. If he could get to the hideout not long after dark, January estimated, Drummond could come and get him well before midnight. Then if Hannibal was on time to meet him, and could get him through Vicksburg's waterfront – or around the town's outskirts, through the dark ravines of the tumbled land beyond its boundaries – without him getting kidnapped or picked up by the pattyrollers, he might actually be able to get some sleep tonight.

Was that what had happened to baby Charlie's mother, he wondered. Had she simply gotten lost in the cane-brakes, in unfamiliar territory, and been picked up by the militia?

No, he thought. *No*.

'*We think she got to be hiding someplace near, sir . . .*'

He remembered how Isaiah's glance had shifted as he'd said it.

With Drew Hardy's dogs out all over the countryside?

If she's dead, why not say so? None of the hotel servants had mentioned her capture.

And if she didn't return – *by an' by* – what would become of that tiny child? Dosed repeatedly with opiates, all the way up the river? Maybe by people too preoccupied to count the spoonfuls? Who would make sure he was fed, and his soiled clothing changed, his bottom and thighs washed in the wake of the inevitable diarrhea? Who would fight to make sure he got his share of the water?

And if he did survive, what then? What would become of him when they reached freedom on the Illinois shore?

Who would take over the care of a child not their own?

A few steps away, someone was bawling his opinions about why no one had caught the slave Quinto yet: 'It's the abolitionists hidin' him! Them an' the damn free colored! Can't trust a one of 'em! Them dogs of Hardy's, they wouldn't miss him!

And I tell you, he damn well better *not* let hisself get caught by them dogs. Ol' Drew don't feed 'em, hardly, an' no meat, less'n they catches a nigger . . . That boy'll be lucky they don't eat HIM 'fore Drew gets 'em off . . .'

On the other side of the buggy, a man groused about the ingratitude of his wife's 'wench' – 'She'll steal any food in the kitchen that's not nailed down! Sugar, coffee beans . . . Saw her sneak a ham hock into her apron pocket t'other day! I tried whippin' her, twistin' her ears . . . I even took an' welted her 'cross the arm with the hot end of a poker—'

'Why'n't you just sell her?'

'Well, Mrs Hicks would take on if I did that. The girl's her daddy's, an' they was brought up together—'

'Well, there's your trouble, Hicks. These stuck-up yeller gals, they give themselves airs—'

January murmured, ''Scuse me, sir,' to Cain, and got down from the buggy. 'If you don't need me, I'll go watch the horses in the roundhouse . . .'

'Here I thought you was gettin' ready to go over an' paste that loudmouth a lick,' sighed Cain. 'I was gonna ask you to hit him another one for me.'

January laughed – they both knew this was, almost literally, an impossibility – and moved away from the buggy through the knots of men, horses and wagons that jammed the ferry deck. Boze stood on a sort of platform suspended above the turntable of the roundhouse, directly behind the horses Samson and Jeptha, touching them now and then gently with a long stalk of cane and calling down curses, threats and imprecations on their glossy quarters: 'Step out there, you sorry dog meat . . . you think that's trottin'? I seen a three-legged pig with two broken ankles trot faster'n that when it had the consumption. Oh, hell, sir—' he added, to one of the white men grouped around him – 'not to contradict a gentleman or nuthin', but I think that race Saturday's gonna be Marse 'Zekias's Big Brownie by three lengths and the rest of the field noplace. Stallions always got the stones to outrun a bunch of geldings . . .'

'And you think we could interest Mr Drummond in bein' one of the stewards?' asked one of the men, removing his low-crowned hat to thrust back his rather greasy shock of red hair.

'You'd have to ask him yourself, sir,' replied the ferry driver. 'I think he'd hesitate, bein' as his own horse is runnin'.'

'It's not like he's going to judge,' urged a man in a loud checked coat. 'And nobody in the county knows horses like your master does.'

'Have you any objections to us riding along when you take the ferry back up? If it wouldn't be an imposition on him to have us come to the house . . .'

The red-haired man replaced his hat and turned, scanning the approaching Louisiana shore, and January, with the shocked sensation of having been unexpectedly stabbed at by a hidden enemy, ducked behind the nearest stanchion and turned his back.

The red-haired man was a scoundrel, slave-stealer, and former river pirate named Levi Christmas, whom January had last seen three years ago when he – January – had smashed Christmas over the head with a pistol butt on a sinking steamboat.

January hadn't forgotten the occasion, and he was fairly certain that Mr Christmas hadn't either.

SEVEN

'He's going to Drummond's,' whispered January, when Cain loafed over to the roundhouse. Thick gold sunlight glittered off the murky water. Men and horses shifted around, positioning themselves to disembark. 'He might recognize me even from a distance. At my size, he'd remember me.'

Cain made a comment that reflected as badly upon the parents of Levi Christmas as upon the man himself.

'When the crowd shifts I'll come back over to the buggy. He'll stay where he is – he's riding the ferry when they work back upstream to the main landing. You drop me about a half-mile inland. I'll hide in one of the cane-brakes near Drummond's until I see Christmas leave.'

The purported slave-dealer gauged Christmas's position – still back near Boze on the other side of the roundhouse – and how visible January would be if he simply returned to the buggy now. There wasn't a man south of Mason's and Dixon's line whose eye wouldn't be drawn to a black man January's size, with a mental comment on his market value, even as they would look at a pretty white woman and – aware of it or not – comment on her beauty and possible availability. He grunted, and returned to the buggy. A few minutes later the ferry put into the small 'downstream' wharf, and under cover of the jostling around the gate in the rail, January moved casually – scalded with consciousness that he might be watched – back to the vehicle and climbed in.

'I do begs pardon, Marse Cain,' he murmured, for the benefit of anyone close enough to hear, and Cain rumbled, 'Not at all, not at all.' Through the tiny oval window at the back of the buggy, January satisfied himself that Levi Christmas – unmistakable despite his respectable dark coat, his reddish beard, and the fact that he'd invested in a glass eye and dispensed with the piratical-looking eyepatch he'd worn during January's previous acquaintance with him – was still chatting with Boze.

And Boze had better watch out, reflected January grimly, *if Christmas thinks there's any chance of getting him alone.*

'Watch out for yourself,' murmured Cain, when January drew rein where the track from the ferry joined the trace that ran down the length of DeSoto Point and thence on to Richmond, the parish seat. 'If he's working with a gang these days, any one of them might be prowling this side of the river.'

'I'll keep back from the road.' January slipped the straps of his satchel over his shoulder and shaded his eyes to scan the countryside that stretched northeast: barely higher than the gravel bars they'd been steering around, knotted with cane-brakes and thickets of swamp laurel and cottonwood that grew like weeds in the black alluvial soil. 'It can't be more than two miles.'

He slapped the flank of the rented horse as Cain gathered up the reins: 'Good luck with Sheriff Brister.'

'Damn Sheriff Brister and his kind all to Hell.' Cain drove off.

Clinging to the fringes of the woods – avoiding the stretches of open ground where at six feet three he'd stand out like a tree – January encountered marginally fewer mosquitoes than he would have following the river road, but this was the only thing that could be said for keeping inland. The undergrowth tangled his feet, and the mushy ground still sent up clouds of gnats at every step. The sun dipped toward the wall of cottonwood swamps on the riverbank to the west, and the air seemed to thicken without appreciably cooling. It would be nearly dark, January reflected, before he reached Drummond's door. Probably after dark, before Christmas got on his way again.

In the sugar country below Baton Rouge, a hundred and twenty miles to the south, they'd be in the swamps cutting wood, preparing for the *roulaison* season when the weather turned cold. The women would be gathering the first of the produce from the 'shell-blow grounds' – tomatoes, yams, bright green runner beans, enough if they were lucky to take them into New Orleans on Sundays and sell them at the market on Congo Square.

And in New Orleans, Rose would be tending her own little garden in the crooked courtyard of their big crooked house on Rue Esplanade. Refurbishing the tiniest of Baby John's shirts and dresses to welcome Baby-Rosie or Baby-Ben . . . *Good God, it's less than two months!*

Two years after the bank collapse of 1837, life was slowly returning to normal. Normal, that is, he reflected, for those who had the privilege of leading ordinary lives, the sort of life he'd be living had he remained in France (except that had he remained in France he would not have met his beautiful Rose). Normal, if he and Rose lived in Boston or Philadelphia (and if he had the wits not to go answering newspaper advertisements for work in strange towns).

The sort of life people would live if their grandparents or great-grandparents hadn't been Africans, minding their own business when slave-traders descended on their village . . .

It is for them, he thought, *for Arthur and Isaiah and Deya and Giselle, that Drummond left his congregation and his friends and his life in New York state. I only said 'Yes,' when Cain asked me to start concealing runaways in my house, in the town where I have friends and family. It's easy, and compared to Drummond's life in this place, it's safe.*

Drummond gave up what he had known – gave up even the comfort of sharing with his wife what lay in his heart – to come to this place . . .

Hooves.

He felt their vibration in the ground, sensed them at the edge of hearing.

Oh, shit—

He hadn't even spotted a thicket to run toward when the dogs started baying.

They were close. He threw a fast look around him at the twilight countryside: a mile and a half to Drummond's, maybe more, and Levi Christmas there . . . *He'll know me. And Drummond can't lie for me, not and keep his own position.*

There were trees to his left, half a mile distant on the low crest of the point, the best he could do. He flung himself at them, panic flooding like cold acid through his veins, a thousand nightmares . . .

'*He damn well better not let hisself get caught by the dogs*,' the men on the ferry had said. '*Ol' Drew don't feed 'em, hardly, an' no meat, less'n they catches a nigger . . . That boy'll be lucky they don't eat HIM 'fore Drew gets 'em off . . .*'

He didn't look back, but the clamor of the pack grew louder.

Brush and sedges tore at his legs through his trousers; he heard men shouting, and the thunder of hooves, somebody's high-pitched hunting yell and someone else hollering, 'There he goes! See 'im?'

Damn you – January crashed through stringers of laurel, nearly stumbled on the roots . . . *Damn you all may you burn in Hell and all white men with you—*

'It's him!' yelled another voice, far back, too far to call off the dogs when they'd seize him.

The dogs were close, closing. He could hear their breath, the rip of their feet on the ground.

I'm not going to make it . . .

Teeth tore his calf and he leaned into the last few yards. Something struck his foot— *Dear God don't let me stumble now—*

There wasn't time to pick his tree, in the grove at the top of the ridge. Cottonwoods, the nearest with branches eight or nine feet from the ground. He flung himself up, wrapped his hands around the lowest, and felt fangs rip his legs again, the weight of the dogs dragging at his boots. He kicked, writhed, felt his hands slipping on the rough gray bark and knew that if he fell the pack would probably kill him. Heaved, clawed, twisted his body and felt the dogs drop off him.

Dragged and scrabbled at the branch, and only then, as he swung his body over (*Thank you God!*) did he look down and see them, leaping up at his legs above them, eyes gleaming in the twilight. Five of them, two bloodhounds and three mastiffs, lean gaunt shadows against the tangle of the undergrowth. He could hear the men riding up, whooping and laughing and making what they obviously considered to be witticisms among themselves: 'How you likin' it up in that tree, boy?' 'You really think you could get away?' Before they came too close he slipped the strap of his satchel from his shoulder, thrust the bag deep into the fork of the branch above him.

With any luck, it would be there when he got back . . .

'Why'n't you come on down, 'fore we shoots you down outta there like a coon?'

January knew the reply that was expected of him and wasn't about to risk a beating – or a lynching – by a display of either pride or courage. Leaving Rose a widow, Baby John fatherless, was far more than his pride was worth. 'Please, sir, please, you call off them dogs, sir!' He used the worst cane-patch English he could muster; he'd heard white men at the balls and parties he would play at in New Orleans speak casually of beating black men for 'talking uppity'. 'I ain't run off from noplace, sir! I swear I'm just takin' a note to Mr Drummond for Marse Pinkerton! I got me a pass!'

'You're a lyin' nigger.' One of the men nudged his horse closer to the tree, shotgun raised, though January guessed it was too dark to aim properly. His clothing was dark, and the fluttering cloud of the leaves gave him concealment. By the last of the fading daylight he made out the man's face, thin and hawk-nosed and dark, an Indian's face or French-Indian, a relative of those who had so recently been swept out of this land. 'Now you hop down outta that tree 'fore I shoots you out of it.'

'Not down with them dogs, sir, no, sir, please, sir.' January could just see the man's white-toothed grin, enjoying his victim's fear. 'Please, sir, I got my pass here from Marse Pinkerton – Marse Cyril Pinkerton, that's stayin' at the Planter's in Vicksburg—'

'You lie one more time, Quinto, an' I'll blow your lyin' head off. Who wrote you that pass? And where you been hidin''?'

It's him, they'd shouted, triumph in their voices. Triumph at seeing five hundred dollars in their grasp. He knew upon whom they'd take out their disappointment and rage, if he proved them wrong.

'Please, sir,' he cried, in as terrified a voice as he could produce – and the terror was almost as real as he spoke it, 'that ain't me! I ain't that Mr Riley's boy Quinto, sir! I'm Ben, that belongs to Marse Cyril Pinkerton! You ask Mr Drummond, sir! He knows me, I spent last night at his house with the snakebite! Please, sir, you send to Vicksburg an' ask Marse Pinkerton!' He'd already pulled the pass that Hannibal had written for him from his pocket, and waved it like a flag of surrender.

The Indian scowled and raised his shotgun again, but a thin man beside him with a saturnine brow spit tobacco on the ground, said, 'Let's see that pass, Colvard.'

'Fuck him, he's lyin'!' The Indian's face darkened with thwarted anger.

The thin man rode forward, held out his hand. January handed over the pass; the man turned back to the third rider, a leathery youth with spiteful discontented eyes. 'You bring that lantern, Punce.'

The youth had a lantern hung on his saddle horn, and brought it up and lit it with an old-fashioned Lucifer match. The stink of the sulfur was like a whiff of the Devil's fart in the dark. 'It's gotta be him, Mr Hardy. Ain't no other nigger in the parish that big.'

The thin man held the pass close to the yellow light, studied it with an expression of concentration that told January – with sinking heart – that the man probably couldn't read. He held it out to the Indian Colvard. 'What's it say?'

'Fuck him!' Colvard crumpled the pass and made to throw it away. Drew Hardy took it from his hand, and rode back under January's tree.

'Let's see that letter you got for Drummond.'

January produced it. It contained a fictitious offer to purchase horses, but all Hardy looked at was the address, probably one of the few passages he could recognize. January ventured, 'Mr Drummond tell you who I am, sir.'

'Yeah, tell us you're not Quinto an' then get the reward himself.'

Hardy slid from the saddle, snapped the short whip he held, driving the dogs back from the tree, then turned to look back up at January. 'Get down out of there, boy.'

January obeyed, his heart pounding, but the dogs, growling, stayed back. From one of his saddlebags Hardy took what smelled like smoked pork, and threw pieces of it to the dogs, who fell on it with hair-raising snarls. When this was done, Hardy picked up the lantern again, and held it close to January's face.

'This him?'

''Course it's him,' retorted Colvard sullenly. 'Riley's Quinto's the biggest nigger in the parish.'

'Punce?'

'Could be him,' said the boy. 'I only ever seen him but once, an' then I was at the back of the crowd, time he beat the hell outta Farrell's Tom down in Natchez.'

Hardy stepped back to his horse and pulled a coil of light rope from the saddle. 'Hold your hands out, boy.' He passed the lantern up to Punce, knotted one end of the cord around January's wrists, then swung back up onto his mount. Shivering with anger and reaction to the chase, January supposed he ought to be glad they hadn't put the rope around his neck.

The dogs trotting behind, the three riders set out back along the point, picking up eventually the road that led along the river's bank, south toward Diamond Bend. The horses walked fast but January was able to keep up – he suspected if he'd been linked to Colvard's horse he'd have been in for a much worse time – and the dogs, evidently recognizing that their part in the events of the evening was over, behaved amicably enough. As the shock of panic eased, January's legs screamed in pain from the bites, but he guessed the wounds weren't deep. He guessed also they were taking him to Maury's, and hoped he'd get the chance to boil some water and cleanse the wounds.

With any luck Drummond – who would almost certainly search the countryside for him as soon as it grew light – would find his medical satchel, and guess what had happened to him . . .

Provided Marcus Maury didn't simply decide to sell him and keep the money.

In a sweat of dread, he followed the horses into the cricket-creaking dark.

EIGHT

The only respect in which the slave jail at Indian Mound Plantation could be considered an improvement over being locked into a half-caved-in icehouse twenty-five feet underground was that it was somewhat less damp, and wasn't also occupied by five other adults and two children.

It was, January estimated, roughly the same size – about eight feet by ten – and the brick of the walls was just as filthy. There were two windows, each the size of January's palm: one in the iron-strapped door and the other where the rear wall met the roof, a foot above January's head. These let in clouds of mosquitoes that hummed shrilly in the darkness. By the brief glimmer of Mr Colvard's lantern light when the men shoved him inside, he could see there was no latrine bucket – from the look of the walls, the far corner of the room served that purpose – and nothing resembling a bed. Roaches and palmetto bugs spotted the walls, and didn't even bother to flee the light. The floor was dirt and wasps' nests covered about a quarter of the inside of the unceiled roof.

You don't bother them, they won't bother you . . .

His stomach sank all the same.

Shackles were mortared in the wall – some at waist-level and others up beneath the ceiling – and a meat-hook had been set into the roof's center beam, but the three patrollers simply padlocked the door from the outside. When they'd ridden past the wagon track that led to the Big House among its trees – and, farther off, to the ragged collection of cabins that constituted the quarters – January had seen only two lights in the house. As the men walked away from the jail toward the house he heard Colvard grumble, 'Bet he's gone to that goddam church committee meetin' in town . . .'

'Yeah,' said young Punce's voice, 'and I bet Shugg is drunk.'

Overseer? wondered January. *Probably.* He'd seldom encountered an overseer who wasn't drunk in the evenings.

He wondered whether Marcus Maury would be moved to simply kidnap and sell a slave dropped thus into his lap. Or if Shugg the overseer and his visitors would drink themselves into a mental condition in which it made sense to simply sell January on to a dealer (*Is Richmond a big enough town that a dealer would be there at this time of night?*) without mentioning the matter to Mr Maury at all . . .

January carefully leaned against the wall, trying to avoid what he'd seen creeping around on other portions of it, and closed his eyes, hating every white man he'd ever met.

Even Hannibal, who was back in Vicksburg in the arms of that trollop Mrs Passmore . . . *No, he's going to be on the bluff at midnight, watching for your lantern light.*

Jubal Cain, white also, and running the risk of his life, to establish the pretense that let him run 'cargos' of fugitives north a dozen at a time . . .

Ezekias Drummond and his sons, living in the land of men who'd hang them or beat them to death . . .

From his pocket January dug his rosary, played the beads through his fingers. *Hail Mary, full of grace, the Lord is with thee . . .*

Thank you for getting me this far alive.

Get me through this night . . .

And he jerked, and slapped at whatever insect it was that crept up onto his bloody leg to investigate the open cut.

He'd just finished binding up every gouge in his legs with fragments of his torn-up shirt when footfalls patted, almost soundless, on the dirt outside. A voice no louder than the breeze off the river whispered, 'Daddy? It's me, Dulcie.'

A second voice – a tiny child by the sound of it – repeated, 'Daddy?' and the first voice – a young girl's, sweet and low as a cherrywood flute – whispered, 'That's not your daddy in there, honey, that's *my* daddy—'

'I'm afraid it's not, honey.' January stood, and pressed his face to the judas in the door. He saw no more than the thinnest edge of starlight outlining a slave-woman's head rag, and the unruly curls of a girl-child – soft curls like a white child's – that she carried on her hip. 'Is Quinto your daddy, honey?'

'No!' she gasped, far too quickly. 'Oh . . . no! Quinto – I mean, who's that?'

'Quinto the fighter,' murmured January. 'Whose daughter I bet Mr Maury would like to get his hands on, to flush her daddy out of wherever he's hiding. You're all right, honey, I won't tell. My master's in Vicksburg and they'll send word to him in the morning—' *Please, Mother of God, let them send word!* – 'so I'll be out of here and Maury's got no hold over me. My name's Ben.' He worked his hand through the bars, and held it out. The fingers that clasped his were small, and rough with lye soap and hard work.

'Maury doesn't know?'

'No, sir. Mr Riley sold me to Mr Maury's brother in Memphis when I was ten, and I only come back here two years ago. Mr Riley never did pay no attention to who was whose daddy and mama on our place. But since I been back here at Indian Mound, Daddy'd sneak out at night – River Grove Plantation's over the other side of Richmond – an' see me when he could.'

She hitched her burden on her hip, and drew around herself and the child a quilt, its faded patchwork of dark and pale squares familiar to January from his own days as a slave-child. Coarse dark fabric, simple patterns of squares and lozenges that his aunties would use at night to tell stories with, like the scattered patterns of dried corn-kernels when Olympe would call on her gods to scry the future. January wondered if the child this girl held was hers. Plenty of planters started in on the girls in their households when the girls themselves were barely into their teens. Reason enough for the lovely Julia Maury to spend her time in Vicksburg rather than on her husband's plantation, and to hell with the Reverend Bickern's preaching.

'Cato said in the kitchen they'd caught you. Everybody was sayin' it was my daddy, I guess 'cause you're big like him.'

'I am that,' said January with a sigh. 'Can you manage to get me some food and water, honey? Even if I'm not your daddy?'

He heard her smile in her voice. 'I can do that, yes, sir. Ben. Them good-for-nuthins Injun Tom Colvard an' Jim Punce, an' Drew Hardy, they're all sittin' around with Shugg playin' cards – Shugg knows Mr Maury'll be putting up tonight with Mr Buck, that was the brother of Miss Emmie, his first wife, over in Richmond. There anythin' else you need? Cato said you got caught by the dogs—'

'I did,' said January grimly. 'So if you could get me hot water, and soap, if you can get hold of it without trouble, and a candle, I would appreciate that more than I can say.'

'I'll see what I can do in the kitchen,' Dulcie whispered. 'They mean, those dogs. Luba, that used to head up the second gang here, tried runnin' off, an' they ran him down near Young's Point and tore him up bad. Mr Maury just sat there on his horse an' watched 'em.'

She hastened off up the path to the house again, and a few minutes later returned, with two pones of corn and a gourd of water, and, wrapped in a napkin, a cake of hard yellow soap and a candle. 'The water in the gourd's hot,' she whispered. 'Watch out, 'cause I got to tilt it to get it through the peephole. An' I got to take the napkin back.'

January carefully untied the bandages and washed the wounds, and – with the aid of the candle's light – used the cleaner portions of what remained of his shirt to re-tie them, swatting aside insects as he worked. The lye soap stung like the torments of Hell.

'Good thing for you that Injun Tom's gone up to drink with Shugg,' whispered Dulcie, as January worked. 'By the time they done, he won't even be able to find his way back here from Shugg's house. He's poison bad, Injun Tom. He says as how his daddy was the King of the Choctaw over the other side of the river, an' how they used to own all the land up the Yazoo, an' he hates everyone, pretty much, like poison, white an' colored alike. Maury's mean—'

She shivered, and the flame of the candle she held twitched, glistening on the backs of the roaches on the wall.

'But he mean all in one direction. He thinks he's pretty much the only man in the world gonna go to Heaven, so he's mean by the Bible. He holds services for us all, Sunday mornin's 'fore he goes off to church in Richmond, an' the field hands all gotta give Shugg part of what they grows in their gardens so he won't tell Maury they work in their gardens Sunday mornin's 'stead of prayin' like everybody's supposed to do all day on the Sabbath. An' the way he treats Miss Julia – Mrs Maury – stands my hair on end. But he's always mean the same way: you do what he says, the second he says it, an' you pretty safe. Injun Tom, he'll tell you to take his horse 'round to the stable an' then he'll lay you one across the face with a switch for takin' his horse 'round to the stable. You ain't heard anything—' She lowered her voice, and tiptoed up closer to the bars, the child held tight against her breast – ''bout whether my daddy got away, have you?'

January finished tying the last knot, swiped for the thousandth time at the mosquitoes whining around his ears, and glanced up, to see her eyes peeking through the judas. Softly, he asked, 'Now, where would I hear a thing like that?'

In a tiny shred of a voice, she said, 'Just around. I heard somebody in town 'cross the river might know such things.'

'You have any idea who?' He stood, looked through the judas as she drew back the candle and shook her head, not meeting his glance.

'No, sir. I just heard.'

There was a long silence. Then she said, 'Thing is, sir, people that help people get away – show 'em where the paths are, tell 'em what signs to look for, on fences or in windows, for people who'll help 'em . . . Lot of 'em are church people. Good people. Daddy told me once there's some – he didn't say who – who think that just 'cause a man's wicked in the eyes of God, an' steals his master's liquor to get drunk on, an' steals stuff maybe to get money, an' bulls all the girls all around the countryside . . . maybe instead of him they'll help somebody who prays a lot and is good. My daddy is good,' she said. 'He's kind, an' helps those he can. He just kind of likes to steal an' drink an' hump women an' fight. It's not fair, to blame him for bein' how he is.'

'No,' said January quietly, sorting out the answers to a number of minor questions in his mind. 'No, it's not fair.'

January felt considerably better after he ate the pones and drank the cooling remainder of the water in the gourd, and even managed to sleep a little, sitting with his back propped against the door. Somewhere in the deeps of the night he heard riders leave – one of them singing drunkenly about the Hunters of Kentucky – and as dawn was breaking was wakened by the door being unlocked. Mr Shugg – heavy-muscled, unshaven and stinking of dirty body linen and last night's liquor – read both his pass and Hannibal's letter to Drummond, with an expression of deepening annoyance, then studied January with angry, piggy eyes. 'Yeah, well, I still don't believe it, boy,' but he sent off one of the houseboys to fetch Drummond, and another – to January's deep gratitude – to the kitchen for a dish of grits and molasses.

'Where's your shirt, boy? What kind of man sends his boy carryin' a message, lookin' like a half-naked pig?'

'I'm sorry, sir. I had to tear it up, tie up the cuts where Mr Hardy's dogs bit me.'

Shugg slapped him. 'What the hell were you doin' wanderin' around where the dogs would get after you in the first place?'

'I dunno, sir. I guess I just didn't think.' He'd found that answer usually shut up a white man, if he wasn't drunk.

It was almost sunset of that day – Tuesday – before Drummond and Hannibal drove up to Indian Mound in a rented buggy – the ferryman having, as January suspected, devoted much of the morning to bringing Rex Ballou and four new windows back to town in his wagon, with many complaints about the quest for glass. 'I sat out on that wretched bluff 'til almost dawn,' whispered Hannibal, the moment he and January were alone beside the buggy. 'Thank God it wasn't raining.' He coughed, with a labored note that January did not like. 'And of course I hadn't the faintest idea where to look for you over here . . .'

Maury was currently exchanging cool civilities with Drummond by the porch of the Big House. He was a tallish, stiff-backed man with smooth dark hair and blandly refined features, eyes pale watery gray behind silver spectacles. ('He looks like my father's rent collector,' remarked Hannibal later. 'He'd eat a tenant's liver and smile.'). He had come to the slave jail mid-morning, accompanied by Shugg and rigid with anger and disappointment; had slapped January in the face, and lectured him for a good half hour on how his own irresponsible conduct had brought him where he was. Then – on the porch of the house and away from the servants – he had excoriated Shugg on his stupidity for apprehending the wrong man. Julia Maury had returned to the plantation from Vicksburg around noon, and January had heard through the open windows at the rear of the Big House her husband's savage reprimands, delivered in a series of chilly statements and accusations and followed by the unmistakable sounds of a beating.

Yet when the patriarchal-looking Reverend Bickern and other members of the church committee had ridden up after dinner around five, the lord of Indian Mound Plantation had been all respectful righteousness. They'd walked past the slave jail on their way down to the quarters, presumably so Maury could show Bickern just how well he treated his bondsmen, and January heard Maury agreeing with the Reverend: 'Of course it's not the same thing! It's not the same thing at all!'

January wondered whether this referred to nigger fights or wife-beating.

In any case, the Reverend Lemuel Bickern was still at Indian Mound when Drummond and Hannibal had arrived, and across Hannibal's shoulder, January saw the confrontation between the two Men of God as Maury came down to the drive, and Bickern remained haughtily on the high-set porch. He heard little of it, because Maury delivered himself of about fifteen minutes on the subject of why Hannibal should never have dispatched his servant with a message to Drummond on Monday evening ('They're never happy if you send them off on their own – Surely you must know they need guidance, and by your actions you have grievously inconvenienced both the militia and my household here—').

But he saw Bickern glare in fury as Drummond drew himself up, saw his stabbing forefinger as he made some reply and the way Drummond's fists clenched, and he heard very clearly the big ferryman say, '*By good words and fair speeches deceive the hearts of the simple—*'

'And what shall we say of *you*,' thundered Bickern, 'who commits adulteries and walks in lies, and leads the sheep away from their true shepherd even to the brink of the pit?'

This startled even Maury out of his discourse, and both he and Hannibal turned in surprise as Drummond went storming over to the buggy, red-faced with anger, climbed in and gathered the reins. To Maury he said, 'And how long do you think that a house built upon lies and false prophecies, and falsehoods preached even to those who would believe, shall stand? The breath of the Lord shall tear it all away!'

He flapped the reins, and January and Hannibal barely had time to scramble in as the vehicle moved off.

'False prophet!' shouted Bickern after them.

'Antichrist!' yelled Drummond back.

'It makes me quite long for our Irish estate,' murmured Hannibal, 'and those peaceful Sabbath evenings when Father Mulrooney and the Reverend Coldkirk would get drunk together and discuss theology – *Glory, the grape, love, gold, in these are sunk, The hopes of all men, and of every nation*. Are you well, *amicus meus*?'

'There's nothing wrong with me,' sighed January, 'that a hot bath won't cure.'

NINE

Following a hot bath, however, January and Hannibal slipped out the back entrance of the Planter's Hotel and walked across to Clay Street, to rap softly on the rear door of Rex Ballou's white-painted camelback house. The kitchen was the only room on the ground floor still usable: 'They did a prime job of that fire, I'll tell you that,' sighed Ballou, sinking onto one of the battered bent-willow chairs.

Hannibal made sure the windows were not only shuttered but curtained, peeked cautiously out the back door, took a candle and a bucket and went out to the pump in the yard. January lit another couple of candles from the lamp in the center of the table, and unpinned the bandages around Ballou's chest. 'You all right so far?' Hannibal had, on the way from Indian Mound and across on the ferry, provided a detailed account of a morning spent demonstrating to every busybody in Vicksburg that Rex Ballou – other than the fatigue that came from firefighting and traipsing around half the countryside looking for window glass – felt perfectly fine.

Ballou leaned back in the chair and nodded, face drawn with exhaustion and pain. By the lamplight January saw how blackly his eyebrows stood out against the café-crème complexion of a quadroon.

'And how's everyone down there?' he asked, as Hannibal returned and knelt by the old-fashioned hearth to stir the fire.

'Well.' Ballou's voice was hoarse with pain. 'Cramped as hell.'

It was on January's lips to speak of baby Charlie and the laudanum he was being fed, but knew that now was neither the time nor the place. He brought the lights closer, and examined the wound closely as the water heated. Somewhere in the neighborhood, someone played a Scottish ballad on a piano slightly out of tune.

'It's only 'til Saturday.' Hannibal coughed, clinging momentarily to the corner of the chimney. 'The town's plastered with handbills for the circus, and I have it from the ladies of the church committee that people are coming from as far away as Monroe, either for the races or the fights or to hear the Reverends Bickern and Thorne condemn horse racing, fights and circuses to Hell. *Suum cuique itur ad astra . . .*' He brought the water over to the table. 'In any case, everyone in three counties will be at the subscription ball that night in the ballroom upstairs from Goodings' Confectionary, by which time, please God, your friends will be miles away.'

January dipped clean dressings in the water, wrung them out.

'There is also what is locally known as a "darky party" to be held the same evening at Gibbs Crawford's livery stable . . .'

'Every time Theophilus Gooding holds a ball at the confectionary,' affirmed Ballou, 'Gibbs Crawford donates his big carriage house, so all the coachmen and valets can have a place to hear a little music and cut some capers themselves. Mrs Dillager – the lady I've been boarding with—' His gesture indicated a large brown house at the end of the block, on the corner of Cherry Street – 'turns up her nose and says she'd no more be seen at such a gathering than she'd let herself be seen walkin' the waterfront in a red dress, but it's good music and good dancin'. That's where I'll be.'

'Well,' said January grimly, 'you dance carefully. No sense in you falling down and springing a leak in front of every valet and coachman in three counties.' Word got around fast in the slave community, and from there it needed only one talkative valet for gossip to pass to some white man that Rex Ballou had been wounded after all.

'You have darky parties in New Orleans, Ben?'

'Uptown they do,' said January. 'Mostly in the American churches, the Protestant churches. My mother wouldn't go to one if they were handing out money under the punch cups.'

'Benjamin!' Hannibal looked shocked. 'What a thing to say about your mother! Of course she would!'

Ballou laughed, and flinched with pain as January rinsed the wound with spirits of wine. The flesh was healing, and neither looked nor smelled putrid, and Ballou's face, though ashen in the lamplight, felt neither unnaturally hot nor unusually clammy.

Cain was right. He IS strong . . .

Hannibal went on, 'You think any of the local yahoos might

reach the conclusion that our friend Quinto's going to have the same idea, and be on the look-out during the hours of the show?'

'I doubt any of 'em's that smart,' whispered Ballou, his voice still hoarse with pain. 'But I'll start puttin' it around Friday that Quinto was caught up at Milliken's Bend – enough so men'll think, *Hell, it's all right now for me to go see that show . . .*'

'I understand Cain spent the better part of the day up in the 'delta' searching for this Mrs Walker, to no avail—'

'Eliza don't come out of the shadows,' said Ballou, ''til she's good and satisfied that nobody's following you. And if she's heard anything of this Levi Christmas fellow that you spoke of bein' in town, I'm guessing she's being extra careful.' His fingers tightened around Hannibal's wrist, as January pinned the clean bandages on the wound.

'There's an old Chickasaw farm where Glass Bayou joins up with Chickasaw Bayou; there's a sort of pond they call the Lagoon. She'll hide up there sometimes, or sometimes in the outworks from the Spanish fort that was here in Revolution times. She'll be all right.'

'And how about you?' asked January. 'Will *you* be all right?'

'I got to be seen,' insisted the barber. 'Lively and dancin'.'

'Can you do that?'

'Or I'll die tryin'.'

For the next three days January made himself unobtrusively useful around Ballou's barbershop. He was supposedly being rented by the barber from Hannibal to assist in the repair of the shop, but his actual task was to make sure Ballou was on his feet and fit to be seen by the white population of Vicksburg.

Though there were, as Ballou had predicted, men who came to be shaved Wednesday morning (complaining that they'd missed their 'regular' spots on Tuesday), most of the barber's customers asked after his convenience, and were put off ''til the place gets fixed up a bit'. One man even offered to help. By dark Wednesday January had the new windows of the shop framed in; by midday Thursday he was applying the first coats of whitewash to the new boards on the front while Ballou shaved his customers with a perfectly steady hand.

By that time, Vicksburg was agog at the well-advertised prospect of the All-American Zoological Society's Traveling Circus and Exhibition of Philosophical Curiosities. Boarding at Mrs Amanda Dillager's on the corner – along with the dozen or so free blacks of the Vicksburg community – January heard the gossip of preparation for the horse races, cockfights, dogfights and slave matches being planned, even as he heard from Hannibal of the byzantine intrigues among the Methodist ladies over the management of the 'Tabernacle in the Wilderness' to be erected, and over whose house would be graced with the honor of the Reverend Bickern's company. There was much talk also of the darky party, which January would have liked to attend – partly to keep an eye on his patient and partly because he knew the music and the company would be better than at Gooding's subscription ball. But rumor was already going around that Theophilus Gooding was making arrangements to hire the musicians from the circus, and he guessed he'd be one of them.

Likewise from Hannibal, on the occasions when the fiddler stopped by the barbershop, he heard that Cain continued to ride out, ostensibly trawling for 'stock' among the few small farmers in the jungly morasses of the Yazoo country north of town, leaving signs for the elusive Mrs Walker.

'Eliza'll send him word when she's ready,' Ballou repeated.

'Personally,' opined Hannibal, when January walked up to the Planter's with him Thursday evening, 'I think he's just trying to avoid Guy Fenks – who spends half his time drinking on the porch and the other half trying to either buy you or sell me one or another item of what he calls *fancy goods*. Thank God I'm in sufficiently good odor with the local ladies to take refuge in their parlor. I've been reduced to getting Mrs Passmore to escort me in and out. Presumably Fenks hasn't the temerity to even approach her presence.'

'No slave-dealer would,' said January. 'That's one of the rules in this country. No lady, even if she owns slaves, will so much as admit that a dealer exists. "Servants", as ladies call us,' he continued drily, 'just appear in their households – or disappear. Dealing with the logistics of owning other people – and getting them to do your bidding – is the province of men. Ask any white man.'

As he was speaking, January saw Jubal Cain dismount in front of the hotel steps, and hand the reins and a five-cent piece to one of the hotel's stablemen – and indeed, the stout Mrs Haffle, descending past him on the arm of her husband, turned her eyes away from Cain like a duchess ignoring a leper. Her husband, whom January knew played chess with the slave-dealer in the Best Chance Saloon down the street, likewise made no sign of recognition, and the little group of Jackson ladies who followed Mrs Haffle all but drew their skirts aside from his very shadow.

But as they passed, a slim, gray-clothed form detached itself from the group and crossed the nearly empty porch to intercept Cain as he strode up the steps. It was – January recognized her dress, which seemed to be the only one she had – Julia Maury. She spoke quickly to him, standing close, her face raised to his.

Cain removed his hat, looking down at her gravely. Her glance fleeted around, touched January and Hannibal in the sunlight of the drive, and she withdrew a step, and said something at which Cain bowed. Agreement, acquiescence, *Whatever you wish, m'am . . .*

She hurried back into the hotel. Cain, after a moment to let her get clear of any association with him, followed.

Thursday night, heat-lightning flared beyond the hills north and west of Vicksburg: flared and died, flared and died. Grayish with exhaustion from his first full day of work, Rex Ballou walked over to Mrs Dillager's boarding house, January pacing cautiously at his side.

Mrs Amanda Dillager was a good cook, but few had appetite for her dirty rice and greens that sultry night: there was much talk of Saturday; talk also of the rumor that had begun to go around that Quinto had finally been caught, up on Milliken's Bend. 'I heard tell it from Injun Tom's boy, Roane . . .' 'Huh. I wouldn't believe a member of that blood, if they said they saw the sun risin' in the east.' 'Tom claims his daddy was King of the Choctaw,' explained another boarder to January, 'an' goes on how he'd own all this land from here to Texas, if it weren't for the white men. And that son of his is just a no-account trapper.'

'With any luck,' said Ballou, when January steadied his steps through the heavy dusk back up the steep hill of Clay Street, 'Injun Tom and Drew Hardy and the rest of their lot will take the day off looking, and go to the races and the fights.'

'Just what I need,' sighed January. 'A bunch of drunk patty-rollers in the audience,' and Ballou laughed.

But the recollection of that little tribe of fugitives, sweltering all these nights in the stinking limbo underground, pulled at him, and he asked, 'Did you hear anything yet of the woman Cindy?'

Ballou kept his face immobile, but January – who had his hand under the barber's elbow – felt him jerk.

Ballou's voice was casual – so casual that it made January's nape prickle. 'Why do you ask?'

What the HELL—?

'I'm worried for her child,' said January. 'All this time down there, and getting laudanum, and who's going to look after him if she doesn't turn up? They kept saying, "Your mama will be back by and by," but what if—'

'She'll turn up.'

January stopped in his tracks, trying to pierce the darkness, to see Ballou's face.

Quickly, Ballou went on, 'I don't like drugging the boy any more than you do, Ben, but—'

'I know he has to be kept silent,' said January. 'I understand that. What happened?'

'I don't know.' Ballou quickened his steps, and staggered: he should not, in January's opinion, have been on his feet at all. 'She'll be all right,' he added, as they opened the door, entered the stifling dimness of the little house. 'The boy'll be all right, once we get them out of there. There's nothing to worry about.' He crossed to the single lamp that had been left burning, turned down low; lit a heat-bent tallow candle from its wick. 'And nothing we can do about it. Will you lock the place up? I'll be bidding you good night.'

He retreated to his bedroom behind the shop, and shut the door.

TEN

On Friday morning the circus arrived, its ten wagons trudging up the road from Grand Gulf in a cloud of dust and including – to the almost-unbearable delight of every child for miles around – Martha the Elephant *and her baby*, painted like Jezebel for the occasion and caparisoned in crimson and gold. Hannibal and January met the company at Haffle's meadow, and while the roustabouts were setting the tents, January assisted their fellow musicians in the less demanding task of carrying in musical instruments, dressing tables and chairs, scenery for the 'minstrelsy show' and the assorted props and costumes, while Hannibal joined the Boneless Monzonnis and Maryam, Princess of the Desert (in her clothed, American incarnation as Annie Garrett) in driving the hordes of local children out from under everybody's feet.

'Is all well with your sister?' asked Tavish, the moment he'd quit shouting the first spate of orders and dropped off his horse to clasp January's hand.

'All well.' He smiled as he would have, had either of his own sisters been spared the danger he'd conjured a week ago. 'A false alarm . . .'

'Never say it!' Tavish shook his leonine head. 'Better twenty false alarms than losing a bairn. You were well missed in Grand Gulf . . .'

'Everything was missed in Grand Gulf,' grumbled the Mighty Hercules, a.k.a. Francis O'Connell, looking slightly out of place as he always did in wool trousers and a neat linen coat instead of the somewhat moth-eaten lion skin he wore onstage. 'Blessed if I ever knew such places existed! There couldn't have been five white women in the audience, and a jungle – a veritable, blessed *jungle* complete with alligators and wolves and Indians, I daresay, not five miles outside the town! The whole place dead as mutton an hour before we went on.'

'That's because nine-tenths of your audience risked a thrashing if they left the fields a minute before their betters did,' returned

January with a wry grin. 'And from here north to Memphis,' he added, 'it's worse. There's pretty much nothing ashore: swamp and cane-brake and forest.'

'We heard wolves howlin' last night,' agreed Tavish. 'Scared poor Jackson half to death.' Jackson was the lion.

'*Sultana* scares Jackson half to death,' January reminded them, Sultana being Jackson's formidable lioness. 'And he should know by this time that she'd never let wolves hurt him.'

Both men laughed, and everyone returned to the exhausting business of getting the show set up for the morrow: tents pitched for the menagerie (Martha and Baby Muffin, Jackson and Sultana, three camels – Socrates, Plato and Aristotle – two porcupines, two zebras, a colony of five monkeys and a long-suffering orang-utan named John Quincy Adams), for the Exhibition, and for the show. Smaller dressing tents and a mess tent were set up, along with a traveling kitchen; the kitchen and all the dressing tents had to be stocked and benches arranged in the show tent; and everything festooned in bunting. Painted (and startlingly inaccurate) advertisements were hung.

Tavish exclaimed in disgust when he saw the Tabernacle in the Wilderness being raised on the other side of the Springdale Road – complete with a cross which could have accommodated a giant – but agreed that at least half its congregation would slip away to pay their twenty-five cents to see the minstrel show as well.

Later on, the owners of three of Vicksburg's many taverns appeared, with their own workers and marquees to sell beer on the following day. Wagons arrived from the town's livery stables, with fodder and bedding for the animals. Uncounted buckets of water were lugged from Mint Spring Branch. An American flag was raised.

Late in the afternoon January encountered Ezekias Drummond by the makeshift horse track, which had been laid out in Haffle's meadow behind the circus's horse lines. Young Solomon was with him: 'He'll be riding Big Brownie in the race. And I'll be here—' Drummond lowered his voice – 'for all the town to see. Is Ballou well?'

'Well and working.' January shook his head. 'If ever I needed proof that God strengthens the arm of the righteous . . .'

'Righteous indeed,' sniffed the ferryman, with a glance toward the Tabernacle and its cross. 'At least I know I lie when I spout pap about God cursing the African race! That Pharisee strains at a gnat, while the camel of slavery slips by him unremarked! *Servants, obey in all things your masters* . . . Pah!' His face twisted. 'A hypocrite and a false prophet! The Book of Job praises the hand of the Creator in the beauty of the warhorse: *He paweth in the valley, and rejoiceth in his strength . . . he swalloweth the ground with fierceness and rage.*'

'I think you're the only preacher I ever encountered,' smiled January, 'who didn't denounce horse racing as sinful.'

Drummond's mouth tugged sidelong in an unwilling grin, the first time, January thought, he'd ever seen the man actually smile. 'How can man's heart not rejoice in the most splendid creation of God? And like the Israelites,' he added, lowering his voice, 'we will use the plunder of the Egyptians against them. Their whoredoms, and their blasphemies, and their drunkenness . . .' His gesture took in all the anthill activity of the teeming fields. 'These shall cover the deliverance of God's servants from out of the hand of iniquity.'

January raised his brows, inquiring. Drummond touched his lips for silence. 'She left word last night. They'll meet at sunrise, and go to the landing place to wait.'

Cressets were set up outside the Tabernacle. By the time January had changed Ballou's dressings and returned to the circus that evening, men and women were arriving, and the Tabernacle's canvas walls glowed from the lanterns within.

'Serve 'em right,' muttered Tavish, 'if their bloody tent burns down.'

January had paid his shot at Mrs Dillager's that afternoon and collected the small bundle of his possessions from Ballou's that afternoon, before going to help Hannibal – who had more luggage – shift quarters from the Planter's to the circus. 'And you have me to thank,' purred Mrs Passmore, encountering them in the hotel's garden as they were leaving, 'that any woman in this town is still going to speak to you in the street after this, you naughty man.'

'I told them all I was a musician,' protested Hannibal, and gallantly offered a match to the cigar that the confidence-woman had stolen away from the parlor to puff ('That's the WORST thing about acting respectable, you can't IMAGINE how I miss my cigars!')

'Playing in a minstrel show?' She blew a smoke ring and traded an amused glance with January, whom she had guessed early on wasn't actually a servant. In less than ten days, Cornelia Passmore (though January didn't believe for a moment this was her real name) by a combination of sympathetic listening, a heart-rending tale of misfortunes bravely borne, and a great stock of carefully expurgated worldly wisdom had made herself the new dearest friend of half the women on the church committee. It would be child's play, January reflected, for her to steal the money they raised.

'I painted them all the most touching picture of an ailing daughter back in New Orleans, and a devoted father – your handsome self, Hannibal – immolating himself on the altar of gimcrack jingles and cheapjack jigs – with the help of your faithful valet – in order to maintain her in a decent boarding school through the summer, until you can go back to playing at the Opera. I said nothing,' she added, 'about card playing.'

'I kiss your hands and feet, *domina*.'

'I scratch your back,' she returned with a smile, 'since you've been so obliging as to scratch mine. Thank you for the warning about that scoundrel Levi Christmas being in town, by the way. I knew him back when he was robbing riverboats . . . Out to get his grubby card-sharping mitts on the church money, I'll wager. And as for you, Mr *Pinkerton*—' She raised her eyebrows archly at the assumed name – 'you're very likely to have formidable deaconesses like Laetitia Purley coming up and clasping your hands in the street and telling you how brave you are, so do remember to mention your daughter.'

'Has she got a name?'

'Viola, I think. Julia Maury is the only one who seems to question the story – she asked what you'd been doing in Indiana when you supposedly met me, the minx – but since you saw her in converse yesterday with that slave-dealer Cain, I'd say your secret is safe. They met Wednesday.' She glanced around her at the green thickness of the arbor that hid them from the hotel, and lowered her voice. 'That husband of hers is a jealous brute. Julia has a cottage about a mile north of town that she stays in when she's in town, where the road goes down from the hills into the bottomlands: the last fragment of her father's property, I think. Cain rode out in that direction late this afternoon – What on earth would a slave-dealer be doing down there, if not paying her a visit?'

January could have told her, but held his peace.

'So I think you have little to fear of her telling anyone you're a card-sharping reprobate without a daughter in sight.'

She smiled, and touched Hannibal's cheek.

'That is a gross slur upon my character and if I weren't a coward I'd call you out.'

'There.' She took one final draw on her cigar, and handed it to January. 'I must return . . . Will you go to Bickern's sermon this evening? I need to be seen there by my sisters in Christ – there's something about night meetings that seizes the hearts of the listeners, and I gather the plan is for him and the Reverend Thorne to go on, turn and turn about, all night.'

'I will never,' sighed January, as he and Hannibal left the garden in the gathering twilight, 'understand this American craze for standing up and testifying before the congregation. Irish Protestants don't do that, do they?'

'But we're all Church of England,' the fiddler said, after a moment's consideration. 'And why anyone would be a Dissenter in Ireland I haven't the faintest notion: all the legal inconveniences of Catholicism without the comfort of getting drunk with your neighbors every night. Of course,' he went on thoughtfully, 'the same could be said of being a Dissenter in America. What flavor of religion does the Reverend Drummond espouse, by the way?'

'Some form of Protestantism, I should expect. You find more abolitionist Protestants than you do Catholics.'

'I should be curious,' said the fiddler, 'to hear him preach. He hails from the upstate counties of New York, and the western woods, I understand, are host to strange sects and curious beliefs: ritual dancers and communes of free love, people finding mysterious golden tablets buried under rocks, and getting revelations that the world is going to end four years from next October. Men seek treasure there with the aid of magical stones, or hear the voices of angels instructing them in curious doctrines; women seek the vote and hold conversations with the dead.'

'And people even believe that the Bible is wrong,' added January, 'when it says that slavery is the Will of the Lord.'

Protestant or Catholic, when January and Hannibal returned to the fields along the Springdale Road and dropped their meager satchels in the tent shared among the musicians and acrobats of the company, they found – in addition to the expected offer of employment from Theophilus Gooding for the subscription ball – a general movement afoot among their colleagues to cross the road and observe the enemy on his home territory.

'I *live* in New Orleans,' protested January. 'I've already seen enough Protestant evangelizers to guarantee me and my whole family passage through the Pearly Gates, always supposing my mother would go—'

He was shouted down, two of the musicians and all five 'minstrels' hailing from New York City or Britain: 'It's the duty of an actor to observe the human condition,' proclaimed Tavish, with a gesture worthy of Mark Antony orating on the corpse of Caesar.

'And Angelo's going to go up and be saved,' added Nardo Monzonni, slapping his brother on his muscular shoulder, 'and tell the whole congregation how he rogered an entire shipload of Irish girls on his way over to this country, and killed and ate a priest.'

January rolled his eyes, but followed them across to the Tabernacle tent in the same spirit that he'd have settled down to playing 'Beggar My Neighbor', if that were the entertainment agreed on by the company for the evening, with the mental reservation that he'd slip away at the end of a half-hour and get a well-earned night's sleep. The tent glowed with lantern light and its benches were already packed; buggies crowded the open ground beyond it, hub to hub, watched over by a scattering of black grooms and coachmen who were undoubtedly making a few extra cents keeping an eye on the equipages and saddle horses of the poorer members of the flock as well. From within rose the sound of 'My Faith Looks Up to Thee', and above it, like a Heldentenor's leitmotif riding above the chanting of a chorus, Lemuel Bickern's beautiful voice proclaiming God's forgiveness for all those who would renounce the evils of this world and set about transforming themselves – and all their neighbors – into a Kingdom of Righteousness.

Periodically he would break off his exhortations and turn to the row who stood before him, mostly women but with a scattering of young men and adolescent girls, some on their feet, others kneeling, some in tears and others keening with a high-pitched hum of formless grief. 'Are you ready to give up sin?' he would cry, sweeping the air with his arms. 'Are you ready to accept your own sinfulness?'

Nothing that January hadn't seen before.

A second preacher moved among the penitents, like a sheep-dog keeping the flock in order: catching a woman's hands here, a youth's arm there, speaking to them softly, gazing into their eyes, earnestly listening to their stammered words.

A red-haired preacher, tallish and thin . . .

January recognized a group of the washerwomen from the Planter's, standing – like the musicians and acrobats – at the back of the tent among the sweating, singing mob. He eeled his way to them, asked, 'Who's that?'

The hotel's chief chambermaid turned to him with eyes shining with the fervor of spiritual exaltation – as Mrs Passmore had said, there was indeed something powerful in the energy of a night meeting that seized and comforted the heart. 'That Reverend Thorne, from Jackson,' the chambermaid said.

January looked swiftly around at the packed congregation – at his height he could see over the heads of most crowds. He spotted the ladies of the church committee – the delicate, white-haired Laetitia Purley and the robust Caroline Haffle, standing as far away from the Jackson church contingent as was possible. Marcus Maury stood between them, but instead of singing he was glancing around him with cold anger in his eyes.

Julia Maury was absent.

Nor did January see Mrs Passmore – *And no wonder*, he reflected, edging his way to the door.

For the red-haired Reverend Thorne, piously leading converts to the front of the Tabernacle and salvation, was none other than the slave-stealer and river pirate, Levi Christmas.

ELEVEN

The show would be at noon.

As he stood in line to take his turn at the washtub behind the men's tent in the first light of what promised to be another gluey-hot day, January wondered whether part of his morning's activities would involve tracking down Hannibal, whose camp bed next to his was empty and pristine, and getting him onstage at the proper time.

'At least,' he sighed, when Tavish brought the subject up through a face-full of shaving soap, 'since he gave up drinking he's easier to locate. But waking him up without a hangover is no easier than waking him up with one.'

'That's the Irish.' The Scot shook his head. 'Best argument I've heard against the Devil possessin' the lot of 'em. Too fond of their pillows to be much use to Old Harry. If the Old One wants evil done, best he tempt a Scot or a Jew into it. At least he'll get a proper job for his money.'

'Except every Scot or Jew I've ever met,' agreed January, 'would figure out a way to get out of the contract before the due date.'

'Aye,' agreed Tavish. 'There's that.' He glanced across the road toward the Tabernacle, whose doorways still glowed with lantern light in the dove-gray dawn. Voices thin with exhaustion wailed 'From Greenland's Icy Mountains'; shadowy figures passed among the half-dozen horses and buggies still gathered in the field beyond.

'Never saw the like.' He flicked open his straight razor, narrowed his eyes at the square of mirror hung to a post beside the washtub. 'Congregation never got down below twenty, guzzlin' salvation like Socrates and his brethren—' He nodded toward the camels – 'emptyin' pails of water.'

'Did Angelo really get up and confess his sins?'

'Oh, aye. With the whole of the congregation cheerin' him on. Meant to rock 'em back on their heels . . .' Tavish wiped the soap from his blade. 'Not one of 'em turned a hair. Half a minute later some blackguard from the wharves stood up and confessed to burnin' down a Creek meetin'-house in Alabama with twenty people locked inside it . . . and I don't think he was funnin' like Angelo was. Congregation said God would forgive him for that too, an' cheered him on for confessin' it. I think it took Angelo aback some. What does it take in this part of the world to send a man to Hell?'

January sighed. 'I wouldn't know.'

He lent a hand – everyone did, including Maryam, Princess of the Desert, the two midgets and Mozambia the Bearded Lady – bringing water up from the spring for the animals, and paused to watch Jackson and Sultana breakfast on a goat carcass their keeper tossed to them through a high window in the back of their cage. By the time the animals were fed and the human portion of the company had finished their own sustaining breakfast, the first of the town boys were dashing around the tents, though at this point there was little to see. In the shelter of their own quarters, Mozambia washed and combed her beard on its stand, and dressed in a décolleté gown of blue and gold, and she and Maryam put up each other's hair. Francis O'Connell (a.k.a. Hercules) oiled his muscles and donned his lion skin which, January was aware, discreetly concealed a truss. ('It's one thing to make a livin' pickin' up your piano, Mr J., but I ain't stupid.')

But all this formed no more than a backdrop to January's thoughts. Every time he crossed between the tents, or walked out to the field where the race would be held, his mind and his eyes were drawn to the glint of the river, gold in the first of the morning's sunlight beyond the jumble of the Walnut Hills.

The show would be at noon. *How long does it take, to get eight people into a wagon and across to the . . . rowboat? Skiff? They can't take the ferry, everyone in town would see it . . .*

He walked into town to Ballou's, found a sign reading 'Closed for the Day' on the newly painted front door, and the barber finishing his coffee in the kitchen. 'I'm well,' he said, to January's query. 'Feeling better every day. I'll walk over to the racetrack with you, if you've no objection, and let everybody in town see me with Mr Drummond. It's my job – yours too, if you and "Mr Freepaper" are willing– to say *Oh, Drummond was just here, I think he's in the show tent* . . . or gone across the road to throw rocks at Bickern, or wherever . . .'

'I think we can do that.' January smiled wryly. 'It's just about all we've been able to do—'

'Never think it!' Ballou set down his cup, his hazel eyes earnest. 'I owe you my life – and more, I think. This is – This is more than an army, fighting side by side and covering each other's backs. What we do is – is like the acrobats in your circus, every man doing his part: you, Mr Cain, Mr Drummond . . . Eliza Walker coming all the way downriver to gather her flock, your friend Mr Freepaper—' He grinned a little at the alias – 'without whom you'd spend half your energy dodging slave-stealers yourself in this town. Drummond and his boys and I are seen by everyone in town at the races—'

'Along with every man in three counties—'

'Drummond slips away when it's done, walks down to the end of Chickasaw Bayou, takes his skiff across to the point. Moves the cargo across the point by wagon, and off from the other side to the bayou again, where Mr Cain should be waiting with Eliza by now . . .'

He spread his hands. 'Mr Cain comes back quiet-like before the end of your second show, I turn up at Crawford's tonight with a tale of how I did this and that with Mr Drummond and his sons all day, while you – and Mr D. and Mr Cain – all speak to everybody at Goodings' like you just had a good day seein' the elephant.'

'And the only person on the point to see our friends off on their journey,' said January, 'with any luck, will be Quinto – who if he's smart, will ask for a ride over in Mr Drummond's skiff.'

He'd been changing Ballou's dressing as they spoke, and felt the sudden stiffening of his patient's muscles under his fingers.

'What is it?'

'*Church people. Good people*,' the girl Dulcie had said. '*Just 'cause a man's wicked in the eyes of God . . . maybe instead of him they'll help somebody who prays a lot and is good.*

'*Not a man who likes to steal an' drink an' hump women an' fight.*'

'Quinto Riley . . .' Ballou hesitated. Debating what he could or should say to a relative stranger.

Quinto Riley doesn't deserve freedom?

Very quietly, January said, 'Did he come to you?'

'I didn't know he was planning to run.' Impatiently, into January's heavy silence, Ballou added, 'He drinks. And when he's drunk he'll say anything to anybody.'

Is that you who decided that, or Drummond? It was a pointless question and none of January's business, so he went on pinning the bandages tight.

After a moment Ballou said, 'It's all of us working together, Ben. Our lives lie in each other's hands. But Drummond makes the final decisions. Without him there wouldn't be any of this.

'He's saving lives: not just the lives of those people down in the pit there, but the lives of their children, and their grandchildren who'll grow up in freedom. I couldn't do it. Not as who and what I am here. I can organize it, I can get them to him, but I can't do what he does. I'd be watched. I'd be taken. And then everybody'd be back where they were. A soldier wouldn't be asked to undertake this in battle, because this battle never ends. He was willing to give his life, that men might be free.'

Does that give him the right to say Quinto Riley doesn't deserve freedom?

No, reflected January. *But it's sure as hell better than nobody acting as ferryman at all.*

Ballou spoke as if unwilling to utter the words. Or unwilling to utter them unreservedly. 'A good man can do . . . bad things, sometimes. But he's a great man, nevertheless.'

January reflected for a moment on what it would do to him, what it would cost him, to shut Rose out of his life. To shut everything out of his life, to masquerade day and night as something he wasn't . . .

'I suppose he is.'

By the time he returned to the race grounds, the sun was well up and Hannibal, washed and tidy and sporting a new black velvet ribbon at the end of his long queue, was escorting Mrs Passmore around the horse lines with the tender deference due a 'widow'. 'The nerve of that bastard Christmas,' she fumed, and glanced back over her shoulder in the direction of the Tabernacle. 'May Buck – the sister to Marcus Maury's first wife

– tells me their “dear Reverend Thorne” has been preaching in Jackson for seven months now, just about exactly as long as Bickern’s been working to raise funds to get his own church here in Vicksburg. So of course Bickern’s taken him to his squalid little heart. And after standing in that reeking tent listening to Caroline Haffle get up and wail for two solid hours about the sins she’s committed in her heart – without once mentioning that she treats her daughters like dog shit in the road and has a mouth on her like a cat-o’-nine-tails!’

‘Are they still at it?’ inquired January politely.

‘Can you ask? Ten minutes before the race they’re going to troop the whole choir from Jackson out in front of the Tabernacle, to make sure the ladies have time to drag their menfolks away from the sin of horse racing . . . and I’ll have to go in and be seen, naturally—’

‘Then I shall go in and be seen with you,’ responded Hannibal with a bow, ‘lest evil tongues whisper that I brought you away not for the sake of the clean morning air but to engage in flirtation.’

‘I trust, Madame, that you understand the greatness of my friend’s love for you . . .’ January removed his straw hat and placed it reverently over his heart. Across the field movement caught his eye, Ezekias Drummond signaling him from the shade of the trees beside the spring. ‘Shall I put a dollar on Big Brownie to encourage him to run faster?’

Hannibal dug into his pocket, produced one, then glanced at the *soi-disant* widow at his side. ‘*Domina mea?*’

She abstracted two from her reticule, pressed them into January’s hand.

He bowed, settled his hat on his head and crossed to the cavern of cool green where at least a dozen horses were tied.

Rex Ballou was seated with an air of sublime laziness on an upturned bucket, watching young Solomon as he checked the girths on a flat-seated English hunting saddle that he had just cinched onto the tall bay beneath the tree.

‘Might I count on you,’ Drummond asked softly, ‘to join us when we group around Solomon here at the conclusion of the race? Your friend, too . . .’ He glanced around for Hannibal. ‘The more people gathered here under the trees the better when I slip away.’

January took a quick tally of the potential 'crowd': himself, Hannibal, Rex, Solomon . . .

'Will Mrs Drummond and her daughter be here?'

Drummond shook his head dismissively. 'Mrs Drummond has no interest in horses. And these days I've thought it best that Rachel keep a little distance from the townsfolk. A girl her age—'

His lips tightened. January followed his eyes, to a young man who had been loitering – rather pointedly – a few yards away. An embodiment, January reflected, of all the reasons a stepfather of deep religious principles would want to keep a sixteen-year-old girl away from tent-shows and horse races. Startlingly handsome, with dark eyes and a Cupid's bow mouth, he was dressed in the stained and faded hunting shirt of a swamp-trapper, coarse moccasins, patched wool pants of the sort that a small farmer might wear. The long black hair under his billycock hat was greasy, and accentuated his Indian features. A foxtail dangled from his hat brim, and he wore a foot-long hunting knife at his belt.

For a moment the young man's eyes met Drummond's. Then the youth hunched his shoulders, turned sharply on his heel and disappeared into the crowd.

It took January a moment to identify who the young man reminded him of.

Injun Tom Colvard, of the pattyrollers.

The son they'd spoken of at the boarding house? No wonder Drummond hesitated to bring his stepdaughter here. He'd have to take his leave immediately after the race too, and presumably Mrs Drummond couldn't be trusted to keep her daughter's suitor at bay.

Whether forbidding the girl to attend an event that every other young person in two counties would be at was the best way of dealing with her resentment, January wasn't at all certain.

There was a stirring across the road in front of the Tabernacle, but no choir emerged. Only the fragile Mrs Purley, gesticulating furiously, and a half-dozen of the Jackson ladies.

'Will Mrs Drummond and Miss Rachel be at the dance tonight?' he asked.

'Oh, aye.' Drummond relaxed, probably because the son of a swamp-trapper wasn't likely to be doing reels and cotillions with the sons and daughters of the local planters. 'There's nothing wrong with rational exercise, you know. Though my wife—'

He broke off, and turned his head as hooves thundered on the slope beyond the stream. Coins of sunlight flashed on the linen jacket of the rider, and the next moment Jubal Cain drew rein among them and flung himself out of the saddle, his pock-marked face set like stone.

Drummond said, 'Cain—' and stepped toward him, one hand held out.

Cain grabbed the ferryman's sleeve, and without change of expression yanked him into a punch in the face delivered with such strength that January was surprised – thinking about it later – that the impact didn't break Drummond's neck.

Drummond went staggering, almost under the hooves of Cain's horse and Big Brownie – everyone, including January, shouted or exclaimed in astonishment. Cain didn't wait for Drummond to get up, but pursued him, dragging him to his feet and knocking him down again, kicking him as he lay. January made half a move to grab Cain and stopped himself, decades of instinct freezing him – no black man *ever* laid hands on a white – and Solomon sprang belatedly to his father's rescue. Cain threw him off as if he'd been a child.

By this time half the planters and townsmen who'd been gathered among the trees – and even a dozen of the men from the Tabernacle – had come on the run. Men grabbed Cain and dragged him off Drummond, while others shouted things like 'What the hell—?' and 'Break it up!' Drummond staggered to his feet, bleeding from his lip and nose and above one eye, and someone had to grab Solomon as he threw himself at Cain again.

Cain ignored him, wolf-yellow eyes on Drummond. Quite quietly, he said, 'You fucking blackguard, if you cross my path again I'll kill you.'

Men were still running up to see the fight when he twisted free of those holding him, caught the rein of his horse, and plunged away down the gully at a gallop, to disappear down the Haynes Bluff Road that led to the bayou.

TWELVE

'You, boy—' Drummond grabbed January's arm as January made a move to follow. 'Get me some water. Damn fool nearly broke my jaw.'

Rex Ballou drew January out of the swelling crowd around the ferryman and his son.

'What the *hell*?' January whispered, as the barber picked up the nearest bucket and headed for the stream. 'Do you know—?'

Ballou's face was without expression. 'I always heard Cain's a man you don't want to get foul of.'

'*Always heard . . .?* Why would Drummond cross him now?' They scrambled down the path, still smoking with the dust Cain's horse had thrown up, and picked their way up the rocks to a little fall, barely knee-high, where the water of the Mint Spring Branch tumbled from higher up the hills. 'I know Cain's no Puritan . . .'

After a long hesitation for thought, Ballou said, 'Looks to me like someone in town might have told him some lie. Bickern, maybe. He'd welcome the sight of Drummond kicked down in the dust.' But the words fumbled, like a man improvising a half-truth.

Whatever it is, he knows . . .

Drummond, the blood on his face roughly smeared aside, was on his knees, examining Big Brownie's legs minutely when January and Ballou returned: 'It wouldn't take but a minute, for someone to slip up and run a knife into his tendon. God damn it, give us some room!' He glared furiously at the men who still swarmed around them, talking and gesticulating and generating stories about Jubal Cain and every other fight any of them had ever seen.

Shocked, Solomon said, 'You mean somebody just – just got Mr Cain mad to bring a crowd?'

'What other reason can you think of, boy?' Drummond snapped. 'Will somebody throw those gawpers out of here?'

'I'll do it, Pa.' The boy began to herd the men away.

His father meanwhile tenderly examined the big stallion's fetlocks and hocks. Big Brownie lowered his head, and gently nibbled his master's collar. 'Either that or to delay the start of the race – easy, my boy, easy—' He stood, and caressed the animal's neck – 'or throw him off his stride. Upset him—' His big hands passed gently over the horse's face. 'Look how he's trembling!'

'He all right?' Theophilus Gooding, sweating like a pig in natty English tailoring, came up on the horse's other side.

And the tall, grim-faced Sheriff Preston of Warren County asked anxiously, 'He be able to run?'

'He's all right.' Drummond looked around irritably. 'Could I get you good folks to clear off, let him calm down a little? Thank you—'

'You want the race put off a little?' asked Preston. 'We can hold it thirty minutes.'

Drummond did a hasty mental calculation, glanced at Ballou, then shook his head. 'Make it fifteen,' he said. 'Easy, my friend,' he added, his face close to Big Brownie's sharply turning ear. 'Easy. All done now. You're all right, everybody's all right . . .'

He hastily washed the blood from his face, watching the horse like a worried mother as he did so. Across the road, the ladies of the Tabernacle clustered, milling about as if uncertain what to do. Solomon came back, looking far more shaken by the fight than his father.

'I've heard of it being done with racehorses in England,' remarked Ballou, when Drummond shook off any attempt to bandage his cuts and had returned to the task of gentling his horse. 'There's English stables that will give a prize racer sometimes a pony, sometimes a goat, like a pet, to keep him company in his stall at night. Makes them quieter, happier. I'm told there are touts who'll steal a champion's goat the night before the race, to upset him so's he won't run as he should.'

January glanced along the line of the shade trees by the spring, each tree sheltering its own little group of owner, horse, grooms, friends. Cinches being tightened, last-minute instructions being given: 'Hold him on the turn, work him toward the inside . . .' 'Don't let him run all-out 'til you're in the stretch . . .'

'You think somebody told Cain something, just to put Brownie off his stride?'

'It makes sense.' Ballou brushed his unruly black forelock aside, and January thought for a moment that his brow cleared a little . . . *Why?* Because it was a better explanation than whatever else he feared had really been going on?

'Or else as Mr Drummond feared, hoping to sneak up during the fight, and put him out of action. A couple of chunks of sugar with laudanum dripped on 'em would do it. Wouldn't hit him, 'til he was halfway through the course.'

The barber frowned, watching as Drummond helped his son to mount, led Big Brownie into the line of horses making for the starting line of the course. 'What I'm fearing,' he continued softly, as he and January followed the crowd, 'is that whatever it is – or might be – will hit Brownie mid-course. Bring him down . . . If he's really hurt, I don't think – I can't imagine Mr Drummond leaving him—'

Or leaving Solomon? wondered January. *If the horse comes down and Solomon breaks his leg or his neck?*

And what happens then? With Cain still furious and believing the worst, and this 'conductor' from Paducah, Eliza Walker, waiting in the bayous for a 'cargo' that doesn't come? With Saul Drummond – and Boze – waiting for his father, and the prisoners in that pit waiting for deliverance, and the hours sliding away in which nobody's going to be watching the river or the point . . .?

Men might have come to the races under the impression that Quinto had been captured, the reward claimed, but at a gathering like this, that rumor would be quickly scotched. They'd be on the watch again tomorrow, sharp as ever . . . and it wasn't a trick that could be played a second time.

January watched the tall bay horse's arched neck, its nervously twitching ears, as the animals took their places. Big Brownie visibly upset – *From the fight and the chaotic surging of the crowd too close around him, or from something he'd been fed, invisibly gripping his guts?* Solomon Drummond leaning forward to stroke the sweating shoulder, whispering encouragement, reassurance . . .

Drummond, standing at the start line, his face taut under the smears of dirt and blood.

Who the hell in town would Cain BELIEVE, if they told him – told him WHAT? – some lie about Drummond?

The starter's gun went off. The horses leaped forward like the breaking of a wave.

And Big Brownie ran like Bucephalus treading the foes of Alexander beneath his feet, like Copenhagen at Waterloo, effortless, proud, head up, steady as the arctic wind. *He swalloweth the ground with fierceness and rage . . .*

The race was over, it seemed, almost before it began. Brownie galloped in, breathing easy, barely sweating, two lengths in front of the next competitor, men crowding around him and cheering, even those who'd bet on other horses. Even those who owned other horses, shouting with the pleasure of men who like to see a good race well run by beasts who truly were the handiwork of God.

Solomon slipped down from the saddle laughing – the only time January had ever seen that sober-faced, anxious youth relax – and his father flung one powerful arm around his shoulders, the other over Big Brownie's withers. 'Now, let's get this boy rubbed down!' cried Drummond. 'He's well earned his feed! Good boy, lad! Good boy!'

The other men went to lead off their own horses, to foregather with their friends, to wrangle over money, little knowing they'd just contributed the one hundred dollar prize to the eventual escape, perhaps, of their own field hands. Still no sign of the Tabernacle choir – January wondered if one or both Reverends had slipped away to watch the race on the sly. He, Hannibal and Ballou closed in behind Drummond as they walked the horse back to the shade of the trees, January already mentally mapping times, speed, places, plausible excuses . . . In half an hour he'd have to be onstage playing 'The Bee-Gum Tree' for Mr Tambo and Mr Interlocutor, and all those people in the pit – Isaiah and Arthur, Deya and Giselle, Ason and Randol and poor little Charlie – would vanish like smoke across the river, into the primeval wildness of the 'delta', never to be seen by him again.

Free, to make of their lives what they could.

He barely saw the child who ran up to Drummond, handed him a piece of paper, and darted away into the crowd. When he testified to it later he was fairly certain it was a black boy of five or six, though afterwards nobody was ever able to trace down the child and there were those who swore he was white, or a girl . . .

What remained clearest in January's mind was Drummond's face when he read the paper.

The dusky fury that suffused it. The rage that twisted his mouth and flared from his eyes.

Solomon stepped back from him as he would have done from the door of a blast furnace suddenly opened. 'Pa?'

Drummond shoved him out of the way, threw himself up onto Big Brownie's back, and spurred at a headlong gallop across the stream and into the woods that cloaked the hills.

Come, listen, all you girls and boys,
I'm just from Tuckahoe;
I'm going to sing a little song,
My name's Jim Crow.
Wheel about, and turn about, and do just so;
Every time I wheel about, I jump Jim Crow . . .

Jacob Blechmann rose from his place in the line of 'minstrels', strutted onto the front of the stage, smiling under the burnt cork, wriggling his shoulders and his hips and now and then stroking back the greased black curls of his wig. Exaggerated buckram shoulders to his long-tailed coat, paste diamonds flashing on his tiepin and pinky rings, checked trousers refulgent in the soft light that came through the canvas of the tent, the very picture of what white people imagined a free black dandy from New York or Philadelphia to be: effete, enormously full of himself, and under the impression he was a lot smarter than he actually was.

And harmless.

I cut so many monkey shines,
I dance the gallopade,
And when I'm done, I rest my head
On shovel, hoe or spade.
Wheel about, and turn about, and do just so;
Every time I wheel about, I jump Jim Crow . . .

The crowd in the tent roared with laughter at his loose-jointed, comic movements – astonishingly graceful, January was well aware, light as a limberjack as he danced his 'gallopade' and wheeled about, turned about, jumped straight-legged up like a machine-piston and landed in an effortless splits . . .

And did Drummond make it, from wherever he went, to meet Saul and Boze? Are they even now bringing the fugitives up from their pit, loading them into the wagon under shelter of the cane-brake, heading for the river?

Did Cain meet with Eliza Walker? Did his riding off in a fury mean he was washing his hands of the whole project?

WHY?

When Drummond gets across the river, will there be anyone there to meet them?

What the HELL was that fight all about? And are Hannibal and I going to walk out of here this afternoon into the arms of the town constable and Sheriff Preston and the Warren County militia with a warrant for all of us, for slave-stealing?

January felt the sweat rolling down his face. Natural enough, in the dense heat beneath the show tent, but as he vamped along behind the spritely banjoes, bones and Jew's harp of the imitation blacks in the front row, he found it hard to concentrate. *Should we even now be heading to the riverfront as fast as we can go and looking for a steamboat for New Orleans?*

Would it be of any help to us if we did?

'Well, Mr Tambo,' said the Interlocutor, 'how's your fine family?'

'Oh, dey's fine, suh, jus' fine!' returned Mel Silverberg, setting aside his tambourine. 'Why don't you come over an' see us?'

'Why, thank you, Mr Tambo. I shall avail myself of your kind invitation at the first opportunity that presents itself.'

'Don't mind no opportunity, suh, jus' come on over any time. Plen'y company there now! We gots all our relations from the country visitin' us. Dey's seventeen of 'em.'

'Seventeen!' Tavish flung up his white-gloved hands. 'Say, that's quite a houseful!'

'You tellin' me, suh! But we got 'em 'stributed around our house. Uncle Zeke an' his boys sleep in with the pig, Cousin Zeb we got in de chicken coop, an' I sleeps in with the cow. She kick a little, but she a good cow. After dinner in de evenin', we hitch up the goat to de wagon, an' all go for a ride.'

'All seventeen of you? He must be a very strong goat.'

Mr Tambo wrinkled his nose and waved as if to chase away a stench. 'Well, suh, he was at first, but we all got used to it now so we doan mind.'

The Boneless Monzonnis (actually two Monzonnis and a Schindler) came on and tied themselves and each other into knots. 'Colonel' Byron Herriott, assisted by his wife and two sons, performed a number of juggling, dancing and acrobatic feats on a rope stretched seven feet above the stage, culminating with a swordfight between himself and his oldest son. Primula Kelly's University of Educated Canines demonstrated that four pugs and a miniature spaniel can be taught to do pretty much anything, including build a five-foot tower and operate an abacus, with interludes between them of song and dance by the 'minstrels'. Owen Tavish came on *in propria persona* to make eggs, silk scarves, flowers and Maryam the Princess of the Desert appeared and disappeared in flashes of light and huge puffs of colored smoke.

In the second row January glimpsed the handsome young trapper who'd attempted to speak to Drummond that morning, laughing and exclaiming with the rest. Did he – Injun Tom's son, January recalled someone at Mrs Dillager's saying his name was Roane . . . Did Roane Colvard plan to rendezvous with Rachel Pryce, Drummond's stepdaughter, when her mother brought her into town for the ball?

Had the note been about them?

January left the stage – and the tent – at shortly after two, to find Cornelia Passmore fuming in the shade behind the menagerie. 'That suck-ass bastard Bickern has taken every cent of the Tabernacle's proceeds to the bank!' she stormed. 'The nerve of him!'

'Maybe he didn't trust the Reverend Thorne after all?' suggested January.

The widow blew an angry stream of cigar smoke. 'Christmas has been gone all morning,' she said. 'Buttering up Caroline Haffle, I should imagine. The tent's practically empty: May Buck's trying to keep the choir going, but without fear of damnation nobody's buying it. Nobody's seen either one of them since ten. Laetitia Purley's practically having a stroke.'

Hannibal, who had sunk down onto the nearest hay bale in a

fit of coughing that shook the whole of his body, glanced up and queried, 'Anybody see Christmas leave?'

Mrs Passmore shrugged, but January caught the fiddler's eye and saw a kind of quizzical concern there, the awareness that the slave-stealer's absence at this particular time might betoken anything.

While the lady expiated further on the Reverend Bickern's morals, anatomy, parentage and probable ultimate destination, Rex Ballou came around the corner of the tent housing the Philosophical Curiosities, and January went to him at once.

'Have you heard anything?'

Ballou shook his head. He looked ashen with fatigue. January took him by the elbow and guided him to yet another bale of Martha the elephant's dinner. 'Wait here.'

All three of the menagerie keepers were on the other side of the tent, stationed along the rope that separated the animals themselves from the jostling throng. January dipped a tin cup of water from the nearest (and freshest-looking) pail before it was carried over to the camels, softly asked the nearest keeper, 'You got a flask? I got a friend back here who's been took poorly.'

The man handed him a flat tin bottle. 'Anything I can do?'

'He'll be fine. It's the sun.' This was a believable lie: the afternoon was as hot and damp as the towels in Ballou's shop. 'He just needs a sit.'

Ballou dumped a little of the rum into the water cup, downed it gratefully. 'Even if – Mr Abel – went straight down to the ferry the minute he took care of his business, whatever the hell that was, he won't be back 'til almost sunset. He'll be at Goodings'—'

Hannibal rose from his own hay bale, and gallantly offered an arm to Mrs Passmore, who ground out her cigar under her heel. As they moved off, Ballou looked around to make sure there was no one in sight. His voice sank to a whisper. 'Believe me, if he'd been caught, this'd be the first place the news would come.'

'What about Cain?' Like Ballou's, January's voice went down to barely a flicker of sound.

In the back of the barber's hazel eyes January saw again the millrace of unspoken thoughts: *What can I tell this man, what do I need to keep quiet about?*

January wanted to grab him by the shoulders and yell, *What the hell is going on?*

Or was it just that, living in secrets and lying to everyone around them for six years, it had become second nature to them to measure every word?

'Cain was mad as fire,' said Ballou at length. 'But I can't see him doing anything that'd put a cargo in danger. Nor would Mr Drummond. For one thing—' And a sudden, unwilling grin cracked his haggard face – 'Eliza Walker'd knock their heads together if they did. She may yet. I just . . .'

He sighed, like a man taking up a burden too heavy to bear, and gingerly rubbed his chest where his mustard-colored calico shirt covered the bandages. 'I just wish it was safe, over and done.'

He listened to January's account of Levi Christmas' absence at just about the time that Drummond had received the note that had sent him riding in cold-faced fury from the racecourse. 'Could it have been Christmas that sent that note? So he could follow him?'

'Could be.' Ballou's face hardened. 'If he thinks he's going to blackmail Mr Drummond into turning those fugitives over to him, he's going to find out his mistake pretty quickly. And given that he's been masquerading for the past seven months as a Methodist preacher in Jackson, I think he'd think twice about jeopardizing ten thousand dollars' worth of church funds – if he can get his hands on them – by trying to run a blackmail game that'd get him six thousand dollars at most.'

'Doesn't mean a member of his gang – if he's working with a gang – wouldn't try it.'

'Christmas'll be fit to skin him – or her.'

Hannibal returned at that point, and January followed him back into the show tent, where Tavish's crew of New York Hebrews was blacking up again for the afternoon show. Theophilus Gooding was there, looking like he was about to strangle on his own high-knotted stock and fussing about the musicians for the ball. All around them, already the talk was of packing up, of tearing down: Maryam, Princess of the Desert, Mozambia and Rosalind Herriott were negotiating the logistics of sharing a stateroom on one of the three steamboats that would carry the circus up to Greenville. Isaiah and Arthur, Deya and Ason, Giselle and Randol and poor little Charlie – and the woman Cindy, wherever she might be – would be on their way through the tangled fastnesses of the Red River 'delta', following the Drinking Gourd past Memphis, to the Ohio River and freedom.

January touched the battered blue rosary in his pocket, and breathed a prayer for their safety. And another for Rose and Baby John.

While all across northwest Louisiana, all across Mississippi and Arkansas and Alabama and Missouri in a few months the cotton harvest would begin, and men would be beaten for not making their two hundred pounds a day, and women would be raped, who happened to catch the master's eye, or the overseer's . . . or that of one of the master's guests or friends. Children would be sold, never to see their parents or their brothers again, not because they had done any wrong but because somebody in the master's family needed money or maybe had just put them up in a poker hand.

Eight running to freedom, thought January, listening to the talk swirling all around him, the small doings of the free, *out of how many thousands, how many hundreds of thousands?*

Mel Silverberg swiveled on his heels and slapped his knees, practicing his 'darky' drawl. Jake Blechmann tried out a new joke: 'Why am one ob does bottles on a cruet stand like a li'l colored boy?'

It's ten dollars a week, January told himself. *I prayed all spring to find work, and this came along. I should take it and be glad, not angry. And at the end of the summer I can go back to Rose, and Baby John, and please God to Baby-Rose or Baby-Ben . . . To family and friends and the way life was lived in the French Town . . .*

But outside the French Town, this land would still be here.

At Goodings', January finally got a look at Constance Drummond, who came in escorted by a starched and dark-suited Solomon, holding firmly to the arm of her daughter, Rachel. Mrs Drummond was a small, fair woman in her early thirties, clothed – like Julia Maury – in a gown that January's first wife, Ayasha, would have identified immediately as ten years out of fashion (but unlike the one Julia Maury was wearing, made up of cheap material which had never really been *in* fashion in the first place). 'Slipping her opiates at night, you said?' whispered Hannibal, delicately adjusting the string of his fiddle on the musicians' dais, and January nodded.

'To keep her from asking questions, Ballou said. And from seeing things she isn't supposed to see. From which I deduce she has never shared in his conversion.'

'Well, whatever's happening at bedtime,' the fiddler returned, 'she's a cat that's found her own way to the dairy by day. Look at her eyes, and the texture of her skin. I wonder if Drummond knows?'

January glanced around the swiftly-filling ballroom, but saw no trace of either the ferryman or his elder son. January had already guessed, from Solomon's look of apprehension, that no word had reached him from his father: January had stopped by the barbershop on his way from the circus grounds to the confectionary shop on Adams Street, and knew that Ballou had heard nothing either. He'd found the barber just emerging from the dead sleep of exhaustion, so there was at least the possibility that someone had brought word but had not wanted to wake him.

Now he shivered with a chill of apprehension.

When Jubal Cain entered the ballroom, like a yellow-eyed Satan in a suit of white summer linen, Solomon crossed to him at once. January saw him shake his head, and in the soft orange lamplight – Vicksburg had nothing so modern as a gas plant in the town – saw his pock-marked face darken, his heavy brows draw down.

Damn it, thought January. *DAMN it* . . .

If he'd been caught, Ballou had said, this'd be the first place the news would come . . .

January knew this to be true. Nobody had come barging into the second show of the 'minstrelsy', yelling that somebody had caught a passel of escaping niggers and that feller Drummond was behind it all along! When he and Hannibal had walked through the showgrounds in the hot twilight on their way into town, the talk all around them from the last of the home-wandering townsmen had been of the dogfights, and the nigger fights, and the horse race that morning.

A musician couldn't walk up to a subscription-paying guest at a dance. At some point, Cain would idle over to chat, and would let him know . . .

What?

The slave-dealer's face was still set and grim. A flicker of the morning's anger still seemed to glint in his eyes.

Solomon glanced back at Mrs Drummond and Rachel, then murmured something else to Cain. Rachel, at least, didn't seem to have followed her mother's path in dealing with the restless malaise that must have been more and more frequent in her life. She was clearly in a state of edgy discomfort, looking around her as if slightly disoriented by the crowd – *Or is she on the lookout for her sweetheart? Or for a way to slip out of the room to meet him?* In the flare of the oil lamps that raised the temperature of the room to stifling despite the open windows all along one wall, her long, vaguely pretty face was pale under a countrywoman's tan, and when she took her mother's arm her hands shook.

She was a tall girl, and sturdily built, but unlike most of the other girls her age in the room she still wore the short frock of a schoolgirl, much turned, altered and faded. Her mouse-brown hair hung down her back to the waist, tied with a schoolgirlish ribbon. The town girls, their stiffly-starched tarlatan skirts let down to their heels, their hair braided up into Grecian knots and masses of curls, whispered and giggled as she passed.

Solomon started to say something else to Cain but Julia Maury, turning from conversation with Cornelia Passmore, caught the slave-dealer's eye with a glance like the single note of a bell. Cain bowed to Solomon and crossed the room to her.

Maury, January noticed, was not in the room.

'And she'd better finish whatever she has to say quickly,' whispered Hannibal, following his eye. 'I understand Mr Maury broke his first wife's jaw, only for talking to Sheriff Preston's son.'

Beaming with good cheer, Gooding called out, 'Ladies and Gentlemen, please take your places for the Marlborough cotillion,' and January had to turn his attention to the music.

Another quick survey of the room, as he struck up the opening notes, showed January that neither the constable of the town, nor Sheriff Preston, nor Sheriff Brister of Madison Parish, were present either. It meant nothing that militiamen like Drew Hardy and Injun Tom were absent – men of their class would no more have been permitted subscriptions to the ball than Rex Ballou would have – but the absence of any of the local lawmen made his heart pound and his attention struggle to remain on the music.

But if there'd been an arrest, Cain would have known, surely? Solomon would have known . . .

Olivettes, passe-pieds, grand chaine . . . The light flourishes of Hannibal's fiddle over the notes, music like a sequined shawl in sunlight. Couples meeting, couples parting; the pat of dogskin slippers on the waxed oak floor and the silvery whisper of silken petticoats.

The Reverend Bickern came in, looking profoundly ill at ease, and was surrounded at once by his chattering flock. Laetitia Purley, his hostess for the revival, put a possessive hand through his arm. *Slandering the Reverend Thorne for disappearing and leaving the choir to look after itself?* January wondered. Julia Maury cast a swift look in his direction and drew Cain deeper into the alcove of the window.

Threading-the-needle, dos-a-dos . . . Candles and laughter. Constance Drummond stepped behind the potted palms beside the musicians' dais and took a quick sip from a bottle she produced from her reticule.

No sign of Levi Christmas. The Jackson ladies kept to their own side of the ballroom, shunning the Vicksburg ladies and watching the door with anxious eyes.

The door of the hall opened. Sheriff Preston came in, followed by the men of the militia – January recognized Drew Hardy, Injun Tom and Jim Punce. None wore evening dress. Marcus Maury was with them, his face like ice, and his wife stepped quickly from the window embrasure and ducked to the protection of Mrs Passmore's black skirts. Mr Gooding hurried to the sheriff, and the lawman said something that made him fall back in shocked confusion. The dancers lost their places in the pattern of the movement. The other members of the little orchestra stumbled in their rhythm. The room fell silent.

January gauged the distance to the window, and estimated his chances of not breaking his leg in a twenty-foot drop to the ground. (*Is there a shed . . .?*)

Sheriff Preston said, 'Jubal Cain?'

Cain stepped from the window alcove. 'I'm here.'

'Jubal Cain, I place you under arrest, for the murder of Ezekias Drummond.'

THIRTEEN

'How the hell should I know what happened?' Cain groped angrily at his pockets, and Rex Ballou, who had met January and Hannibal on their way up to the jail that morning, produced a cigar. In the rectangle of hot early sunlight by the jail's open door, a sour-faced young deputy glowered at them, possibly because the Havana was something he couldn't afford to smoke himself, as well as the obscure sense that a black man – no matter how free – had no business owning such luxuries.

The bell of the Episcopal church chimed gently on the sultry air. Out on the Springdale Road, the All-American Zoological Society's Traveling Circus was striking its tents and counting its money.

'Where was the body?' Hannibal straddled the bent-willow chair that had stood in the corner of the jail's outer room. Ballou and January stood, as black men should in the presence of their betters, Ballou leaning inconspicuously against the barred front of the cell. In the bright morning light, the exertions of the previous day, and of the night he'd spent crossing the river to help escort Mrs Drummond and her daughter home, were clear as the gouges of a chisel.

Cain's glance flickered toward the listening deputy.

'In Julia Maury's cottage,' he said unwillingly, 'on the Haynes Bluff Road.' He groped in his pockets again and January produced, and lit, a match. The Haynes Bluff Road joined the trace Cain had taken, after hammering Ezekias Drummond with his fists and yelling at him, '*If you cross my path again I'll kill you.*'

'Julia Maury's?'

'What on earth was Drummond doing there?' Hannibal's eyebrows quirked halfway up his forehead.

'Meetin' your friend, seemingly,' drawled the deputy, with slow satisfaction, and spit tobacco into the sandbox. The whole jail smelled of it. 'Leastwise them was his gloves we found, layin' beside the body and all covered in blood.'

'*Pro di immortales*,' murmured Hannibal. 'How do they know they're Mr Cain's gloves?'

'They're mine, all right,' said Cain grimly. 'My yellow dogskin ones. Everyone at the hotel's seen them.'

'Stolen?'

Cain's mouth hardened, and he did not reply.

'You surely ain't gonna say,' added the deputy, 'as how you never set foot in Mrs Maury's cottage in your life, now, are you, Mr Cain? 'Cause the cook there saw you Wednesday night . . .'

'Hilding,' growled Cain, 'you talk too goddam much.'

Very softly, January said, in Latin, 'Ask where the body is now.'

'I'm shocked!' Hannibal turned to the deputy. 'I'm sure there's been some mistake—'

'Yeah, like your friend there made a mistake layin' in wait for a man, then killin' him an' leavin' his body, and comin' up with a damn-fool story about where he was all afternoon.'

'If I'd lain in wait for Drummond,' grated Cain, 'don't you think I'd have come up with a better story than the truth? And the truth is that a fellow named Johnson up on the Sunflower River had a couple of likely boys to sell me, and I threshed around for most of the afternoon looking for his damn farm and got nothing but bit to death by mosquitoes for my trouble.'

'There ain't no Johnson up on the Sunflower,' pointed out Deputy Hilding, and spit again.

'Yeah, I did find out the truth of your assertion.' Cain blew a line of smoke in the direction of the door. 'But just 'cause I was fool enough to make and keep an appointment in the way of my legitimate business with some jug-eared drunkard I met over in Richmond the other evening, doesn't mean I'd take time out of my day to stab to death a man I'd already beat the crap out of in front of pretty nearly every man in Warren County.'

'Stab?' said January, and Cain snapped warningly, 'What the hell business is it of yours, boy?'

'My servant was trained by a physician,' explained Hannibal, dividing his placatory glance between Cain – who took care never to look like he was collaborating with a black of any description – and the deputy. 'I've seen him make some quite pertinent observations about wounds. Might there be a chance—' He stood, and slid a hand into his breast-pocket suggestively – 'that I could have a look at the body? Is it on the premises?'

Hannibal liked to quote a great Roman statesman to the effect that no *'No fort is so strong that it cannot be taken with money':* in this case it seemed that the Roman was quite correct. The deputy led Hannibal – with January tagging along like a good servant at his heels – to a small shed at the back of the court-house, roaring with flies and already thick with the stink of mortality. Gold had certainly opened this door: the room was occupied, in addition to Drummond lying naked on a table in the midst of it, by five other men, two of them dressed like planters or well-off townsmen, the other three unshaven roughnecks from the waterfront, all gaping and muttering among themselves, and shaking their heads.

January counted at least six deep stab wounds on Drummond's roughly washed torso. Flies swarmed around his eyes, nostrils and the smaller gashes on his chest, belly and hands. Ants made a black ribbon from the windowsill up the leg of the table, and tiny maggots had begun to creep from the wounds. The deputy having departed ('Now, don't you linger, hear?') – January murmured to Hannibal in Latin, '*Tell me to turn him over*.'

Hannibal, greenish with nausea, obediently piped up, 'Turn him over, Ben, there's a good boy,' and – having given the order – valiantly kept his eyes on the corpse when January did so.

There were another four stab wounds on the back.

The other men crowded in to stare.

'He sure done the job on ol' Drummond.'

'You reckon it was over Mrs Maury, Dan?'

''Course it was over Mrs Maury!' One of the planters spit a brown tobacco wad onto the floor. 'Julia Maury been practically livin' in that cottage since Christmas. Only thing surprises me is it wasn't *Cain* they found cut up there, an' *Maury's* gloves beside *him*.' And, when the other men all crowded around the speaker like a bunch of schoolgirls, the man went on, 'Hell, ever since Cain been in town she's been sweet on him. You seen her, speakin' to him when she'd come by the Planter's for them church committee meetin's. What the hell else would any decent woman want with a man of his type?'

'You think she was doin' Drummond too?'

''Course she was—'

'After all his carry-on about God an' righteousness—'

'Hell.' The planter spit again. 'I never met a preacher yet who could keep his pecker in his pants. You seen the way the Jackson ladies crowd around that pusillanimous Bible-beater Thorne . . .'

Hannibal pretended to be absorbed in study of the corpse, but January could see, beneath the brim of his hat, the fiddler's neck and ears flush red with anger as the conversation turned to pornographic speculation about what Julia Maury would be like in bed. Since it was clear that Marcus Maury violated most of the women on Indian Mound Plantation on a regular basis, January could scarcely blame the man's wife if she had been the Messalina they described, but it was nauseating to listen to.

The men departed, continuing their commentary about Julia Maury and digressions on their own 'wenches'; the moment they were out of sight Hannibal walked to the doorway and stood looking out, breathing deeply and shakily. January immediately probed the muscles of Drummond's arms and thighs – something he couldn't have done with white men in the room – and felt in them the remains of rigor, though the ferryman's neck and jaw had already gone slack. Not a surprise, in this heat . . .

Faint traces of subcutaneous blood could still be seen on his back, though most of the *livor mortis* was on his face, chest and belly.

January turned him over again and stood looking down at that harsh square face, the graying beard stiff with blood and dirt. The man who'd given up everything he'd known in New York state, to come to this place. A man who'd put the freedom of others before his own happiness or comfort. *A harsh man*, he thought. *A strange man*. A man who'd fed his wife and stepdaughter laudanum, knowing what its long-term effects must be . . .

A man who had loved his horses.

Where's Big Brownie? Running loose in the cane-brakes, lost in the woods . . .

Drummond's clothing was folded on a chair in a corner of the shed. January unfolded it, keeping an ear sharp for the deputy's return.

The shirt was stiff with dried blood, and smudged all over, front and back, with dirt and the stains of moss and foliage.

January found himself remembering how violently Cain had thrown him down in the trampled grass of the meadow.

'Julia Maury did seek him out,' murmured January in Latin. 'We both saw . . .'

'You don't think she was connected somehow with the Railroad?' the fiddler returned in the same language.

January shook his head, and picked up the trousers, ran his fingers through the pockets – a pencil, a folding knife, a couple of neatly-wound packets of string. The waistcoat pocket was empty, yet January knew he'd seen Drummond look at his watch before the race. The jacket pocket held a couple of chunks of sugar wrapped in blue paper, and a hoof pick. 'What do those wounds say to you?' he asked.

'*His silver skin laced with his golden blood* . . .' Hannibal didn't turn around from the doorway, and dropped from Shakespearian English back into Ciceronian Latin without a blink. 'Hatred. Rage. One blow won't do.'

'Or panic,' said January. 'Fear. Look at the gashes on his hands. He came after his killer, barehanded, after the killer had struck him in the back.'

'So what do we do? It's not as if we can bring in this woman Mrs Walker as a witness to Cain's whereabouts all afternoon.' Hannibal followed January to the door, then remembered and preceded him through it.

The deputy joined them just outside the shed; when they entered the jail again Ballou, who had been speaking quickly and earnestly with Cain, looked around sharply and stepped back.

'The first thing I want to see,' murmured January, as the deputy slouched back to his desk, 'is that note he got just after the race.'

'The body was found by Marcus Maury.' Ballou led the way down the hill to the half-burned barbershop on Clay Street.

'Somehow,' said January, 'it doesn't surprise me to hear that.'

Church services were letting out. Carriages rattled along Main and Jackson Streets, picnickers bound out of town. Boys were swarming back from the wharves, where they'd been watching the circus board three steamboats for the next leg of its journey up the river. January and Hannibal had taken regretful leave of the show early that morning, amid the noisy chaos of tents being taken down, props packed up.

'I can't explain what I owe Cain,' Hannibal had said to Tavish. 'It's a debt of honor and friendship that goes back years. In honor, I can't leave him.'

The Scotsman had cocked his head, surveying Hannibal and January under those dragon eyebrows, as if he understood that there was something going on that wasn't being spoken of: 'D'you need help of any sort?'

Hannibal had shaken his head. 'I have a little saved.' In point of fact, in the confusion that had followed Cain's arrest and the break-up of the ball last night, Hannibal and January had quietly slipped down the backstairs of Goodings', returned to the Planters' Hotel and burgled Cain's room, eventually unearthing a hundred and fifty dollars of the Philadelphia Anti-Slavery Society's money secreted behind the drawers of the desk ('I'm astonished Mrs Passmore didn't get here first,' Hannibal had remarked). (They'd met her in the hall on their way out). 'As long as I stay sober I should make enough at the poker tables to keep us. I am sorry, truly, to leave you high and dry—'

'Ach, there's worse happens in war.' Tavish clasped their hands in farewell. 'Good luck to the pair of you. You'll look me up when we come back through New Orleans in the fall, and let me know how it all fell out.'

If we're not murdered, January had reflected uncomfortably, watching the Scotsman walk away, *as Ezekias was murdered* . . .

He'd have to write to Rose, let her know that no money would come for a while . . .

He could not keep the thought from his mind: *Was Ezekias Drummond the only target?*

Or only the first?

'*Was* Cain having an affair with Julia Maury?' he asked the moment the door of Ballou's shop closed behind them.

'Maury thinks his wife's having an affair with any man who crosses her path.' Ballou passed through the tidied-up shop to the kitchen, fetched the kettle from the old-fashioned hearth. 'He was like that with Emmie Buck as well – his first wife. Rumor is he beat her to death, though no one's ever proved it.'

'I'll get that.' January took the kettle from his hand. 'You look like you've been horse-dragged. And I'll want to change those bandages.'

'It's better today.' Ballou sank into one of the rough chairs. 'I can feel it. Itches like the devil.'

'Good,' said January. 'That means it's healing.'

'Julia Maury was trying to get Cain to buy some of her slaves,' said Ballou, as January filled the kettle from the big yellowware water filter in the corner. 'She went to him because he's not well-known here in town. The local dealers know her husband. I think she's planning on running away.'

January recalled Maury's cold voice rapping out imprecations and questions, through the open window at Indian Mound. The slap of leather on flesh, and the woman's sobs. 'Did Cain – or that deputy – say anything about a note being in Drummond's pocket? The one that child brought him—'

'Is that where he got it?' Ballou straightened a little in his chair. 'Jim Litharge's horse kicked up a fuss just then and I had my head turned. When I turned it back Mr Drummond had the note in his hand—' His voice broke off and he looked aside, unable to go on.

The man was alive. Breathing, triumphant, aglow. *And now he's gone.*

After a moment, Ballou said, his voice thin with emotion, 'He had his faults. Bad ones, some of 'em. How do you weigh that against the good he did?' He rubbed his face with his hand. 'I helped Solly take the ferry back last night . . . *Every* damn passenger wanted to talk about it with poor Solly. And with Mrs Drummond, and Rachel: people who wouldn't have given either of them the time of day, just twitching for gossip.' His fists bunched briefly, then he put the thought aside. 'Saul said he'd waited with the wagon in an old barn near the pit, 'til dark and after. It wasn't until he saw the ferry's lights coming back that he returned to the house to learn what had happened.'

'What did Cain say about it?'

'That he waited with Eliza Walker in the cane-brake near where they'd planned to land.'

'What did he say about the fight?'

Ballou hesitated. January saw the man's eyes shift.

At last: 'He said it was between Mr Drummond and him. That it had nothing to do with anything.'

'And you *left* it at that?'

Ballou sat for a long time, hands folded on the table before him. Silent as a mouse, Hannibal removed the steaming kettle to the back of the range, then returned to his chair. January looked down at the man before him, recalling his silence in the pit . . .

'He said it wasn't any of my business.'

'What does this have to do with this woman Cindy?' asked January quietly.

Ballou twitched, just slightly, as if his flesh had been touched by a hot wire. 'There's nothing it could have to do with it. Nor with Mr Drummond being killed.'

'Why not?'

The barber looked up at him again, hazel eyes bitter under the silky forelock of his hair. 'Who'd kill a man over the honor of a black girl?' he asked softly. 'What's done is done.'

'And what,' returned January, 'exactly, was done?'

FOURTEEN

'The man had his faults,' Ballou said again, softly now, as if arguing against his will.

'You keep saying that. What faults are we talking about?'

In his heart, January knew. It was like watching a building collapse, inevitable, unstoppable. Knew, and was sick in his soul.

'He saved hundreds from slavery,' said Ballou. 'Gave them new lives. He didn't have to do that. He had a home in New York state, a congregation who respected him, a calling . . . He left all that, to come down here. To do what we do. Not another man in a thousand, in five thousand—'

'He raped her,' said January quietly. 'Didn't he?'

'I don't know if you can call it rape—'

'What else do you call it,' returned January, 'when a woman says *No*, and a man goes ahead and has her anyway?'

Ballou didn't answer.

Hannibal suggested, 'Slavery?'

'He was saving her from slavery.'

But January heard the defeat in his voice. The bitterness of betrayal. The blistering shame at his own silence.

'Where is she?'

'I don't know. He has a place somewhere this side of the river, another of his hideouts, deep in the swamps. Maybe more than one . . .'

January felt cold inside, as if he were about to vomit something poisonous. Cold that turned to heat. 'You mean, Cindy isn't the first.'

Ballou looked down at his hands. 'No.'

Or the second . . . or the third . . .

January walked over to the stove, filled a washbowl with the steaming water and carried it back to the table. As a barber, Ballou had drawers full of clean rags and towels, neatly folded. Methodically January brought them over, along with the spirits of wine that were part of the barber's trade. He didn't trust himself to speak.

Hannibal said, 'It sounds to me as if Cain might have encountered this woman in his search for Mrs Walker in the swamps on the other side of Chickasaw Bayou—'

'She should have hid from him!' burst out Ballou. 'She didn't know who the hell he was—'

January said nothing, but he saw that his patient had heard his own words as they came out, and knew them for what they were: *She should have kept her rapist's secrets, just like I did . . .* Heard them and hated them, and himself.

Ballou turned his face away, eyes shut and mouth twisted, as if physically unable to look at what he'd been avoiding . . .

For how long?

Then he sighed, and looked back at January. 'I never knew what to do,' he said simply. 'I needed a white man. A man who could own property, a man who could act without always looking over his shoulder the way I have to do; without having to fear he'll be beat up or killed for saying the wrong thing to the wrong person, for things that have nothing to do with the Railroad. Maybe for nothing at all.' He glanced across at Hannibal, then back at January. 'A man like your friend Mr Freepaper.'

January unpinned the bandages from his shoulder, and unwrapped the wound. Only a few of the free blacks in Vicksburg and Natchez were legally deemed permanent residents of the state: it took a special act of the legislature – in effect, a special, personal law, sponsored by the well-off whites in the town. At Mrs Dillager's boarding table he'd heard men talk of the proposal under discussion in Jackson, the state capital, to ban all free blacks from the state, under the presumption that they would 'inflame' slaves to revolt.

'When I bought myself free I swore I'd come back here, to help those that didn't have the chances God gave me through no deserving of my own. And Drummond was brilliant. He was crafty, he was strong, he rode with the militia and there wasn't a man in Madison Parish that thought he'd be working for the Railroad. And this – with Cindy, and the others . . . This was something you can't know, just from looking at a man.'

Still January didn't speak. Couldn't. Church bells were ringing again up the hill. A couple of women walked by on Clay Street, talking about hats. January wrung out a rag in the hot water, and examined the wound. The swelling was going down. There was no pus, and it smelled clean.

'It was two years,' said Ballou, 'we'd been working together. Harriet Wells from Monroe sent us a cargo, two men and a woman . . . Tina was the girl's name, eighteen years old and pretty as a kitten. I took them to one of our hideouts and when I came the next day, to tell them of the plan for moving them on, Tina was gone. Her brother – he was one of the men – said Drummond had come in the night and took her away, and told them not to speak of it to anyone, that she'd be well. He said Tina had told them everything was all right, but, he said, he knew her, and knew by her eyes that it wasn't. But what could I say?'

What indeed? Through a silent scald of rage, he guessed that for the girl Tina it had been a question of *This is the price I have to pay for freedom*. And Drummond – at a guess – would simply have thought, *She's been bulled who knows how many times by her master, and probably every guest who came to his door. What's one more?*

What indeed?

'When I got the others across the river Tina was there with Drummond at the meeting place. There was no chance to speak to either her or her brother alone. To this day I don't know the truth of what happened . . .'

And what COULD he say? January pinned the clean bandage in place, a little surprised at the steadiness of his own hands. *Stop that or I'll send you back to New York?*

All that would get would be, *The girl lied. Her brother lied.* Like nearly every man he'd ever met, black or white, confronted by a woman's accusations.

And the search for a white conductor on this critical river crossing, this critical station on the invisible 'railroad' to freedom, would have to begin all over again.

Stop that or I'll beat you up?

As if a black man could get away with striking a white man.

January held his silence. He had learned this as a tiny child, when he was weeping and cursing inside. Being beaten with a wire-wrapped cane-stalk for *Get that look off your face, boy*, had been a great teacher . . .

Hannibal asked, reasonably, 'Did you ever speak to him of it?'

Ballou shook his head. 'You know how you do, when someone's lying and you just . . . you just *look* at them, like, *I know you're lying* . . . But he'd just meet my eyes like there was nothing wrong. Not even, "What you lookin' at, nigger?" Just flat. Blank. Maybe I should have spoken—'

'He'd either have lied,' said the fiddler, 'or he'd have said what Father Mulrooney said back home, when he'd help himself to the collection-plate to buy his booze: *Thou shalt not muzzle the ox that treadeth out the corn*. Do you think his boys knew? Or Mrs Drummond?'

'I'm not sure about the boys. They worshipped him.'

'Doesn't mean he wasn't teaching them that it was something *they* were entitled to.' The words tasted bitter in January's mouth. Ballou flinched again at the extra handful of ordure smeared on his dream.

'Mrs Drummond, no,' the barber went on after a few moments. 'I sat with her a little last night, 'til Saul gave her some "headache medicine" and got her to bed. Toward the end she wasn't watching what she said, but never was there a word of suspicion, a word of resentment and anger.'

'And how *would* she know?' asked January wearily. 'If she was taking "headache medicine" every night. That was the point. Did he care for her at all?'

'He did. But on his own terms. Mrs Drummond was one of his congregation back in New York state: Mrs Pryce, she was then. I've heard him preach how woman is the "weaker vessel", that a wife should be subject to her husband. When the first Mrs Drummond died he was shattered, sick with grief. For the first few days, his boys feared for his reason. Constance – Mrs Pryce – had always adored him. Most of the women of his congregation did, and his congregation – so Solly tells me – was about three-quarters women. It's an isolated place, Genesee County, farms and deep woodland . . . Mr Drummond sent her a letter and she came down with her daughter at once.'

'And was she,' inquired Hannibal, 'a habitué of "headache medicine" even then? That must have made it easy,' he went on, when Ballou nodded. 'It's astonishing what you don't notice, once you get to the point of taking a spoonful or three just to get you through the day. Though it certainly won't hurt us to ask, I suspect one of the things she didn't notice was whether her husband had any particular enemies in the county . . . How long has she been here? Three years? No rumors about her, for instance . . .'

Ballou looked momentarily puzzled, then shocked. 'Unthinkable, sir,' he said firmly. 'She worshipped him—'

'Well, our whole problem turns on the fact that you can't judge a Bible by its cover,' pointed out Hannibal, as January emptied out the basin of water, and made a package of the soiled bandages, for disposal where they couldn't be traced to Ballou's shop. 'And God knows there are men enough who worship *him* and still betray his commandments and precepts all over the landscape. As Saint Augustine prayed, *Da mihi castitatem . . . sed noli modo*. It doesn't sound as if she ever ventured far from her own doorstep—'

'Never. I was surprised she was at the dance last night, in fact.'

'Was that her own choice?' asked January. 'Or part of "being subject to her husband"?'

'Her own choice,' said Ballou. 'Being from Upstate New York, she doesn't have much use for the other women in the district. Not for the planters' wives, if they have them; certainly not for the wives of the crackers and swamp-trappers on the Louisiana side of the river.'

'Well, that certainly displays a Christian charity.'

'Maybe. But with Rachel getting older, and making eyes at Injun Tom's boy, Roane, Mrs Drummond kept even more to home.'

'All the same,' said January, 'I'd like to talk to her, if you think it would be possible.'

'The boys, yes. Mrs Drummond I left ill with grief—' *And probably in an opium stupor* –'and under her daughter's care. The boys will know if there was anyone in the district who hated their father enough to lure him to Maury's cottage and kill him. But I doubt it had anything to do with the girl Cindy – or any of the girls he . . . he *used* . . .'

The word *raped* still stuck in his throat.

'No,' murmured Hannibal. 'I don't know of anyone – except Jubal Cain, of course, and Benjamin – who'd even get angry over the honor of a black girl . . . certainly not angry enough to kill somebody over it. And we all know where Cain and Benjamin were at the time . . . What was the time of the killing, anyway, Benjamin? Could you tell?'

'Judging by the size of the maggots in the wounds,' returned January thoughtfully, 'I'd say Drummond was dead about twenty-four hours. That puts the time of his death shortly after he rode away from the race grounds, which was, what? Eleven in the forenoon?'

'Just after eleven,' said Hannibal. 'I looked at my watch when the race started, and when Big Brownie crossed the finish line, to see what kind of time he made – fifty-two seconds, which is up to the best of any I've seen.'

'And the trail Drummond rode down, into the gully and into the trees,' said January, 'leads straight past Julia Maury's cottage. Did Drummond have anything to do with Julia Maury?'

'Not a thing.'

'That we know of.' January packed up his medical kit. 'But since I'm also guessing that Maury would have taken a strap to his wife for speaking to Drummond, I'd like to have a look around that cottage, and see what we can see.'

As a well-known personality in Vicksburg, Rex Ballou expressed little apprehension about crossing on the ferry to be of whatever assistance he could to the family of his friend. If he disappeared, his white customers would probably go looking for him, if only to avoid having to 'break in' a new barber.

January, on the other hand – contemplating the prospect of venturing back to the trampled acres of Haffle's meadow three-quarters of a mile outside of Vicksburg, where the woods that cloaked the Walnut Hills came down close to the Silverdale Road – lost his nerve. In New Orleans he wouldn't have hesitated to send Hannibal on a quest for Julia Maury while he himself followed Drummond's probable route to see what he might see along the way: a much more efficient use of their time before the arraignment tomorrow.

But the thought of leaving the limits of the town, of poking about in those thickly-wooded gullies alone, with no one knowing exactly where he was or when he would be back, struck him as foolhardy in the extreme. Poor Arthur Dane, trapped in the pit with the rest of the 'cargo', wasn't the only man he had met who had been kidnapped and sold as a slave simply because his kidnappers knew they could get away with it. With Levi Christmas in town he wasn't taking any chances.

Fortunately Hannibal agreed with him, and found nothing timid or unreasonable in the suggestion that they investigate the woodland path together. 'Should anything befall you I would be obliged to marry your beautiful Rose,' explained the fiddler, as they followed the dusty Springdale Road out of town. 'And dearly as I love her – and I hope I would serve as a worthy stepfather and mentor to your children – I fear I would live in daily dread of being blown sky-high by one of her chemical experiments.'

'You can't think about things like that,' replied January serenely. 'I never do.'

'But how does someone who's given up drinking *not* think about things like that? Or any of a dozen other things I could name . . .'

'It takes practice.' January patted the fiddler's shoulder comfortingly. 'You'll get used to it.' He moved slowly across the trampled grass between the beaten flat of yesterday's racecourse, and the line of trees along the creek where the owners had tied their horses. That sycamore there, trunk pale in the dark lake of its shade, was where Big Brownie had been. To that place they'd been leading him back, when that little black boy had squirmed his way through the press around the victors, and put a folded piece of paper into Drummond's hand.

'And she'd henpeck me.'

January nodded, his eyes on the ground. 'She would. You can't let yourself think about that, either. Did you see when that child handed Drummond the note?'

Hannibal shook his head. 'I mean, I was standing next to him and yes, I suppose I saw it out of the corner of my eye, but I was looking for Cornelia Passmore—'

Of course Hannibal was looking for a woman. Hannibal loved women, not as a libertine in the hopes of bedding them (though he would happily bed any woman who'd let him) but because he genuinely enjoyed their company and conversation.

'You didn't happen to see if he put the note in his pocket, or threw it on the ground, did you?' January fluffed his foot through the trodden grass, noting the variety of detritus that the menagerie, the race, the crowd and the circus had drawn to the pasture . . . Cigar stubs, sprinklings of oats and hay, broken Lucifer matches, women's hairpins, a scrawled paper that proved to contain somebody's bets on the race.

Nothing that would have contorted Drummond's face with that icy rage.

They followed the trace that grooms in quest of water had beaten to the creek and walked on into the woods.

The Maury 'cottage', as it was referred to, stood a mile and a half outside of Vicksburg, where the town's bluff flattened out a little before descending to the tangled bottomlands of Chickasaw Bayou. The land around it had been partly cleared at one time – for a garden or a vegetable patch – but had been allowed to run back into saplings and young pines. The house itself – two or three rooms at most, plus a loft, January guessed – was well maintained and had been painted yellow within the past year, and the wood bin behind its kitchen – free-standing in the old-fashioned style – was stocked.

The windows of the cottage were shuttered and the door locked. But when January circled around to the back a woman appeared from the kitchen, neatly dressed in reasonably new calico, and barefoot, like most slaves, in the summer heat. 'Can I help you, sir?'

'If I could trouble you for a cup of water for my master—' January raised his hat, and gestured toward where he'd left Hannibal in front of the house out of sight – 'and another for myself, we'd be grateful, m'am. My master came to town this morning looking for Mr Maury, and heard he stays out here sometimes. We heard too some kind of uproar about there bein' a killin' here yesterday—Here, let me get that for you, m'am,' he added, as she picked up a pitcher from the worktable outside the kitchen door, and moved toward the well. 'On a hot day like this—'

'Well, that's kind of you, sir.' She smiled at him, and relaxed;

a sturdy little woman in her thirties, though hard work had aged her face. The cottage wasn't far from Mint Spring Branch, and the well water was fresh and cool.

'Ben,' said January with a smile, and lowered the bucket.

Her returning smile showed three teeth missing. It was common lore among women that a woman lost a tooth for every child. 'I'm Minnie. Mr Maury's in town—'

'And Mrs Maury? My master was friends with them both.'

'Miss Julia gone back to Indian Mound, and the house all locked up by the sheriff. You heard right,' she added, relishing January's look of astonished inquiry. 'There was a killing here, the ferryman from Vicksburg, Reverend Drummond – a good and godly man, that preached over in Young's Point Sundays.' Her brow knit with anger. 'It was a slave-seller who killed him, a yellow-eyed sinner. He'd come walking up Wednesday evening, to try to talk poor Mrs Maury into selling some of her husband's slaves. She sent him away, but yesterday I think he must have been waitin' here for her when poor Reverend Drummond come by.'

'Was he – this slave-dealer – was he pestering Mrs Maury,' asked January, eagerness at the melodrama of it all blazing in his voice, 'and the Reverend tried to drive him off?'

Minnie looked wise and reproving at once, as if to say, *I wouldn't put it past that sinner to try anything*, but with a kind of regret she shook her head. 'No, 'cause Miss Julia was at the revival in town. I was only left here to keep an eye on the place. I think that Cain feller just broke into the house when I was back here in the kitchen. I didn't know a thing about it, like I told the sheriff. Far as I knew the house was locked up tight. I think the Reverend Drummond musta came by an' saw the door open. First I knew about it was when Mr Maury came riding up from town, and left his horse tied right to the well, right here where we're standing—' January, pouring water from bucket to pitcher, exclaimed suitably – 'and went in at the back door. Then the next second he came running out, with one of Mr Cain's gloves in his hand, all soaked with blood, yellin' as how he'd found Drummond's body in the parlor, with the glove beside it.'

'You was back here while all that was happenin'?' January cast a half-scared glance toward the house, which lay some fifty feet across the yard and which, he observed, completely blocked any view of the trail that led back toward town. The Boneless Monzonnis could have done their entire act before the front door and nobody in the kitchen would have been the wiser. 'He could have come back here and killed you, too!'

Minnie widened her eyes and nodded, reveling in the closeness of peril now that it was safely gone away.

'You wouldn't—' He lowered his voice. 'I couldn't get you to let me – and my master, too, of course – in to have a look would you? He just loves to read all about that kind of thing in the newspapers.'

The unquestioning promptness with which Minnie fetched the keys and unlocked the back door told January that it was unlikely that Sheriff Preston had said anything resembling *Don't let anybody in* or, *Don't touch anything 'til I've had a look at it . . .*

Or maybe she simply didn't care, particularly not when Hannibal handed her a twenty-five-cent piece. The money also purchased a more detailed recounting of Maury's discovery of Drummond's body, delivered to Hannibal in hushed tones while January studied the parlor where the body had been found.

Dark blots marked where the half-dozen wounds on Drummond's chest and abdomen had drained onto the oak floor, six feet in front of the door. Traces of earth seemed to indicate where tracks would have been, had the previous two weeks not been dry. The rag rugs on the floor were unruffled, the furnishings – two upholstered chairs, three wooden ones, a largish pedestal table in the center of the room and a smaller sewing table in a corner – all stood firmly on their feet, and from what Minnie said of her own activities on Saturday, both before the discovery of the body and afterwards, it didn't sound as if she'd come in and done any tidying up once the body was removed.

Nor, apparently, had she heard any sound of struggle or raised voices. No indication that anyone was in the house at all.

'. . . Going over the laundry for repairs, for work on the Sabbath I will not, and it's something that can be done while the dough is rising and the corn soaking . . .'

Given the heat of Saturday, she'd probably done her work at the rough table outside the kitchen door, in the shade. The house and the dark-leaved laurels surrounding it might have blocked out the sounds of arriving hooves, but the small stable attached to the property lay a little distance from the kitchen, and, January ascertained with a few more casual questions, Marcus Maury had not been staying at the cottage with his wife. Why bring the horse around to the yard to tie it up, if he intended to go in, like a white man, through the front door?

Nor had she actually heard anyone come or go.

January guessed, also, that had he and Hannibal both come into the yard at the same time, the white man's presence would have intimidated the servant. But, introduced by January, Hannibal was able to practice his considerable charm on the woman, and to move easily from discussion of the events surrounding the murder – as she surmised them – to Cain's earlier visit Wednesday night.

'Coming around when all honest folk were thinking about their beds, and pestering poor Mrs Maury! She begged me say nothing of his visit, when I sort of mentioned that I'd seen him – "You know how afraid Ginny and Stan are about being sold off the place," she said to me, Ginny and Stan being the laundress over at Indian Mound and Mr Maury's coachman. "I would never for the world want to make them upset," she said, and promised me no matter what that Cain said to Mr Maury, she'd never let any of us be sold.'

Minnie's lips tightened and a hard fear glimmered in her eyes, the fear January had lived with, day in and day out, in his childhood: the nightmare that he'd be sold, or his family would be sold away, leaving him alone.

'And wasn't Mr Maury wild, when he came to town next day, and learned Cain had been out here! He's a jealous man, Mr Maury,' she went on grimly. 'I never seen a man that jealous, and for no reason, none! No matter what trash like Injun Tom and Jim Punce say! And him lookin' so smooth an' talkin' so pious. But I've seen him black her eye, over her just speaking with a man. I think if he had another plantation farther from town he'd send her there, to keep her away from her friends. He came storming out to the kitchen Thursday morning shouting had Cain been here, and struck me when I said "No." I think if Mrs Maury had been here he'd have taken his riding whip to her, as he has before—'

She shook her head. 'I feared for her,' she said. 'I warned her when she came back that afternoon from her church meeting that he was sure Cain had been here. But she told me she'd met Mr Maury in town, and he'd said nothing of it, so he must have cooled off. It's a pity he did,' she added. 'And that he didn't take a whip to that slave-monger and turn him out of town, before he could come back like he did, and do murder in this house.'

'Just as well,' remarked Hannibal, when at last he and January walked back down the path to the dusty road, 'that her testimony wouldn't be admitted to court in this benighted country. Obviously it wasn't Cain who was here yesterday lying in wait for Drummond. By the look of the front door, and of the window casements, nobody forced their way in. If the door lock was picked, whoever did it was awfully good. Whoever was here—'

'Nobody was here,' said January. 'There wasn't enough blood soaked into the floor for a man to have been lying there from eleven in the morning until five in the afternoon, when Maury ran into town yelling to the sheriff about finding the body. Drummond was stabbed ten times, and his hands and arms were gashed in the struggle as well . . .'

'And he didn't cry out?'

'He may have,' said January grimly. 'But I'm guessing he wasn't anywhere close enough to the house to be heard.'

FIFTEEN

They found the first spots of blood on the trail a dozen yards beyond the house.

'Ah.' Hannibal straightened up from the dark little crust in the scuffed dirt. 'So Maury found Cain's glove in the house when he was there Thursday and raised such a fuss with poor Miss Minnie – the glove would have been left Wednesday night. When he came upon Drummond's body yesterday – God knows what he was doing in the woods! – he lugged it up to the cottage . . . There seem to be tracks here of a dozen horses, coming and going along this way, can you tell them apart? Neither can I. As Aristotle has conclusively proven, *Et omnes infiniti idem color equorum crura*. Where is our friend Lieutenant Shaw when we have need of him?'

'Getting his head broken on the waterfront at New Orleans . . . There's another.'

'*Out, damned spot, out, I say* . . . It answers the question of why there's no sign that the cottage door was forced. Of course Maury would have a key.'

'Which won't help us in court,' January said. 'A good lawyer could argue around it. That didn't look like a particularly difficult lock to pick—'

'It isn't.'

'—And the only witness we have as to whether or not there was outcry at the time of the murder can't testify.'

Hannibal swore in Homeric Greek. The road dipped down the slope toward the bayou, and the smell of the swamp rose to meet them, a musty compound of water and decay. Cypress and cottonwood began to mingle with the loblolly pine of the hills. A spotted gopher snake whipped away into the ferns.

'We need to get Sheriff Preston out here,' said January, when they found a third dot of blood. 'Thank God it's been dry.' He drew his watch from his pocket – it was ten past one – and squinted at the sharp yellow sunlight stabbing down through the leaves.

'My understanding,' returned Hannibal, 'is that Preston isn't a man to go drinking with the militia at this hour of a Sunday afternoon. But depending on how far into the swamp Drummond was actually killed, I should hate to try to display evidence once the *light thickens, and the crow, Makes wing to th' rooky wood* . . . I'd offer to run back to town and fetch him, but quite frankly, *amicus meus*, I'm not altogether comfortable at leaving you out here in the rooky woods by yourself *whiles night's black agents to their preys do rouse*.'

'To say nothing of the fact that I'd rather have a look at what's at the end of this blood trail,' added January, 'before we fetch the sheriff. I should hate to find that something really damning fell out of Drummond's pocket when he was killed – like a list of every Underground Railroad station in the state, for instance.'

'Hmmn,' said Hannibal. 'There is that. *Adde parum parvo* . . . If Maury lugged Drummond's body all the way back to his wife's cottage, it can't have been too far, can it?'

'We can but hope. *Solvitur ambulando*.'

They moved forward. The church bells of Vicksburg grew muffled by the trees. Though the river, somewhere to their left, was low, these bottomlands were still a squishy tangle of marsh and pond, and the hot air grew stifling in January's lungs. He probed the overgrown trail before them with his stick, and his scrutiny of the ground yielded fruit: gouts of dripped blood, black and swarming with flies, at long intervals in the dirt.

'I suppose if Julia Maury were planning on fleeing her husband, she'd need to raise the wind somehow,' said Hannibal after a time. 'I can't imagine Cain would have encouraged her to believe he'd buy any of her slaves – in any case, she wouldn't have clear title to them, would she?'

'If everyone in the Mississippi Valley thinks he's a dealer, he could hardly refuse outright. And her title would depend on the terms of her father's will. Here we are.' He stopped before the rucked-up tangle of undergrowth just to the right of the path, where quite clearly a fatal struggle had taken place.

Hannibal echoed Lady Macbeth's whispered words: '*Who would have thought the old man to have had so much blood in him?*'

Black stains still darkened the ground, splashed the flattened sedges and soaked into the earth in a huge stain where the body had lain. Its smell still lingered in the air. 'Walk carefully,' added January, as Hannibal began to pick his way around the place, examining the ground gingerly in quest of either a possible list of every Underground Railroad station in the state, or whatever else might have been dropped from Drummond's pockets in the fray. January studied the broken foliage and wished he had his friend Abishag Shaw's skills as a tracker. January, who could name a piece of music after hearing two bars of it or distinguish from a strand of hair whether its owner had been black or white, couldn't tell horse prints from those of a mule and considered himself lucky if he could tell either one from dog tracks. But the gouged clay, the torn-up undergrowth, spoke unmistakably of a struggle. In a thicket of swamp laurel not far from the scene of the killing itself, January thought he found a place where the killer had waited for Drummond to come riding by, though the foliage made it impossible to distinguish more than a few heel-gouges where the killer had strode forward.

'Why a knife?' Hannibal turned from his investigation of the surrounding sedges. 'Drummond was a big man. He's not someone I'd care to take on hand to hand, not even in the robust vigor of my youth.' He coughed, his hand pressed to his side. 'Not that in the robust vigor of my youth I was ever sober enough to wield so much as a butter knife without hurting myself. So far as I can tell, Drummond didn't drop any lists, and the killer neglected to drop his visiting card.'

'A knife is quiet.' January straightened up from examining the ground. 'And you can hide it.' He mimed concealing such a weapon between his forearm and his body.

'You think Drummond knew his killer, then?'

January looked around at the green stillness of the marshy woods. 'Would you dismount in this place for a stranger standing beside the path?'

'So that note he received said something like, "Meet me by the big magnolia tree where the path rises".'

'I think it must have. And it was from someone – or it said something – that made him angry enough to set off at once.'

'Wouldn't shooting him from ambush be safer?'

'You ever tried to shoot anyone from ambush, Hannibal?'

'Ah,' said Hannibal. 'Hmmn. In plays and novels the hero always seems to manage . . .'

'Most people, their aim is just not that good. Especially not trying to hit a rider on a moving horse. And if you miss, you've told Drummond someone's out to kill him – and because he came here in the first place to meet you, he knows the killer is *you.* Damn these weeds,' he added, looking at the calf-deep greenery around their feet. 'Personally, I'm wondering if the killer acted alone.'

'If I were tackling a man of Drummond's size with a knife,' remarked Hannibal, 'I'd certainly bring help – always supposing I could trust my confederate. It would explain why there were so many wounds, but it opens the question of why he'd stop for *two* people – unless one was in hiding.'

'The ground's too torn-up to tell. And why wouldn't he, if he knew them? If he suspected nothing – if he was angry about something entirely different connected with his killer: the feed bill from the stable, or Bickern calling him a false prophet in church.'

'Why would the man who sells him horse feed wait here to murder him?'

'Drummond was a man with a secret,' returned January quietly. 'More than one secret, it seems. If one, or two, or several of the local slave-owners learned the truth of why he'd come to Madison Parish – the truth of what he was doing for the Underground Railroad – I think it very likely they'd ambush him. But it raises the question, if they knew that much, what else did they know? And what do they propose to do about it? Do I tell Ballou and Drummond's sons to bolt like scared rabbits for the north? Not to mention you and I? Or do we sit tight and see what happens?'

They walked a little farther down the trail, until it lost itself in a morass of shallow ponds, crisscrossing game trails and murky little waterways that ultimately joined the bayou itself. Ten-foot spiderwebs stretched across some of the trails; now and then on the rough gray bark of a cottonwood tree, January saw the scratch marks that had to be either bear or cougar.

Having satisfied himself that there was nothing either incriminating or obviously indicative of the true murderer farther down the trail, January turned back, Hannibal trailing gamely behind him. The fiddler's breathing had thickened to a painful rasp, however, and his pace slowed: January didn't like the waxy pallor of his face, long before they were even halfway back to town. There was, however, no question of his returning to Ballou's to rest. No white officer of the law in the State of Mississippi was going to listen to anything a black man had to say.

Enquiry at the jailhouse elicited the information that Sheriff Preston would be back Monday. He was a strict adherent of the Third Commandment. 'And God help you,' added the deputy, scratching his greasy hair, 'if you goes and interrupts him while he's havin' Sunday dinner with his mother.'

As afternoon services were just letting out, however, January took a guess and made for the First Presbyterian Church, and several blocks along Monroe Street encountered that tall, grim-faced form, tenderly escorting a white-haired woman nearly as tall – and every bit as hatchet-faced – as himself. A wife, four cowed-looking children, two menservants and three maids trailed meekly in their wake.

'God help me,' whispered Hannibal, 'that mother of his looks like she can smell a sinner at a hundred feet, and kill him at fifty.'

'Not on the Sabbath, surely.'

Hannibal crossed the street, removed his hat to the ladies, and bowed.

'Cyril Pinkerton, at your service, sir.' He proffered one of Mr Pinkerton's cards. 'M'am.' His next bow divided equally between the elder and the younger Mrs Prestons. 'Mr Preston, might I beg the favor of a word with you?'

'If it's on any subject but that of a man's salvation,' returned the sheriff repressively, 'it'll keep 'til Monday.'

'Perhaps a meditation on the thirteenth chapter of Luke, verse fifteen?' inquired Hannibal, standing his ground. The sheriff's eyes narrowed, as if suspecting sarcasm.

'It better be a good one.' He turned to his wife. 'Mrs Preston, would you be so good as to take Mother home and see to it dinner's laid out? You're the feller who came and spoke to Cain, aren't you?'

'I am, sir.'

'How well you know him?'

Something in the sheriff's tone made January's nape prickle, and Hannibal answered without hesitation, 'I've known him in a business way for two or three years, sir. He lent me money at a time when I sorely needed it, without security or any guarantee that he'd ever see it again—'

Preston's glance went to January, speculative, and Hannibal finished, 'I did return the money to him when I was able—'

'So he had nothing to do with you coming to Vicksburg?'

Hannibal shook his head, innocent and – by his expression – a little puzzled by the question. 'I was pleased to see him . . .'

That steel-trap mouth flexed, as if to comment that a strolling musician WOULD scrape acquaintance with a slave-dealer.

'You ever heard anything about him, beyond what you know of your own knowledge?'

Hannibal looked startled, and shook his head. He had always, January reflected, had the most amazing ability to appear innocent as a newborn babe. 'I've never inquired—'

Damn it. January's heart raced. *Damn it—*

'Not that he had any connection with helping slave runaways?'

Hannibal's timing was perfect. 'You mean like the slave-stealers who pretend to offer freedom to get men to run from their masters, and then sell them in the Territories? Or real runaways?'

'Real runaways.' Preston's dark eyes seemed to dissect Hannibal's face like a mathematical diagram. 'You ever heard any rumor about Cain only pretending to be a dealer, so he can move fugitives through to the north?'

DAMN IT—

'Great Heavens!' Hannibal's eyebrows bowed upwards toward his hairline, then sank in puzzlement. 'But I've seen him sell slaves – where was it, Ben? In Mobile, anyway—'

'The Tombigbee House.' January kept his voice slightly constrained, as if washing his hands of the whole business. Jubal Cain – alias Judas Bredon – had never actually sold a slave in his life. 'When you went looking for him to return that money, sir.'

'Good Heavens—' Hannibal shook his head. 'Where on earth did you hear—?'

'Feller named Poger.' Preston's hard mouth twisted as if the word were foul on his lips. 'Another dealer.'

If you think they're so distasteful, reflected January, keeping his expression one of stony stupidity, *where'd you get your yardman and your mother's coachman? Pick them off a bush?*

'Maury knows him – sent for him. He said he'd heard a rumor about it in Mobile.'

DAMN IT!! thought January. *Who the hell—?*

'You still got words to say to me about Cain bein' innocent?'

'I can't believe it.' Hannibal shook his head wonderingly. 'I should be anxious to hear—' He broke off, frowning, then went on, 'To my sorrow, sir, I know what rumors are, and I know that either way, you – and Judge Griffin – will sort out the right of it. But in the meantime, did Mr Maury mention to you that he'd moved the body? Moved it a distance, I mean,' he added, as the sheriff opened his mouth to snap the obvious remark that you don't find a corpse in your parlor without turning it over to see who it is.

'I strolled in the direction of the murder cottage this morning,' explained Hannibal with a cough. 'Ten or twelve feet beyond its door I found dripped blood, and more on the trail that leads down to the bottomlands. Being – I confess – of an inquisitive turn of mind, I followed this trail and found what appears to have been the scene of frightful butchery: blood soaked into the ground, undergrowth torn up, every sign of a struggle . . .'

'Why do you say it was Maury who moved the body?'

'I thought—' Hannibal – and January as well – were momentarily totally nonplussed.

Why indeed?

'Why would the killer have moved it?' was all he could eventually answer.

'That's something,' said Preston, 'that I'll be able to tell you better after I've seen this battleground of yours.' He took his watch from his waistcoat pocket, glanced at it and then at the sun, his eyes no longer those of a patriarch leading his family to Sabbath dinner, but of a lawman, gauging the light. 'And maybe had a word with this man Poger. If you'd be so good as to follow me to my mother's house for a few moments while I change my clothes, sir, can you then show me the place?'

Hannibal inclined his head. 'With pleasure, sir.'

SIXTEEN

His sister's face returned to his mind as they walked; the sound of her voice . . .

The smell of smoke and swamp-water in the maroon camp in the *ciprière*, all those years ago.

Olympe will know . . .

Will know what? Hannibal walked ahead with Sheriff Preston, trying – with the discreet air of one who would never indulge in gossip unless it was absolutely necessary – to get Sheriff Preston talking about Maury – who seemed to have made enemies of just about everyone in two counties – Mrs Maury, the rumor-mongering slave-dealer Poger, and whatever else he might have learned about either Ezekias Drummond or Jubal Cain.

'If Cain is working for the abolitionists,' grunted the sheriff, 'it would explain why he hated Drummond. There's nothing one of those self-righteous whining Quakers hates so much as a real man who'll turn their come-to-Jesus excuses back on themselves with the real word of God, the actual word as it's found in the Bible. If there's one thing in this world that sets my back up,' he added, 'it's a hypocrite.'

Evidently, January gathered, it would never occur to any slave in captivity to try to escape, were it not for white Puritan abolitionists coming south and encouraging them to run away. His mouth grew almost sore with the effort of not asking Preston how the hell HE knew so much about what slaves thought and felt about their lives.

'Maury always suspected Cain had something to do with that boy Quinto running off. And Cain did show up in town just two days before it happened. Myself, I think it had just as much to do with Cain taking seventy-five dollars off Maury at the Best Chance over on Adams Street, the same night Quinto disappeared. Next day Maury shows up in my office to swear out a complaint saying Cain had kidnapped Quinto and was going to sneak him out of town on the steamboat and sell him in New Orleans.'

He shook his head. 'Did he have any reason to think this? That I don't know. But he may have written Poger about it, in which case it would make sense that Poger would write back to say, "*Far from it, the man's working for the Underground Railroad*."'

'I've heard tell,' said Hannibal delicately, 'some rumor about him hating Cain because Cain was a little too friendly with Mrs Maury—'

'Now that,' retorted Preston sharply, 'is a damn lie, and the kind of damn lie you'd expect—!' He paused, visibly gathering himself in hand. 'Where'd you hear that from, sir? Some of those roustabouts at that circus of yours?'

Hannibal gave him his most honest and innocent expression. 'To tell you the truth, I can't recall just where I heard it, sir.'

Preston sniffed. 'Then my advice to you, sir, is you keep your mouth shut about any lady in this town, if you don't know what you're talking about. Julia Maury would no more have to do with a man of Cain's class than she'd steal from the church poor box. And if you haven't sufficient experience of ladies, in your line of business, to know that, Mr Pinkerton, I suggest you don't go around speaking of them.'

Red flared along Hannibal's thin cheekbones at this slur on his upbringing, but he cast his eyes down and said, 'I would not have done so now, sir, were not a man's life in danger. And I certainly hope I have better manners – and better sense – than to do so to any man other than an officer of the law in the pursuit of his work.'

The sheriff rumbled in his throat. 'Quite right,' he said unexpectedly. 'Quite right, sir, and I apologize for my hasty words.'

January wondered if Preston's deputy Alf Hilding had ventured to comment on the subject in his employer's hearing.

'I intended no offense. But it gets my goat—' Anger crept into the sheriff's tone again – 'to see Marcus Maury accusing his wife of flirting with every man who comes through town.' He stopped where the path turned toward the cottage, half visible in the trees, stood for a moment looking at the neat little structure with narrowed eyes. 'Her grandfather settled here when the Spanish still owned the territory; Julia Maury was brought up in that cottage.'

He looked like he would have said something else, but frowned again – insofar as his expression ever strayed from a perpetual frown – and walked on. 'Where's this blood you claim you found?'

At the scene of the killing itself, while Preston poked around in the brush (trampling, January feared, any marks that might have revealed the actual killer, or some evidence of the true sequence of events, to someone who knew what the hell he was looking at), Hannibal stepped close to January and whispered, 'Should I ask him about other ruins farther up in the 'delta'? Places where Drummond might have hidden that poor girl Cindy?'

'We can get that out of Ballou, or one of Drummond's boys.' January watched as Preston made his way slowly around the clearing, nudging at the undergrowth with his boot toe now and then, hands clasped behind his back, never bending or kneeling for a close look. 'He's too close already to Cain's tracks.'

'Do you think the boys knew?'

'I think they suspect.' January remembered the way Saul had averted his face on the wharf at Vicksburg, when he'd asked him, '*Did the others get away?*'

'He could have been sharing her with his boys, for all we know.'

Hannibal said, 'Faugh!' and Preston returned to them, hands still behind his back, his dark eyes somber.

'It was done here, all right,' he agreed. 'And I thank you for coming straight to me, Pinkerton. But it doesn't follow that Maury was the man who hauled poor Drummond's body up to the cottage to take revenge on Cain. It's just as likely that Cain hauled the body up to the cottage himself, either to put the blame onto Maury – who as good as called him a slave-stealer over that Quinto business – or to get revenge on Julia Maury for rejecting his advances. Or simply to get the body out of sight. It's the nearest house.'

'It doesn't mean the killer was Cain!' protested Hannibal.

'After that affray Saturday morning,' returned the sheriff, 'it's a good guess that it was. And by what I've heard around the barrooms,' he added drily, 'Cain's a good man with a knife.'

'But wouldn't "a good man with a knife" have finished his

victim off with one or two blows instead of – what was it? Eleven? Twelve?'

Preston regarded him with cold distaste. 'You ever killed a man with a knife, Mr Pinkerton? 'Specially a big man like Drummond, who's fighting to live?' He turned back along the road to town. 'Cain said before witnesses that he'd kill him. Cain's glove was found by the body, soaked with blood. That's good enough for me.'

Hannibal coughed, and hastened to catch up with the tall sheriff's longer strides. 'Did you happen to look at the rest of his clothing, as well as the glove? Or search to see if anyone had thrown bloodstained garments away?'

The sheriff halted and faced him in glowering irritation. 'You are bound and determined it ain't going to be your friend who did it, aren't you?'

'He isn't—' began Hannibal warily, but the sheriff went on.

'And I'll warn you, Mr Pinkerton: don't leave town. The arraignment is tomorrow; the preliminary hearing's set for the following Monday, the seventeenth. When Mr Poger arrives here from New Orleans, Judge Griffin is going to want to hear what you have to say about Cain in response to Mr Poger's assertion that he's working for the Underground Railroad.'

'No chance of just breaking Cain out of jail, I suppose?'

'Vicksburg's the county seat,' said January. 'That jail is new, barred with iron all the way around, and right down in the middle of town by the courthouse.'

Both men stood for a time at the corner of Jackson Street, watching the sheriff's stiff-backed, high-shouldered form retreating toward his mother's house and the Sunday dinner that is the reward of the virtuous.

'Bloody hell. *Ab honesto virum bonum nihil deterret . . .*'

'The best we can do,' said January, 'is find out whose movements are unaccounted for between eleven and one yesterday.'

'Aside from Cain's, you mean?'

'Yes.' January sighed regretfully. 'Aside from Cain's.'

At five o'clock, under a sky like a bowl of incandescent brass, January, Hannibal and Rex Ballou joined the rear of the little crowd that followed the Drummond wagon down Clay Street to the waterfront, and so along it to the ferry landing where Drummond's beautiful horses waited to draw their master across the yellow-brown waters one last time.

Here, at least, there was no trace of the Sabbath above. Tinny piano music jangled from the barrooms, whores lolled from windows and doorways, sweating men unloaded sacks of flour, barrels of sugar, crates of liquor, bales of clothing and shoes. Dogs slept or scratched in the alleyways; down near the Forty Thieves Saloon a man was beating a mule.

Most of the men in the crowd, January observed, were crackers, the small farmers of the backwoods of Madison Parish across the river who made up the backbone of the 'militia' that patrolled the roads at night to discourage late-walking slaves: illiterate, hardscrabble men who owned no slaves but fought stubbornly for the right to do so when and if they had the chance. Listening to them – and Hannibal had a genius for getting conversations started – January gathered that most of the men in town took it for granted that Jubal Cain had done the murder: 'Hell, Marcus Maury found his gloves right there beside the body!' Opinions varied as to motivation, from murky tales of Drummond's contempt for Cain's occupation to Cain's gallantry toward Mrs Drummond ('Mrs DRUMMOND???' murmured Hannibal) to rumors about Cain having, two years previously, kidnapped Drummond's previous stableman—

'Which is true in its way,' whispered Ballou, as he and January stepped to the rail of the ferry, to let the wagon pass. 'A man named Tom Spracklin worked for Drummond before Boze did. He left, suddenly, about two years ago – went back up north, though of course nobody could say so, and it was Cain who arranged for him to get there.'

January glanced sidelong at him, as Boze and Saul Drummond – looking more than ever like his father – cast off the ropes. 'He say why he left?'

Ballou read his glance, shook his head. He repeated – his eyes going to the coffin where it lay in the wagon bed a few yards from where they stood – 'He did great good.'

The horses in the roundhouse leaned into their collars. The side wheels of the ferry began to turn. Sunlight spangled the water, blindingly. Farther along the waterfront, a crew of stevedores hauled on a crane.

'If you can't come,
If you can't come,
If you can't come, Lord,
Send one angel down . . .'

The melismatic wail brought back the voices of January's uncles and aunties, of the other children of the hogmeat gang in his childhood at Bellefleur, the patient call-and-response across the cane-fields in the blistering afternoons. In his years in France he'd scarcely thought of his home or his childhood – the dark beauty of swamp and woods, the thrum of cicadas and the incessant peep of frogs when the sun went down. Childhood's wonderment braided together with constant fear. Since he'd been back – seven years it was, now – those memories had pushed forth from the grave in which he'd buried them, to be re-accepted into his heart.

'If you can't come, Lord,
Send one angel down . . .'

An angel named Ezekias Drummond?

Would I be able to go on working for a man, who did what he did – in order to help those that he helped?

January didn't know, and looked sidelong again at Ballou's averted profile. Then beyond him, to Boze, gently clucking to the six laboring horses, his goblin face like stone. The slave-dealer Fenks stood beside Saul Drummond, talking quietly and gesturing now and then in Boze's direction: *You really are trying to buy a slave from a young man whose father has just died,* thought January in disgust. *Whose father's body still lies in the coffin, unburied . . .*

Drummond had taught his sons well. Saul didn't throw Fenks over the ferry's side into the river, which, in January's opinion, showed more than Christ-like forbearance (the Son of God having lost his temper a time or two on the earth) and an iron determination never to appear averse to slavery in any way, shape or form.

'What was Maury doing,' asked January softly, 'during and just after the race?'

'Listening to the preaching, I expect.' Ballou turned his gaze away from the river, as if glad to focus on something other than the conundrum of whether a good man could do evil things, or an evil man good ones. 'The slave matches didn't start 'til three, and after Quinto ran off I'm not sure the man could have stood to watch . . .'

'Wherever he was at eleven—' Hannibal returned to their side – 'he wasn't listening to the Word of God. Remember that Thorne went missing just before the race started, and Bickern went off to take the proceeds to the bank . . . But according to Mrs Passmore, he was an unconscionable long time doing it. He didn't return until nearly three.'

'And Thorne?' asked Ballou. 'Not that Thorne had any reason to murder Drummond—'

'That we know of,' said January thoughtfully. 'Hannibal?'

'Not the slightest idea. Other than being a slave-stealer and a crook. It might pay us,' he added, 'to look into Bickern's movements at the time.'

'Personally,' sighed Ballou, 'I can't see one preacher doing more to his rival than tearing his hair out, over religion.'

'You've obviously never been to Ireland,' returned Hannibal. 'Personally, I should be curious to learn whether Drummond had enemies back in Genesee County.'

'Who'd come all the way down here to find him?'

'We're talking about a man,' pointed out January quietly, 'who considered it his right to abuse any woman who put herself under his protection. It could have taken a man – or a woman – in Upstate New York seven years to locate him, particularly if there were some triggering event involved: a deathbed confession, a lost letter or diary coming to light. Anyone could have handed a child a penny to take him a note after the race, and then lain in wait for him beside the trail . . . Anyone could have then walked down to the landing and stepped aboard a steamboat, leaving Maury to find the body – hours later, by the look of the *livor mortis* – and make whatever other arrangements he pleased. Would his sons know?'

'Saul was sixteen when Drummond came here,' replied Ballou. 'Solly only eleven. There was a third brother, David, who died the year before last of a fever – I'm not sure what they would have known, if their father hadn't told them.'

'So it's only Mrs Drummond who might know.'

'She was in his Genesee County congregation . . .'

'And from the sound of it,' sighed Hannibal, 'she'll need a certain amount of sobering up before we can get anything out of her. God knows whether what we learn will make sense or not. If Cain is bound over without bail, how long do you think he has before this fellow Poger arrives from Mobile and gets him lynched?'

SEVENTEEN

As neither Rex Ballou nor Hannibal was in any shape to follow Drummond's coffin the six miles to the Sanctuary of the Spirit in Young's Point, as most of his thirty-two-person congregation was prepared to do, they settled for paying their respects at the Drummond home. They found a dozen members of the militia gathered in the bare, whitewashed parlor with young Solomon Drummond, waiting for the main procession to begin.

Solomon, red-eyed from weeping and looking deeply confused, managed to reply to Ballou's gentle question that his stepmother was in her room, with Rachel looking after her. Did he think she might be able to talk to a gentleman about if Mr Drummond had had enemies back in New York state? Men who might have done this terrible thing?

'I – that is . . .' The youth glanced around the parlor, dim with the sinking of the sun behind the wall of poplars that surrounded the house, as if trying to remember who was in on which secrets. 'She's pretty broke up.'

'If it's at all possible,' said Hannibal, 'anything she might tell us would be appreciated.' The movement of his eyes was like a reminder that nobody, for the moment, was in earshot. 'I think we all know that Mr Cain isn't the culprit, and since the arraignment is tomorrow it's fairly urgent that we have something to go on besides Maury's accusation.'

'You're right.' The boy pulled himself together, drew a steadying breath. 'I'll—'

He turned as another young man came up to them, silent as a puma, in the gathering gloom. 'There anything I might do for your mama?' the newcomer asked, and January recognized the dark eyes and Cupid's bow mouth of Injun Tom Colvard's son.

'Thanks, Roane. That's kind of you. I don't think—'

Saul Drummond broke abruptly from the group of militiamen around him, strode across the parlor. 'We got all the help here we need, Roane. An' if you're thinkin' just 'cause Pa's gone, the likes of you can come sniffin' around our sister, you got some more thinkin' to do.'

Black fire leaped in Roane Colvard's eyes. 'You plannin' on keepin' her on as a servant like your pa did, then?'

'Keepin' her within a God-fearin' family, rather'n see her the whore of a half-breed swamp-rat? Yeah, I do.'

Colvard's fist twitched back; Ballou looked as if he would have spoken, but clearly didn't dare. Hannibal put a hand on the young man's wrist. 'Gentlemen, please,' he said – an interpolation which, January recognized, took a lot of courage, since Saul Drummond's hand was already on the knife at his belt. 'I'm a stranger here and it isn't my right to speak, but a woman has been widowed in this house—'

For a moment January thought Saul actually was going to go after Hannibal, but Solomon came forward and took his older brother's arm. 'He's right, Saul.'

You shut up was almost visibly on the older brother's lips as his head snapped around, but the words seemed to sink in. To Roane, he grated, 'You stay away from my damn sister,' then wrenched himself clear of Solomon and strode back to the men on the porch. Roane followed him for a moment with a cold glare, then made for the door. In doing so he passed within a foot of his father, Injun Tom; but Injun Tom, in the group around Saul, only watched him go with chilly contempt.

It was obviously not the moment to pursue inquiries of any kind, so Hannibal only bowed to Solomon, said, 'I apologize again if I presumed—'

The youth shook his head, gestured an acceptance he was clearly unable to frame in words.

'Might we call tomorrow?'

'Uh – sure. 'Course. Rex—?'

'Please let her know this is important,' said Ballou softly. 'There's a feller on his way from Mobile, claims to know something of Cain's involvement with the Railroad. We got to find who did this, and fast, for her sake, and your sister's, and us all.'

Solomon's eyes widened in shock at this news, and he managed to whisper, 'I'll do what I can.'

Ballou gripped his arm. 'Stay strong.'

By the door, men were shaking Saul's hand in departure. Others, some with their wives, were climbing into buggies and wagons down in the yard, forming up the procession to Young's Point. Torches and lanterns were kindled in the blue dusk; Ballou went out and lit a spill from one of them to light the single lamp on the table. Its dim glow emphasized the barrenness of the room, furnished with nothing but the family dining table, two benches against the wall, and a hearth swept and cleansed like bridal china. No pictures, no whatnots, no shelves. The plank floor bare, the walls naked of anything but whitewash. January followed Ballou and Hannibal out onto the high porch, and down the steps to the yard, and from there glanced at the windows in the short wing. Only one showed a smudgy reflection of what looked like a single candle within, and a woman's voice lifted in an inarticulate wail, which a moment later resolved itself into words: '*Have mercy upon me, Oh Lord, for I am in trouble! Mine eye is consumed with grief . . .*'

She came to Louisiana for love of him, thought January. *Gave up HER life at home. And her daughter's. And now he is gone.*

Saul at the reins, the wagon drove off down the track that led to the river, and thence along its bank to Young's Point. The men of the congregation followed, and those who'd ridden with Drummond in the militia.

Somewhere close, among the tangled swamp and cottonwood enclosed in the hairpin turn of the river, January heard the baying of Drew Hardy's dogs.

January dreamed that night of Olympe.

She'd run away from their mother's house, to one of the maroon villages in the *ciprière*. She was always doing that; even as a small child she'd run off to the fugitive settlement deep in the bayous near Bellefleur. Like January, she had been freed when St-Denis Janvier had bought their mother and made her his mistress, but she would not take even freedom from the hand of any white man.

She knows the answer, he thought, as he searched the hot darkness of those monochrome woods. *She can tell me . . .*

Tell me what?

He didn't remember where the settlement lay, and he feared

that he'd become lost in that world of gray moss hanging from the trees, of the thrumming drone of the cicadas.

I have to find her . . .

Waking, he lay still in the indigo hush of Rex Ballou's attic, to which he'd returned with the departure of the circus. The fire had destroyed the gable end of the building, and though he'd repaired the framing he could look out through it to the fading stars.

Olympe knows the answer.

He lit his candle, and went downstairs to the little corner cubbyhole that served the barber as an office. It, too, had been gutted by the fire, but had at least been swept out and scoured, and a makeshift desk built of planks. He took a sheet of paper from beneath the hair oil bottle that weighted it down, sharpened a pen, and in the warm gloom wrote Olympe a letter in the rough cane-patch patois of their childhood, French words strung on the warp of African construction.

Nobody who hadn't been raised in the quarters would understand it, but Olympe had scorned to learn better French than that.

His heart at rest, he softly climbed the attic stairs, and returned to his bed.

On the following morning Jubal Cain was arraigned for the murder of Ezekias Drummond, the preliminary hearing to be the following Monday, June 17, 1839.

Bail was denied.

Like the seven runaways in the darkness of their pit, he could only wait on events beyond his control.

With the money they'd taken from Cain's room – property of the Philadelphia Anti-Slavery Society – Hannibal retained a local lawyer named Butler Leeland, whom Ballou recommended, a tiny old man whose sharp features were at once thin and oddly puffy – kidney disorder, January identified the signs uneasily – and whose long fingernails were stained yellow with nicotine from incessant cigars. He duly protested that no evidence of any kind existed that his client had murdered Drummond – a man whom he'd met on only a handful of occasions and with whom he had no connection – and was overruled by Judge Griffin and by Marcus Maury's evidence. 'Likely,' the lawyer remarked in his high, creaky voice when Cain was returned to the jailhouse later, 'owing to your unwillingness to explain your remarks of Saturday morning to the effect that if the deceased ever crossed your path again you would kill him.' He leaned a patched elbow on the table and raised an eyebrow at Cain: Sheriff Preston had permitted them the use of his office, with Alf Hilding standing guard (and doubtless eavesdropping, reflected January dourly) outside the door.

'It has nothing to do with the case at hand,' returned Cain stubbornly.

Rex Ballou, January and Hannibal, gathered, at Cain's request, in one corner of the office, said nothing, and Leeland glanced over at them as if for clarification.

'I was riding up the Sunflower River looking for a lying pye-dog named Johnson who supposedly had a couple of likely boys to sell me,' Cain went on, his pock-marked face grim. 'And if I didn't happen to think to haul along a witness to the fact that I was going about my lawful affairs, that shouldn't be the business of the State of Mississippi or of anybody else. And even if I had murdered Drummond, why the hell would I have dragged his body up to Julia Maury's cottage?'

'You were seen keeping company with her,' pointed out the lawyer. 'And that's enough for Marcus Maury to come up with some good reason for that surely unreasonable piece of behavior by the time the hearing rolls around.'

'I was engaged with Mrs Maury in a matter of business. Ask her.'

'I will. Mr Ballou, you've known the deceased longer than anybody in town – I think you're probably the only Negro I never heard him say a bad word about. In six years, he wouldn't happen to have spoken of anybody back from wherever he came from – Upstate New York, was it? – who'd want to do him harm? Didn't run off with the church funds or kiss the mayor's wife?'

'He never spoke of it, sir,' responded Ballou. 'Mr Pinkerton and I—' He nodded toward Hannibal – 'will see if we can speak to Mr Saul after the funeral this evening.'

The lawyer nodded, and for a moment regarded January as if he would have spoken to him as well. But he merely said, 'Let me know what you find out, Ballou. Because, Mr Cain, I can tell you this. Juries are stupid. If you think they won't hang you on the grounds of whatever cock-and-bull story Maury's cooked up in his head about you and his wife—' He held up a hand against Cain's irate protest – 'then I have to say that I hope you don't find you're mistaken. And if this Mr Junius Poger gets to town in the meantime with that folderol Maury told Preston about you bein' an abolitionist slave-stealer—'

'That's ridiculous!'

'That's as may be. But it bein' ridiculous won't keep some of the local militia from arrangin' a necktie party, all for your benefit, before your case comes to trial.'

Upon leaving the courthouse, Hannibal rented a buggy and, because neither the laws of Mississippi nor Louisiana permitted men of color to do likewise, engaged in the charade of picking up Rex Ballou half a mile beyond the ferry landing on the Louisiana shore and letting him off in the cottonwood swamps just before they reached Young's Point. A dozen militiamen would be at the funeral. It was known that Ballou was a friend of the family, but word would spread if any collusion or understanding seemed evident between him and the so-called Mr Pinkerton, friend of the man accused of his murder.

Had Rex Ballou had the strength to walk the six miles from the ferry landing to the Sanctuary of the Spirit, January would have suggested that Hannibal remain back in Vicksburg, while he – January – accompanied the 'friend of the family' afoot. But the prospect of being kidnapped was too likely for him to go alone, and in fact, despite all that he knew, Ballou *was* a friend of the family. The man who had first asked Drummond to give up his life in New York, to engage in this risky venture. The man who had been Drummond's partner in saving hundreds of men and women from hell.

Six years. He looked back over the side of the buggy as they drove on ahead toward the little cluster of unpainted plank houses that surrounded the wood lot that was the settlement's primary reason for existence. *Knowing and not wanting to know. Telling yourself lies and making excuses for what you suspected . . . Seeing the good that he did, and knowing the man for a monster.*

As he approached the Sanctuary, a plain box of a building

constructed on stilts, like most in these low-lying lands, January heard the voices of the congregation chanting what he eventually recognized as a rewritten version of the forty-fourth psalm. The building itself was no more than a single square room, but it had a separate side door reserved for blacks – not, he suspected, that there were many in that community of Madison Parish who would give up their Sunday rest to listen to Drummond's brand of preaching.

The chapel contained not even benches, let alone an altar. The coffin lay on trestles beside a pulpit that resembled a packing crate. The congregation stood. Saul Drummond preached the sermon – nearly two hours of it – very much in what January guessed to be his father's style and presumably designed to cement the young man's position with the slave-holding community as someone who would never even think of being involved with the Underground Railroad.

January saw no sign of Constance Drummond, nor of her daughter. Nor, he noticed, was Roane Colvard present, though Injun Tom was in the crowd, falling to his knees and weeping – as several others did – and smelling of liquor at twenty paces.

With both sons, and Boze, at the funeral, would the girl be able to slip away from her mother for a few kisses behind the barn?

Let's just hope if she does, Mama doesn't find the laudanum bottle for a few extra sips to hold her grief at bay . . .

The woman has just lost her husband, he reminded himself. *The man whom she worshipped – almost literally – for years, as a member of his congregation; the man for whom she abandoned her own family and life in New York state, when he wrote to her asking her to be his wife in Louisiana . . .*

She knows of no reason to remain sober now.

Whoever had translated the psalms into liturgy – and it was probably Drummond himself – had done himself proud on the thirty-seventh: *The arms of the wicked will be broken, but the Lord will uphold the righteous; The Lord knows the days of the righteous, their inheritance shall be forever . . .*

Chanting about how all their enemies would perish, the congregation, plus a few extra militiamen and Hannibal, with January,

Ballou and Boze the only three blacks present, followed the coffin back to the wagon, and drove the six miles back to the house.

Thus it was almost sunset, before Hannibal – with January standing respectfully behind him – sat down at the table in that bare box of a front room, to talk to Ezekias Drummond's wife.

'Oh, my husband hated him.' Constance Drummond fixed Hannibal with enormous blue eyes, which seemed bluer, because their pupils were contracted almost to pinheads with opium. Her short, lye-reddened fingers picked and toyed with the grain wood, as if she could smooth it to a different shape.

Beside her on the bench her daughter Rachel watched her worriedly, as if she feared that her mother would suddenly do or say something inappropriate. The girl herself, as she had at the ball, looked pale and ill, controlling her face into an expressionless mask with visible effort, her big, square hands clasped hard around each other in her lap. A farm girl, brought up in the western woods of New York state, she already looked older than her sixteen years.

'My first husband,' explained Mrs Drummond. 'Joshua Pryce. Rachel's flesh-father, though of course Mr Drummond was the true father of her spirit, in her own eyes, and in the eyes of the Lord. Isn't that so, darling? Mr Pryce started out giving his heart to God in the proper way, but later he slandered Mr Drummond, bore false witness against him, and in the end divided the congregation, and drew off half its number after him into damnation.'

'And no loss,' sniffed Saul, on the bench beside Hannibal. 'Let the dead bury their own dead. Once the congregation split—' He turned to regard his guests – 'many of the men who had turned against my father hated him for continuing to speak the truth in the face of their iniquities. *They that hate the righteous shall be desolate . . .*'

'And who's in charge of that part of the New York congregation now?' inquired Hannibal.

'Oh, Joshua is.' Mrs Drummond blinked at him, like an owl in daylight.

Hannibal looked startled – *as well he might*, thought January. 'I – ah – I'm sorry,' said the fiddler after a moment. 'I thought Mr Pryce was dead.'

'He is dead to me,' declared Mrs Drummond. 'He is dead to the congregation, and to the Lord. From the moment he turned against Mr Drummond, he was given to the outer darkness and all its evil works. He should have been proud,' she added, when Hannibal – possibly for the first time in his adult life – had nothing to say. 'When I was chosen—'

'Chosen?'

'To be Mr Drummond's bride.' Constance Drummond spoke as if the matter were written above her head in letters of flame and her guest was simply too obtuse to notice it there. 'The other men in the congregation deeply felt what an honor it was, when their wives were chosen—'

January's gaze cut sharply to Saul's face – which wore the same wooden expression that masked Rachel's, as if he were listening to shipping information being read from the newspaper – and then to Rex Ballou's. Ballou was managing to keep his countenance, but his eyes were wide with protesting shock. This was clearly news to him.

'Pardon me, Madame,' said Hannibal uncertainly, 'but wasn't it just three years ago that you became the Reverend Drummond's wife?'

'The *second* time,' the little woman explained, as if speaking to a not-very-bright child. 'The *first* time was in 1830 – and it became clear then how deeply the Devil was embedded in Joshua Pryce's wicked soul!'

'You mean to tell me that Mr Drummond – ah – *chose* wives from among his congregation while their husbands were still living?'

'All were married in the New Covenant of the congregation,' Mrs Drummond assured him earnestly. 'As he had blessed our unions, he of course had the right—'

'The time of that chapter of the Covenant,' put in Saul, his voice flat as an iron table, 'is over. Pa was washed free of his former life, and became a new man.' He fixed his gaze on Ballou, the man who had called Ezekias Drummond to the higher purposes of Abolition and the Underground Railroad. 'When he was *called*, he left that part of his life behind.'

Which doesn't mean, reflected January, *that IT left HIM behind . . .*

'I – uh – see,' said Hannibal, nonplussed. 'In your opinion, Mrs Drummond, did Mr Pryce hate your husband enough to follow him down here? To do him harm?'

'Oh, yes!' Mrs Drummond nodded with such vigor that the stray tendrils of hair around her face bounced around the frame of her white house cap. 'Why, the night I left his house to go to Mr Drummond's, he said—'

'Yes, but Mama,' Rachel spoke for the first time, her voice a soft mumble, as if she feared its being heard, 'Pa – *Mr Pryce*,' she corrected herself self-consciously, cheeks blotching red, 'got married again, don't you remember? To Mrs Brattle.'

Her mother bristled. 'Effie Brattle! That hussy—'

Rachel turned to Hannibal, her face grave with anxiety. 'I honestly think my fa— Mr Pryce – wouldn't have left his wife, and his congregation, to come all this way. Others would have,' she added grimly. 'The Lord pointed out to Mr Drummond – to my *father*—' Her mother had nudged her sharply – 'ladies among the believers whom he wished my *father* to take unto himself. And their husbands, or their fathers, sometimes were angry: I know Mr Snow was angry enough to come down here after my *father* – Buford Snow – and Mr Sanders, I don't remember what his first name was—'

'Theodore,' provided her mother. 'He had a brother named Michael; Mr Sanders' wife was Rosalie, a very holy woman in the work of the Lord.'

'Mr Sanders moved away to Brooklyn,' added Rachel. 'But he said, in front of the whole congregation practically, that he'd have his revenge. And don't you remember me telling you, Ma, just this past Saturday morning, after Pa and the boys left for the race, how I thought I'd seen a man who looked just like him, on the road near the ferry?'

Mrs Drummond looked startled, clearly not recalling anything of the sort, then said quickly, 'Yes, yes of course you did, dearest.' At a guess, reflected January, the minute Pa and the boys left for the race Saturday morning, Mrs Drummond had refreshed herself from one of her hideout bottles and was in no condition to remember who had said what to her.

As Saul conducted them down the steps to where the buggy waited in the now-empty yard, he said, 'Most of our neighbors in Genesee County hated my father.' His voice was non-committal. 'Our congregation lived by its own rules of holiness. The evil are always abashed in the face of righteousness.'

Hannibal bit what was almost certainly – January was willing to bet – a facetious remark that would not have improved the situation at all. Rex Ballou elected to remain for a time, to help the family put the house in order and to help Solomon take supplies to the fugitives after mother and sister were abed. But as January and Hannibal drove away, January said quietly, 'It makes me wonder whether Ezekias Drummond's "conversion" to the cause of abolitionism had something to do with his making Genesee County too hot to hold him.'

'It may not have been.' Hannibal leaned around the side of the buggy for another look at the rambling wooden house, the quadrangle of stables, smokehouse and workshops, before the square of cottonwoods hid them from view. 'My uncle Bellingham would convert – quite sincerely – to a different religion about once a year: I remember when I was eleven him combing the London waterfront for a Chinese who knew enough English to teach him about Buddhism, and the following year he insisted on having himself baptized a Catholic. My aunts on that side of the family tried for years to have him declared insane, but he was perfectly sane and made a fortune speculating on trading ventures to the Indies. He would just cast himself, body and soul, into new recipies for salvation – when it wasn't the Quakers or Islam, it was vegetarianism or hydrotherapy or having himself beaten by his valet with birch twigs.'

'Which is not the same,' pointed out January, 'as multiple adultery with the wives of his neighbors – a practice which Drummond may not have forsaken, the abuse of fugitives notwithstanding, upon coming to Madison Parish.'

'I notice nobody mentioned a divorce of any kind . . .'

'I'm not sure they could get them, in New York state.'

'*Fronti nulla fides*. I can see that some more tea and gossip with the ladies of Vicksburg is in order.'

EIGHTEEN

That evening Hannibal went to call on Mrs Passmore at the Planter's Hotel. His double purpose was to learn – if possible – the whereabouts of Lemuel Bickern immediately before and after Saturday's horse race, and to reinstate himself – if possible – into the graces of the ladies who led the town's circles of gossip, most of whom had been horrified to learn that the personable gentleman with whom they'd had tea on Thursday afternoon had in fact been a common musician with a traveling circus, who had now taken up residence in the rented attic of a black man's house.

Given Mrs Passmore's recommendation, and Hannibal's facility for telling a convincing story, January had little doubt that the fiddler would be back at the tea tables within twenty-four hours.

Rex Ballou arrived for supper at Mrs Dillager's boarding house fifteen minutes before that redoubtable lady cleared the table. Most of the others who took their meals there had already departed, and though she glared admonishingly at him, she produced the small quantity of chicken stew, rice and greens that she'd sequestered at the start of the meal, a mark – January recognized – of high regard. Ballou and January both remained to help clear up, and only when that was done, and they were walking back to Ballou's burned-out skeleton of a house, did the barber say softly, 'You still want to speak with Eliza Walker?'

Eliza Walker met them in the blackness beneath the trees, where the road dipped out of the hills toward Chickasaw Bayou, not far from where Ezekias Drummond had met his death. Ballou had led the way to the place unerringly, January listening in dread for the sound of hooves on the road that lay to their left. A bare flicker of gold had marked when they'd passed Julia Maury's cottage, where Minnie kept up her kitchen fire. After that they'd moved from tree trunk to tree trunk, as in last night's dream

January had navigated the darkness of the *ciprière*: how many steps, what was the angle of the ground, could you smell the swamp in the darkness? The difference between cottonwood's ridgy roughness and the stringy fibers of cypress bark, distinctive as colors beneath the fingers. The barber whistled like a screech owl, then stood still.

An owl hooted to their right. Then that single spangle of moonlight touched the shoulder of what looked like a boy's shirt, the edge of a boy's braided straw hat. January had the impression of a small woman, barely a gleam of eyes beneath the hat, and a voice like gravel and silver as Eliza Walker whispered, 'Rex?'

January said softly, 'M'am,' and touched the brim of his own hat. 'It's my honor to meet you.'

'And mine to meet you.' There was a note in her voice, a hardness like buried anger. 'Our friend has spoke well of you. How fares he?'

'Well, so far. He's being held without bail. The preliminary hearing is a week from today. Maury's claiming he found his glove beside the body. Maybe because he didn't like the way Mrs Maury spoke to him, maybe for some other cause. Do you know anything? Heard anything? Whisper, rumor—'

'Nothing any white man would get himself into a lather over.' The anger was clearer then, like the glint of a steel blade.

She knows about Cindy . . .

Awkwardly, Ballou asked, 'Did Mr Cain speak of it?'

'Of what?'

'Of what . . . made him angry at Drummond that morning.'

'If you mean the girl Ezekias took to that cabin of his below the Walnut Bluffs and raped,' said Mrs Walker, 'no, he didn't mention it. He was mad still: I could feel it coming off him like heat off a stove. I think he hadn't made up his mind what to do about it.'

She watched Ballou, waiting for what he would say. When Ballou exclaimed, '*Raped* her?' he sounded sufficiently shocked. 'What girl?'

'Cindy. One of the fugitives. You didn't know?'

'No! *Drummond?* Are you sure?'

January bit his tongue, and reminded himself that Ballou's ability to tell a good story was part of what kept him alive.

'Is she all right?'

'She's well.' Some of the tension went out of Mrs Walker's voice. 'Cain took her up to a cave under Snyder's Bluff. I found her there yesterday. I assume that's why he was late getting to me. We were to have met at daybreak, at the old Indian farm by the Lagoon. It was mid-morning when he got to me. Cindy told me he'd found her early that morning when he was scouting the area. I'm guessing he rode back to town from there and beat hell out of Drummond. But as I said,' she went on thinly, 'it's not anything a white man would kill over, except maybe Cain.'

'I can't—' Ballou stammered to a halt.

'*Can't you?*' Her eyes snapped fire. 'Do you think just because a man doesn't tie a woman up, or black her eyes for her, that it isn't really rape? If a man had *your* child, and *your* freedom, in his hand, and asked *you* to lie down for him, would you?'

January said, very softly, 'I would.' After a moment he went on, 'And Cain – nor anyone else – never spoke of others who'd hate Drummond? Who'd want to do him harm?'

'White men's business is white men's business,' she replied gruffly. 'If it would have made any difference to what we were doin', Cain would have told me. But he's not a man for gossip. And I'm not in this country often enough to know who's who. He didn't say much Saturday. We rode together down the bayou and round to the end of the bluffs, where the land shelves down to the swamp, a mile downriver of the bend where you can't see it from town. That whole point of land, 'tween the bayou and where the Yazoo goes into the big river past the bend, it's all swamp and woods you can't hardly get a horse through. There we waited, from noon 'til it grew dark. And in all that time, he barely spoke five words to me.'

'And you've never heard others speak against Drummond? No rumor?'

'Who would care?' she asked bitterly. 'Those poor souls fleeing this so-called "cotton kingdom" that white men brag of: they know nothing of Drummond 'til they meet him, and nothing of him once he sends 'em on their way.'

'Only that he's helped them,' said Ballou, 'across the river to freedom. And risked his life to do it.'

January started to speak, but in the same moment that Eliza

Walker put a warning hand on his wrist to silence him he heard the muffled clop of many hooves, some dozen yards to his right – on a trail or path, it sounded like – and saw the glimmer of lanterns through the trees. All three fell silent, January wondering how the hell he was going to get back to town if the patrol detected them and they had to split up. He heard one of the men speak, retelling some story of being cheated by a storekeeper in Warrenton, and the voices faded.

The fear he felt, he understood, was what they wanted him to feel. Fear that would keep him and others of his heritage indoors, like good little niggers . . .

He remembered the dense hot stink of the slave jail at Indian Mound, the pain of his dog-bitten leg and the terror that had ridden him through the sweltering night that the overseer would take the opportunity to sell him rather than return him to his 'owner' in town . . .

'And what about those he doesn't help?' asked January softly. With the hot smell of the slave jail came back the voice of another girl, coming out of the darkness, sweet and soft as a cherrywood flute. 'What about those who steal and drink and hump women and fight, and who still seek to flee. Did Drummond hold out his hand to help *them*?'

Ballou turned his head sharply. Eliza Walker only tilted hers, puzzled. 'Who would ask such a question as that?'

'Maybe one who feared betrayal,' returned the barber.

'In all the years I've led folk through the 'delta',' she replied, 'I have never yet met a black man stupid enough to think that turning Judas wouldn't get him betrayed by the whites in return. Or who thinks that there's anywhere he could run, where he wouldn't meet revenge.'

On the way back to town, January asked, '*Did* Quinto come to you, asking to be helped to flee?'

Enough moonlight filtered through the trees from the roadway that he could see Ballou nod.

'And was it Drummond who refused?'

'I agreed with him,' said Ballou. 'You can't trust a man who can't keep his mouth shut when he drinks.'

When January said nothing, Ballou went on, 'I wake up every

mornin' wondering if the day will end with me getting my neck stretched by pigs like Injun Tom and that cracker weasel Punce. And sometimes I lie awake wonderin' if somebody was about to shove a red-hot poker up my asshole, would I *really* keep silent? Or would I turn over everyone I know, everyone who's ever helped me, just to get out of havin' that done? All it would take is one word . . . One word from the likes of this dealer Poger who's comin' upriver to tell what he knows about Mr Cain. You think about it, Benjamin. You think about if you're willing to put your life in the hands of a man who shoots off his mouth when he drinks.'

Still January did not reply. In time, Ballou added, 'Besides, Quinto didn't know about Drummond. If he'd been killing mad, he'd have come after me.'

But we don't know WHAT he knows.

'And where is Quinto?'

'No idea. But nobody's claimed that reward, and they've got men looking as far as Memphis.'

Between waking and sleep in the charred-out attic of Rex Ballou's house Monday night, listening to the drumming of the cicadas, the hoot of the hunting owls, January again dreamed of looking for that maroon village in the *ciprière*. Of looking for Olympe.

He knew it lay somewhere out past the crumbling city wall. In his dream it was summer, and the river was low; now and then moonlight would gleam in the gold eyes of alligators in the bayous.

His mother had shrugged, and said, '*She be back by an' by.*' January knew their mother had never had much use for Olympe. Nor had she for January. Both were African-black like their father, living proof that their mother had once been a slave, and like a slave had been given to a field hand as mate.

January had accepted her neglect, had taken greedy advantage of the schooling and training her white protector offered him. Olympe would have none of it, and had taken instead to going to the voodoo dances on St John's Eve out on the bayou; to running away from the nuns who tried to educate her.

And now this.

He had cried to his mother, '*She's only fourteen!*' and his mother had replied, '*I can't do a thing with her.*'

And so he had gone out to search. To the place slaves went to, when they ran away.

But the darkness only grew deeper, and the fear grew in his heart.

Olympe knows the answer. That's why I have to find her. She knows who killed Drummond . . .

His adult self wondered at this, because that wasn't what he'd written to her about in the pre-dawn blackness that morning.

Then it seemed to him then that he came to a clearing in the trees. Instead of darkness the air was filled with cool gray light. As if, like Jesus, he'd been lifted to the top of a mountain his vision changed, and he saw the whole of the United States laid out below him like a map, from the ocean on the east to the borders of Mexico on the west. He saw the forest in which he'd searched as the green place of safety, not danger. All around those green hidden pockets he saw the lands of slavery, crawling with the armies of slave-takers, kidnappers, militia patrols.

New Orleans – made of glass and no bigger than the nail of his thumb – gleamed amid that green darkness. With precise, miraculous clarity saw his own house on Rue Esplanade, like the diamond in a ring. His beautiful Rose, sitting on the porch, bespectacled and gawky and incomparable, corrected the mathematical proofs of her three students (*A miracle! Three!*), while her son – *their* son – solemnly built walls of blocks and her next son – in his dream January knew it would be a son – grew strong and sturdy in her belly, waiting to be born.

And around them – outside the city – those crawling armies of slave-takers and patrols crept like lines of red ants, chewing into the green safe places, until those places were safe no more.

Crawling over the roads. Cutting off the route to freedom.

He saw the river closed off, and the port, and all the roads north. He tried to shout to her, *Run, Rose! Take Baby John and run!* but she couldn't hear him. *Run to the* ciprière*, run to the north! Follow the Drinking Gourd. The seven stars will point you to freedom . . .* The safe places on the map crisped and burned, as if the map had been laid on a fire. Rose raised her head, startled, and he heard the clatter of hooves in the street, and the wild baying of Drew Hardy's dogs.

NINETEEN

'I'm begging you,' a woman said in the yard below. 'My very life depends on your silence.'

'Is it true?' Hannibal returned in a reasonable tone.

By the stars, still visible through the open framing of the attic's rear wall, it was halfway between midnight and mid-summer's early dawn. January calculated he had been asleep barely two hours. When he and Ballou had returned to the house on Clay Street the fiddler had not yet come in, and had presumably either lingered at the Purleys' sociable, or had gone down to the waterfront to see what information he could pick up in the gambling-hells.

'I have to get away from him.'

Julia Maury . . .

'I have to get money from somewhere. No man's going to buy the cottage, no matter what my father's will said. My husband will never let go of title. Any purchaser must know the battle in the courts could go on for years. Slaves, it's different.'

'And you'd rather have your husband think you were encouraging the romantic attentions of a slave-dealer?'

'My husband thinks I'm encouraging every man's romantic attentions merely by going out of the house. If he weren't so desperate to be thought godly by the other members of the church, I think he'd literally keep me a prisoner. But when I come into town to stay for a night, Stan, the coachman, has orders to spy on me; my maid as well. And he makes certain I never have a penny more than I have to – as any woman in town can tell by looking at my clothes,' she added bitterly. 'I could take a steamboat upriver as far as Greenville, maybe, but how would I live then? There's not a great deal a woman can do. And he would pursue me.'

January slipped from beneath the mosquito-bar that surrounded his pallet, and crept to the edge of the broken floor. By the glow of the lantern that Ballou had left burning above the back door, he could make out their dim shapes in darkness, and the pale blur of faces.

'Please,' she said softly, 'I have no doubt whatsoever that it is as you surmised to Mrs Passmore: that my husband found Mr Drummond's body in the woods and carried it to my cottage, with the sole purpose of incriminating Mr Cain. Mr Cain *was* there Wednesday evening . . . But what you said about me seeking to sell the slaves my father left me – as you are a gentleman, I beg of you never to speak of it. If he even suspects I'm trying to get money to leave, I will be kept prisoner indeed. And I beg of you, tell Mr Cain that if he speaks of the matter at all, to anyone, I am lost. It can't make any difference to Mr Cain what my husband believed was going on.'

'On the contrary, *mea tu belliata*,' said Hannibal, a little diffidently, 'I suspect it will make a great deal of difference to a jury whether a man on trial for murder is believed to have been wrongfully accused because he was dealing with a woman in a business way – at her instigation – or whether he is believed to have attempted to force his attentions on her. And I regret to assure you that there are men in this town who are all too ready to believe the worst of your – or probably any woman's – intentions.'

'I will deny it. I will swear that he was the pursuer. It will be his word against mine. Denying it will not save him, and it will damn me who would be damned in either case.'

In the silence that followed January guessed that Hannibal regarded her steadily, letting her hear her own words, because when she spoke again her tone was pleading.

'He is a monster, Mr Pinkerton! Cold-blooded, cold-hearted and suspicious of everyone and everything. Tomorrow morning, my maid is going to report to him that I stayed out late; I'll be questioned like a thief as to where I was at this hour and why. Saturday, when neither the Reverend Bickern nor the Reverend Thorne could be found, rather than let me have a little time to enjoy the menagerie or – God forefend! – see the minstrelsy show, he dragged me with him all over town while he searched for word of them, convinced to the marrow of his bones that they were trying to abscond with the church money. And convinced that if I wasn't with him, I'd be . . . *disporting* myself in some ungodly manner that he wouldn't approve of!'

'That's a little harsh,' remarked Hannibal, 'for a man who paid three thousand dollars to put another man into fistfights.'

She sniffed. 'Not *fistfights*, he would tell you – as he told *me*, for forty-five minutes when I was so foolish as to disparage this obsession of his . . . An *agon*, he called it. An all-in struggle that – how did he say it? – that *displays the iron core of the human heart*. He calls watching it *muscular prayer*: spiritual inspiration to every man who sees it, in a way that women aren't capable of understanding. He says the same of dogfights. He is mad,' she added, in a tiny voice. 'Mad in a way that nobody will believe.'

Looking down on them from above, January saw her move toward Hannibal, take his hands in hers.

'Mr Pinkerton . . .'

Hannibal gently took her wrists, and stood her away from him. 'And did your husband,' he asked, 'ever locate the Reverend Bickern or the Reverend Thorne?'

'I don't think so,' she replied after a time. 'The Reverend Bickern returned at about three and commenced preaching – he and my husband spoke a little outside the tent. My husband gave his *kind consent*—' An edge hardened for a moment in her voice – 'for me to remain and listen, in company with the other ladies of the committee. He left, I assume, to watch his disgusting *agon* . . . I didn't see him again until Mr Cain was arrested.'

'Whereas in fact he was in the swamp along Chickasaw Bayou,' murmured Hannibal, 'finding poor Drummond's body. You have no idea what the Reverend Bickern said to Mr Maury?'

'None. There was a good deal of noise around the Reverend Bickern's return, and Caroline Haffle was right beside me, trumpeting orders like a sergeant of the grenadiers. Mr Pinkerton, I am begging you—'

'And it is my turn, *acushla*, to beg you. If you can learn for me where the Reverend was between ten in the morning and three? If you can find out that, we may both of us – all of us – completely avoid any question about what Mr Cain's gloves were doing in your cottage or who walked up and said what to whom.'

'You don't think . . .?'

January could hear the widening of her eyes in the sudden hush of her voice.

'You're not saying the Reverend Bickern could have . . . have *murdered* Mr Drummond? They despised one another, had contempt for one another, but surely, as a man of God . . .'

'My dear Julia,' said Hannibal softly, 'every man of God from the prophet Joshua on down will tell you that it is perfectly acceptable to smite the enemies of the Lord on the edge of the sword – laudable, even. And at the moment, Be—' He stopped himself from saying, *Benjamin and I*, and changed it to, '*I* am not concerned with who thought what or would do what, but just who *could* have been in the woods waiting for Mr Drummond to ride by at shortly after eleven o'clock. Just learn for me where he was – and where the Reverend Thorne has got himself off to, if you can – and we'll see where we are from there.'

January was sitting at the top of the ladder when Hannibal, candle in hand, climbed to the loft. He heard the fiddler stop in the kitchen after closing and locking the door, and cough – with excruciating violence – for a good five minutes before proceeding, a sound that filled him with both grief and dread. Since he'd known Hannibal, he'd watched the older man's struggle against the slow advance of consumption, periods of relative wellness alternating with debilitating bouts of infection, fevers and weakness. His friend's decision to give up a lifelong dependence on opium, laudanum and jaw-dropping quantities of liquor had probably saved his life, but January knew well that it couldn't reverse the damage. A bout of pneumonia would kill him.

And though it made him writhe with shame to do so, January could not keep himself from praying, *Please, PLEASE don't let him come down with pneumonia when we're clear the hell up in cotton country and it's a long way back to New Orleans . . .*

Candle flame wavered down below, and a moment later Hannibal's head appeared in the opening in the attic floor.

'I'm sorry,' said the fiddler promptly. 'Did that little scene in the garden wake you?'

'Doesn't matter. And I'm afraid that much as I sympathize with that young woman's desire to get the hell out from under the thumb of a lunatic like Maury, I can't say I'm delighted at the idea of her selling people to God knows what kind of new masters to facilitate her escape.'

Hannibal clambered up the last few rungs, seated himself on the floor at January's side and set the candle between them. 'It seems at least Maury has a witness for his movements at the time of the murder itself. Were you able to speak to Mrs Walker?'

'I was. She says Cain was with her – with allowances for how long it would take him to ride from Haffle's meadow to the head of Chickasaw Bayou – pretty much from eleven o'clock on.'

'And after he'd found Cindy and beat the tripes out of Drummond,' agreed Hannibal. 'A sentiment with which I find myself wholly in sympathy, but which does us no good whatsoever in terms of exculpating Cain.'

'And was the Reverend Bickern at Mrs Purley's this evening?'

'He was. Exhausted and distracted, and no wonder. The original plan was to spend the evening with the committee counting the loot, but owing to the Reverend Thorne's continued absence, the Jackson contingent started demanding that any vote or decision be postponed until he could join them—'

'Did Bickern have any explanation of his absence Saturday?'

'After a fashion. Bickern says he carried the money away from the Tabernacle in his red leather valise with the silver fittings, and deposited it in the Vicksburg and Natchez Traders' Bank. He then returned to the Purley house for a spell of prayer and meditation in the garden, believing that his "associate" Thorne had things well in hand at the Tabernacle. Of course, the Jackson contingent, still striving for the deciding vote about who will control this new church, took immediate exception to his implication that the Reverend Thorne was in any way delinquent.' He shook his head. 'A frightful evening. *Chaos umpire sits, And by decision more embroils the fray* . . . And of course since all the Purley servants were at the menagerie that morning, Bickern could have been anywhere, doing anything, from ten until three – and I can't think of anyone else whose note could have elicited that look of rage on Drummond's face. *Meet me in the woods, you sinner* . . . Only of course the same theory applies to the Reverend Levi Thorne Christmas, always supposing he had a reason to hate Bickern. I suspect Christmas would be considerably handier with a knife than Lemuel Bickern.'

'There's no reason for you to suspect that,' returned January somberly. 'A man can do a lot of things before he decides to start preaching the gospel of the Lord – look at Saul of Tarsus and St Ignatius Loyola. But in fact,' he went on, 'in spite of what Sheriff Preston says, those wounds did look . . . amateurish. Most of the lividity was in Drummond's back: his attacker stabbed him repeatedly and left him lying. By the blood in the clearing, Drummond wasn't able to get up and follow: he lay there and bled out. Cain – or Christmas – or Lieutenant Shaw back in New Orleans – would have finished by cutting his throat. Our man didn't.'

Hannibal said, 'Hmmn.'

'Does Bickern go back to Richmond tomorrow? Today, I suppose we now have to call it,' added January, listening to the sudden crowing of the first cocks in the yard below.

'Tomorrow,' said Hannibal firmly. 'I refuse to close the book on today until I have sought my well-earned bed. He has a christening to perform in Milliken's Bend, and will return Wednesday, to count the money before Thorne and the Jackson ladies go home, and I trust,' he added anxiously, 'there's no pressing reason for me to be present at that engagement—'

January shook his head. 'See what you can find out,' he said, 'about when Bickern actually took that money to the bank – and what he might have had time to do afterwards. Whatever you can learn about Levi Christmas's movements during that time will help also, but I'm guessing it'll be harder—'

'And I'm guessing,' said Hannibal, 'that Cornelia Passmore might know – she's worked more than one confidence game with him – and might be persuaded to tell me.'

Tuesday morning Rex Ballou arranged a meeting between January and Nell, the Purley housemaid. January took over the early-morning chores of lighting kitchen fires and starting the boiler in the barber shop going, while Ballou set forth, shortly before daylight, to catch the Purley slaves at their early-morning chores before 'the family' were up and about; he returned with the information that Nell thought she could get away that afternoon after dinner.

'Is she loyal to her mistress?' January poured out hot water into a can for Ballou to wash and shave before his first customers arrived. 'Will she think it her business to let the Purleys know somebody's asking questions about the Reverend Bickern? Is she loyal to Bickern, for that matter? I think I saw her in the Tabernacle—'

'They took turns,' Ballou reported with a grin, 'sort of milling around in that tent, letting Mrs Purley see them – so she'd think all of them were at the Tabernacle and not the circus.' He gathered up a clean towel and the brass can, paused in the bedroom doorway. 'And since she calls the Reverend Bickern "Reverend Fish-Lips", I'm guessing she'll be perfectly happy to tell you whatever you want to know about him for twenty-five cents.'

So it proved. Because several of Ballou's 'regulars' came early, the barber breakfasted on cornbread and hard-boiled eggs, which Mrs Dillager put up for him the night before, and Hannibal, January knew, wouldn't stir from his blankets much before noon. Thus he was able to have his own breakfast at the boarding house, and offer to help the handsome widow with her own chores ('Now, did Mr Ballou send you over to butter me up?' 'M'am, he knows you're stern, and not subject to buttering . . .'), and received in exchange all the gossip of the town, about who else might have wished ill to Ezekias Drummond, and why.

These included most of the Bickern contingent, the Reverend having regularly described his rival from the pulpit as the Antichrist, and many of the free blacks of Vicksburg, thanks to Drummond's skill in deflecting even the slightest suspicion that he might have been in league with the Underground Railroad. 'I never did see what Rex saw in the man,' sniffed the landlady, scooping soft soap onto a rag and attacking the pile of dirty queensware bowls stacked beside the sink. 'Most white folks in Vicksburg, you don't cross the line with them, they're just as happy to deal with you like a regular person. They ain't gonna step off the sidewalk to let you pass, but they'll give you good mornin' when they see you in the market. But Drummond was a northerner, and didn't grow up around black folk. He'd look through you like you wasn't even there.'

She grimaced, shook her head, and called out to the slave-girl Hetty on the other side of the kitchen, 'Slice them carrots a little thinner, honey. Remember Mr Brand got sore teeth this week.'

'Yes'm.'

'Injun Tom Colvard, now.' Her mouth pursed tight. 'Whether

he wished Mr Drummond harm or not would depend on what time of the day it was. In the mornin's when he's sober, he's a prayin' member of that Salvation Sanctuary – probably 'cause Drummond has no objection to a man taking a drink now and then. But folks say when evening comes and Colvard gets his load on, he rants and spits on Drummond's name for insulting Colvard's "blood" by warning off his stepdaughter from his son, never mind that Colvard doesn't have a lick of use for that son of his himself. Roane Colvard left his father's house – *if* you can call it a house! – when he was thirteen years old . . . But get Injun Tom drunk, and he's fit to kill any man who forgets his father was a king among the Choctaw, for all he's a drunken wretch whose kin no man in his right mind would consent to let a daughter wed.'

'And what did Roane Colvard have to say about all that?'

Mrs Dillager shrugged. 'Roane doesn't say much to anybody. He lives like an animal in the Yazoo swamps, trapping muskrat, and comes into town barely once a month. Keeps himself to himself, and well he should. I suppose that makes him a better citizen than Injun Tom.'

She glanced down sidelong at her big gray tomcat, inspecting the corners of the kitchen for lizards or mice. 'But by a long chalk, Jehoshaphat there is a better citizen than Injun Tom.'

An interesting supposition – and several more disreputable stories about Injun Tom and his son surfaced during the course of the morning that January spent at Mrs Dillager's – but January well recalled seeing Injun Tom in the crowd around Drummond immediately after the race. And Roane, he knew, had attempted to speak to the ferryman just before Cain's appearance, leaving the young man very little time to get out to the woods, lay his ambush and still be seen in the front row of the circus.

'He could have managed it on horseback,' Hannibal pointed out, when January returned to Ballou's and found the fiddler sleepily dressing in his attic cubbyhole.

'I don't know where he hid his horse while he lay in wait, then,' returned January. 'And where he hid his horse's droppings. I saw no sign of either in the clearing.'

Shaved, tidy and smelling faintly of Rex Ballou's bay rum, Hannibal sallied forth to the bank, and to see if he could locate

Julia Maury before her husband obliged her to return to Indian Mound. He had not returned by four, when January set out, via the alleyways that were the usual routes of travel for the unfree of the town, to meet the Purleys' servant-woman Nell.

Nell was tall, stout and dressed in print calico that attested to the Purleys' consideration for their bondspeople: anyone could want their indoor servants to be clean and tidily dressed, but the frock clearly hadn't been re-cut from somebody's hand-me-down, and was new enough to tell January that it wasn't worn every single day.

'My master,' he told her, in the rough English that he was familiar with among the Uptown New Orleans slaves, 'is a good friend to Mr Cain, that was arrested for killing Mr Drummond Saturday: he's bound and determined Mr Cain didn't do it.' He handed the young woman a silver twenty-five-cent piece. 'And he thinks it's mighty convenient, that just by chance the Reverend Bickern happened to have disappeared right before he calculates Mr Drummond was killed. His daddy was a doctor,' he added, to Nell's announced disbelief that anyone could tell what time a man died.

'Not unless he been dead and rots,' she opined.

'I guess doctors can do that,' January asserted. 'To within a couple hours. An' he says as how Mr Drummond was dead by noon. I hear tell you was at the Tabernacle yourself, and know the Reverend went missing before the race started—'

To his surprise, Nell giggled. 'Oh, yeah.'

January raised his eyebrows. 'You know where he went?'

'I don't know where he *went*,' she said. 'But I sure got a good guess what he was doin'. It was my job to pack up his things, 'fore he left town this mornin' – pack 'em up neat, my missus says . . . the stingy old fish.'

Since this was exactly what January had wanted to ask the maid about – servants routinely packed up the effects of guests for their departure – he put on his most fascinated expression: not a deception. He'd hoped to encounter puzzlement or a frustrated '*and one of his shirts is missin'!*' – an indication that a bloodstained garment had been disposed of. Instead . . .

'Don't tell me you found rouge on his shirtfront,' he joked with a grin, and she responded with a huge grin of her own.

'Not just rouge,' she said. '*Perfume*.'

It was the last thing January had expected and he must have looked suitably nonplussed, because Nell let out a crow of laughter.

'Rouge—' The white ladies of the French and Spanish Creole communities – and the fairer-skinned among the *plaçées* – routinely colored their cheeks, but in Vicksburg, the only women who would have painted would be prostitutes.

'And *perfume*.' Nell was practically hugging herself with glee. 'And a couple of gold hairs. And serve him right, the old goat, when everybody in the town find it out, the way he starin' an' squeezin' an' strokin' at me, when I'm unpackin' his things in his room . . . After all his carry-on about sin! Hmnf!'

'You tell Mrs Purley?' asked January, fascinated.

'An' get a lickin' for speakin' lies about the servant of God? Not damn likely.' She grinned again. 'But, my goodness! It just makes me smile to know.' She cocked a bright eye at January. 'So you tell your Mr Pinkerton that the Reverend Fish-Lips couldn't'a been a murderer 'cause he was too busy bein' a gold-plated hypocrite. Ain't that a joke?'

'It is,' agreed January, and handed her another twenty-five-cent piece. 'It is indeed.'

TWENTY

January returned to Ballou's through the thick hot gold of late afternoon, and wasn't entirely surprised to find Hannibal still absent. Thunder growled in the west, but the river remained low, the sky dry. 'If it'd rain we'd be all right,' muttered Ballou as they walked down to Mrs Dillager's. 'We could get those folks out of that cellar and down to the river without worryin' about giving ourselves away. But Sheriff Preston's got it into his head – he told me this morning – that it might have been Quinto that killed Drummond, because Drummond spoke out against abolition, so we still got hunters out all over the countryside, sniffin' for the least trace of scent. And Saul and Solly haven't got the faintest idea what to do.'

'And where's Mrs Walker?'

'One of Ezekias' hideaways in the 'delta'. There's a sycamore where the trail turns off toward Haynes Bluff, got a fork in its main branch. If we need to meet with her, we cram a bundle of leaves and sticks, like a bird nest, into that fork; she'll go to our meeting place with her, at the east end of the Lagoon, just after sunset. But we got to come up with something soon, to clear the hunters away so the cargo can move. They can't stay down there forever.'

'No,' said January softly. 'You give that much laudanum to a child, you'll either kill it . . . or it'll cry so bad that you'll have to keep drugging it, all the way north. Not something I'd want to see happen to any child, not the son of my worst enemy.'

By eleven o'clock that night, when Hannibal still hadn't returned, January began to feel uneasy. 'He's a nightbird,' he said, as he and Ballou packed up their cribbage game and made one final check of the shop to make sure everything was laid out ready for the morrow. 'He might have taken the opportunity to sit in on a card game somewhere, or he and Mrs Passmore might be . . .' He hesitated, '*playing cribbage* on their own account. Even so . . .'

He walked out onto the burned-out porch of the little house, gazed at the darkness of Clay Street. Here and there, windows still smoldered with the dim glow of candles and lamps. A couple passed in the gloom: January smelled the man's cigar, the woman's perfume. Recalled with an inner chuckle the Reverend Fish-Lips and the rouge on his shirt . . .

Even if it did destroy a promising alternate suspect. He'd gone in the afternoon to visit Cain in the jail, and had found the slave-dealer pacing uneasily. With Alf Hilding at his desk in the jail's main chamber, little information could be exchanged, but Cain had seemed glad at least of the company. He'd growled loudly, 'No word of that idiot Poger yet, I suppose?' and January had shaken his head. 'The man's a liar and a cheat,' Cain had continued, chiefly, January guessed, for Deputy Hilding's benefit. But Cain was clearly deeply worried.

As well he should be, thought January.

Ezekias Drummond – a conductor on the Underground Railroad – had been killed; Jubal Cain – likewise connected with the Railroad – faced hanging at the hands of either Mississippi state justice or an angry mob . . .

And Hannibal Sefton (or Cyril Pinkerton) was also in league with the Railroad.

As was January.

'But if it's somebody who knew about the Railroad,' pointed out Ballou, when January came back indoors, 'they could just tell the local slave-holders who we were. They wouldn't have to sneak around and commit ambushes or tamper with evidence. Nobody in this county – in this *state* – would raise a hand if we were lynched or bother to seek out those who did it. You're just jumpy.'

'I suppose I am.'

January was woken at midnight from a restless sleep by pounding on the back door. He heard Ballou's footsteps clatter on the kitchen floor and rolled from beneath the mosquito-bar, and went to the open end of the gable in time to hear the door open.

'Rex?' said a voice in the darkness, and an instant later candle-light shone in the lightless garden, enough to outline a shadow there.

'Bart?' Ballou sounded sleepy. January hoped he'd put on a nightshirt to cover the bandages on his chest. In this heat he himself certainly wasn't wearing one.

'That white feller Pinkerton still stayin' here with you?' asked Bart. 'From the circus?'

Ballou must have nodded.

'He over at the Best Chance. Feller set on him in the alley just outside, stabbed him and broke his head. Nick thinks he's dyin'.'

The gambling room at the Best Chance got very silent as Rex Ballou and Benjamin January entered.

Somebody'd brought in a bench from the sidewalk outside. A mangy-looking blanket had been thrown over it; Hannibal lay on this, with his coat rolled up under his head. A knife-slash crossed his right shoulder; blood glistened in his dark hair. His eyes were shut, his breathing barely a whisper. Sheriff Preston straightened up from beside him, nodded at January, and said, 'Ballou. This man with you this evening?'

'Yes, sir.' Ballou looked startled by the question.

'All evening?'

'Yes, sir—'

A harsh-faced man in a blue frock-coat said, 'You trust a nigger's word?'

'I trust Rex Ballou's word a hell of a lot more'n I'd trust yours, Wagget,' the sheriff retorted. To Ballou he said, 'Nick behind the bar says the man that did for him was big like Ben.'

'*Did for him . . .*'

Cold shock went through January as if his own flesh had been gashed.

Carefully, he said, 'My master back in Mobile, 'fore I come to Marse Pinkerton, was a doctor, sir. Might be could I have a look at him?' Now was *not* the time to impress white men with good English.

Somebody else said, 'Don't let him. Doc Ford'll be here in a minute. If it was him that knifed him, he'll finish him off—'

'Ben's been with me all evening, since supper time,' Ballou said. 'What happened?'

Nick the barkeep – who also boarded at Mrs Dillager's – said,

'I heard a shout out in the alley, an' a crash like somebody rammed into the back wall of the place. Mr Purley'd just left, an' I thought somebody might have gone after him, since he'd been winnin' all evening . . . So I ran out and saw a big black man with a knife, droppin' down to stab a man on the ground. I yelled out, an' the man ran for it.' He shrugged. 'That's all I know.'

You're a slave, January reminded himself. *You can't ask things like, 'What time was that?' and 'Had he been here earlier this evening?'* Nor could he push to the fore . . .

He tried to catch Ballou's eye, but the barber in his turn knelt at Hannibal's side. 'I don't smell no liquor on him,' he said. 'And I know he wasn't a drinking man.'

'Well, he was sure as hell a card-playin' man,' retorted Wagget, around a cud of tobacco. 'He took thirty dollars off me, last Wednesday night.'

Ballou – *finally!* – turned back to January, said, 'You think he can be moved?'

'Let me have a look at him, sir.'

Wagget opened his mouth to complain again but Sheriff Preston moved back.

And at that moment a stout man in a black coat shoved his way into the room, snapped, 'Get away from that man, boy!' and four men grabbed January and thrust him aside.

Somebody said, 'He been stabbed, Doc!'

'Somebody bust his head.'

'I see.' Dr Ford whipped a stethoscope from his pocket – the long wooden tube stuck out nearly three inches and distorted the hang of his coat – flipped Hannibal over as casually as a butcher turning a slab of meat on a counter, so that his forehead cracked audibly on the bench, yanked the fiddler's coat down to his elbows, and listened to his heart (in the wrong place). January's jaw ached as if it would break with the effort not to shout at the man, knowing that one word at this point would land him in jail.

'This man needs to be bled,' Dr Ford pronounced, and spit tobacco on the floor.

January could smell the liquor on him from where he stood. Behind him, he heard the slave youth Bart say to Nick, 'Thank God he was only down the street at the Delta Palace . . .'

While somebody fetched a chamber pot – clean and still smelling of turpentine – from the back room, Ford turned his patient over again briskly and tore up a bar towel to bandage the superficial gash on Hannibal's shoulder. Wagget asked Ballou, 'You got a razor on you? – Hmph! Whoever heard of a barber that don't got a razor on him?'

Sheriff Preston produced a knife.

They'll kill him. Despair flooded January as blood poured from the severed vein and Hannibal's face grew waxy. *They'll kill him, and I can't speak a word . . .*

'Anybody got some feathers?' asked the medico, when Hannibal (not surprisingly, considering the amount of blood he'd lost) didn't respond to smelling salts. Bart dashed out – presumably there was a pillow somewhere on the premises – and Ford slapped Hannibal sharply, yelling, 'Mr Pinkerton? Mr Pinkerton?'

Burnt feathers didn't revive him either.

'Can anything be done for him?' asked Ballou

Ford grimaced as he tied up the cut with the rest of the bar towel. 'I'm afraid not. Traveler, was he?'

'With the circus,' said Wagget, and the physician shrugged dismissively, and spit again.

'If it's all right with Mr Roper—' Ballou named the owner of the Best Chance – 'Ben and me could take him back to my place and make him comfortable . . .'

Mr Roper – who'd come in midway through these events, visibly uneasy already at the thought of someone dying in his saloon, not to mention losing business for the rest of the night – agreed at once. Wagget and Dr Ford put up another fifteen minutes of argument that January should be arrested for the attempt on his 'master's' life, but in the end Preston said, 'You swear you'll be responsible, Ballou?' and let them go. Roper even sent the slave Bart along, to help carry the makeshift litter down Cherry Street and over to the barbershop.

'How bad is he?' asked Ballou softly, as they walked along with the light burden between them.

'Worse than he was before he had three pints of blood taken out of him.' January took a deep breath, fury and grief ebbing before the growing chill of fear. 'I don't know,' he added. 'With a concussion it's hard to tell. It looks like he was thrown back against the wall, and that can kill a man . . . It doesn't sound like he was gambling there earlier, but it still could have been a robbery. Does this kind of thing happen often, in this part of town?'

'It's gonna happen anyplace there's money changing hands this late at night. Still, we're pretty far uptown.'

'You believe that?'

There was long silence. Then Ballou said, 'No.'

Back at Ballou's, in the downstairs bedroom by the light of every lamp and candle in the house, January turned back the lids of Hannibal's eyes, though with only two lamps and a few candles anybody's pupils would be dilated. The fiddler's pulse was as thready as his breath, and he gave no sign that he was aware of anything as January felt the back of his head, then clipped some of the hair away to gently wash the abraded bruise there.

The skull (*thank God!*) felt unbroken. There didn't seem to be any damage to his neck. But he lay like a corpse as January cleaned and re-bandaged the shoulder wound, and sat with him in Ballou's downstairs bedroom through the remainder of the night.

Ezekias Drummond.

Jubal Cain.

January leaned back in the bedside chair, closed his eyes.

But Ballou was right. Who would take the trouble to kill secretly, if the reason had anything to do with the biggest and deadliest secret of all?

On the borders of sleep, his mind drifted back to the day when he was fifteen, when he'd gone into the *ciprière* to search for Olympe.

Olympe, who had turned her back on the generosity of their mother's protector, that had opened such doors to January. That had paid to enroll him as apprentice to a free colored surgeon, and to have him taught proper French, proper English, Latin and a smattering of Greek

He remembered as if it were yesterday, searching for the maroon village in the swamps, where all paths looked alike and earth and water changed places with eerie ease. Following what might or might not be the path his sister had taken when she'd fled.

What was she fleeing?

She was already free . . .

Voices in the shop on the other side of the thin partition wall. Morning light filled the window. Ballou's morning 'regulars', men who'd book shaves by the week with haircuts thrown in at a discount: clerks, shopkeepers, employees of the banks. Men who had to be at their jobs early. Meaningless as the blundering of bees in the rafters, and occasional laughter.

Ballou laughed along with them. That was part of his job.

Footsteps in the kitchen, a woman's heeled shoes. Mrs Passmore's soft contralto voice: 'Ben?'

'In here.'

She'd let herself in through the back door. No woman could hope to enter the barbershop from the street and retain her respectability.

The widow – if she was a widow – carried a rush basket, and a pottery bottle of ginger water; January took these from her and went to the kitchen to fetch himself a bent-willow chair, surrendering the upholstered one to her.

'Who did this?'

January shook his head.

'Is he – Will he . . .?'

'It's early yet. He has a concussion – the cut on his arm is nothing.'

'Could it have been someone hired by Levi Christmas?' She leaned over to touch the bandage around Hannibal's head, but brought her hand back, as if she weren't certain how to show tenderness. 'He was the one who walked off with the money, you know,' she added, when January looked puzzled. 'Levi Christmas. That's what Hannibal found out at the bank yesterday. He came and told me yesterday evening. That – That *polecat* Bickern never took his little red satchel of money to the bank. It seems he met a young lady on the way, one of those who'd been at the Tabernacle, she said—'

January groaned.

'You heard about that?'

'From Nellie. The Purleys' housemaid. Rouge on his shirt – *and* perfume . . .'

'And instead of "meditating and praying" in the Purleys' garden he was falling for the oldest panel house rig in the world. Some people shouldn't be let outside without their mothers.' She neglected to mention that this was what she herself had been planning to do.

'Which explains,' sighed January, 'where Christmas was at the same time. Hiding under Bickern's bed in the Purleys' guest room, or waiting outside in the garden for the girl to drop the satchel full of church money down to him while Bickern snored.'

'And there's nobody in the world easier to seduce than a preacher just off an all-night revival meeting.' She looked down at Hannibal again, and this time, very gently, touched his hand. 'I expect Bickern has packed his things and fled from Richmond by this time. He'll never be able to clear himself. Christmas hasn't been back to town either, the one-eyed weasel. As far as I can tell, he isn't working with a gang. May Buck from Jackson is going frantic, thinking up tales of what might have befallen him . . .'

She frowned. 'But why hire someone to kill Hannibal? Yes, he was asking questions at the bank, but what could that tell him? Christmas left town Saturday afternoon. He's got to be in Memphis by this time. Can I do anything?' She looked back at January. 'Do you need anything?'

'I'm all right so far.' *Free papers? Fast passage back to New Orleans?*

Leaving Hannibal here to die? Cain here to hang?

Poger could turn up at any hour today. If a lynch mob formed, how long *would* it be before his own name was mentioned? He felt sweat on his forehead that had nothing to do with the summer's heat, and looked down at the still, thin face on the pillow. *And how the hell would I get him out of town?*

Sometimes the only thing you *could* do was run. But was this one of those times?

'Has he not come to yet?'

Again, January shook his head. 'In cases of a heavy concussion he may not recover his senses for days.'

'Does he have family? Friends?'

January sighed. 'Only my wife and myself.'

'Poor soul,' she whispered. 'Poor lost soul.'

TWENTY-ONE

Julia Maury came later in the day, with a stoneware jar of broth and an offer to send one of the Indian Mound slaves to help January with the nursing. She confirmed Mrs Passmore's surmise that the Reverend Bickern had vanished: 'My husband is beside himself, and swears that abolitionists assassinated him on his way to that christening in Milliken's Bend—' She hesitated. 'He swears that Mr Cain was behind it all . . .'

That's all we need . . .

'And now Mr Pinkerton—'

'As far as I know, m'am,' January said gently, 'the Reverend Bickern was robbed of the church money Saturday afternoon. And as far as I know, the thief seems to have been the Reverend Jeremiah Thorne.'

Her mouth fell open for a moment in shock. She started to speak, then stopped herself, and he saw her eyes, just for a moment, shift at some second thought. Then she said, 'Mr Maury never trusted him. That's who he went looking for, Saturday afternoon, after the Reverend Bickern returned to the Tabernacle. Someone must have told him that the Reverend Thorne rode into the woods . . .'

'Probably,' said January, 'to hide the loot. And what point would there be anyway in Mr Cain being "behind" the Reverend Bickern's disappearance, even if he was – God only knows who started that story! – an abolitionist? I've seen the man sell slaves in Mobile,' he added mendaciously. 'I've seen him buy them in Grand Gulf.' He let the anger he'd felt, when he'd actually seen men and women bought and sold in New Orleans, come into his voice: 'Believe me, m'am, Mr Cain is no abolitionist. And you can tell Mr Maury that—'

'No.' She flinched. 'Mr Maury . . . believes what he believes. I no longer try to get him to change . . . anything.'

January was silent, remembering the thwack of a belt against bare flesh in the afternoon stillness.

'I beg your pardon for asking this, m'am,' he said after a time. 'But . . . you're from hereabouts. Is there anyone you know of, who hated Mr Drummond as your husband hated him?'

A small upright line appeared between her brows. 'You still seek to help a man like Cain?'

'I seek to help my master,' said January quietly. 'He's said to me, more than once, that he would not be alive today were it not for what Mr Cain did for him. I have to do what I can. And given what happened to Mr Drummond, I can't help thinking what happened to my master is somehow connected. He was asking questions . . . Was there anyone who would have wished to do Drummond harm, anyone he wronged?'

'Other than his poor wife?' Anger tightened her mouth. 'Whom he keeps as close a prisoner as my husband keeps me, only he uses God as the guard he sets on her, rather than his coachman . . . Who is outside, by the way, watching the door. As close as my husband kept his first wife, though at least Mrs Drummond is spared the humiliation of lying awake at night listening while her husband . . . *disports* himself . . . with his daughter's nurse-maid. Every time I see that poor woman – which isn't often, for she never comes into town – I want to run up to her and shake her and say, *Why don't you leave him?* God knows I would leave Mr Maury, if I could. Yet she adores him.'

'*He for God only*,' January quoted, '*and she for God in him . . .*'

Mrs Maury smiled. 'One can tell that you've been with Hannibal for a long time . . . Do you know what that's from?'

Reminded that he was supposedly a slave, January looked self-conscious, and said, 'Somethin' called *Paradise Lost*, he said. About sin and God and the Garden of Eden. None other, that you can think of?'

'Roane Colvard,' she said. 'He's been sweet on Rachel for over a year now. Drummond's stableman Boze, if he knocks him around as Mr Ballou said he mistreated poor Tom – the man he had before him, and who finally ran off . . . It's all you can do, you know, with people like that,' she added softly. 'Just get away from them, if you can. Break your chains, and never look back.'

From the kitchen door January watched her go, circling the house to where a low-slung barouche waited for her in Clay

Street. Evidently Marcus Maury had no objection to spending money on things that were too cumbersome for his wife to sell for getaway money – he had noticed again how she wore no jewelry.

Just get away from them . . . break your chains . . .

But not without money in hand, he reflected drily as he turned back into the house. Getting away, for her, included selling men and women to a slave-dealer – who might peddle them on to the sweltering hell of a Louisiana sugar plantation, where field hands lasted seven years if they were lucky. Or to a drunkard like his old master Simon Fourchet. Or a man who considered a black woman's body as the handiest receptacle for his seed whenever he had an itch in his pants.

The girl Cindy – wherever she was – had fled with nothing. The woman Giselle had fled with nothing. Deya, Isaiah, Arthur, Ason, Randol had fled with nothing, never looking back; as his own first wife, Ayasha, had fled her father's *harîm* at the age of fourteen, rather than be married willy-nilly to a business partner.

Olympe. His mind snagged the old memory. *Olympe had fled . . .*

That's why I was looking for her.

A note was waiting for him when he and Ballou returned from supper that night.

Garden at the Planter's, it said. *9 o'clock. I have learned the name of the man.*

– Cornelia

He reached the hotel at eight thirty. After spending most of the day in the stuffy bedroom, watching over Hannibal, even the sticky heat of the dusk was welcome. Fireflies danced in the dark hedges; another storm rumbled far to the west, filling the sky with horizon-wide flashes of light. From open windows, open doors, all along those little houses on the fringes of the fashionable district, he heard the voices of children, of mothers telling old tales of High John the Conqueror and Br'er Rabbit, of men and women speaking softly of the business of the day, with the intimacy that darkness brings.

The garden of the Planter's was surrounded by a tall box hedge.

Oak trees grew outside the hedge, stretching their branches over and through it, and instead of walking down the driveway in the new-fallen darkness, he approached from the hedge side, and climbed one of the trees.

The waxy smell of the gardenias was sweet as a drug in the night. Away on his right he could tell where the jasmine lay, and farther off the honeysuckle, like pools of invisible color. When, fifteen minutes later, the stench of cigar smoke and clothing that hadn't been cleaned quite recently enough rolled into the garden, it was like a shovelful of stable muck on silk.

There were three men. One of them took his post behind the gardenia just beneath the branch on which January lay. Another – January could just see movement by the reflection of the lights from the Ladies' Parlor – concealed himself behind the bower of ivy.

He smelled the combination of dusting powder and cigar smoke, and heard the silvery whisper of Cornelia Passmore's skirts when she descended the garden door's shallow step.

'I think you'll find everything in order.' She handed something – January could just see her movement in the glow of the windows – to the third man, who stood in the little plot of grass. He held papers up to where the window light would catch them. 'Mr Pinkerton came to this afternoon, and we had a long talk. He understands he's not going to be able to work for the rest of the summer, maybe longer than that.'

'You sure his title's clear?' The nasal voice was that of Fenks the slave-dealer.

She handed over another piece of paper. *She must*, January reflected furiously, *have been forging it – and the sale papers – all afternoon.* 'He said he'd send Ben along at nine. He hadn't the heart to tell him he'd sold him – he's grown extremely fond of him – so . . . Well, be as gentle as you can, would you? It'll come as a terrible shock to him.'

Not as much of a shock as you think, you conniving witch. The rage that swept January almost entirely drove out panic and fear.

And if you've forged Hannibal's signature onto sale papers – and forged papers giving HANNIBAL title to a slave named Benjamin – if I just slide down this tree and head back to Ballou's you'll get the sheriff and won't I look silly, yelling 'No, no, I'm free and here's my papers . . .'

And then it'll all come out that Hannibal's name really isn't Pinkerton and Cain's name really isn't Cain and we're all working for the Underground Railroad . . .

And you'll get the sheriff if I don't come walking down that drive by nine fifteen.

He slipped his hand into his pants pocket and brought out the heaviest thing he had on his person, the silver watch he'd bought in Paris. It was the first thing he'd purchased when he'd begun playing music for his living, when he'd given up the attempt to make a decent livelihood from the practice of surgery . . . When he'd realized that even in the land of *liberté, égalité, fraternité* no white person was going to hire a black surgeon.

When he'd gotten the news that St-Denis Janvier had died, and that he, Benjamin, was on his own.

And could live perfectly well on his own.

It was either that, or the brass tube in which he habitually carried friction matches and a little kindling, and he knew he'd need those.

He kissed the watch goodbye, and threw it as hard as he could in the direction of the drive.

'What's that?'

Fenks and Mrs Passmore whirled, and strode a step or two toward the shadows that lay pitch-black along the side of the hotel. 'Ben?' she called.

January slid as quietly as a serpent down the oak, and headed straight for the edge of town.

His first thought was to make his way to the waterfront, on the possibility that the ferry was still on this side of the river and hadn't been shut down for the night. He discarded the scheme almost immediately. It was the first direction they'd look.

Going to Ballou for advice or assistance was out of the question. He had great respect for Mrs Passmore's intelligence and knew she respected his: if she hadn't sent the sheriff to Ballou's already, she'd do so the moment nine o'clock passed and he didn't put in an appearance in the Planter's House garden.

Useless even to consider that Ballou would be able to testify in any court in the State of Mississippi – or anywhere below Mason's and Dixon's line – that Hannibal hadn't been conscious that day and couldn't have signed Mrs Passmore's sale papers. He'd told the barber where he was going and why – and why he was leaving an hour early to scout the ground ('Any man who'd trust Cornelia Passmore with as much as twenty-five cents needs to be confined for his own safety . . .'). So Ballou wouldn't be much surprised by a visit from the sheriff with a warrant to transfer possession of Benjamin January to Guy Fenks, slave-dealer . . . who was probably leaving town in the morning. Ballou would come up with a story of some kind, which would at least buy him time.

Time for what?

Other than for this man Poger, whoever he was and whatever he knew about Jubal Cain, to make his way up the river . . .

Time to flee Vicksburg, leaving Cain alone to face the noose?

Time to leave Hannibal alone and injured? Prey to a lynch mob himself? They'll burn the shop over his head.

Even if he managed to get to the waterfront before Mrs Passmore and Fenks set up a hue and cry, he doubted he'd make it back to New Orleans.

He tried to remember, as he walked, Eliza Walker's description of the old Chickasaw farm on the Lagoon, and how to reach the place. Tried also to recall what he'd said to Ballou about dealing with deep concussion, and whether he'd expressed his opinion of the methods of American doctors with sufficient vehemence to keep the barber from calling in Dr Ford or one of his intellectual equals to bleed or puke or purge the fiddler again. He hoped, too, that Ballou had been paying attention earlier when Hannibal had spoken of his struggle to free himself of opiates and liquor, to the point that he would respect what his guest had gone through and not simply spoon Godfrey's Cordial down his throat the way the fugitives in the pit were spooning it down poor little Charlie.

It's out of my hands now. Out of my hands, and in the hands of God.

There were times when he hated white people.

And those times, he reflected bitterly, seemed to coincide with every occasion on which he emerged from the French Town and ventured any distance into cotton country . . . Or any other territory occupied by Americans.

He worked his way north through alleyways and cow yards, and breathed a blessing on the week he'd spent in Vicksburg which had given him a rough idea of the quickest way into the surrounding hills. The lamps and candles were being put out, the little cottages of seamstresses and shoemakers, warehouse clerks and mule drivers, darkening. Day was done. Past First Street the cottages turned to shanties, set in vegetable gardens or warrens of chicken runs and pigsties. These in turn yielded to the uneven fields where the hills wrinkled up below the bluff. He listened all around him for the sound of hooves. Skirted Haffle's meadow and heard in the night stillness the cluck of the stream, and followed the edge of the thicker trees to where the road dipped to cross it. There was enough moonlight to cut himself a snake stick from a cottonwood sapling, before he ducked into the shadows of the trees.

A mile and a half up the bayou, on the other side, Ballou had said. Beside the Lagoon where Glass Bayou runs into it. Would she be there?

The road ran along the high ground, skirting the line of bluffs. He left it and descended, scrambling in the thickets toward the murky smell of the swamp.

TWENTY-TWO

It took him until after midnight to reach the Indian farm. Once he heard the clatter of hooves on the track behind him, and stayed still until the sound died away. Now and then the tree cover would break, and January tried to take his bearings from the stars, seeking the Drinking Gourd whose handle pointed north, to orient himself toward the bayou to the west.

Mostly he groped like a blind man with his snake stick, barely able to make out stray edges of moonlight on the tree boles before he ran into them. His legs ached from scrambling over fallen trunks, last week's dog bite a painful reminder of what he fled. He was back in his dream again, looking for Olympe.

The ground fell steadily. Creepers clutched his ankles and mosquitoes whined in his ears. Twice he tripped on traps that someone had set for small game, triple-braided horsehair tough as silk, nooses delicately set along the game tracks or laid as snares beneath the undergrowth. Town slaves, he guessed: men bought for the gangs that worked the waterfront or cut trees for the wood lots, trying to supplement their monotonous rations of salt pork and dried Iowa cornmeal, or to make a little extra money selling squirrel and rabbit in the market. He well remembered his father back on Bellefleur Plantation taking him out before dawn to check the traplines and snares that provided their little family with the only fresh meat they ever got.

He remembered, too, how his father would sigh and tighten his jaw when he found one that some clumsy idiot had stepped on or kicked into. But the darkness was too thick for him to reset the traps, and he had long ago lost whatever knack for it he'd had. He whispered an apology to the unknown trapper – and to his father's patient shade – and moved on.

One more thing to worry about, he reflected, as the ground turned squishy beneath his feet – swamp-trappers like young Roane Colvard would have their snares set down by the bayou, and the last thing he needed was to get himself tangled up in their heavier lines or, God forbid, in the steel traps that waited for lynx and puma down near the water.

At least there was mud here. He scooped some up gratefully to smear on his face, neck, and hands as protection from the mosquitoes. It smelled of all the greenish oozy decay of the swamp, and he hoped desperately that the Indian farm had a well or a spring of some kind nearby. Thirst had set in, and he sweated in the night's heat.

Just keep going. This is better than getting caught.

Anything is better than getting caught.

Ballou, he guessed, would come looking for him in the morning.

Bringing food, I hope.

Moonlight glimmered, and the undergrowth grew thicker. Shrunken in these days of low water, Chickasaw Bayou was still like a minor river before him, two or three hundred feet across and velvety with duckweed. Nearly sick with dread, January walked a little upstream until he found a place where there were relatively few snags and deadfalls, then pulled off his boots, tied them up in his shirt, and – praying to the Virgin and St Christopher – slipped into the moonlit water and swam like hell for the opposite shore.

Is there a patron saint to ward off alligators?

Or pattyrollers?

St Christopher – patron saint of river crossings – was evidently on the job that night. January scrambled, dripping, out of the muddy water and made off down the bank in the direction of the main river, for nearly a hundred yards before doubling back on his trail. Dogs would follow his tracks in the direction of the river. The men would assume, even after they lost the scent, that he'd continued that way.

Only when he returned to the place where he'd come out – when there was utterly no other option – did he wade into the bayou again, and swim northward through the still, terrifying water.

He kept to the center of the waterway, putting off from minute to minute the voice in his head that urged him to swim to the bank and rest. Gators would be in shallower water, in the maze of fallen trees, along the bank. *A few yards more . . .* Every second he expected to feel teeth on his ankle, pulling him under.

The farther up he went the greater were the chances that if the patrols *did* bring dogs up the bayou, they'd turn back before they caught his scent. *A few yards more . . .*

Once he saw, a yard or two distant from him, the black triangular head and the moon glimmer on the wake of a cottonmouth swimming . . . *St John Evangelist, turn it away . . .*

As a child he'd been abjectly superstitious – like most of the slaves at Bellefleur – and had always assumed that it was his later education that had cured him of this system of belief. Now he understood, with terrifying clarity, that his superstition had been born of utter powerlessness and daily terror, dispelled only because once his mother had been freed – once he himself had been given his freedom – he had had the luxury to look at the world as a place subject to human reason.

Thirsty, exhausted, in deep water with alligators and poisonous serpents, Montesquieu and Locke and Voltaire had very little to say to him.

St John Evangelist, turn that serpent aside . . .

Only when he was trembling with fatigue did he swim – as swiftly as he could – to the bank and scramble up, scraping his shins on half-submerged deadfalls and cypress knees, and sit for a time, shivering, on a log. The mud had washed off him and every mosquito in the State of Mississippi returned, singing the Devil's anthem, around his ears. *Did Noah actually save two mosquitoes on the Ark or did Satan invent them later?*

Wearily, he mudded up again, and moved on.

Three hundred yards farther, the bayou widened into the Lagoon, something over a quarter-mile across and nearly twice that in length. The surrounding woods pressed close on the shore, but January patiently circled it, a stone's throw inland from the water, and in time found what he sought: a tumbledown cottage, raised on six-foot stilts against the chance of floods, and behind it what had probably once been a stable.

January was still far too conscious of the possibility of detection – Roane Colvard supposedly had a cabin a mile or so farther up the bayou, at Lake Thompson – and far too wet and tired in any case, to attempt to strike a light of any kind, but enough moonlight leaked through the stable's broken roof to show him the remains of a ladder on the ground. This he used to scramble up into the loft, and hauled the ladder up after him. Something scurried and squeaked in the blackness around him, but it sounded like only mice, and he was long past caring about anything smaller than a full-grown bear. He said his prayers – piously refraining from a personal request that God strike Mrs Passmore with leprosy before morning – and fell asleep.

It had been a long day.

Hunger woke him, and the excruciating itch of mosquito bites on his neck and arms.

Birds were singing, waves of sound that seemed to pass over the broken rafters of the stable and fill the gray warm air.

He had dreamed, he remembered. Dreamed he'd found the runaway camp in the *ciprière*.

Olympe had been there, not the furious, defiant fourteen-year-old she had been, but her adult self, her woman-self, still thin as braided whipcord, still standing with her arms folded and her long elegant hands callused with work, but smiling, as she'd never smiled as a child . . .

Olympe has the answer . . .

He woke wondering why he'd thought that, for it hadn't been to seek an answer that he'd followed her to that place in the summer of 1811.

In those days, he remembered – the days before the war with England, the days when New Orleans had been still a tiny French–Spanish city surrounded by swamps and sugar plantations – if a man ran away from his master and went out to hide in the *ciprière*, his friends back on the plantations would often know exactly where he was, and would bring him out food, when they could get away. The runaways in those little *ciprière* villages would fish and trap, but they'd seldom grow food, for fear of being found.

Many times, the runaways returned to their plantations of their own accord, because they missed their wives and children, or because – as the Israelites discovered when *they'd* escaped slavery – freedom often meant an empty belly. Because there was really nowhere else to go.

Looking up into the weatherworn rafters over his head, January thought about food.

It was far too early in the year for berries – except strawberries, for which it was far too late. There'd be walnuts in the woods, cattails by the bayou. Turtles could be trapped, though the logs on which they basked were also lurking places for alligators. Both cattails and turtles involved cooking: January hoped his matches were still dry. It was a nuisance to strike the back of his knife on the flint he always carried as well. And fire meant the smell of smoke. Among the mountain men of the West January had heard tales of survival in the wild involving the consumption of grubs, frogs and worms, but put those possibilities aside for the moment.

He had no fishhook, and no real desire to risk losing a leg by wading in the bayou again in an effort to club a fish that would then have to be cooked. His momentary wish that he'd thought to raid one of the snare traps he'd tripped over last night – it had left a thin bruise across his shin as if he'd been hacked with a metal straight edge – dissolved on the same grounds: rabbit meant cooking meant smoke.

Fenks would be angry enough, and determined enough, to be looking for him, today and almost certainly tomorrow as well, particularly if Mrs Passmore had pocketed whatever money Fenks had given her and high-tailed it out of Vicksburg on the next boat. (*And I hope its boiler blows up.*) If the pattyrollers came this far up the bayou, they'd be smelling for smoke.

There was a great deal to be said for hiding in a hole in the ground for ten days, if someone was willing to bring you food and water.

January lowered the ladder, climbed cautiously down (*Do NOT break your ankle at this point . . .*), and emerged into what had once been the yard. By the height of the swamp laurel that choked it – there were cottonwoods nearly adult size – the place had been deserted for many years, since Americans had begun to move into the Mississippi Valley and drive out the 'civilized' tribes: Choctaw, Chickasaw, Creek, Cherokee. The ruin of the house was barely visible in the trees. The kitchen – when January finally came on it – had long since been devoured by the woods. The stone curb of the well had crumbled in, but when he looked down it – the morning sky now bright behind his head – he could see the reflection of light on water.

And me with no bucket or cup.

A patient search of the ruins – first the kitchen, then the house – yielded a large wooden bowl, weathered and warped and half-covered with the dirt in which it had been buried, but January scraped it clean with handfuls of leaves, tore the sleeves of his shirt into strips to make a sort of rope, and, finally, was able to get a drink.

Ballou is on his way. Unless Fenks is watching him . . . which given the fact that I've been staying with him may well be the case.

Wait? Keep on fleeing north? All the way to Ohio?

Leave Cain and Hannibal? Lose my freedom, and with it whatever chance I have of ever seeing Rose again, or my son – my children . . .?

January waited.

Listening all around him with an intensity that made his head ache, he searched the woods around the ruin for walnut trees – though wild walnuts, he was well aware, would be almost impossible to crack. He found three trees, in addition to two apple trees near the house – the fruit barely set and smaller than the ball of his thumb – and settled himself to the tedious chore of searching for a piece of wood that would serve as a cracking-pincer to hull the walnuts, since pounding them with a rock would be audible for miles.

Returning to the broke-down house, he'd managed to crack about four walnuts when Nick, the barkeep from the Best Chance, emerged from the woods and looked uncertainly around the yard. 'Ben?' he called out, in that hushed flat tone of one who doesn't want to be heard. 'Ben, you here?'

Lying along one of the rafters of the stable loft, January remained silent, surrounded by his litter of walnut hulls.

The young freedman looked around the overgrown yard, set down the basket he carried and hurried away at once.

The food would be from Mrs Dillager. Had Ballou arranged this?

Or had Fenks?

After a long time January slipped down the ladder, and stood waiting in the shadows of the stable's broken doorway. Even if Nick wasn't working for the pattyrollers, he would have been easy to follow from town, had anyone seen him strolling into the woods with a basket. *I cross to the basket, the pattyrollers step out of the woods, and I'm . . .*

I'm gone.

Rose will never know. My children will never know.

He waited, not moving, for nearly an hour. Listening. Hearing only bird cries.

They have to be gone by this time . . .

He stepped forth, crossed the yard quickly, caught up the basket and dodged back into the stable. One of his own clean shirts covered it, and a pair of his pants – Ballou gave it to Nick, then. Which means he himself couldn't get away.

Or that someone searched his place and took them . . .

There was bread, cheese, sausage and two bottles of ginger beer.

He was just tearing the paper wrapper away from the bread when a shadow darkened the stable door.

'You need to get deeper in the woods,' said Eliza Walker's husky voice. 'They're all up and down the bayou like ants at a picnic.'

TWENTY-THREE

Seen in daylight, Eliza Walker reminded him a little of Olympe, especially Olympe back in their schooldays in New Orleans, not that Olympe ever attended school if she could get out of it. As Olympe often had, Eliza Walker wore boy's clothing that hung baggy on a thin, sturdy frame, and had cut her hair to a short fuzz that could easily be hidden under a head rag if she had to switch to a dress. Her face was a network of weathering and wrinkles, and the gaps of two missing teeth showed in her smile, which was bright as sunlight on the river. Her strong square hands, like Olympe's, were callused with lye soap and hard work. She led him out the back of the broken stable and into the woods without a moment wasted.

'They got dogs?' was his first question.

'Only that sorry old mutt of Alf Hilding's that couldn't find its own butt if you stuck a sardine up it.'

'They likely to follow me here?'

'Not for what the court'll pay 'em to recover a runaway. They're all counting the minutes 'til they can go back to DeSoto Point and look for Quinto. But better safe than sorry, and this place is a little close to the bayou and a little close to Roane Colvard's place. He sets traps in the woods clear to the river, and he'd notice your tracks around the well.'

'What's happened in town? Do you know?'

'Only that Rex thought it was important enough to send out somebody with food.'

'I hope Nick makes it back to town safely,' returned January, and for the hour or so that he followed Mrs Walker through the marshy, bug-ridden woods, he related in an undertone all that had happened since last they had spoken in the darkness. She made an angry hiss when he told her that Ballou had in fact known not only about Cindy but about the women who had come before her: 'Damn him,' she said. 'Damn them both.'

'It was a hard choice to make,' said January. 'Ballou knew nothing of it until Drummond was here and established. I'm not saying I agree with his choice, and I know what I'd like to think I'd do in the same circumstances, but I don't, for sure, for certain, know what I'd actually do.'

'I'd thought better of him.' She said it like a curse. 'Rex is like a lot of abolitionists – and a good many Christians I've met. He sees things in terms of a single goal. You save black men before you save black women, and if sacrifices have to be made, it's the woman who's expected to make them.'

Cindy was waiting for them in a shallow cave under the bank of what had been, in the distant past, the bed of the Mississippi River. Some long-ago flood had cut it off as a sort of lake or bayou attached to the Yazoo. She was, January guessed, seventeen or eighteen years old, small and pretty with a snub-nosed face that looked as if its habitual expression was cheerful. When she sprang to her feet as Mrs Walker and January scrambled down the bank, however, he saw the marks of anxiety grooved deep around her mouth and her eyes.

'This is Ben,' Mrs Walker introduced them. 'He's been lookin' into who it was, who did for Mr Drummond – that is, 'til the white man he was workin' with got himself cracked on the head, and one of the dealers in town started claimin' he'd sold Ben to him . . .'

Cindy's eyes filled with real distress, as if she'd never heard of such perfidy before. 'Will he be all right?' she asked. 'Your master?'

Like everyone else, he reflected wryly, she thought it was the white man who ran the partnership.

'My friend,' he said, sitting down and unashamedly helping himself to the contents of Ballou's picnic basket. 'I'm a free man – I have my papers—'

'You lucky they ain't been tore up yet,' remarked Mrs Walker, and drew a cupful of water from a small basin, set in the back of the cave. There was food there, too, in baskets hung from roots that protruded from the walls and the low clay of its roof. January wondered if Ballou provided it from town, or if it had come from Drummond's farm.

'I've seen Charlie,' he said then, and gave her news of her son, while she clung to Mrs Walker's shoulder and wept.

'I did it for him,' she said, over and over. 'I did it for him . . . He said I wouldn't never see my boy again, 'less I did what he asked. So I did what he asked.'

As his mother had done, January reflected, when Michie Fourchet would tell her to go service one or another of his house guests who'd admired her beauty . . .

The thought snagged at his mind. *Olympe . . .*

That was why Olympe ran away when she was fourteen . . .

He remembered now. He'd tried for years to put it aside.

His dream returned to him, Olympe standing in the doorway of one of the maroon huts, her arms folded, her eyes bitter as black coffee. '*Maybe I don't want a thing to do with him,*' she had said. '*Or his . . .*'

'Did he hurt you?' asked January gently, and Cindy shook her head.

'No, sir. Not on purpose.' She wiped her eyes, her face relaxed with the peace of knowing, at least, that Charlie was alive and in good hands, even if it was in a sweltering hell-pit . . .

Hesitantly, he asked, 'Did he ever bring anyone with him?'

She shook her head. 'No, sir.'

'We'd been thinking,' January continued, 'Mr Sefton and I, that whoever killed Drummond – whoever sent him a note after the race, and lay in wait for him by the trail – might have been someone from his past, someone he knew in New York State, where he'd made enemies. You weren't the first woman he abused – according to his wife he'd made a habit of it. So there was the chance that he was killed by someone from New York State, who could have just walked back into town and taken the next steamboat for anywhere between Warrenton and Timbuktu. But the fact that my friend was attacked after he'd been asking questions about Drummond's past means that the killer was probably someone in either Vicksburg or Madison Parish.'

'Makes sense,' agreed Mrs Walker, and Cindy nodded, wide-eyed as if at a tale.

'Cindy, did Drummond speak to you at all of enemies in the parish, or in Vicksburg? Of people who would have done him ill?'

'No, sir.' She looked aside, and for a moment her dark eyes were a thousand years old. 'Mostly he didn't talk to me at all.'

In the thick belt of snags and brush along the water below them a horse nickered. January swung around, his heart in his throat, and Mrs Walker laid a hand on his shoulder. 'It's ours,' she said.

'Yours?'

'We found him in the woods,' explained Cindy. 'He's penned up down by the water. When we can finally get moving again, he can carry the boys – Randol and Charlie – and we can move faster.'

January drained the last of the ginger beer and rinsed the bottles with a little of the water from the basin. He stood up, bending to keep his head from colliding with the roof of the cave. 'Let's see him.'

The horse was Big Brownie.

The women had made a pen of brush and deadfalls. Saddle and bridle were hidden a little distance away, under a granny knot of snags that had in years past washed up out of the Old River at high water. Cindy scrambled into the pen, and smiled – for the first time – as the big stallion came up to her and rubbed his face against hers. She scratched his white forehead, then knelt before him and unwound the rough strips of torn calico that had been bound like bandages around his front legs.

Brownie's forelegs were cut, just above the hocks, a straight slash as if someone had razored the animal across the shins. The wounds had been carefully cleaned, and were beginning to heal.

January stood looking at them for a long time. Then he bent, and pulled up his trouser leg far enough to display an identical, bruised slash across his own shin.

'What happened?' exclaimed Cindy, straightening up. But Mrs Walker didn't ask.

Just looked, from January's leg to that of the horse, eyes narrowed with thought.

'Tripped on a trapline,' said January quietly. 'In the woods last night.'

'Horse can't get up the speed to hurt himself that bad on a trapline,' Mrs Walker said. 'Not in the woods.'

'No.' January climbed over the side of the pen, gently approached Big Brownie and patted his shoulder, then hunkered down to take a closer look at the cuts. Even in pain, as he must have been, the big stallion let January pick up his feet, turn them to a better angle of the light. 'You know whose horse this is?'

Both women shook their heads. After a moment, Mrs Walker said, 'I think he must have been Drummond's. We found him Monday, way up the bayou. His legs was pretty bad then.'

'The one Drummond was riding when he was killed. The one he galloped off on, in a full-tilt rage, from Haffle's field—' He stood up, as Big Brownie tried to nibble at his ear, as if he had a secret to tell.

But January already knew the secret. Olympe had told him.

'Can you take me back,' he said, 'to the place where it happened? I want another look at the trees there.'

He and Mrs Walker crossed Chickasaw Bayou as the birds were starting up their first waking calls of the morning, the moon down, the bayou barely a glimmer under starlight. Mrs Walker led him unerringly to the trace that led up the bluffs to Vicksburg, moving silent as a pair of shadows in the deeper shadows of the trees, and they waited in the darkness until the second wave of birdsong flowed through the woods, and slowly, slowly, trunks and leaves and brush emerged from the darkness.

Friday, the fourteenth of June.

Nobody was on the road from town this early. January smelled it when in the few cottages nearby – Julia Maury's among them – servants got the kitchen fires started for the day. In the dry weather, Ezekias Drummond's blood still stained the ground, though the passage of horses and foot travelers had obliterated whatever evidence the dirt of the track might once have given. But in the little glade itself, where the track ran through it, January found a sycamore tree whose bark bore a sharp thin gouge, as if struck with a razor, a foot or so above the ground. The big magnolia tree on the other side of the track bore the same gouge, deeper on the side toward town, where the braided trapline had dug when Big Brownie had run into it with the full weight of his gallop.

A little searching even yielded the stout branch around which one end of the line had been wrapped, so that the killer could yank it tight as the horse and rider neared.

'Trapline sounds like Roane Colvard,' said Mrs Walker. 'Doesn't it?'

'Except Colvard can't write. And I saw the young man just before the race, and then almost immediately after it in the show tent. But it sounds like someone who knew him well enough to learn about trapping from him – and who had access to his traplines.'

Mrs Walker was silent, studying the roadway where Big Brownie would have fallen hard after hitting the trapline full-speed. The roadway where Drummond would have been thrown from the saddle, stunning him, so that his killer could rush forth from hiding with a knife. Winded, on the ground, he'd have been an easy target for those first four wild stab-wounds.

After examining Big Brownie's cuts, January had slept for the remainder of the day in the cave by the Old River, still exhausted by his flight of the night before.

Slept, and dreamed of Olympe.

Olympe dressed in a high-waisted gown of white gauze, a grown woman's dress though at that time – the summer of 1811 – she was barely fourteen. The pearls St-Denis Janvier had given her gleamed like moons around her throat. Though she would never be as beautiful as their mother, with her simple *tignon* and long kid gloves she showed the promise of being a striking woman.

Thus dressed, she'd been introduced to St-Denis Janvier's good friend – and business associate – Arnaud Rabutin, who had kissed her hand and murmured, '*Enchanté*,' in admiration. Their mother had smiled in complicity and St-Denis Janvier – the owner of their cottage, the man who was paying for Ben's education and for the lessons on the piano that he so dearly loved – Janvier had relaxed, relieved that his wealthy friend was pleased. Olympe's face was like stone.

Then the dream had changed to Olympe in the dirty rags of her red calico dress in the maroon village, saying, 'I don't want a thing to do with him or his . . .'

Olympe saying, 'I won't ever go back . . .'

Olympe saying – he remembered now – 'I will kill him.'

He'd found her in the maroon village, after she'd run away, and she had said, '*I will kill him . . .*'

And she'd told him how she planned to do it.

There was a stretch of land along Bayou St John, where it ran past the low-lying meadows of the Allard Plantation just outside New Orleans – both January and his sister knew it well. The young men would go there in the gray fog of morning to fight duels or to ride races. M'sieu Rabutin would often do so, racing with his young son. Olympe had collected traplines from several of the fugitives in the maroon settlement, and had braided them into a tough, thin cord, nearly invisible when laid on the ground. '*I'll wrap one end around one of the oaks*,' she'd said to him, '*and the other around a cypress by the water, with a stick tied to it, to help me pull it tight when he rides by. It'll bring down the horse, and while he lies stunned on the ground, I'll cut his throat*.'

January, horrified, had begged her to put the thought away from her, and when appeal to the Fifth Commandment was met with derision, had fallen back on, '*You'll never get away with it!*'

'*I don't care if I get away with it!*' his sister had retorted. '*I will not be that man's whore!*'

She'd turned as if to run away then, and when January had grabbed her by the arms, struggling vainly for some other argument, she had looked into his face with that bitter close-lipped smile and said, '*You just want to keep on Michie Janvier's good side so you can stay in school. So he'll go on paying for your piano lessons, and for Michie Gomez to teach you medicine. Like Mama wants me to please him, so she can live in a nice house*.'

And the word *NO!* had stuck in his throat, as if rammed back down his gullet by those African-dark eyes. The words *M'sieu Janvier wouldn't do a thing like that . . .*

The words *Nor would I ever let him . . .*

At that point the headman of the fugitives, Suma, had taken Olympe aside into one of the huts, and when Olympe came out she'd agreed to return to New Orleans with her brother. He'd heard no more of murdering M'sieu Rabutin – who had taken a different concubine shortly after that, a much fairer-complected girl named Alys Bassineau, much to their mother's disgust – but for years he had watched Olympe nervously, knowing then what she was capable of. He had tried for years to go on thinking that St-Denis Janvier wouldn't push Olympe to become *plaçée* like their mother. But their mother had tried to introduce her to two other prospective 'protectors', both business associates of St-Denis Janvier, and in 1815 had borne another daughter, a beautiful quadroon princess: '*She'll train that one up from a pup to do what she wants*,' had jeered Olympe.

When Olympe was sixteen she'd run away to the voodoos, and January – deep in his studies then of surgery and music – had not seen her again until his return from France, nearly twenty years later.

Opening his eyes from his dream, he had smelled the swamp, and heard Cindy humming to herself as she climbed the trail to the cave with a couple of fish on a line, and he had recalled what she'd said.

'*It was for Charlie . . . I wasn't going to say no . . .*'

As his mother wasn't going to say no, when a man whom she barely knew took a fancy to her beauty and brought her to New Orleans to be his concubine. Freedom, and a life for her children – even if she understood from the beginning that it would mean handing her girl-children back into concubinage when her protector required it.

Swimming in a bayou full of alligators was the simple thing to do, to win and keep freedom. He understood that it could have been much, much worse.

Standing now in the pre-dawn stillness where Drummond had fallen, January said quietly, 'I saw Drummond's face when he read that note. He was half-blind with rage. I'm guessing it said something like, *Cindy has fled*. It wouldn't even have had to be true. Setting aside that no man's going to sit still for his women-folk to flout him, Cindy knew too much by then. Of course he'd ride for the cabin where she was hidden at a hell-for-leather gallop.'

'Roane Colvard could have found the cabin where she was,' agreed the guide. 'He traps this side of the river clear up past the Yazoo. But as you said, he can't write. And even if he could,' she added drily, 'and even if he wrote on that tree there, *Roane Colvard done it*, your word in court counts for nothing. Even if you could walk into a court, at this point, without bein' impounded by the sheriff like a stray ox and turned over to Guy Fenks . . .'

January shook his head, still looking at the torn-up undergrowth of the glade, the shadow of all that blood. *I have to get word to Ballou . . .*

Mrs Walker had spent most of the previous day scouting the edges of the woods, waiting near the sycamore tree for Ballou to appear. Ballou could get the lawyer Leeland out, to witness the marks on the trees, but those would be useless without further proof.

They only told him that the proof existed.

And where it would be.

'Not Colvard,' he said. 'He was in on it, to make sure Drummond got the note just after the race. The one who set the trap – who wrote the note – and did the killing – has to have been Rachel.'

TWENTY-FOUR

'Colvard checks his traps in the mornings.' Mrs Walker turned to follow the rising ground, away from Vicksburg and into the ravine-cut jumble of the Walnut Bluffs. 'He sets 'em as far west as Milliken's Bend, nine miles as the crow flies from his place. He'll be gone, all right.'

'Is there any way to get word to Ballou?' The quiet that reigned in this rough country behind the bluffs was broken only by bird-song and the occasional ruffling of the wind in the trees, but still January spoke in a whisper. The land, too broken to be much use for farming, was dotted with grazing cows. Far off he heard the crack of a rifle, where someone hunted for sport. Empty as these hills seemed, there could easily be someone close enough to hear his words, or to see a black woman and a black man making their stealthy way through the thickest of the vegetation, heading north.

'I want to know how Hannibal is. Who's treating his injuries, and how.'

'You're thinking Rachel Pryce got her sweetheart to slug him over the head?'

'Hired someone to do it,' said January grimly. 'People seem to think it was a black man who did the actual violence. Possibly her sweetheart hired him. Possibly one of her brothers.'

Mrs Walker turned her head sharply. 'I thought Cindy said they didn't know—'

'She said Drummond never brought them along. We have no way of knowing.'

He remembered Rachel's pallor and shakiness, both at the subscription ball and on the day of the funeral. He'd thought then that it was only the result of the laudanum she'd been taking for years.

'I think,' he went on slowly, 'and it's only me thinking, so far, I haven't any real proof – that Cindy wasn't the only woman Drummond was using these days. He made sure both his wife and his stepdaughter were drugged every night, to keep them from seeing who came and went. For a man who feels that women can be used like that, I think from there it was a short step to going to Rachel's room, and having her when she was too disoriented to resist. But I have no idea if the boys knew of this, or what they thought—'

'Or if they had her themselves.' Darkness that was more than mere surmise glinted in the woman's eyes. Certainly it was the first thing Olympe would have asked.

After a little silence he said, 'So I can't risk them finding out how much I know or what I think, until I have something solid in my hand.'

'And what's that going to be?' Her voice mocked him, as Olympe's had done. 'Anything you find and bring in to hand to Mr Cain's lawyer, Saul Drummond's sure to ask: *Who says he found that at Colvard's?* That note or trip line or bloodied knife . . . The answer's gonna be the same.'

'Which is why I've got to see what's there,' said January. 'Then I can get word to Ballou, to get word to Cain's lawyer, Leeland. Then Leeland comes out and "finds" it—'

'Butler Leeland is near eighty years old, and a sick man, I hear. You think he's going to ride all the way up to Lake Thompson, through the thick of the 'delta', just 'cause some black man says there's somethin' out there he needs to see?'

'Ballou thinks he will,' said January. 'Myself, I think the old man's just ornery enough to do it. But he won't have the stamina to make a search. I have to tell him where to look.'

Roane Colvard's cabin stood about a hundred yards from the edge of Lake Thompson, a body of water, like most of the lakes in the 'delta', whose size and depth varied with the season. From the marshy ground of the cypress forest, January could see only the clear sky over the lake, and the head-high forest of sedges that grew around its edge. The cabin, rough-built of logs in the American fashion, bore unmistakable signs of frequent immersion to the eaves of its roof.

A raft was tied behind it, in more or less open ground between the cabin and the outhouse. Presumably it was easier for the cabin's owner to load whatever he wanted to save onto the raft when the waters rose, than it was to construct a house on stilts as Drummond had done.

There was no stable, and no kitchen. A firepit close by the cabin's back door evidently accommodated whatever cooking the young trapper might have a taste for, though January observed that skulls, bones, paws and fish skeletons had all been deposited in a midden near the outhouse, not simply dumped around the log near the fire that would be the logical place to sit and eat. January approached the dwelling, scalp prickling with a sense of peril, while Mrs Walker remained in the shelter of the woods.

'I'm sorry, Ben,' she'd whispered. 'If there's trouble, I can't let myself be caught. Too many people need my skill in the woods. And I wouldn't be able to help you anyway.'

'Believe me,' said January, 'I understand. I won't be long.'

He circled the house, keeping to the thicker undergrowth that crowded up close on its rough walls. Neat racks stood all around it, on which hides were stretched: raccoon, squirrel, muskrat, fox, deer. Antlers of varying size made a sort of frieze, a foot below the shallow eaves. The roof probably consisted of oak shakes, invisible under a growing blanket of resurrection fern. A smokehouse stood to the south of the house, a big grindstone near the front door.

Someone is watching me. January felt his heart pounding. *There's someone here . . .*

Birds called on the lake: ducks, a heron, the scream of a red-tailed hawk. Down here in the low country cicadas drummed and throbbed in the trees. Not a breath, not a whiff of untoward sound. Yet January felt it, like a hand laid on his shoulder.

He stole up to the house, ready to bolt like a hare.

Stood beside the door, listening. Feeling exposed to a thousand watching eyes, from the murky cypress woods, the green wall of sedges.

Stepped inside.

Nothing. A narrow bed, made with a couple of very worn sheets and a cheap wool blanket folded across its foot. One table, one chair. On the table, a jar of oil and a bunch of feathers to grease traps, and guns. A bullet mold and a couple of boxes of shot, and a dish of lead scrapings taken when bullets were cast. A pottery bowl contained pieces of a gunlock, extra flints, trap springs, fishhooks and a tiny pincushion stuck full of pins. Another held scraps of tow and wadding, and a spool of thread. A shelf above the table sported two chipped queensware bowls and a plate, of the kind January recalled from his own slave-cabin childhood. A tin cup. A horn spoon.

Pegs driven into the wall held trapline. Black glistening coils of horsehair, braided thin for small snares – weasel, rabbit, muskrat. Steel traps, in graduated sizes: fox, badger, lynx, bear. Beside them, a massive hank of silk fishing line, barely as thick as a lady's hair but strong enough to land a six-foot alligator gar. Braided, it would still be nearly invisible.

Given the cost of such material, he couldn't imagine Colvard throwing twenty or thirty feet of it away. He searched every box, and beneath the mattress of the bed, feeling on him that terrifying unease, but found nothing save further evidence of the young man's thrift. Tools scrupulously cleaned, broken fragments of whetstone saved, dishes re-glued. String and horsehair put aside for repairs. Beside the door a firkin of gunpowder stood in a box of sand. The cabin was ceiled, so there had to be an attic of some kind above this single room, but there was no ladder in evidence, so January guessed it was unused. In any case, his whole being shrank from the idea of getting trapped up there . . .

He searched the smokehouse, and the outhouse as well. Nothing.

After a moment's thought he dug his blue bandanna from his pocket, slipped back into the house, and helped himself to about a half a cup of Colvard's gunpowder.

'I can't say I'm surprised,' he murmured, when Mrs Walker rejoined him in the woods. 'Rachel has to have been the one who set the trap. Colvard was at the circus, and he's probably a good enough shot to have killed Drummond with a rifle, rather than needing to stun him with a fall. But if Drummond had been shot, it would have been too easy for everyone to guess who *was* that good a shot, and who had reason to want him out of the way. Hence his being at the circus, where everyone in town could see him. Nobody was expecting to see Rachel there in the morning and I'm pretty sure her mother had no idea whether she was on the property or not.'

'And Saul and Boze was out on the point,' finished Mrs Walker.

'Waiting for Drummond to land in his skiff.' She froze, lifted her hand at some sound in the woods. Then she shook her head, and they moved on.

After a time she said softly, 'Sounds to me like nobody had no idea where Rachel was nor what she was up to – not then, not for years. Her mama worshippin' Drummond like some tin-pot god . . . What the hell was her daddy, her real daddy, thinkin', lettin' his daughter go off into the household of such a man?'

This was something you can't know, just from looking at a man, Rex Ballou had said . . . 'God knows,' said January. 'Joshua Pryce was part of that congregation, too – and he didn't seem to have wasted any time taking another "wife". Rachel had good cause to be angry.'

Silence fell between them, broken only by the drum of the cicadas, the whine of the gnats.

'Rachel must have searched her stepfather's pockets,' he went on at last, 'to make sure the note wasn't found on him – the note that probably said, *I am leaving – Cindy.* Can Cindy write?'

Mrs Walker nodded. 'Her mama was a housemaid. I think one of the little girls in that household taught Cindy, before she was sold. She'd have known about Cindy from Roane?'

'If Roane found Cindy's hiding place he may well have overheard Drummond speak her name. Once Drummond was dead, and Rachel got the note back, she had to get rid of the snare line, and fast, before anyone else came along. She probably needed to change her dress, unless she'd brought spare clothing. She didn't know when her brothers would be back to the house. If she was smart enough to rig up a trap like that, I think she's smart enough not to risk just throwing the trapline into the river. In low water like this there's too much chance it would surface someplace. What would you do with it, if you were her?'

'Throw it down the outhouse,' returned Mrs Walker immediately. 'White folks *never* look there.'

Ezekias Drummond had kept his skiff in a boathouse at the end of the bayou; Mrs Walker had the key to the little building's door. It was a long walk back to the bayou from the site of the murder, by the circuitous route that Mrs Walker chose, and when they passed the Lagoon she unearthed a calico dress and a head rag from a hidey-hole in the Indian farm. She had, January observed, a tin slave-badge and a pass establishing her as the property of Ezekias Drummond of Madison Parish, Louisiana, guaranteeing her an unpleasant stay in a slave jail if she were picked up by the pattyrollers, rather than a flogging and impoundment – and sale – by the state.

Or worse.

He himself spent the hour it took to row across the river glancing nervously all around the little boat, as if every raft, every flatboat, every steamboat and keelboat that shared the muddy current with them were alive with watching eyes. At the same time he knew this was foolish. With the sun dazzling on the water, and the comings and goings of rafts and keelboats, of steamboats and small skiffs like the one he rowed, it was nearly impossible to make out the occupants of any vessel, nor where that vessel was making to put in.

'You'll go back across and see if you can make contact with Ballou?' he asked, as he pulled out of the heavy flow of the big river and into the long, tangled zone of snags and deadfalls that fringed the bank.

'The boys on the ferry will know me,' she replied. 'They'll carry word, and get me out of town safe. I'll meet you back at the Indian farm tonight. You be sure to go up along the bluffs, and circle back to the place from the north.'

January blew his breath in a long sigh. 'Thank you. More than I can say.' The thought of separating from this tough little woman filled him with dismay – as much as the thought of crossing the river again after searching the Drummond farm, and working his way back through the rugged ravines beyond Vicksburg and back around to Chickasaw Bayou. But at this point he saw few other options, if Cain was to go free and lay protective claim to him. He had investigated crimes and puzzles in New Orleans on a number of occasions – never before had he been so conscious that in New Orleans, he was recognized as a member of a specific category of society, a *gen du couleur libré* – an actual person who had business walking around by himself. To the Americans, outside that shrinking enclave of French society, every person of color was a slave. In some states – Mississippi was one – even freedmen like Rex Ballou needed specific permission by the state legislature to be considered permanent residents. In New Orleans, January couldn't testify in a court, but he could ask questions of people he met. Here, without a white protector, he was nothing. Worse than nothing, he was worth at least a thousand dollars to anyone who could convince a buyer that he was property – and most buyers these days didn't take much convincing. His dream-vision returned to him, of the green safe areas of the map being chewed away by the army ants of white commerce and white greed. Of the roads north to safety gradually being cut . . .

One thing at a time.

He'd had only a little dried fish and some bread to eat and the mid-afternoon sun smote him, the heat suffocating and the glare on the water among the forest of snags dazzling. And this woman in the boat with him did this, came to this place of danger, twice or thrice a year; sheltered in the thickets and caves of the 'delta' marshes with one ear always cocked for the pattyrollers; watched endlessly . . .

To lead people out of slavery. One by one.

Heaven itself must stand in awe of her, he thought. *And angels salute her with their burning swords.*

He worked the boat in as close to the snags of the shore as he could, and climbed gingerly out onto a half-sunk tree, keeping a wary eye out for cottonmouths. The current of the river was generally too strong for gators, but here in the shallows snakes were always a danger. Mrs Walker pushed the boat back with the oars, working her way downstream along the bank; they'd agreed she'd leave the skiff for him close to the 'downstream' ferry landing, concealed in the brush of the riverbank. From the mouth of Chickasaw Bayou, the current had borne the skiff down just above the 'main' ferry landing, almost directly opposite the Drummond house. From where he concealed himself in the brush and snags on the riverbank, January could see the ferry was gone, across the river in Vicksburg.

He settled down to wait.

And thought about Rachel Pryce.

Sixteen years old. How old had she been, he wondered, when her parents had first joined Ezekias Drummond's New York congregation? What *had* Drummond preached, when he spoke his true beliefs and not what he thought the white men of Madison

Parish wanted to hear? What had seemed to him an idle question from Hannibal was actually a very important one.

She would have been seven, when her mother had been 'chosen' as an auxiliary bride for the head of the congregation – had her father kept her with him then? What sort of beliefs had *he* pursued, in his own congregation after the schism? A child, January knew, will accept almost anything, if it knows no other world. He himself had seldom questioned why Simon Fourchet had the right to tie him up, at the age of five or six, and beat him nearly to death with a broom handle simply for coming into the house. At the age of thirteen, when her mother had received a letter asking her to come to Mississippi to become Drummond's bride for a second time, what other choice had the girl had? Evidently her father's second wife didn't offer to take her in. Did Joshua Pryce know – or guess – or care – what sort of man Ezekias Drummond was?

Rachel Pryce was a big, strong girl, capable of rowing a skiff across the low river and walking the distance necessary to get her upstream if the little boat was swept off course. Raised in the western woods of New York State, she'd have easily picked up a trapper's skills from her sweetheart, if she hadn't known them already. He remembered how she'd watched her mother in that small front room, how she'd steered aside questions about her true father and instead presented arguments for this or that member of the congregation – and had slipped in remarks that implied she'd been at the farm all Saturday morning. Fuddled with opium, her mother was in no state to contradict her – nor to notice if one of her daughter's dresses dropped out of sight. Certainly not in the reverberating aftermath of Drummond's death.

Easy. Easy.

After long listening to the dead stillness of the hot afternoon, with no sign yet of the ferry among the dozens of craft, large and small, bobbing like shards of wood on the yellow-brown waters behind him, January picked his way to the edge of the batture, looked across at the line of cottonwoods that hid the Drummond house. He'd brought Rose's spyglass with him on his journey up the Mississippi with the circus, but it was back in Hannibal's portmanteau—

And he closed his eyes again, and whispered a prayer that his friend was still alive, that Ballou was looking after him, and that something hideous hadn't happened to the barber – the kind of thing that could too easily befall a free man of color in this part of the world . . .

An explosion split the air like the crash of thunder.

Even at a distance of three-quarters of a mile, he heard someone at Drummond's scream.

As smoke began to billow from the deadfalls of the riverbank, a mile to the south, three forms burst from the wall of cottonwoods around the Drummond house, first pointing toward the smoke and then running toward it.

January let them get a hundred yards on their way before he stepped out of his own cover, and began to walk swiftly toward the Drummond farm.

None of the three turned to look back at him.

Mrs Walker had made good use of Roane Colvard's gunpowder.

This, he thought, *had better be fast.*

TWENTY-FIVE

January drew up a bucket of well water and set it near to hand before investigating the outhouse, though like everything else on the Drummond property that facility was clean, solid, and well-made. By the look of the wood – and the glint of the nails that held it together – it had been taken apart and moved to a new location within the last year. On the other hand, in case of the unexpected, he didn't want to lay down a scent-trail for Drew Hardy's dogs the next time they happened to come by the area.

And though the convenience was built solidly and its pit dug deep – well-built, well-drained and well-ventilated – it was still an outhouse in the Mississippi Valley in the middle of a hot June. Interestingly – and fortunately, as far as January was concerned – there was only one. On every plantation and farm he'd ever visited – certainly in most dwellings in New Orleans – there were invariably two: one for the family, one for the house-servants.

Leaving the door open for light, January raised the hinged board that served as a seat, and observed that the place – again, like every other House of Office he'd ever encountered – served a secondary function as the repository for broken and disused household items. In the shadowy light he made out the fragments of broken plates and cups, a small tin pail missing its handle, several scattered piles of walnut shells, an unbelievable number of medicine bottles (*If Mrs Drummond is taking opium daytimes as well as nights, not surprising she'd get rid of the bottles where her husband couldn't see them . . .*) And, on the side of the general effluvia and clearly visible (*Thank God!*), a tangle of what looked like wire-thin black rope.

Silk fishing line, braided into a twenty-foot coil.

He washed his hands swiftly in the bucket, emptied it in the garden. Then he went quickly through the house, observing that the boys slept together in the half-story above the main block while Rachel's room was in the wing at the other side of the building. The narrow stair that ascended to her room was just outside the door of her parents'. He found four bottles of Godfrey's Cordial – a mixture of brandy, molasses and opium – in the kitchen cupboard, and two of Kendal's Black Drop (which Hannibal, formerly a connoisseur of such potions, claimed was far stronger) concealed under the mattress of the room shared by Mrs Drummond and her husband.

At the back of a drawer in the same room January found several short lengths of rope, and a leather riding crop. And that, thought January, sickened, in the bedroom of a man who would never lay such an implement to any of his beloved horses.

There was virtually nothing in Rachel's room – a narrow bed, an open shelf for her two dresses and several folded sets of drawers and petticoats. A chamber pot, a sewing basket and a Bible. January checked under the mattress, but found no sign that a bloodied dress had been hidden there—

Did she burn it already? He counted days in his mind as he hastened down the stairs to the ground floor of that little wing. The dress could be cut to pieces, fed a little at a time into the stove. He guessed she could have shoved the entire dress into the flames with her mother in the room and Mrs Drummond wouldn't have noticed.

If it's here I have to find it. Sheriff Preston was no fool. Stabbing someone like that would have left its traces on the killer's garments – *Like that ridiculous glove Maury claims to have found, soaked in chicken-blood probably.* The claim that Rachel must have destroyed her bloodstained dress would be met with the counterargument that Cain could just as easily have destroyed a bloodstained jacket or trousers – *And we're back to proving a negative.* January cursed the legal system that rendered it impossible for him to go back to the sheriff himself with the trip line – that would not even admit his witness in court. Butler Leeland, old and sick as he was, would have the wits, January guessed, to lead and guide a search party to check the outhouse and wherever the dress was hidden – if it still existed – rather than start in with the claim, *I know the trip line'll be in the outhouse and the dress in the . . .*

In the where?

Smokehouse. Roane Colvard's simple cabin sprang to his mind, the tall column of the hollowed tree standing behind it surrounded by a pile of cut wood.

Nobody goes near the smokehouse from Christmas to first frost. If not the smokehouse itself, the woodpile next to it. A dozen errands take her out to the yard every day; she could make a fire there unnoticed and burn the dress a little at a time. The smokehouse stood apart from the main house, behind the chicken runs. *Boze has enough work in the stables he's kept busy for hours at a time, the girl's on her own . . .*

He stepped out the back door of the house, and found himself face to face with Rachel Pryce and looking down the barrel of her rifle.

He saw her face tense up and flung himself sideways without even drawing breath, and the bullet buried itself in the porch rail. The girl had a pistol hung around her neck on a ribbon, like old-time pirates used to carry them, and January bolted for the tangled bottomlands of the point that lay beyond the line of cottonwoods. Behind him he heard Rachel scream 'Boze!' and cry out something else, and as a black man he had a fairly good idea what kind of an accusation a white girl would fling at him if she suspected he was getting too close to the truth.

Besides, he *had* broken into the house . . .

Cross the point. Get to the batture, lose yourself in the snags . . .

She'll send Boze for the pattyrollers . . .

He dodged into a thicket of swamp laurel, flattened to the ground and crawled. Heard Boze away to his right. Movement in the matted canes beneath him, he pulled his hand away as a four-foot copperhead coiled back beneath a deadfall tree, opened its mouth and hissed. January backed off, deeper into the tangled vines that covered a dying cypress. *If I can keep hid until he's farther off . . .*

Two egrets broke cover in a flurry of wings off to his left and he heard at the same moment someone coming into the thicket behind him, a heavy body swishing through the leaves. *Damn it, where'd they come from . . .?*

Lie still and hope they miss you?

If they trip over you you're dead. She'll make sure you don't survive for her brothers to come back . . . if these aren't her brothers on your trail now. If her brothers haven't been with her in this from the start . . .

It's got to be less than a mile straight west to the river again, and better concealment on the banks.

With a silent curse – and a prayer to whoever might be the patron saint of fugitives (*Is there one?* he wondered) – he edged himself as silently as he could in the direction of the river.

'There he is!' yelled a man.

Damn it—

January launched himself to his feet and ran.

A gun cracked behind him and the bullet tore through his sleeve, grazed his arm like the stroke of a red-hot poker on his flesh. He staggered, saw someone – a black man – running at him from his right, and plunged into the trees, willing himself not to feel the pain of what he knew was only a superficial wound. No dogs – not yet . . . Leaping fallen trees, praying he wouldn't stumble in the vines or step on another copperhead – *If I can get enough distance on them I can lose them on the batture . . . They'll get the others, hunt the point for me, damn it, damn it . . .*

The men behind him were fast (*They haven't just rowed across the Mississippi and walked ten miles before that . . .*), closing the distance. *They're not going to ask for an explanation, they're not going to let you speak. Get to the river, you can swim . . .*

You'll drown in the current.

He knew that. *Is that going to be worse than being beaten to death?*

Rose, I'm sorry.

They caught him a few yards short of the waterside. He heard the other man panting, closing the distance though he dared not look back, felt him running just a yard behind his left shoulder, then a foot. *Just make it to the water . . .*

The nearer pursuer lunged sideways, crashed into him, threw him to the ground, and then they were both on him. January kicked, punched, twisted like a landed fish; grabbed the man's wrist (*It's Roane Colvard . . . long black hair tangled in his eyes . . .*) as a knife flashed above him, and someone kicked him from behind, the black man . . .

January was dragged to his feet and Colvard snarled, 'Fuckin' bastard—'

January kicked him, hard, deflecting a murderous lunge with the knife, and the black man – a ragged Hercules – wrenched his arm behind him and shoved him toward the tangle of snags and water by the river. Colvard staggered to his feet again, scooped up his knife as the black man dragged January to the water, waist-deep, grabbed his hair, and thrust his head under. January kicked, writhed, struggled with the broken shards of submerged branches breaking and stabbing under his feet. His free hand grabbed at the wood and he gouged it at the powerful body bent over his, fought an involuntary gasp as the man twisted his arm harder, shoving him deeper into the murky water.

He stabbed again and this time twisted free, sobbing as his head broke the surface. His opponent grabbed him by the throat, wrenched him to his knees as Colvard came up, knife raised. 'God damn bastard—' the Indian snarled.

January yelled, 'I didn't touch her!' And then, seeing blind murder in the young man's eyes, added, 'And neither did my master!'

Colvard checked. 'You lyin'—'

'What did she tell you?'

The young trapper stood for a moment, looking at him, knife in hand and thigh-deep in the black mud of the churned-up water, but his eyes had changed. Asking himself, maybe, about what Rachel *had* told him.

January said, 'Was it you gave that note to the boy, to give Drummond?'

The anger – the blind rage to protect – eased back another degree. This was a man, January saw, who would kill in hot blood but not in cold.

A little uncertainly, Colvard said, 'How'd you know about that?'

'You know what it said?'

Colvard thought about it for another moment, then said to the black man, 'Let him up, Quinto.'

'*Quinto?*' January had to grab hold of the nearest dead tree, to get to his feet. And hold it, to stay on them. He looked back at Colvard. 'You know what that note was? Or where Miss Pryce was the morning her stepfather was killed?'

The two men, Indian and black, traded an uncertain glance. Colvard started to say, 'What the hell business is it—'

'You ever ask yourself,' January went on, 'why she was suddenly claiming she'd been assaulted by the man who was asking questions about who'd have reason to kill Ezekias Drummond? About the man who was keeping her apart from you?'

He didn't know. He could see it in Colvard's dark eyes. *He didn't know.*

'Go look down the outhouse,' he said quietly. 'You'll find all that fishing line that you've been missing, braided together into one line strong enough to trip a galloping horse. Go look at the glade on the bayou road north of town, by the big magnolia tree just before the road rises, where a man would push a horse faster to take the hill. The ground's still stained with blood and the trees on either side of the road are cut from the trip line being stretched between. If you check in the smokehouse – or the woodpile behind it – you may find part of the dress she was wearing that afternoon, if she hasn't burned it all—'

'You're lyin'.' Colvard's voice was uncertain and soft.

January met his eyes. He had nothing left to lose, challenging a white man, accusing a white girl. 'Go look.'

Quinto spoke, a surprisingly light-timbred tenor for a man his size and with speech surprisingly clear: the man had been a valet, January remembered, and not a cotton-hand. 'That's what you were doing at our place this morning? You thought you'd find the trip line there? I was in the attic,' he added. 'I watched you the whole time. I've been hiding up there two weeks now.'

'That's what I was doing.'

'You're trying to clear a *slave-dealer* of murder?'

'I'm trying to clear an innocent man of murder,' said January. 'A man who saved my life, and my partner's – I'm a free man, by the way, Pinkerton isn't my master. It's a long story. But—'

Running feet crashed in the undergrowth, and Rachel Pryce stumbled from the trees, rifle in her hands. She stopped, her eyes flicking from January's face to Colvard's and then Quinto's.

Without waiting for any of them to speak, she gasped, 'You'd believe this lying . . . this lying *fiend* sooner than you'd believe . . .'

'While you're asking her what she was doing Saturday morning when Drummond was killed,' added January gently, '*if* you're going to ask her – ask her the real reason she would want to kill her stepfather.'

Rachel stared for a long moment into her sweetheart's eyes, her face like brittle stone. Then like brittle stone she broke, turning her face away, her whole body shaking, and started to cry. Not the flamboyant tears of one who seeks pity, but hard-faced, gripped with pain and shame that can be tolerated no more. She dropped the rifle and started to flee, but Colvard moved swift as a snake and caught her arm. She tried to pull free, the sobs coming stronger until her body convulsed with the violence of grief bordering on nausea. When she couldn't flee she only stood, weeping and shaking, as January had seen girls on the auction block weep without a sound, when the dealers would strip them naked before the eyes of the buyers.

Colvard gathered her against him and it was as if an iron skeleton broke within her flesh. She pressed her face to his shoulder, clung to him as if unable to stand, tighter and tighter, neither able to speak.

January touched Quinto on the arm, and together the two men retreated into the deadfall jungle of the batture, leaving the lovers alone.

TWENTY-SIX

'You've been hiding at Roane Colvard's, all this time?'

'He's a good boy, Roane,' said Quinto. 'He hates the planters. They came in and took the land away from his tribe; hates the land-dealers that turned his father and his uncles into drunkards whoring for the white men, and the slave-dealers that drag in men like me, and you. They've ruined the land, he says. Tore it up, cut the trees, killed the game. It'll never be what it was.'

He took a clean bandanna from his pocket, when January pulled his arm out of his torn shirtsleeve to look at the smarting gash that Colvard's bullet had left. 'Lemme see that . . . Roane's not an educated man, but he sees what they've done. He found me sleeping in one of those old farms in the swamp, and he's kept me at his cabin, waiting for the hoo-rah to die down a little—'

'Why?' asked January. 'There's a reward of five hundred dollars out for you. That's four times what anyone around here makes in a year. The best thing you could do for yourself is to get out of here now.'

'We're lyin' low.' The valet shook his head, and wrapped the bleeding cut tight. 'When the shoutin' dies down we'll take the canoe up the Sunflower River to the Tennessee border. But first I got to go back across to Madison Parish, and get my girl.'

And, when January raised his brows, remembering that Quinto had a reputation as a womanizer: 'Dulcie.' Quinto's voice, his face, his body changed at the mention of her name. 'My baby girl. She's nursemaid at Indian Mound. And thank God that swine Maury doesn't know she's mine—'

'Nursemaid . . .' ('*At least Mrs Drummond is spared the humiliation of lying awake at night listening while her husband disports himself with his daughter's nursemaid . . .*')

January took a deep breath, rage flooding over him at the recollection of the girl Dulcie, standing on tiptoe outside his cell to give him hot water to wash his wound. She's what? Fifteen? Sixteen?

Older than Olympe, when their mother had tried to push her into the bed of one of St-Denis Janvier's business friends.

The age at which the daughters of planters were urged to become the wives of their fathers' friends' sons – or their fathers' friends. In Paris the daughters of the demimonde started being brought to the public balls at the Opera at that age, to the salons of this or that elegant courtesan for their mothers or aunts to show them off, seeking protectors as the *plaçées* of New Orleans sought them . . .

And none of them with any more voice, any more choices, any more alternate ways to make a living than Olympe had had, or Rachel. At least Olympe had had the voodoos to run away to.

Dulcie had nothing.

He shut his eyes, let the anger roll over him and past him, as he'd gotten bitterly, savagely used to letting it roll past for all the years of his life. Anger and pity.

'I've seen her,' he said at last. 'Spoken to her. Almost two weeks ago, when the pattyrollers got me in mistake for you.'

'How'd she look?' There was no mistaking the eager love in Quinto's voice. When January had told him about their brief conversation the valet shook his head and said, 'She needs to be more careful. If Maury found out she was my daughter, I wouldn't put it past him to put word around that he'll sell her down the river for a field hand, unless I come in. He'd do it, too.'

Then he, too, was quiet, letting anger pass. 'So what's it to you,' he asked after a time, 'to take up for this dealer Cain? You're a free man, you say. You think you're never going to end up in his hands? He's innocent, you say – you think he doesn't deserve hanging, for all the souls he's traded into Hell? Deserve it more than Drummond's poor daughter? He was doing her, wasn't he? Drummond. Him with his mistress down by the river—'

'Tell me about her.' January pulled his shirt straight, and listened, but couldn't even hear the voices of Colvard and Rachel. The sounds that came across the water to them from the river were faint and far off: the churning of the paddle wheels, the shouts from raftsmen, as they pointed at the clearing plumes of smoke from the explosion that Mrs Walker had set off to draw out the inhabitants of Drummond's house.

'And I won't end up in Cain's hands, even if he goes free,' he added. 'I know the man, as my friends know him, Pinkerton and Rex Ballou in town. Cain is getting out of the business, changing his way of life. He won't be back on selling men the river.'

It was a safe assertion. Even if Cain weren't hanged for murder – even if this Mr Poger didn't appear in Vicksburg until after the hearing – the swirl of rumor would be enough to endanger any future efforts to smuggle slaves north by that route.

And a safer assertion than the truth.

'He's lying.'

'I don't think so. I heard him say this to Ballou well before he was arrested, before any of this ever arose. It was on Cindy's account that he was arrested, you know. Drummond was keeping her there a prisoner; he had her child locked up at another place of his.'

Quinto gaped at him. '*Bastard—*'

'Cain found the cabin where Drummond kept her, near the mouth of the bayou, Saturday morning. He got her out of there, moved her up to a cave under Haynes Bluff, then rode back to town and beat the living crap out of Drummond in front of pretty much everyone in Warren County. And – in front of pretty much everyone in Warren County – said he'd kill him if their paths ever crossed again.'

'And her child?'

'He'll be all right.' January hoped this was going to be true. 'We're trying to get him now, Mr Ballou and me.'

'Damn,' whispered the valet. 'Damn. We didn't know that – just that he was keeping a woman at one of his hunting cabins near the mouth of the bayou. Roane and me, we found his tracks, and heard him speak to her once or twice. But we wasn't about to get any closer to ask questions. You ever hear him preach? God knows what Mr Ballou saw in him, to keep a man like that his friend. When we went checking traps Sunday afternoon we saw she was gone. If we'd known. . .'

'Did Roane tell Miss Rachel about it?'

Quinto nodded. 'Wednesday afternoon. Mrs Drummond nods

off pretty soon after dinner most days, as soon as Mr Drummond went back to the ferry, and then Miss Rachel would walk down to the riverbank, or into the swamp, to meet Roane. Roane said when he told her, she cursed something surprising in a preacher's daughter.'

'And it was after this that Mr Colvard missed his fishing line?'

Quinto shook his head, with an expression of surprise. 'That was weeks before.'

'So she's been planning it,' said January softly. 'Planning for a while. She knew he liked to gallop. It was just finding a way to make sure she'd know when and where he'd be passing. Did she give Mr Colvard a note to have someone give Drummond after the race?'

'He thought it was – I don't know, something about her leaving his place. She'd been talking about it,' he added. 'Myself, I saw nothing but trouble from it if she did. He blacked her eye once, six months ago, when Roane first asked her to marry him. Mr Riley, my master at River Grove, spoke of it. He'd often talk at bedtime of what was going on in the Parish. Not long after that Drummond rode out to Roane's place with the pattyrollers, and warned Roane he'd horsewhip him if he tampered with his "daughter". I'd laugh,' he added bitterly, 'if it wasn't Miss Rachel we were talking of . . . or any girl, really.'

He was silent for a minute, staring at his big, heavy-knuckled hands. 'I ain't sayin' I'm a saint myself or anything,' he added quietly. 'And God knows I've broke my share of commandments, and I've lain with my share of girls not much older than Dulcie or Miss Rachel. But not like that.'

No, thought January. With his handsome features and his pleasant voice, and the easy friendliness of his manners, Quinto had probably never had to coerce a woman in his life.

'And what did Miss Rachel tell Roane,' he asked softly, 'about why he needed to kill my friend?'

Quinto looked aside at that, his lips tightened with shame.

'I assume that's what you and he were trying to do. On the subject of who deserves what, she must have known that with Mr Pinkerton out of the way I'd be impounded to the jail, held for the next of kin . . . or sold off to pay probate costs.'

When the valet still didn't reply, January went on, 'I'm not saying Mr Drummond didn't deserve what he got. But I am saying Mr Pinkerton didn't deserve it – and right now I don't know whether he's alive or dead, a man who has been like my brother, who has saved my life and only came up into this country to keep vermin like Fenks off me. He was only asking questions. And I sure as hell didn't deserve what I've gone through for the past twenty-four hours.'

'She said your friend tried to rape her.'

January nodded, unsurprised. 'And then when you and Roane showed up at the house just now, when I ran off, did she claim that I'd tried to rape her, too?'

'I'm sorry.' Rachel stepped through the brush, her eyes red, her nose swollen like a small potato from weeping. She sniffled, and wiped her nose on a bandanna, and sniffled again. 'What I did was wrong. To your friend, I mean. I was afraid . . .'

Roane emerged from the foliage behind her, his face grave with pain. 'I would have stood by you,' he said softly, 'without lies. And I will stand by you now. Just please don't lie to me again.'

Will a woman who has grown up surrounded by lies be able to learn not to take that road? January wondered.

Can people really change?

Rachel whispered, 'I won't,' in her soft crumble of a voice. She turned to January. 'I'm not sayin' it to excuse myself,' she added. 'But that first day, that first couple of days . . . It's like I couldn't think straight. I knew that medicine he gave me and Mama was bad – it's laudanum, isn't it? I don't think I slept that first night, nor the second, I was so sick. And then Mr Pinkerton came around, askin' questions, talkin' to the boys all quiet in the corner, askin' Mama . . .'

'The boys didn't know about you and Mr Drummond, did they?'

She looked aghast at the idea. 'Good Lord, no! And I think if I'd told them they wouldn't have believed.'

Her hands shook as she brushed the lank, light-brown hair from a forehead washed in sweat. 'I thought – I swear it was the first thing I thought. That if anybody found what I'd done, they'd come after Roanie too. They'd hang him as well as me. Nobody'll believe he didn't know. I am so sorry he had Quinto hurt your friend.'

'I'll do what I can to put things right.' Roane tightened his grip around Rachel's waist. 'I'll go into town tonight, Ben, and see how the land lays. And she's right – Rachel's right. That first couple days after it happened, she wasn't herself.'

'That was the laudanum,' said January softly. 'You haven't had it since?'

Rachel shook her head. 'He'd make me take it. Stand over me when he poured it out. Saul and Solly tried to talk him out of it, but he'd usually send them out of the room. By that time of the evenin' I was feelin' pretty poorly anyway, and Mama would make a fuss if I said I didn't want to. I just . . . I just got so tired of fighting both of them.'

'Did your mama know? Or suspect?'

'No.' The girl sighed, and pushed her hair aside again. 'I told her – I tried to talk to her – about Mr Drummond coming into my room in the middle of the night, and getting in bed with me. She said I was dreaming. She said *she'd* dreamed about him doin' the same, while she was still living with my daddy, my real daddy . . . I couldn't talk about it.' Her eyes squeezed shut, leaking tears, and Roane tightened his arms around her, worried and confused and, January suspected, over his head in waters he had never suspected existed, but ready and willing to help.

'She slapped me,' she whispered. 'Slapped me for lyin'. I thought if I spoke of it to the boys, they'd do the same. An' Mr Drummond . . . Mama loves him. She still loves him. She'd sit me down and tell me about a hundred times about all those ladies in the Bible, that was "in the house" of some patriarch or other, and that he had a husband's rights over 'em, a master's rights. And how it was an honor.'

She shook her head again, unable to go on.

Then after a long time she whispered, 'I had to get out of there. I had to get out. He'd ride with Injun Tom in the militia and drink with him, but he said he'd kill me, 'fore he'd let me marry any of Injun Tom's get. I knew he'd never let me go.'

She turned her face to Roane's shoulder again, trembling once more, shame and grief and terror. Olympe, thought January again, had had the maroon village to run to, and the voodoo queen, Marie Saloppé, who had taken her in as a pupil: a community to which to flee. This girl had had no one.

No wonder she had struck out in terror.

'Was it true what you said,' asked Quinto softly, 'about Mr Cain changing his way of life? Leaving the slave-trade, leaving the valley?' His velvet-brown eyes went to Rachel as he spoke, worriedly, but the girl waved his words aside.

'It don't matter. Roane is right. Mr Cain – I'm glad if it's true,' she added, looking up with a shy fragment of a smile, '—and he has seen God's light – God's *real* light, not what Mr Drummond said – and is turnin' from the wicked path he's walked . . . But it doesn't matter if he goes on sellin' men into slavery and smokin' and drinkin' and chasin' after Mrs Maury, like Mr Maury says he did. He didn't do *this*. Me keepin' silent about it because he's a slave-dealer is just the same as Mr Maury makin' up lies because he's jealous. I just . . .'

Her hand went to the long brown fingers that rested on her shoulder, closed around them tight. 'I gave Roanie that note, sayin' that girl of Mr Drummond's had left his cabin. I told him to pay some pickaninny to hand it to Mr Drummond, right after the race – told him not to let nobody see. He didn't know what was in it, he doesn't read real well.'

By the arch of Roane's eyebrows January guessed that *real well* in this context meant *at all*.

'But that was all he did. All he knew. I told him to stay at the circus, that I'd find him there later, so nobody could say he had anything to do with it. But I felt so sick, and so scared, and all of a sudden your friend starts askin' questions . . . All I could think of was that nobody'll believe Roanie didn't know. I am so sorry Quinto hurt your friend.'

'I'll find what I can about your friend this evenin'.' Roane glanced at the slant of the shadows in the brazen light, at the glare of the sinking sun on the river. 'And about that polecat Fenks. If – if things are bad, I swear to you, Ben, I'll at least get you up the Sunflower with Quinto and Miss Dulcie, and take you across to Tennessee. And then I will come back.'

He turned Rachel within his arms, to look into her face. 'Rachel, I swear I will come back. I will stand by you. I won't let you face this alone.'

She nodded, and pressed her face to his shoulder, like a shabby backwoods Romeo and Juliet. *Facing darkness those silly star-crossed Veronese lovers never dreamed of*, reflected January. Darkness that nobody spoke of, nobody wrote of.

Does she trust him?

Or does she just assume that he will cheat her, the way everyone in her life has cheated her, because that's the way the world is?

Quinto sighed. 'It's a damn shame,' he said, 'we can't just go into town and say that preacher killed him. I mean, he's dead, he can't get hanged for it—'

'He's a damn preacher,' said Roane, exasperated. 'Preachers don't go around killin' each other—'

'Whoa,' said January, remembering everything Hannibal had said about preachers in Ireland. 'What preacher?'

Roane looked as if he were surprised January hadn't known about this.

Quinto said, 'The preacher we found three days ago, dead in the woods.'

TWENTY-SEVEN

It was Levi Christmas.

He'd been shot through the head.

Now THAT, reflected January, *was a man who truly deserved what he got.*

'He was a rogue,' he said. 'A confidence trickster.' He leaned on his shovel, looked across the shallow grave in the clear light of the following morning at Quinto. 'He stole the Tabernacle money from the Reverend Bickern Saturday afternoon – and I don't see any sign of that red leather bag it was in. When I met him first, he was masquerading as an abolitionist preacher, trying to lure slaves into "escaping"—'

'So he could sell them?' Quinto's mouth twisted bitterly.

'Better than that. He'd "sell" them at six different small towns up and down the river, then they'd "escape", meet him outside town, he'd "sell" them again . . . and eventually kill them so they couldn't tattle on him. He'd slit their bellies open before dumping them in the river, so they wouldn't blow up and float.'

Quinto whistled softly. 'Your friend Cain's lookin' better by the day.'

Roane was back at the cabin with Rachel when they returned. Rachel was pale and sweating from a wave of sickness but assured them, as January and Quinto came in, 'They're getting less awful. I actually slept a little last night. Mama . . .' She hesitated, and winced. 'Mama's still trying to convince me there's no harm in taking "medicine" all day, the way she does.'

'It'll get better,' January promised. 'It takes a long time. Even after you stop being sick, you'll find yourself hit by darkness, blue-devils fifty times worse than what you've ever known, for months, maybe years. But in time, those pass, too. My friend Mr Pinkerton's done it. Stay busy. Make friends. Pray. You'll have to help her with that, Roane.' He looked at the young man, sitting anxiously on a corner of the table, holding Rachel's hand. 'Be patient with her. It's as if she'd had her leg broken, and healed short.'

'There, see?' He managed a smile, which Rachel managed to return. 'It's all just a broken leg, honey.' He kissed her hand, then leaned to kiss her mouth.

'It'll be a hard road,' warned January. 'Harder than any you've ever walked.'

'There speaks a man,' returned Roane with a crooked grin, 'who never grew up in the same house with my pa.'

It had been full dark the night before when Rachel and the three men had returned to the trapper's cabin on Lake Thompson – far too dark to dig up shallow graves in the woods. Colvard had gone on into Vicksburg to learn the news of Hannibal, while January walked the mile back to the Lagoon, listening behind and around him for pattyrollers and dogs. There he'd learned from Eliza Walker the same news that Colvard brought back to the cabin long after midnight: that the fiddler had regained consciousness, and, upon learning from Julia Maury the details of January's 'sale', had immediately sent for the sheriff and instituted proceedings against both Guy Fenks and Cornelia Passmore.

'And of course they've both left town,' added Hannibal, when January – accompanied by Roane Colvard, just to be on the safe side – finally walked into the downstairs bedroom behind the barbershop on Clay Street on Saturday afternoon. 'No sign yet of Mr Poger.'

'Mrs Passmore left only this morning,' affirmed Mrs Maury, who had been sitting beside the bed wringing out a cloth in a basin of cold water for him when the men had come in. 'I would never have suspected her of such – such *perfidy* . . . Except that before she left, she gave me a letter to bring to Mr Pinkerton, that reveals a degree of familiarity with . . . well . . .'

She blushed furiously, while Hannibal groped for the folded sheet that lay on the white linen counterpane. Under Julia's damp compress his forehead was ridged with pain, and he looked haggard and ashen; January made a mental note to ask Ballou if any of the local doctors had come in and bled him. The curtains were drawn, and Hannibal squinted and flinched a little as he tried to read the note, then passed it to Mrs Maury.

'*My dearest Hannibal,*' she read. '*The sucker-bait you're looking for is named Kitty O'Toole, she works mostly at the House of Parliament—*'

'That's down on Levee Street near the wharves,' provided Hannibal.

'*—and is silly and greedy enough to* – um, I'm not sure what she means here but I'm sure it isn't nice . . . *for two dollars, let alone tell you, for that sum, what she was doing Saturday morning. I'm sure it's what Levi Christmas paid her to drop Bickern's red leather valise out the window. Please extend my apologies to Ben. It is a harsh world, and a woman must live.*'

January stifled his observation about Mrs Passmore out of regard for Mrs Maury's sensibilities and Roane Colvard's sense of proprieties. Mrs Passmore had, after all, only done what Mrs Maury had earlier proposed to do with her own slaves. A harsh world indeed. Even if a woman were proved a thief and a whore, if she was white, a black man took his life in his hands pointing out those facts.

Colvard said, 'Hell, I know Kitty! Sorry, m'am,' he added, with a glance at Mrs Maury.

'Pretty much every man in town,' observed Hannibal wanly, 'could say the same. I believe I have made a handshaking acquaintance with the young lady myself. There was a pawn ticket enclosed.' He held it up between his first two fingers. '*Silver watch* is written on the back . . .'

January took the ticket, wondering how much that enterprising lady had gotten for it.

At least I'll get it back . . .

'And now Levi Christmas is dead,' he said thoughtfully.

'I found him Sunday morning,' agreed Roane. 'Deep in the woods, near the hollow oak. Qui— *I* buried him,' he corrected himself, 'and searched around some, but found no red leather valise, and sure as hell no money, so it sounds like he was killed for that. I had no idea who he was.'

'If we could get Miss O'Toole to testify that the Reverend Thorne was actually a thief and a slave-stealer,' mused Ballou, leaning with one shoulder in the room's doorway, 'we could probably put the blame on him for Drummond's death—'

'Or on whoever killed him.' January felt Hannibal's pulse, got up from the edge of the bed where he sat, tweaked open the curtain a crack, and peered into his friend's eyes. They seemed to be dilating and contracting normally. Looking up, he met

Colvard's gaze, wide with hope. 'The presence of another killer in the woods on Saturday morning – or at least of a robber with a valise full of church funds – may be enough to cloud the issue with the jury . . . particularly,' he added, with a glance at Mrs Maury, 'if you're willing to provide evidence as to your husband's jealousy, and his . . . *misinterpretation* of, shall we call it, Cain's efforts to talk *you* into selling some of your late father's slaves?'

'You told him to go away and chase himself, of course,' added Hannibal.

'I think I can do that.' Mrs Maury smiled, a little bit dreamily, as if her mind were suddenly elsewhere. 'In fact, it will be my pleasure.'

Butler Leeland arrived then – Ballou had sent one of Mrs Dillager's sons for him immediately after January's arrival – and Mrs Maury remained long enough to assure the old man that she was willing to testify that Cain had spoken to her of business only. 'God knows, m'am,' grunted Leeland, 'half the men on the jury will have had that husband of yours accusing them of improper conduct with you, or with your predecessor. It's only scum like Jim Punce and Injun Tom – 'scuse me, Roane—'

'Hell, I knowed my old man was scum 'fore I could tie my shoes.'

'Well, it's only their sort that believe it.' Throughout the conference, Leeland kept glancing at Colvard, then at Ballou, as if sensing that the young man was present for a reason but biding his time, like a slow old tortoise, as he marshaled the arguments that would dismantle Maury's contention that the murder had taken place – and that Cain had dropped his bloodstained glove – in the cottage. 'Don't mean they won't hold him for trial,' he said, as he walked Mrs Maury to the door. 'But if you make a man look a liar on the stand, you're halfway home even when he tells the truth. Not,' he added, 'that Marcus Maury ever told the truth about anythin' in his life . . .'

His creaky voice faded down the path as he walked the woman to where her carriage – and the watchful Stan – waited for her on Clay Street, leaning heavily on his walking stick. When Leeland returned, Hannibal said, 'I hope her speaking against her husband's word in court isn't going to bring her harm. Is there a way she can be protected against that?'

'She's his property.' The old man's mouth twisted. 'Same as that boy Quinto he's got everybody in the countryside out lookin' for. Legally, he can beat her if he wants to. I advised her to find some relative to go visit right after the trial, but she's got to go back to him sometime. She's willing to do it.' He shook his head, and settled back into the bedside chair, his yellowed hands shaking as he fumbled for a cigar. 'And it may come to no more than a few slaps for comin' to the courtroom at all.'

With an air of having satisfactorily settled the matter – reminding January of the men who shrugged off beating their slaves with '*A lick or two more or less never hurt anybody*' – he lit his cigar, turned to Colvard and raised his sparse white brows. 'And where do you come into all this, young man?'

The Indian took a deep breath, glanced at January as if for support, then said, 'I come into this because Mr Cain never killed Ezekias Drummond, sir. Drummond was killed by his stepdaughter, Rachel. She's the one asked me to come here and speak to you.'

Leeland listened quietly to Colvard's account of Rachel's dealings with her stepfather: her mother's devotion to him during their days in New York State, his iron control of their lives once they came to Madison Parish. 'She says he changed, when he came down here, sir. He had this . . . He called it medicine, but he sometimes spoke of it as somethin' God wanted her and her mother to drink—'

Colvard shook his head, like a horse beset by flies. 'I don't understand that very well, sir, but my thinkin' is, this Negro woman Cindy he was keepin' out on the bayou wasn't the first. I think he made sure his wife and his stepdaughter were drugged, so he could go out in the night to meet these women – maybe bring 'em into the house. You seen how quick he gets rid of the hands that work in his stable. Boze's only been there a year or two – the feller before him didn't last but a year.'

'It's true, sir,' put in Ballou. 'Begging your pardon for speaking against a white man – and a man who's been my friend for many years. But I knew him in New York state. And he was often in trouble there, for meddling with the women of his congregation.'

Speaking with difficulty, Colvard went on, 'Rachel says – and she told me to tell you, and says she'll swear to this under oath – that her stepfather would come up to her room and have his way with her, when she was too woozy to know what was happening to her. Her mother swore it was just dreams, and struck her for havin' dreams of that nature about her stepfather. But Rachel says she'd find bruises on her body, an' . . . an' blood on her sheets, an' know it wasn't no dream. An' I know most men will side with her ma, and say it was just a girl's dreamin'—'

'Well, I ain't one of 'em,' said Leeland. 'So go on. I take it one day she decided she'd had enough.'

'I told her about this woman Cindy out on the bayou,' explained Colvard. 'Rachel . . . Rachel braided some of my silk fish-line together into a rope; she wound one end of it round that big sycamore, just where the road starts to rise up 'fore it goes down to the bottomlands, wound the other around the magnolia on t'other side of the trace. She'd give me a note when I crossed to see her the night before, told me to hire some pickaninny from out of town at the circus, to hand him the note right after the race was done. I didn't know what it said but I guess it said, *I am leavin' you, Cindy*. Later she got the note out of his pocket and burned it. She knew he'd take the trace down to the bottomlands, and take it at a gallop. She dressed herself up in her brother Solly's things, and crossed over the river on the next ferry, which was so jam-full of folk goin' to the circus Boze didn't even see her.'

'And I reckon her ma hadn't the slightest idea she was even gone.' There was no question in the old lawyer's voice, and Colvard shook his head.

Leeland sighed. 'Another reason for his keepin' Mrs Drummond out of town. Not that there ain't women enough in town who couldn't get past that time of the month without "medicine". The stuff takes hold fast.'

'Particularly,' remarked Hannibal, 'if one doesn't especially want to know what's happening under one's nose.'

'You go out to the grove where the blood was found,' Colvard went on after a moment, 'and you can see the marks on the trees, from the trip line. Ben here—' He nodded to January, who had sat in the silence deemed appropriate to a man of his color –

'found Mr Drummond's horse loose in the woods, with its shins tore up from hittin' that line. It's at my cabin now. Rachel took her steppa's skiff back across the river, and burned the shirt she'd been wearing, and Solly just thought Mrs Drummond had lost it in the washin'. If Mr Cain hadn't been accused of the crime, and facin' the gallows for a murder he didn't do, Rachel wouldn't have spoke. She figured – and I figure – that Mr Drummond deserved what he got.'

'It's no more than any man would have got,' murmured Leeland, 'from any girl's pa . . . if it hadn't *been* Rachel's pa, or steppa anyway, that was doin' it. Or from her brothers, if she'd had any—'

'Or her husband,' said Colvard. 'Which I will be, soon as this hearing's over. And I swear to you I didn't know what was in that note, nor what she planned to do, but if it comes to court – if it comes to Mr Cain bein' declared guilty – I will swear to it in court that I handed that child the note, and stood at a distance and watched him deliver it; watched Drummond ride off in a rage. As Rachel will swear to it what she did, and why she did it.'

The lawyer drew on his cigar – which had gone out – and set it aside. He studied Colvard's face as if adding what he saw to an invisible sum of things remembered, or as if peering into some future unrealized.

'She's at my place now,' Colvard went on, uneasy into his silence, 'still sick from the laudanum he gave her and her ma all those years. Only reason she didn't come with us to speak to you is, she didn't want the talk there'd be, were she to come to town.'

'The word that interests me,' Leeland remarked after long silence, 'is *if*.'

The ensuing conversation occupied much of the rest of the afternoon. Rex Ballou came and went, attending to customers in his shop: January heard his light, cheerful voice bantering with the gentlemen of the town, joking about local gossip, now and then refereeing the games of chess or checkers when two or three men were waiting to be served. As Leeland went over all specifics of the case again, the barber was called in to provide details, and at no point – January noted with admiration – did even the possibility of Drummond's secret life stir the surface of the story. As the only black member of Drummond's congregation – as the man whom the ferryman had repeatedly referred to as '*the only Negro in this town worth a damn*' – his word was accepted, though Leeland mapped out carefully how the things he attested might be brought into the case without mention of the fact that their source was a black man.

Likewise, when Hannibal – gray with nausea and exhaustion – swore that anything his servant Ben said, he himself would back up under oath, the lawyer had merely nodded and made a note, before the entire discussion was moved out into the kitchen, so that the fiddler could sleep. Leeland lit up another cigar.

'We found a dead man in the woods,' said Colvard. 'The Reverend Thorne, Mr Ballou tells me, that come out from Jackson to preach with the Reverend Bickern last Saturday. When we're done here we're goin' over to tell Sheriff Preston—'

Leeland's white eyebrows shot up.

'Only come to find out he's really a slave-stealer and a river pirate, name of Levi Christmas, that ran off with the church money Saturday . . .'

And the whole story emerged, with a wealth of corroborative detail and Mrs Passmore's note, and January's account of his conversation with the Purleys' servant Nell – whose testimony, of course, would also be legally inadmissible.

'What my master suggested,' said January at last, 'is this. The hearing Monday isn't about who killed Ezekias Drummond, or why. Marse Pinkerton has a great deal of compassion for Miss Pryce – as do we all, I think.' He glanced around the kitchen table, at which Ballou had joined them again, one ear cocked for the bell over the door of his shop. 'But the hearing tomorrow – he has pointed out – is to decide whether or not *Jubal Cain* did that murder. Nothing else. And none of us – my master doesn't think—' he was careful to add, and caught a glint in Leeland's eye that told him that the old man knew perfectly well whose idea all of this truly was – 'is really interested in bringing the actual killer to the vengeance of the State of Mississippi.'

'You are suggesting in fact,' pointed out Leeland, rekindling his cigar, 'that we all of us become accessories after the fact to Mr Drummond's murder.'

'Yes, sir,' said January. 'I guess I am.'

'Well, hell!' Colvard sprang to his feet. 'It sounds like *you're* suggesting – Mr Leeland – if you'll excuse me sayin' so – that we all become accessories to *Rachel's* murder. You think those brothers of hers ain't gonna shoot her, 'fore they'll let her get up and dishonor the man they think was next to God? Or if not her brothers, some other man in his congregation? You think her ma's gonna back up her story? Half those militia hog farmers that'll be on that jury have frigged their nieces or stepdaughters or whatever hired girls their wives got in, an' come up with reasons why there was nuthin' wrong about it – you think they'd find *any* girl who fought back, or took revenge, guilty of less than murder in the first degree? You really think *any* girl in this state is goin' to get justice for killin' a man who raped her?'

'I'm suggesting nothing, son.' The old man blew a smoke ring, with great attention. 'Except that you damp your boiler a little and listen to me. You sound off like you're doing and there won't be a man in town who won't say you're pleading your own cause. Drummond made no secret of it that you was after the girl, nor that he thought, and her ma thought, she was a long sight too good for the likes of you. And if she's been out at your place, there goes any chance of any doctor proving what she says—'

Rage flushed the young Indian's cheekbones and he jolted to his feet again, fists clenched. The lawyer waved him down again as if he were no threat: 'Her brothers know where she is now?'

Struggling to hold his temper, Colvard said, 'She wrote to them yesterday. I left a note for them last night, at the ferry landing. And my father – who I passed on the way there, laying dead-drunk in the middle of Clay Street in his own vomit with his privates hangin' out – says *our* family is too good for the likes of Drummond's blood. *He's* the servant of God – *we're* the Kings of the Choctaw.'

Leeland chuckled, like a tree creaking in the wind. 'So he does,' he agreed. 'So he does. And believe me, young man, when I came into this country in 'seventy-eight I knew your granddaddy and he was no more the King of the Choctaw than I am. An honest farmer, and a good one, 'fore Jackson put him out with that treaty . . . And I been in the law long enough to know there's a difference between justice an' vengeance, an' when you talk about who has the right to do what to who you're on shaky ground with a jury. 'Specially the quality of jury you get in these parts.'

The filmed blue eyes shifted to Colvard. 'I'm an old man,' he went on quietly. 'Dyin', that doctor from New Orleans tells me. I think you're wrong about her brothers, but juries . . .'

He shrugged, dismissing most of those he'd seen.

'Let's say this, then. We will present Mr Cain's case on its merits, an' point out that there was at least two *bona fide* killers out in the woods that day: Levi Christmas, who could have killed Drummond protecting his own ill-got goods; and whoever it was who did for him. I'll go down to the House of Parliament tonight, and see if I can find Kitty O'Toole . . . and I must say I'm surprised at Lemuel Bickern, falling for a game as old as that one. That'll teach him to scorn the waterfront and hold up his nose against ill companions – every man in town must know that girl by sight, at least from her chin down. We couple that with showin' up that whole silly glove story for what it is, and we've got us a good chance of gettin' Mr Cain off without mention of who else might have done the deed.'

'If you can't,' said the young man, 'Rachel and I are prepared to swear before the court, to what I've told you today.'

'Fair enough.' The old man sighed a gusty cloud of nicotine. 'I don't imagine you'd have told me all this if you wasn't ready to go through stitch with it. And then we'll see,' he added, with a curious sidelong glance at January, 'if Mr Cain truly means to change his way of life.'

Through the open windows of the kitchen a gray breeze stirred. Far off, January heard the whisper of thunder.

The old man took his leave then, Ballou guiding him gently out through the shop with a promise of service and attention whenever he chose to come by. Colvard followed him, pausing only to shake hands with January and Ballou. 'I hope to see you at the hearing,' the young man said. 'What we're doin' is right – Rachel and me – and I don't think I could live with a woman who . . . who'd let a man go to the gallows in her place. Or even in *my* place. Even a slave-dealer. You think the old man can be trusted?'

'I gave up a long time ago,' sighed January, 'thinking I could say what any man would do or wouldn't do. When a man's dying it changes his view of the law, and of men . . . and of juries, I'd imagine. We trust Cain, for what he'll do with his life if he walks away free. And Leeland trusts you.'

'A damn sight more'n any of us,' returned the Indian grimly, 'trusts the State of Mississippi.'

A troop of militia rode by on Clay Street, the men slouched in their saddles, rifles on their shoulders, joking and spitting tobacco. Three or four hounds snuffed and quarreled around the trotting hooves.

'Hell,' added Roane, 'we should have damn little to worry about for the jury, anyway. Most of the men who're dumb enough to believe Marcus Maury's story are still gonna be out, riding all over Madison Parish lookin' for Quinto . . .'

And he paused, sniffing the air.

Very softly, Ballou said, 'Weather's changing. Storm on its way.'

TWENTY-EIGHT

That night the river began to rise.

Lying in his attic at Ballou's, January heard the far-off grumble of thunder, watched the flicker of distant heat-lightning reflect in a sky clear and hard as black glass. Sunday was hot, and still as death. January wrote to Rose, and, there being no Catholic church in Vicksburg, walked up to the Planter's and across to Mrs Dillager's every hour or so, to listen to gossip, picturing a thousand times in his heart the arrival of a steamboat from New Orleans, and the slave-dealer Junius Poger striding down its gangplank . . .

Late in the afternoon, in response to a note from Hannibal, suitably garnished with the coin of the realm, Kitty O'Toole came knocking at the rear door of Ballou's. What she was expecting January had no idea – she was gowned in yellow silk cut for evening wear and painted to the eyebrows – but her discovery of Butler Leeland there as well as Hannibal elicited only the remark, 'It's a dollar extra for two.' And then, 'Why, Mr Leeland, fancy meeting you here!'

'Storm's coming,' said Ballou, an hour or so later, when Kitty departed, still dressed and reassured that Levi Christmas was dead and that it was in her own financial interest to keep her mouth shut about her upcoming testimony until the trial. 'Tomorrow afternoon, I'd say.'

January whispered, 'Thank God.'

Roane Colvard agreed with this prognostication, when he arrived after the fall of darkness Sunday night with Quinto and Rachel. Rachel was rather gray around the mouth but determined to make what amends she could to Hannibal, who by this time was sitting up in bed with a throbbing headache. 'I'm sorry,' she said, holding out her hand. 'I did you a harm, and an injustice, but I was afraid . . .'

'You had an injustice done to you.' The fiddler kissed her fingers, to Rachel's blushing surprise. 'And a very great harm – two very great harms, considering what you're about to go through if you have the courage not to go back to laudanum. My advice is to stay away from liquor as well – from my own experience I can tell you it's perilously easy to slide from one to the other, especially if you've found out how delightful opium dreams can be—'

'Roanie don't touch it.' She spoke rather shyly. Her long hair was coiled up now, like a grown woman's. She had on a different dress, January noticed. She must have gotten her things from Drummond's. 'After growing up around his pa, who would?'

Hannibal sighed. 'You'd be surprised, *acushla*.'

From the kitchen, Ballou called out, 'Ben?' and January went to join them in the candlelit room.

Colvard was saying, 'It's good of you to help us, Mr Ballou – to help Quinto . . . You sure this scheme of yours for getting him away is going to work?'

'Any scheme can fail,' returned Ballou. 'But if you're determined' – He glanced across at the valet, big and genial in his red calico shirt and blue suspenders – 'to fetch away your daughter from Indian Mound, I think this is the way to do it. Ben?'

January nodded. 'I'm willing. I owe your daughter for two pones of corn and some hot water that might just have saved my life.'

Quinto laughed, and gripped his hand. 'Bless you, then. Bless you both.'

'We'll need all the blessings we can muster,' sighed January, 'if this is going to work. You be in Drummond's skiff that'll be drawn up just south of the ferry landing before ten.'

'And Drummond's boys won't notice that somebody's got their daddy's skiff out?'

'They'll likely be at the hearing,' said Ballou blandly. 'If they ask, I'll just say it was me.'

'I can't ever pay you back for this.' Quinto pressed Ballou's hand, then Colvard's. 'Not any of you.'

'Just do what you can,' said the barber, 'to help others down their road. Ten o'clock, now—'

The wind had shifted by the time the trapper and his friends were leaving, the hot sky filled with puffy, sticky-looking wads of cloud. Colvard sniffed the darkness of the yard, said, 'I'd say that storm should hit around two.'

* * *

January's greatest fear, Monday morning, was that the militia, Drew Hardy and the dogs would be near their projected landing place, which he'd estimated would be some two miles downriver of Vicksburg on the Louisiana side. It was in fact farther down, for the river's strengthened current had filled the great stream with uprooted trees, branches, fence posts and the carcasses of animals, and it took all January's strength, and Quinto's, to bring the little craft to shore. The water was already several feet deeper in the belt of snags, and lapped more than two yards inland of where it had been the day before. They halted the boat in the midst of the snag forest and sat for a time, listening to hot noon stillness.

But no sound broke the silence save the chatter of the birds in the deadfalls and the whining of mosquitoes around their ears.

January looked at Quinto, that big good-natured man who loved to fight but didn't want to do it for blood or for the amusement of white men. A drinking man. A whoring man. A man Ezekias Drummond had considered 'inappropriate' to save – but a man who'd put his head back into the lion's mouth to bring his daughter out of bondage. 'You ready to do this?'

Quinto grinned. 'Only one way to find out.'

Long after Quinto, Colvard and Rachel had departed the night before, Saul and Solomon Drummond had slipped in through Rex Ballou's kitchen door, and with them, Eliza Walker. The planning had gone on until nearly dawn, and afterwards January had been too keyed-up to sleep. He felt slightly light-headed now, and a little as he would in the moment before the curtain went up on the tent-show: keyed-up and running through the order of events in his mind: who needed to be where, when, and what part they had to play. He half expected someone to start strumming 'The Bee-Gum Tree'.

He and Quinto hauled the skiff out of the water, far enough to be noticed but not far enough for it to be obvious that they *wanted* it noticed. It just looked like a bad attempt at concealment. Just before setting forth from Vicksburg, Quinto had taken a turn along the waterfront, long enough for a few people to say, when questioned later, 'Oh, yes, a man of such-and-such a height, of such a darkness of complexion, wearing a red shirt and blue suspenders – he was in here . . .'

Together, and moving quickly, January and Quinto set off across the point, beneath a darkening sky.

Upriver, anvil-headed clouds towered thousands of feet, riding on a base of shadow. January could smell the storm, even as he'd felt it in the pull of the river's current. They kept to the thickets. Last night Ballou and Saul Drummond had drawn up a map of the point in minute detail, and Quinto knew the landscape already from surreptitious visits to his daughter.

Saul had asked after his stepsister, awkwardly but without either anger or defensiveness; when January had reported, 'She seems happy with Colvard,' the young man had nodded.

'Pa never liked him . . .'

Ballou had said, 'I think your pa was wrong,' and Saul had said, 'I just don't want to see her hurt.'

They didn't know, thought January. In a life already tangled with secrets, Drummond had at least kept that second, deeper secret folded away behind the first.

Like Leeland, January suspected the boys were unlikely to kill, if the truth emerged, but one never knew.

Right now, it was enough to pray that at that very moment Junius Poger wasn't stepping off the *Vesuvius* onto the wharves at Vicksburg, striding up the hill toward the courthouse . . .

And to pray that today wouldn't end with him getting shot himself.

One thing at a time.

He prodded a knot of dead wood with his snake stick, and stepped back quickly as three copperheads whipped forth and darted away. *Perfectly straightforward*, he thought, compared to the nest of snakes in that rambling brown house in its square of cottonwoods . . . *And potentially less deadly.*

A long slough lay at the heart of the marsh, leading off in the direction – eventually – of Indian Mound. According to Quinto, the ruin of another Indian farm stood near the water, almost hidden in the cane-brakes but with most of its roof intact. It was here in fact that Roane Colvard had found the runaway valet on the morning after his flight from the River Grove Plantation two weeks ago. 'You watch your feet,' said January, as Quinto pulled off his shoes. 'And watch your back. Good luck to you.'

'And you.' The valet shook his hand.

'Give my regards to Miss Dulcie.'

'I'll do that.'

As Quinto waded off down the length of that winding sheet of water, mud and reeds, January hitched his blue suspenders on his shoulders, shrugged a little more comfortably into his red shirt – which was not quite the right size for him, though identical in color to that of his companion – and continued through the woods.

Listening, he heard no sound yet of pursuit. When Roane excitedly put the word around that Quinto had been seen in Vicksburg, some of the militia would set off in skiffs of their own. Most would cross on the ferry, where Saul and Boze would exclaim at the news in astonishment. Boze would ask the men what they'd do with the five hundred dollars Marcus Maury was still offering for his absconded property. Saul would think hard all the way across, then exclaim, as the ferry touched the landing, 'I'm coming with you, boys! I know this point like the back of my hand!' There'd be a horse – saddled – in the shed by the downstream landing.

Then the chase would truly be on.

January swung southwest, moving fast – Ballou had given him a compass – and keeping to the woods of Lexington Bend. He found without trouble a huge old swamp willow that Ballou had described, and sure enough, a rope had been tied around its branches, concealed in the tree's hollow. With blessings on Boze and the Drummond boys – whichever of them had come out in the dark before dawn to set this up – he clambered easily into the tree, detached the rope and hid it in a high crutch of the branches, then cautiously stepped from its boughs into the crown of a white oak that grew nearby. According to Saul and Ballou, the thicket here beyond the willow was dense enough that it was possible to pass from tree to tree for some distance, and this turned out to be true.

He descended from the trees a hundred yards away, and headed into the hazel thickets along another slough.

Not escape them, he had said to the little group gathered around Ballou's kitchen table in the deep of the previous night. *Just delay them. Lead them up the garden path . . .*

The garden path that would lead, with luck, all the way to

Young's Point and would leave DeSoto Point denuded of militia for a good two hours, while the storm washed out any scent of tracks.

It was rather like watching Owen Tavish perform his feats of prestidigitation, or the Herriott family toss one another casually around the stage – or even, he supposed, Levi Christmas's neat-handed robbery of the Tabernacle church funds. *You have all the strings in the right places, you have everyone briefed on their part in the act, you have the script written out in advance and your audience* – whether it consisted of the population of Vicksburg, or poor Lemuel Bickern, or the militia of Warren County and Madison Parish – *would follow under the impression you were making it up as you went along.*

The only problem, reflected January, was the dogs.

Dogs were less easily fooled, though Saul, Solomon and Boze had left tracks all over the point, leading away from the area where the cellar hideout lay.

He heard Drew Hardy's pack baying just as the first huge drops of rain began to fall. *Right on time.* Eliza Walker had calculated how long it would take January to get to approximately where he was at the moment – half a mile from the riverbank on the outside of Lexington Bend and about three miles from Young's Point. He quickened his pace, listening behind him, gauging where they'd be. He'd climbed trees twice more, moving through the branches so that the hunt would stop, the dogs cast in all directions until they found his scent again. His heart pounded fast at the sound of the pack, and he drank the last of the water gourd he'd brought with him, and flung it into the next pond he passed. It wouldn't do for him to look too prepared.

He glanced at the sky. In Vicksburg, the hearing would be over by now, for better or for worse. Had Marcus Maury found someone to take him across the river in time for him to join the hunt? He would save himself the five hundred dollars reward, if he could claim that *he* was the one who captured Quinto. Would his rush to do so give his wife time to get herself to a place of safety, before he took his revenge? ('*No more than a few slaps . . . a lick or two more or less never hurt anybody . . .*')

On DeSoto Point, the fugitives in the root cellar would be emerging, blinking and shaky, from their long imprisonment, rain pattering around them as Ballou and Solly guided them at a run toward where a skiff would be waiting on the river. Eliza Walker would be watching them from the bluff above the mouth of Chickasaw Bayou, a mile away across the brown-yellow surge of the rising water. Lightning flashed, half a dozen bolts snaking from sky to earth. The rain would wash any trace of the escapees' tracks, any marks or prints along the bayou.

January trotted, listening behind him, pacing himself. Thunder split the sky, less than a second on the heels of renewed lightning, and the rush of the storm wind, like the cherubim of the Bible, poured a blessing over his sweating face. The dogs were getting nearer, baying on his trail; all the cottonwoods and swamp laurel lifted their branches in the ravening torrent of the wind. He came clear of the trees, and broke into a run, through the fields of the Anderson Plantation, dull green and just beginning to speckle white with the cotton bolls coming ripe. They'd come out of the woods and see his red shirt, and follow like the pack of British aristocrats they liked to pretend they were. In the fringe of cottonwoods that marked the boundary between the Anderson place and the next plantation he turned, and yes, it looked like every militiaman and every dog in two counties was out . . .

Now, he thought. *Now*.

He leaned into his speed, heading for the tiny cluster of white houses, huddled in the rain around the wood yard on Young's Point.

The dogs came on with horrific speed. He plowed between the cotton rows, thinking as he ran; the rows ran down to the river, and he had to take care as he crashed through one line of standing plants after another; the thing he could not afford to do was trip. If they got too close he'd head for the river, but the men would be so angry after the long chase – and now soaked in the rain – there was very real danger they'd shoot him, or beat him to death, or simply leave him to be killed by the dogs, when they found that no, he wasn't Quinto, and nobody was going to pay more than fifty dollars reward for all their trouble . . .

And Quinto would have time to get to Indian Mound, and speak to his daughter.

He ran, and behind him he heard the thunder of hooves and the wild hallooing of the men. If he made Young's Point there would be witnesses. Several were members of Drummond's congregation, and might even recognize him from the funeral. With the noise the hunt was making – with the countryside in a state of excitement over the reward – they'd come out of the little grocery there, out of the offices of the cotton-press and the wood yard . . .

A snake-rail fence. Pastureland. A new house off to his left, half built, some man who'd borrowed money to buy land and slaves, hoping to pay off his loan on the first crop and with that credit buy more land, more slaves – slaves bought new, sold away from their families or kidnapped from the streets of Philadelphia or Washington. Wealth enough to contribute to Congressmen and Senators who'd vote against anything that might interfere with slavery; wealth enough to run for office himself, if he was lucky. Certainly wealth enough to lend money to poor men in trade for their votes, men who wanted badly to believe that black men deserved their slavery . . .

The dogs were twenty yards behind him and the first buildings of the settlement a hundred yards away. The smell of smoke and privies, of the rain and the river. He veered right and headed for the water, clear of snags on the inside of the bend but churning and heaving like yellow-brown milk. Branches, fence posts, what looked like half the ruin of a house thrashed by on the current, and he waded in, his feet slipping on submerged deadfalls, in many ways the most dangerous part of this little play, this little performance . . .

DO NOT FALL. DO NOT TRIP. The current clutched at him and he knew if he lost his footing he would be swept away and drowned. This was the great god of the continent's center, the Father of the Waters, and He did not approve of being used as a toy in a game like this one.

January stopped, at the very edge of the zone where the current grew overwhelming, and raised his hands in supplication. The dogs lined up along the bank, barking and snarling, but had more sense than to follow him in. The men pelted up behind. Marcus Maury, riding in the lead with his spectacles all fogged with the rain, leveled a shotgun at him but January was pretty certain that by this time the powder would be as wet as the planter's court-day linen suit.

Injun Tom yelled 'That's him! That's Quinto! We got him!'

'Don't hurt me, sir!' January called out. 'Don't hurt me! I'll go back! It's me, Mr Pinkerton's Ben! I wasn't really runnin' away!'

'You lyin', nigger!' yelled Injun Tom, but Saul Drummond nudged his horse forward, his head bare and his long hair slicked to his shoulders.

'That's Pinkerton's nigger, all right,' he said loudly.

Half a dozen voices shouted disagreement. Men were running from the settlement, yelling both affirmation and disagreement, but men who would bear witness now to whatever took place on the river's brim.

His face a mask of cold fury, Maury raised his shotgun and fired.

And indeed, the powder was soaking wet. January made sure to flinch like a whipped dog. *It's part of the act . . .*

Part of the minstrelsy.

Say there, Mr Tambo, what you know about Matthew Matticks?

It's not my job to change them, he thought. *Or to take revenge. Only to participate in what will hurt them most: the wholesale theft of their property, and the insult to what they conceive of as their manhood.* The thought made him smile, invisibly in his heart.

Isaiah and Deya, Art and Ason, young Randol and Giselle holding poor little Charlie in her arms, would even now be scrambling ashore on the Mississippi side, invisible in the downpour. Cindy would run down the bank in the rain to gather up her child, and they would follow Mrs Walker up Chickasaw Bayou into the impenetrable tangles of the 'delta'.

'Don't hurt me, sir!' he pleaded again, imitating Jacob Blechmann for all he was worth. 'I come along quiet.'

Saul swung himself down from his horse, yanked a line of rope from the back of the saddle and waded out to where January stood. He cuffed him – hard – and January cringed, and meekly held out his wrists to be tied. When Saul led him ashore Maury raised his shotgun as if to club him with the butt, but Saul said, 'Now, none of that.' With his long hair slicked onto his shoulders and his wet beard plastered to his chin, he looked more than ever like his father, his gray eyes an avenging angel's.

He looked around him as he mounted, wrapped the end of the

rope around his wrist. 'I'll lock him up at my place tonight, take him back to town in the mornin'. I don't imagine Pinkerton's going to let him get away with this.'

Like Hannibal, reflected January, keeping his head well down, Saul Drummond spread a sort of cloak of white ownership over him. Reassured those who owned black men that those black men were strictly under a white man's control.

And they were reassured. Marcus Maury looked around at them, as if gauging how much they'd let him do, then jerked his horse's rein, and cantered away across the pasture, mud splattering up onto his clothes.

Their momentum broken, what could have easily turned into a mob became again just a gang of disappointed pattyrollers, wet and thinking about the nearest place they could get a drink.

The rain that washed their spit off January's face and arms was the same rain that obliterated the fugitives' tracks.

TWENTY-NINE

Jubal Cain was waiting at the Drummond house. He stayed within the shadows of the porch until the last of the militiamen rode out of the yard, crossing to the ferry where Solly and Boze waited to take them back to Vicksburg. Extra horses had been put on the treadmill, but January guessed the vessel would still overshoot the town by more than a mile. Hannibal was still at Ballou's, asleep, with the barber and Mrs Dillager to watch over him.

'No problem at all,' Cain said, when he and Saul walked over to the stable after dinner, where January was allegedly imprisoned. 'Once Leeland cut the legs out from under Maury and his damn "blood-soaked glove" story, the jury was perfectly happy to believe that whoever shot Levi Christmas also ambushed and knifed Ezekias Drummond. Maury tried two or three times to drag in the rumor about me being a secret abolitionist, but nobody on the jury believed a word he said by that time, and Leeland played him like a fish. That Poger fellow never did show up, thank God.'

January's breath blew out in a sigh. 'Thank God. I wrote my sister Olympe Monday morning, and asked her to arrange with some of the gangs on the wharf to steal his luggage. But I had no way of knowing if she got the letter.'

Cain laughed. 'Looks like she did! I owe your sister a bottle of French champagne, next time I'm in town . . . and you, too, of course. And your beautiful, patient wife.'

'We'll look forward to the honor of sharing it with you, sir.'

The big man's smile was crooked. 'Glad you still think it is one, Ben, after all this. Looks like you weren't wrong, when you told the Colvard boy I was changing my way of life. That Poger fellow – or somebody like him – could show up any day – any minute. So, I'll be riding up to Young's Point in the morning, to take the next boat for Memphis. I'm afraid I'm out of the slave-dealing business.'

'Pity.' Saul adjusted the flame in the lantern that stood on the table between them. 'It was a good blind. People really believed you were a dealer. You did good work.'

'Had to happen sooner or later. And I'll be back.' He grimaced. 'Playing a different game. Maybe looking a little different than I do. And I wouldn't worry,' he added more gently, 'about your sister and Colvard. I think in time you'll find he's more to your way of thinking than your pa would admit.'

'If he hid Quinto all these weeks,' agreed the young man slowly, 'you may be right about that. You didn't—' He raised his head, and looked again from Cain to January. 'There's a cabin,' he said, 'near the mouth of the bayou . . .' He hesitated, struggling for words.

'If you mean the woman Cindy,' said Cain, 'she's safe. She's rejoined the others.'

Saul closed his eyes, as if in prayer. 'He was a great man, Pa,' he said, after a long time. 'A man of God. He just . . .' His lips tightened. 'I went up there Monday, after the funeral, but she was gone. I'm glad she's all right. Was that why you beat him up?'

Cain nodded, and the young man sighed, as if the older man had answered another question that Saul could not bring himself to ask.

After a moment, Saul went on, 'And I never did like that business with the laudanum. He always said it was because they couldn't be trusted, but I was always worried, when we were out in the night, that the house would catch fire. Rachel tells me your friend Mr Freepaper used to be as bad about laudanum as poor Constance is – Mrs Drummond. You think maybe, before you leave town, I can get him to speak to her a little on the subject?'

'He'll be happy to speak to her,' said January. 'But she's got to be the one who wants to change. Will she stay on here with you?'

'Of course.' Saul looked surprised that she might go elsewhere. 'She is of our family now – and she has always been good to us. And she'll want to stay near Rachel. She has said also,' he added, 'that she wants to be close to Pa's grave.'

Just before sunset the storm had settled into a distant series of grumbles. Rain drenched down from a flat black river of sky. It would be wet out in the 'delta' tonight.

'Did no one have an idea as to who did kill Pa?' asked Saul after a time. 'I'd have said Maury, but they say Mrs Maury was with him up 'til nearly noon . . . How'd he take Mrs Maury's evidence about you chasin' her only to buy her slaves, sir?'

'Cold,' said Cain. 'The minute she gave her evidence she kind of excused herself and went out of the court, and didn't come back – she must have seen his face the same as I did. Leeland kept Maury on the stand, askin' him this and that, for long enough for her to get clear away. He was still at it when some feller comes in shoutin' as how Quinto had been seen down on the waterfront, and it was like Maury'd sat down on an anthill.' He grinned, with huge satisfaction. 'Out of this whole sorry business, that's my best memory: Maury torn between takin' his vengeance out on me by slanderin' my name, and rushin' off to capture Quinto and save himself his reward money.'

'His wife had better watch herself,' said January somberly. 'He's not someone you want to cross.'

A quick knock sounded on the tack room door. Saul got to his feet and opened it, and a slim little figure slipped in, dripping with rain; January recognized her voice when she said, 'Mr Drummond?' A soft alto, like a cherrywood flute. Her eyes went to Cain, then quickly to January, as if taking reassurance from the presence of a man of her own color in the room.

'You'll be Dulcie?' Saul held out his hand to her to shake.

'And we've met before,' added January, standing – as Cain rose, too – to offer his own hand. 'I'm Ben.'

Her face broke into a sunny smile. 'How's your leg?' she asked.

'Well enough this afternoon to run from the dogs again.'

'That was you?' She laughed with delight. She didn't resemble Quinto much – which had probably saved her, January thought, from being used by Maury as a hostage – save in the eyes, velvet-dark under long lashes. Her complexion was lighter than her father's as well, light enough to show the final, fading remains of a bruise on her cheekbone, as if she'd been struck hard by a man wearing a signet ring. 'Mr Maury was fit to be tied, when he got home! Even before he heard about Mrs Maury, and found the box—'

'Box?'

'Mrs Maury?'

'The box under his bed,' explained Dulcie, as Saul brought her up a chair. 'A strongbox with a lock on it – he keeps his banking things there. When he came in, with his suit all sticking to him and covered with mud, first thing he asked was, was Mrs Maury home from town yet? Cato told him she'd come in, and then gone out for a walk, and wasn't back yet, though it was past dinner time and pouring down rain. Then he ran up the stairs to his room, and yanked out the box from under his bed – he was so upset he left the door open, which he never does, so of course we were all out in the hall watching him. And he opens the box, and pulls out this leather valise – red leather with silver fittings, and sort of turns it upside-down, though he must have seen already that it was empty—'

Cain said, 'Well, I will be dipped.'

Saul looked blank. January explained, 'That's the valise the Reverend Bickern put the money from the Tabernacle in. The valise that Levi Christmas – the Reverend Thorne – paid some tart from the House of Parliament— Did Kitty O'Toole testify at the trial, Cain?'

His grin went from ear to ear at the memory. 'Oh, yes. In a purple silk dress you'd have to see to believe . . .'

'He paid her to steal it from Bickern and drop out the window. That's what Maury was doing out in the woods when he found your father's body,' January went on. 'Looking for Levi Christmas and the church money.'

Cain said, 'Looks like he found him.'

January laughed, picturing the man's rage, but after a moment Saul said gravely, 'That hypocrite blackguard. To kill the thief, and then keep the money for himself. He can't have meant to return it. He's had a week to reveal that he had retrieved the money – a week during which poor Lemuel Bickern has fled the state in disgrace, accused of a theft he didn't commit. Pa called Bickern a false prophet, but the man himself never showed anything but kindness to Constance and Rachel. My understanding was that for all his wrong-headed doctrines, he was a good man.'

'You mean—' Dulcie gazed from one to another, her eyes wide and slightly shocked, – 'Mrs Maury got it? The only thing left in the box was a gold watch on a fob. I think it was the Reverend Drummond's.'

'It was.' Saul's mouth twisted with distaste. 'A thief, as well as a murderer. To rob Pa's body when he moved it—'

'Would certainly explain where Mrs Maury disappeared to,' grinned Cain. 'And why she sneaked out of the courtroom so early. She knew Maury'd be tied up for the rest of the afternoon, trying to put Drummond's murder onto me.'

'She must have realized yesterday that Maury'd killed Christmas,' said January, thinking back. 'When we told Hannibal about finding Christmas's body. She knew her husband had gone into the woods searching for him. And she'd know he'd never have brought the money back to the church.' He turned his head as another knock fell upon the door, and Quinto stepped into the dim-lit room.

'Baby!' he strode forward, and folded his daughter in his arms.

'Thank you,' he added, looking over at January, Cain and Saul once their delighted embrace was done. 'More than I can say. The river's still high, but we can probably land where Big Bayou runs into the main river, south of town. Mrs Walker's waiting for us by the Lagoon, with the others—'

'How's Cindy?' The plunge of Cain's eyebrows turned his yellow-hazel eyes even more like a wolf's. 'And her child?'

'They're well.'

Saul said, quietly, 'Thank God.'

'Poor little Charlie's fussing and sick, of course, but Mrs Walker says, for the next ten days we're not going to come anywhere near a settlement, so there's no need to keep him silent. Cindy—' He glanced across at Saul.

'Tell her for me . . .' The young man hesitated, unable to speak. Then, 'Tell her I beg her forgiveness, on my father's behalf. He . . .' He stammered to a halt.

'His accounts are paid up now,' returned Quinto. 'She's free. They're all free. Across the river and free.' He turned back to Dulcie with a smile. 'We're all free—'

'Tell them to keep on going,' advised Cain, ''til you get to New York or Boston. Ohio's too close to the border. The more the Railroad operates the more slave-catchers are being sent to the north. Some judges'll demand proofs from 'em, others'll just take ten dollars and sign a warrant for your arrest, papers or no papers.'

'And don't expect it to be like here,' said January. 'The rules are different. You're not going to be welcome. Most white men up north don't want to see a black man taking a job *they* could get. A lot have started pressuring factory owners not to hire blacks at all. A lot of white men won't work next to black ones. The bank crash, and the hard times this whole country's been going through, will just make it worse – and the fact that more and more black men are coming north. That's no Promised Land up there. It's a land like any other – and you're probably going to spend the rest of your life looking over your shoulder. Tell the others that. Make sure they understand.'

Quinto nodded, sobered.

'Tell them to learn to read,' added January. 'And tell them, they're in my prayers. Every single one of them.'

'And you're in ours. Every day we live.' Quinto took his daughter's hand. 'Let's go, Baby Girl. We got to get clear around the back side of Vicksburg through the ravines. Time to start walking.'

'I can't.' She stepped back from him, to the length of her arm.

'What?'

'I can't.' Gently, Dulcie drew him back to her. 'I guess I mean, I won't. I came to tell you. To tell you to your face.' Her eyes flooded with tears, and she drew a deep breath. 'I can't leave Emily.'

'*Who?*'

'Mr Maury's little girl.'

Her father was staring at her as if she spoke some language he did not understand. Despite her tears her voice remained steady.

'His daughter by his first wife. Miz Julia never cared for her. It's not just she was happy to leave her with whoever wasn't busy – she just didn't think about her *at all*. No more than she thought about the kitchen cat. And Mr Maury goes for weeks without seeing her or asking for her. It's like – nobody cares for her. Nobody speaks to her. Nobody but me. Now Mrs Maury's run off, it'll be worse.'

'That ain't your business, Baby Girl.'

'Then whose business is it?' asked Dulcie softly. 'I seen dogs treat their young better than they treat that little girl. I been Emily's nurse since she was born. And they only made me her nurse 'cause I couldn't embroider. I was the only one ever changed her diaper, even 'fore they made me her nurse; nobody looked to make sure she was clean, they were all scrapin' so hard to do their own work 'cause Mr Maury keeps everybody he can out in the fields. Nobody ever checked that she'd been fed. They don't now. You don't know what that house is like, Daddy. Miz Julia would go off to town, leavin' her behind, for days. Other day, Mr Maury give me a big bottle of laudanum to keep her quiet 'cause he doesn't like the sound of a child cryin'. Nobody in that house – *nobody* – thinks of her, or looks after her, or picks her up, or speaks to her, 'cept me.'

January remembered the moonlight on the peaks of Dulcie's head rag, and how it had caught in the tousled curls of the child she carried on her hip: pale curls, like a white child's.

He realized that had probably been Emily.

Charming Mrs Maury, sweet as sugar candy, pleading with Hannibal not to betray her, speaking to himself of her need to escape.

Like Cindy – like every black woman who dreamed of flight – she knew that a child would weigh her down, drag her back. Be a danger to her, prevent her from fleeing.

Besides, it wasn't her child.

'*. . . listening to her husband disport himself with her daughter's nursemaid . . .*'

He closed his eyes, red rage flooding him. *Bitch. Whore and bitch . . .*

Dulcie said, 'I won't leave her.'

'He'll sell you,' said January quietly, 'when he gets tired of you. You'll have given up your chance to run, for nothing.'

'Not nothing.' She wiped her eyes. 'I can't. She needs someone.'

'She'll have someone,' snapped Quinto impatiently. 'White girls always get someone. Doesn't have to be you.'

January thought of Rachel, Dulcie's age, raised by whining fools and human wolves and betrayed by those who should have cared for her. *White girls don't always get someone*, he wanted to say, but couldn't and didn't.

'*You think them white girls is free, brother?*' Olympe had said to him once. '*You think Marie-Louise—*' She had rolled the name of St-Denis Janvier's white daughter off her tongue with spiteful relish – '*is gonna get to pick and choose who marries her? They're property, same as us. They just get to dress better.*'

'It's not your business,' Quinto was saying again, desperately now. 'It's not your business—'

Neither, reflected January, was the Underground Railroad.

Not his, not Saul's, not Rex Ballou's.

Not Ezekias Drummond's, who had helped so many hundreds to freedom . . .

'I can't,' Dulcie said again. 'Papa—' She put her arms around his neck. 'Go. Go on to New York, go on to Boston. Send me word if you can where you are, and I'll come to you one day. When she's big enough. When things change. But I won't leave a child alone in that awful house.'

'He's made you his whore!'

Her face froze, just for a moment, as if he'd struck her; or as if some feeling had gone through her, more than she could bear.

Very gently, January said to her, 'Don't do this.'

A tear slid down her face; she brushed it aside. 'And if I don't,' she returned, 'how many years is it going to take for me to quit hearing that child crying, every time I shut my eyes at night?'

'Nobody's going to thank you for it. Not even her, after he sells you off—'

Nobody ever thanks the women, thought January, *for what they do*. He felt suddenly sick at heart, an ant-sized Sisyphus confronted by a boulder the size of the Himalayas, knowing that it would not be moved in his lifetime.

Quinto left at last, weeping with frustration and anger, and for the child he was leaving in the land she had chosen, disappearing into the night. The rain was easing, though January smelled more on the way. The river was filled, now, with the trash of a continent, swirled together and pouring down to New Orleans. From the doorstep of the tack room he could see it, where stray fragments of moonlight flashed on it.

The river would bear him and Hannibal back to New Orleans

as well, as soon as the fiddler was able to be carried down to the wharves. January understood that, whatever rumors and trouble might be circulating around Vicksburg, he'd remain there until his friend could travel. It was dangerous and foolish and not his business to look after a wastrel white fiddler, not with Rose depending on him, Rose and Baby John. But he knew he wouldn't leave his friend behind. Maybe there'd be enough left of the summer, then, for him to find the American Zoological Association Traveling Menagerie and Exhibition of Philosophical Curiosities, but without white protection he wasn't sure he'd have the nerve.

In New Orleans, he recalled, he'd start teaching piano students again when cold weather came, for the first time since the bank crash. Rose would have students in her school. Life would return to normal . . . Whatever *normal* was, for the free who were not really free.

Saul clasped Dulcie's hands, towering over her, a bearded young patriarch with a mission from God. 'Come here when you feel you can, Dulcie. You know you won't be alone. Or go to Mr Ballou in town. Not a word . . .'

She shook her head.

'. . . but that's where you can come.'

'Thank you,' she said. 'It's good to know.'

She hugged him, and Jubal Cain, and January. Her tears were drying. She had made up her mind, and her feet were already set on her new road. 'I'll pray for you all,' she said.

And walked away, back toward Indian Mound through the dripping black of the evening. Turning her back on the northern sky, where the clouds momentarily parted to show the seven stars of the Drinking Gourd, that pointed the way to freedom.

As January himself, he reflected, would turn his back on them to go home to New Orleans.